Nikolai's War

Also By
HOWARD BERK

Novels

The Hero Machine
The Sun Grows Cold

NIKOLAI'S WAR

A Novel by Howard Berk

iUniverse, Inc.

New York Lincoln Shanghai

Nikolai's War

iUniverse books may be ordered through booksellers or by contacting:

iUniverse
2021 Pine Lake Road, Suite 100
Lincoln, NE 68512
www.iuniverse.com
1-800-Authors (1-800-288-4677)

This is a work of fiction. All of the characters, names, incidents, organizations, and dialogue in this novel are either the products of the author's imagination or are used fictitiously.

ISBN: 978-0-595-41024-8 (pbk)
ISBN: 978-0-595-67861-7 (cloth)
ISBN: 978-0-595-85377-9 (ebk)

Printed in the United States of America

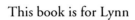

This book is for Lynn

Surely, if there was no god,
there was at least a frolicsome
force that arranged things,
like an eccentric uncle.

—Nikolai Granger

PART I

▼

ESCAPE

CHAPTER 1

▼

On the first day of July 1941, a horde of Germans swept onto the quaint streets of Riga, and the Russians, who had swept in only a year earlier, now found themselves fleeing Latvia. The Russo-German Non-Aggression Pact was over; Russia was under attack. It was a bad time for history.

In Independence Square, it was a bad time for Nikolai Granger. With guns roaring from every direction, he fled through a downtown choked with invading Germans and retreating Russians. Both sides indiscriminately fired at anything in their paths. Through narrow, Hanseatic streets, small-bore artillery sent shells hurtling through the flesh of the city, deflected to human height. Limbs and cobblestones flew through the air like hailstones.

Nikolai ran wildly. All around him, bullets gouged masonry and spattered chips of concrete with mad abandon. He broad jumped two huddled bodies cut down by shell fragments: two women holding bread like babies, one with her throat ripped apart by slivers of white-hot metal, the other so peacefully dead that she might have chosen the moment. He felt a sickness rise in him, the beginning of his love dance with death.

Most of the gunfire was German, the popping of Mausers, the ripping voice of the Schmeissers, then the small flurries of Mosin-Nagants, wheezing weak defiance in the retreat to the east.

He was twenty-two years old, lean and hollow-cheeked, with straight, black hair. His full name was Nikolai Arliss Granger. His friends thought of him as American, but there was a Russian cast to his face, which came from his mother, the eternally lovely Tatiana. His father had been Russian too, but of him there was not even a fragment of memory. Nikolai's connection to America came by virtue of Tati's marriage to Lionel Granger, who was attached to the American Embassy in Riga in the years 1932 to 1936.

Suddenly aware of a shrill wind, Nikolai made his way past the rear of the National Museum. The weather was mild, but the wind went through him in a cold wave, an augur of worse to come. Between the detested Russians and the despised Germans, both of whom had devastated Latvia for a thousand years, there was little to choose. Every century or so, one would roar in on a pale horse, proclaiming that the scourge of the other had ended.

Nikolai had arrived from London several days before, home for the summer— a misleading term conveying a normalcy that did not exist. Europe was at war, and the Nazis had already swallowed half of the continent. The manageable route was London to Sweden by neutral steamer and then by another to Riga.

He was in his third year at the London School of Economics. He was indifferent to trade and finance but had succumbed to Tati's hectoring. She had insisted that he become a person of substance: "The world is a hard place. You must facilitate it with money." She clung to this mantra, using the word "facilitate," a deliberately exalted term to impress him. It did not. Nikolai had no objections to money, but a mercantile life held no appeal.

The streets had grown strangely quiet. From time to time, people would scamper out of doorways and race down the alley, their shoes clicking frantically across cobblestones like rat nails. In one strange, ballet-like confrontation, Nikolai and a wild-eyed man of about sixty crashed into each other when rounding a corner. The man's glasses flew off, and Nikolai automatically plucked them out of the air as they sailed over his head. He handed them back, politely murmuring, "I beg your pardon," but the man was already clattering off.

Lindgen Square was even quieter. His apartment building, Number 62, was unmarked but strangely empty, not only of sound, but of life. Where was the clatter of humanity that went with the building?

Nikolai was amazed to see that the elevator panel was lit. It was an old cage with double doors, and one door was half open. He ignored the creaking elevator and dashed up three flights of stairs to the shadowed hallway and the eerie silence.

He slid his key into the lock and pushed open the door. A corona of light shone into the living room from the balcony and blinded him to everything but the silhouette of his mother, seated. One arm was languidly draped over the chair, and her face, hidden by the backlight, was turned as if in query.

"Tati!" he called. He had never called her anything else; his first word had been "Tati," not "mother." It was not Tati who replied but Katya, whom he had not seen in a year. Wraithlike, she materialized from the shadowed hallway.

"Oh, God, Nikolai! She's dead!"

It was so absurd a remark, so at odds with what he could see, that he snapped, "What the hell's the matter with you?" He bounded toward Tati's quizzically skewed head and softly arched arm, and the truth came into focus with a blinding flash.

Tati's neck was a dark-red swath. A torrent of blood had poured out of the wound as though from a spout; it had flowed down her neck onto her wheat-colored dress, soaking her body and staining the floor.

Katya was beside him now, holding his shuddering elbow. "I found her on the balcony. I dragged her to the chair."

"How?" he finally managed.

"I don't know. She must have been watching. Out there, watching!"

Now he could make out the jagged chunk of metal that had spent itself in the dark wood of the living-room ceiling: Tati's killer. He stared at the liquid slouch of her body; hopelessly tangled in grief and bewilderment, he waited for a flicker of life.

Katya touched his arm. "Nikolai?" He looked at her eyes and saw her concern. "We've got to go."

The war seemed to grow noisier, as though reclaiming its proper rank in the scheme of things. Thumping cannon fire reverberated throughout the city, machine guns sputtered, and rifle fire crackled in nearby streets.

"I can't just leave her," he said, as though Tati, deaf forever to life, would be lonely. There was a large, woolly throw on the sofa, and he picked it up and hastily wrapped her in it; the mummy-like sheath obliterated the evidence of death but bizarrely proclaimed it at the same time. He looked at what he had done. He could see himself, mouth agape, not in a mirror, but in his mind's eye.

It was all too preposterous. He could not think. Explosions peppered his brain, tiny electrical jolts in search of connective tissue. But nothing came. Tati was gone. She was dead. But she could not be dead, so she must be alive. And yet her body was shattered, and beneath the throw was the dried waterfall of blood. *You must sing. You must always sing, because if you sing, people will assume you are happy and have acquired the secret of life, and they will respect you.* It was an early aphorism of Tati's.

Katya read his crazed mind. "You can't take her," she said. He nodded at last and broke free, and in the same moment, shouts and rifle fire sounded from the street below. In the lobby, hobnailed boots thudded on marble floors and then the marble stairs.

"Germans," he said. "Out the back."

He led the way past the rear door and along the hall. They started down, then stopped abruptly. Clacking boots had entered the rear stairway. Nikolai opened a broom closet and tugged Katya in with him. Through a hairline crack, he could see soldiers coming off the landing and swirling past in a field-gray blur.

Inside the musty closet that reeked with the stench of ammonia and damp mops, they pressed together in breathless silence. As always in war, the Germans gutturally croaked, shouting from apartment to apartment: "Anybody?" "Nothing!" "Anything?" "Nothing!" And then: "Here's one!" And a second voice: "Not bad looking, but she's dead!" And someone else: "Fuck her before she gets too cold, Willy!" followed by a wave of laughter.

Katya felt Nikolai tensing, close to erupting, and she ran her fingers down his face, a contact so unexpected, so personal, that he sought her eyes in the darkness. He could not find them, but he understood her touch, and his rage eased.

He took her hand and sucked in his breath, then let it out in a soft, controlled hush to say he was all right. A whistle blew from somewhere below, and the gray-green uniforms moved past the crack in the door and down the back stairs toward the street. The soldiers were noisily carefree. Nikolai pressed his eye to the crack in the door and saw that their arms were filled with bottles of wine.

Nikolai listened intensely for the sounds of a trap. He and Katya breathed in small gasps; in the bleak, dark world of their silence, they could almost smell the Germans waiting to unleash a torrent of bullets. But there was nothing, only another whistle from further down the street, where the Germans were regrouping to fine-comb another block.

Nikolai pushed open the door. The rear balcony was empty, the building quiet. Through the balustrades, he could make out the tail-end of the German patrol rounding a far corner.

"Now," he said. Katya came into the light, and just then, Nikolai was struck by the eruption of femininity that had transformed her from schoolgirl to young woman in the past year.

They were friends and confidantes, but never had been more. Katya's mother, long gone, had been Tati's second cousin. With Nikolai away for years on end (first in Switzerland, then in England), Katya had become a familiar presence in the apartment. In the summers, she and Nikolai would rediscover their friendship, which remained uncomplicated and undemanding.

"What do we do?" she asked.

"Christ, I don't know. Get out of here. Stay away from the Germans."

"I heard the army tried to stop them at Jelgava." She shook her head. "I heard they were wiped out."

"Maybe we'll head south, cut to the coast," he said. He glanced back toward the apartment, and they started down. They picked their way through the streets to Forest Park, a huge tract of grass and trees that stretched several kilometers out of the city. They met other furtive, fleeing figures, but no soldiers, neither German, Russian, nor Latvian.

"What about your father?" Nikolai asked.

Katya said, "I don't know where he is." She had returned from school in Stockholm on the same day Nikolai had arrived from England. "Maybe you didn't know. Papi was a member of the council. When the Germans attacked, he went off to emergency meetings, but he never came back. Then the guns started, and I ran to the apartment to be with Tati."

Past the park and the forest preserve, they took the road south. It was clogged with refugees, most carrying bags or packs, pushing carts, or riding horse-drawn wagons heaped high with household goods. An occasional car slid in and out of traffic, almost comically packed with disjointed arms and legs.

Nikolai and Katya had nothing, not even water, jugs and bottles of which people clung to the way they clung to their children. There was no authority, only the mindless drive of fear. Trudging along, Nikolai mused that things could not be worse: Tati was dead, Latvia was in chaos, and he was on the road to nowhere.

Attached to his heavy-hearted predicament was an odd relief and an even odder irony. His return to Riga had masked an announcement to Tati, one he had never quite made. He had dropped out of the London School of Economics, and he had no idea what he wanted to do next. Of course, he had been waiting for the right moment to tell her, which had never come, because the Germans had come first. The only redeeming aspect of this tragedy and disaster was that Tati had been spared his bad tidings. As for himself, he was now free to pursue a new future—a future admittedly dampened by the fact that he was running for his life.

A murmur swept the column: the Germans had set up a checkpoint several miles ahead. The refugees stopped, anxiously questioning each other. What could it mean? Should they turn back, or scatter into the forest? Some were already peeling off and heading back—but to what? The war they desperately sought to escape?

A few hardy souls struck into the forest, but only a few. People circulated stories of cutthroats waiting to pick off such foolish strays. Most people waited; surely there would be a development.

It came within a half-hour, racing with telegraphic speed down the line. The Germans had no interest in the refugees. They were barely glancing at IDs, waving people through. Cheery rationales sprung up like summer flowers: Of course the Germans didn't care where the refugees fled, so long as they did not clog the arteries of attack! And what could be more obvious? Not a single German soldier seen, not a single Wehrmacht vehicle, not a single Luftwaffe aircraft! This was not an artery of attack! The Germans had no interest in them!

Nikolai had been inclined to try the forest, but he could not make up his mind. Katya bit her lips, ready to follow, unwilling to lead. And then came the news that the checkpoint somewhere ahead was benign, and the column was moving again. With a shrug of concession, Nikolai rose from the ground and tugged Katya to her feet. They plodded on.

Several miles down the road, new rumors floated back: The Germans were even handing out rations! Water and food! A boy came running back along the line. He stopped exuberantly before his parents and a younger brother. He had gone ahead to see for himself, and it was true! He had seen the checkpoint! He had seen the soldiers! They were friendly! They had mechanized vehicles and motorized cannons! All brand-new! And their uniforms were smart: black with lightning bolts on the collar!

Nikolai pulled Katya out of the column. He was tugging her toward the forest. "What are you doing?" she said.

"It's no good. They're SS troops."

"What's the difference?" she asked. "If they're behaving decently, isn't that all we have to worry about?"

"Katya, they won't behave decently."

But she was frozen, more frightened by the forest, her mind filled not only with fresh stories of throat-cutting thieves but fairy tales involving rapacious wolves and Latvian trolls who turned children to stone. She knew they were foolish stories, but she felt like a child now.

Meanwhile, the column had taken on a new life as an energized mass mindlessly shuffling forward. Katya tried to pull free to join them, but Nikolai would not release his grip, and he tugged her toward the darkness of the woods.

In fact, Riga's criminal population was small and had fled the city along with everyone else. The people they encountered in the forest growled to keep them at bay, wary of newcomers. When the afternoon light faded, some of the larger families dauntlessly settled in for the long night; fires were lit, sentries posted.

Moving past one such fire with supper pots cooking, Nikolai ignored a snarled warning from a trio of men and aimed his smile at several women around the fire. He gestured back to Katya, who was hugging herself against the evening chill, and conveyed her apparent condition with a sweeping motion over his belly. The women gave them bowls of stew and chunks of bread.

They ate quickly, and Nikolai handed back the bowls. He thanked them, and one of the women went to a cloth sack and pulled out a thick, moth-torn sweater. Nikolai handed it over to Katya and thanked the group, offering money for their hospitality, but one of the husbands said, "Just go."

They stumbled on, dead reckoning from fire to fire, but soon there were no more fires, and they were alone. A half moon came out and painted the forest a murky silver. Clouds covered the moon, and it began to rain, but a Travelers' Rest hut loomed up out of the dark, and astonishingly, it was empty.

Inside was a rough-hewn table and a few chairs. There was a fireplace too, but no wood. Enough could be gathered—Nikolai even had matches for the half-pack of cigarettes in his pocket—but they were two people, not six, and a fire would draw attention. The chairs were huge, almost the size of love seats, and they settled in and scrunched together for warmth.

An owl hooted in the distance. When it stopped and there was nothing more, Katya's eyes began to close, and soon she was asleep.

Wide awake, Nikolai thought of Tati and then tried not to think about her, but he could not stop the onslaught of memories, and when he finally slept, it was in a swirl of dreams about her.

She had been born fifty miles from Moscow in the turbulent times before the Great War. Her delicate features and lissome beauty were perfectly matched for the Moscow Art Theater. A creature of stunning familiarity, she conveyed stereotype and mystical status all at once. She was selfish, willful, flighty, and neurotic, but these were failings rescued by charm, and her career flourished; that is, until the entire country crashed down into revolution. She fled the chaos that was Russia and settled in Latvia, carrying with her an unborn child, the fruit of a brief liaison with a White Russian captain executed by the Reds. His memory was a gossamer thing she brought out on special occasions, but without obsession.

In the mid-thirties, sensing the next European debacle, she married Lionel Granger, who was with the American state deperțment in Riga.. She was not always rational, but her survival instincts were keen; she reasoned that an American connection in the new, once again unstable Europe would eventually make up for Lionel's shortcomings. In this, she was wrong. Fate is not a neat thing.

She accompanied Lionel when he was transferred to Washington, and while she was fond of America, she became less and less fond of Lionel. When she expressed an interest in Hollywood, Lionel was appalled—his lifestyle mirrored the discretion of his trade. His was a world of whispers and asides. He even coughed quietly. A theatrical wife was something of an exotic asset; a Hollywood wife would stamp him as a fool.

One day, on a whim—Tati had just finished an American tour of *Ah, Wilderness!*—she packed her bags and headed for Latvia.

In the game of life, the circumspect Lionel was never more than a spectator, a man who understood everything but altered nothing. When Tati packed up and left, he watched but did nothing about it. Lionel noted Tati's departure in silence. He let her go and never saw her again.

Tati returned to Riga, to the National Theater. She had retained her stage name, Tatiana Ulanova, but the late thirties were an uphill struggle; she pitted her intensity against time's voracious appetite. She never regained her popularity, but there were always admirers.

In his dream, Nikolai was one of them, beaming from the front row of the National Theater as Tati bowed to tumultuous applause … but a strange light fragmented his view of her and then obscured her entirely, and he awoke.

No less than three heavy-duty military flashlights bobbed before his eyes. Next to him, Katya grunted in surprise, and Nikolai started to jerk out of the chair. He received a blow across the forehead from one of the flashlights and went to his knees.

He heard the clank of equipment and then the voice of one of the soldiers. "Stay where you are, pig." Another soldier roughly searched him for weapons, and he saw Katya being pulled to her feet. Outside it was almost dawn, a somber, gray day with scudding dark clouds.

"What are you doing here?" one of the Germans said in a Swabian monotone.

"Refugees," Nikolai replied.

The soldier who had spoken was a sergeant, a man who looked like Hitler down to the mustache, except that he was a thick-set giant. "Identification cards, and fast," said the sergeant.

The soldier behind Katya slapped the back of her head. "Move, bitch."

The sergeant looked over the IDs and rapped them against his palm. "What did you do with the guns?"

Nikolai and Katya stared back in bewilderment. The soldier behind Katya sliced a palm against her neck. She stumbled forward, gasping in pain. The third soldier smacked her face, and the stinging blow brought another cry. At the same time, the sergeant brought up his knee sharply into Nikolai's groin. Nikolai fell back to his knees with a silent cry.

"Schoffer, take a look," ordered the sergeant. The soldier searched the tiny cabin, which required little more than a spin on his heels. He shrugged to the sergeant: *Nothing.*

The sergeant turned wrathfully. "You stole them. They're not here, so you handed them over to your partisan friends. That gets you a bullet in the head, patriots."

The soldiers shoved them out of the hut and marched them through the woods along the edge of a creek, then over a rise into a small forest-preserve warehouse that had been turned into a German rear-echelon arms depot. Trucks roared in and out, raising clouds of dust. Fluent in German, Nikolai pieced it together: The depot had been raided during the night. It had been a small, well-executed robbery, and the German guards had failed to detect it. It was embarrassing, the sergeant said, then added reasonably, "So somebody must pay. Am I right?"

Nikolai pleaded their innocence, but the sergeant waved him off with thick fingers. "Nobody knows anything. Nobody ever knows anything." He said it with a comedic edge, and the other two soldiers laughed. Warming to his audience, the sergeant added, "Of course, it's possible that you're telling the truth, but you're still going to get shot. Mark it up to wrong place, wrong time, bad luck," he said, so good-natured that his men laughed again.

The entourage halted before a tent. Within it sat two officers bent over paperwork. The sergeant entered and spoke to one of the officers. The officer shrugged impatiently and said something. The sergeant came out and pointed to an incoming convoy of a half-dozen transports. A number of soldiers were moving toward them. "There's a rush on. We've got to pitch in."

"What about them, Sergeant Mueller?" asked the soldier who had slapped Katya around.

"If we shoot them now, we have bodies stinking up the place until we bury them, and Hocher would chew my ass out. So we'll put them in the storeroom in the back. Let's move."

The soldiers prodded Nikolai and Katya around the side of the concrete building to its rear. They stopped at the door while one of the soldiers took a heavy key from a nail near the door and grated it in the lock. The sergeant looked along the gray slab of wall and decided, "We'll shoot them right there."

The door squeaked open, and the prisoners were pushed into the storeroom. The door was closed, the lock turned, and the key returned to its peg. "You've got about thirty minutes to live, so go to it!" the sergeant called after them— another performance for his men, who roared.

There was nothing in the storeroom but bags of cement. Damp walls rose twelve feet. Light came in from a single slit of a window high up on one wall. Katya sank to the floor with a quiver of despair. Her arms crept around her body. "No," she said again and again, a soft, rhythmic chant, a hopeless prayer.

"We'll get out," Nikolai said, so dauntlessly that it sounded even more hopeless. He tried the door, then flung himself at it and kicked it in wild rage. It was so thick that the thud did not even reverberate to the walls. A truck approached. The two swallowed their breath, expecting that it was the sergeant and his men returning to shoot them. But the truck moved past.

The minutes flew by with frightening speed. Any second now, their executioners would be back. And then they were out of time. Footsteps crunched on gravel as someone cheerily whistled. Nikolai and Katya looked at the door as though peering through to death on the other side. But the whistling continued past the door, and the footsteps were those of one person, not three.

"Quick!" hissed Nikolai. He jumped on some sacks of concrete and motioned to Katya. She broke out of her desolation and offered her back. He got one knee to her shoulder; she rocked, wavered, and almost fell but recovered. He got the second knee up to the other shoulder, propped against the wall, and straightened up, with one foot on each of her narrow, swaying shoulders. "Move over!" he hissed, and staggering, she edged along the wall until he was at the window slit.

He could see out on a flat trajectory, but the whistling soldier was nowhere in sight. Nikolai's heart fell. The man had moved beyond earshot. "Oh, God," he moaned.

"*Was?*" asked a surprised voice, almost below the window. It was the soldier who had whistled; he was out of sight, seated against the base of the wall. He was on a smoking break, and a thin cloud of smoke drifted into Nikolai's nostrils.

"Who's down there?" Nikolai asked authoritatively.

"Wollens," said the soldier. "What's going on?"

"Wollens, listen. It's Schoffer." Nikolai mimed Schoffer's voice and accent as best he could—another Swabian. "I'm stuck in this fucking storeroom. Jesus Christ, get me out of here, will you?"

"What do you mean, 'stuck'? Where's the key?"

"If I had it, I wouldn't be stuck in here, for Christ's sake!" Nikolai exploded. "Mueller locked me in by mistake!"

A silence hung in the air like a terrible weight. Nikolai closed his eyes, waiting for the soldier to unravel the strange and unnatural exchange. Why hadn't Schoffer called out when Sergeant Mueller had locked him in? And how could Mueller have been so absent-minded as to lock someone in the storeroom only seconds after opening the door?

Indeed, Wollens was stumbling through this tangled terrain when Nikolai impatiently sputtered, "For God's sake, Wollens, Mueller played a trick on me!"

Wollens grinned. Now it made sense, and he snorted. *What a* dummkopf! He said, "Hey, Schoffer, want to buy a three-legged horse?"

"Ha, ha, ha. Come on, Wollens, let me out."

"What's it worth?" Wollens asked shrewdly.

Nikolai grunted, a man trapped. "Twenty marks, you miserable bastard. Okay?"

"Deal!" said Wollens, and he took the key from its peg and slipped it into the lock. He pushed open the door. "Twenty marks! Pay up!" Wollens stuck his head in the room. "Where the hell are you?"

Nikolai was standing behind the door, with Katya hidden just beyond, and when Wollens came into view, Nikolai slammed the sack of concrete down on his head. Wollens crashed to the floor.

Katya looked away. "Is he dead?"

For a moment, Nikolai stared. More death, he was thinking, and this time, he was involved. He knelt beside the soldier and listened to his chest.

"There's a pulse on the neck. Right here," Katya said, demonstrating with a finger to her own neck. Out of the corner of her eye, she could see a thin flow of blood from Wollens's head.

Nikolai tentatively touched the man's neck, feeling for a pulse. He looked around in relief. "He's breathing!"

They edged out of the storeroom and surveyed the immediate area. In the distance, preoccupied soldiers were unloading the big trucks. They hugged the wall, moving past the proposed execution site, then cut into the open and broke into a wild run to a nearby fringe of woods.

For the next hour, they were running, slowing, gulping air, and running again, always moving. Nikolai kept looking back—the Germans were partial to dogs—but they saw nothing and met no one.

From a distance came the washboard ripple of machine guns and the pops of rifle fire. At first, Nikolai thought that some isolated Latvian unit or other was putting up a fight, but then he realized that the firing was too measured; it lacked the fierceness of battle.

Nikolai and Katya followed a gully and picked their way through a thick copse of trees until they reached the edge of a clearing. There, an SS *Einzatsgruppe* was dispatching dozens of victims at a time. Forty or fifty would be culled from the head of a long column that stretched far beyond sight down a dirt road through the woods. There was no discrimination. Families of men, women, and children were peeled from the top of the column and rushed into place, a narrow depression that Nikolai now realized was a continuation of the same gully they were in.

They watched as crying children and begging mothers were gunned down. For the most part, the men seemed too stunned to protest, except for the occasional youth who would make a mad dash for freedom. But peripheral guards had been stationed around the clearing, and with the leisure of sportsmen, they tracked and cut down the renegades.

Katya's trembling finger pointed to the next batch of victims being prodded into position. Nikolai recognized among them a family that had been close by in the column the afternoon before, including the two brothers; it was the older brother who had brought back news from the checkpoint.

In that second, Nikolai saw something incredible. The father whispered something to his sons, and the two boys suddenly bolted from the line and ran off. They were so fast that everyone watched in surprise, the two boys running like the wind, the rest a frieze of hapless parents, doomed refugees, and amused SS. Frozen like the others, Nikolai and Katya saw only that the boys were headed directly for their hiding place.

Two SS soldiers raised their Schmeissers and unleashed a withering fire. Nikolai pushed Katya's face into the earth. All around them, bullets were shredding shrubbery and thunking into trees. The two boys, borne aloft as though at the end of a frenzied dance, cartwheeled to a sprawling finish and lay still. Just as Nikolai glanced up, the execution squad went back to work. The father leaned into the rain of fire, eager for death. The mother's mouth was open when the bullets reached her; her hands were raised to the sky in protest, and she fell into the ditch that way.

The two young, riddled bodies were no more than ten or twelve feet away through the shrubbery. If the Germans came over to deliver a coup de grâce, Nikolai and Katya would be seen. But the SS guards stayed where they were, alert for attempts to escape.

Already, the new lineup was ready for extermination, and gun bolts and priming levers were rasping and clicking into place. "When they shoot, we go," Nikolai told Katya.

The firing began, and Nikolai grabbed Katya's arm, but she was dead weight. He pressed his mouth to her ear and whispered, "Come on!" But she could not move. Her eyes were fastened to the death scene; nothing else penetrated the madness of the moment. Nikolai slid his hand across her mouth; he was afraid she would cry out. She remained silent, but his hand came away with blood where she had scarred her lips with her teeth.

"Katya," he said in appeal, and her head finally came around. Her eyes were crazed, but she nodded in comprehension. They waited for yet another batch of firing, and this time, when the executions sounded, they used elbows and knees to back up until it was safe to rise and run off in a half-crouch.

Through the long day, they wandered alone with no further reminders of the war, and the SS killings became flashes of memory that would not go away. In the afternoon, a soft summer rain pattered through the trees, and then the forest gave way to large estates surrounded by orchards and vineyards. The trees budded with early growth but offered nothing to ease their hunger.

Now they could make out a tiny village just beyond a sturdy bridge. It was bisected by a cobblestone street, but the street and the town were empty. They slipped closer, moving through a meadow, where a few cows placidly chewed grass. A dog slunk by and disappeared behind a building.

They inched past a low-slung house that was built of ochre-colored stone, like everything else in the town. There was a flurry of movement down the street as an elderly couple emerged from one house and furtively disappeared into another. A few villagers remained, after all—the ones who could not easily flee. In any case, Nikolai reasoned, the Germans had ignored the town. What could they want here, anyway?

He tried the back door of the low-slung house, and to his surprise, it was open. They pushed inside to a country kitchen of no great charm, but it was well stocked with bins of fruits and vegetables. Behind a gauze curtain in the pantry, they found half a loaf of dark bread. There were bottles of wine too, and they ate ravenously, but they were tense with every bite and every swig. A German patrol could roar into town at any second.

They gulped their food and left, cutting south out of the village on a narrow dirt road that climbed a shallow ridge and brought them to a vista overlooking the Baltic. The rain had stopped, and the mist had thinned, and brilliantly clear shafts of light cut through the woods. Far, far away, a gigantic swath of golden sun spread like butter across a silky sea.

"That's Horseshoe Crab Beach down there," Katya said. As children, they had shared visits to that irrecoverable world. Spontaneously, their hands slipped together.

"Maybe we'll go down and take a dip," Nikolai said.

"Maybe we'd freeze our behinds off," Katya said, with the first glimmer of a smile in two days.

Nikolai looked around uneasily. They were on a commanding knoll, but not the highest, and they were out in the open. "Let's get out of here," he said. Hand in hand, they cut back to the cover of the woods.

But it was too late.

CHAPTER 2

▼

Baron Reinhard Ernst von Hartigens-Hesse was a descendent of the Teutonic black knights who had ravaged the Baltic states throughout history. In this more civilized age, Prussian aristocrats like the Hartigens-Hesse family were prominent by virtue of their holdings in agriculture, lumber, cement plants, and shipping interests. In the old days, the black knights had hit and run; later, they expropriated timber and farmland, which they managed from the Prussian homeland. Still later, having carved out huge Baronial estates, they built manor houses and installed their families in the "new land."

They straddled two worlds: the prestigious world of their noble origins and the expanded power that came with their new holdings. Their loyalties were not divided—they were Prussian to the core. They maintained estates, though usually more modest, in the "old country," and their politics were Prussian politics, not Latvian, Estonian, or Lithuanian.

This is why the Baron was furious. The man across from him at the terrace table on the west veranda was an arrogant SS general named Pforzheim. The Pforzheims were from Saxony, and the father had been a low-level bureaucrat, yet this street-brawling politician-cum-*offizier* had the gall to insinuate that the Baron was not a true German. "It must be difficult to see your new homeland so roughly handled," Pforzheim had said, feigning tact.

The Baron took enormous delight in his emotional control. He was forty years old. His face was oval, almost round, his nose rather thick and long; his lips were full and red, which gave him a sensual look. His hair was dark and thinning.

"I can assure you, my dear general," he had responded, "that Germany is my homeland, not Latvia. I can further assure you that the elimination of the Russian plague from Latvia has been my dearest wish for many years."

"Of course, of course," Pforzheim said. He had a way of smiling with his teeth, curling his lips back but moving nothing else. He had expected his visit to the Baron's estate to culminate in an easy success, but it was turning out badly. As sometimes happened (and he was aware of this fact), his contempt seeped through, and he had nothing but contempt for this fop of a "baron" whose family had deserted Germany but who made himself out to be the purest patriot since Bismarck.

As *Gruppenführer* of an SS unit more than a little responsible for the dazzling drive into Latvia, Pforzheim had assumed that Hartigens-Hesse would be delighted to hand over his manor house. Instead, this puffed-up little robin had turned him down cold—without so much as an apology. Hartigens-Hesse, occasionally lifting large Zeiss binoculars to his eyes to scan the hills and valleys, the forests and lakes that were his domain, had suddenly stiffened in his chair and coldly announced that his property could not, under any circumstances, be used for anything "other than family purposes"!

Pforzheim revealed nothing, but inside, he was shocked at this impudence. His staff had selected the Hartigens-Hesse manor among other estates in the area because of its convenient location, but when the proper petition had been ignored, Pforzheim—who saw himself, not unjustly, as a key figure in the war—had taken matters into his own hands.

So it was that the general and his entire staff had piled into three staff cars and wound their way up the twisting road to a dominating hilltop. They had passed through flanking entrance gates featuring the Hartigens-Hesse crest, then rolled along the quarter-mile driveway of sentinel-like elms, at the far end of which sat the manor house itself. At the general's request, the entourage had halted to take in the magnificent, funnel-like view of the structure. Pforzheim was duly impressed. What a magnificent place! It had the rough charm of a hunting lodge but was the size of a hotel.

Pforzheim had expected a fawning host, but Hartigens-Hesse had first kept him waiting, then listened coldly to Pforzheim's request. Without a second's hesitation, he had said, even more coldly, "That is impossible."

Stunned and not a little embarrassed, the general had suggested that they talk in private. In doing so, he had taken on a glacial countenance of his own: what his staff called his "Death-head Mode." The Baron had led the way to the terrace.

Here, they had settled at a table, and a servant had brought a cut decanter of wine. Pforzheim, enjoying this small conquest almost as much as the larger ones of the last two days, had brusquely informed the Baron that his stay would be lengthy, perhaps as long as the war itself, that his command situation would require full use of the manor house, and that he would also require the Baron's entire staff to remain in service during this period. He had said he regretted the fact that the Baron would be required to leave the manor for whatever period the war entailed.

At first, Pforzheim had thought that the Baron's expression was obsequious, but then he had realized that it was something quite different. The Baron had picked up a large pair of binoculars and proceeded to toy with them, focusing here and there, as though marking his territory like an animal. When the glasses came down, the Baron had said, "I must repeat, General Pforzheim, that your request is quite impossible. I must therefore ask you to leave."

Again, Pforzheim was shocked. The bastard was not only turning him down but throwing him out! Once again, he felt foolish, realizing how badly he had miscalculated. His mind sputtered: *Imitation Prussian! Pretentious shit!* For one delirious, bile-surging moment, he thought about pulling out his Luger and emptying it into the sallow-faced turd. But he had come a long way since the beer-hall days.

"My dear Baron, I come to you first because of your standing. As a loyal German, I am sure you recognize the high honor that comes to those who aid the fatherland in its time of need. May I provide a small example? During the western campaign—to which, in all modesty, I contributed my leadership no less significantly than in the present campaign—the Dutch family Leiten, a family of some substance, like your own, and loyal to the fatherland, like your own, promptly volunteered its estate at Mechelen to my command needs."

"How commendable," said the Baron. And he picked up the binoculars again.

"Then you refuse this official request to aid the German high command," Pforzheim said flatly.

The Baron lowered his binoculars with deliberation. "If this was an official request from the high command, I would evaluate the need. But it is not. It is a personal request, which I therefore cannot in any way seriously consider."

Pforzheim's eyes flew wide. He was so incensed that in rising, his knees shook the table. His glass tipped, and the wine ran down onto his uniform pants.

"Are you calling me a liar? Are you calling me a fool? You will regret this!" Pforzheim raged.

The Baron smiled back. People like Pforzheim did not frighten him. For one thing, his rank in the reserves was the equivalent of Pforzheim's. For another, the general had foolishly failed to investigate his intended host; if he had done so, he would have known that *Reichsmarschall* Göring was a personal friend of the Baron's; in fact, the families had adjoining estates in Prussia before World War I.

One other factor determined the Baron's lack of hospitality: his anger at the killing of two valued members of his household staff earlier in the day. One was a first-class pastry chef named Jurgens, and the other was a new and promising *sous-chef* named Loebel. They had been trapped in Riga by the invasion, then caught up in the river of refugees escaping the capital, then executed along with six or seven hundred others in a typical SS "object lesson."

Killing Jews and establishing "object lessons" was all very well and good, but the indiscriminate murder of two members of his staff revealed negligence at the highest level. It was a supreme irony that the very man responsible for this criminal act should have come to him seeking favors.

While Pforzheim's motorcade retreated down the road, the Baron again focused his binoculars, trying to locate the earlier movement that had aroused his curiosity. He located his assistant, a whip-thin man in his thirties named Rolf Helger, and spoke to him briefly. Helger took another man with him, and they descended a path that ran down the opposite side from the entrance to the estate.

Helger was a particularly skilled hunter. Within the hour, he was able to track down the two people the Baron had spotted with his binoculars. They were dipping their feet in an icy pond below a series of cataracts. It was still light, but it was darkening fast now that the sun was gone.

"Long walk?" asked Helger. He was squatting on a narrow stone ledge above and behind them. Nikolai whirled in surprise, feeling as awkward as a crane; his feet squished in mud, and water lapped at his ankles. Katya turned so fast that she started to fall, then straightened with a splash. Now Nikolai could make out another man, separated from the first, also at a height above the pond. Helger was smoking a cigarette, luxuriously puffing. "You come from Riga?"

"Yes," Nikolai replied.

"We're not Wehrmacht," Helger said. "What's your name?"

"Granger."

"Sounds English. How about the young miss?"

"Katya," Nikolai said uneasily.

Reassuringly, Helger said, "You're not the first ones to come through here." He angled his thumb toward the manor house, half hidden far above. "We've been watching refugees all day."

Nikolai looked up, making out a roofline and some of the structure. "You live there?"

"We both do. This is the Hartigens-Hesse estate. Perhaps you know of the family."

"Yes, I've heard of it. Baron von Hartigens-Hesse. Are you the Baron?"

Helger flipped the cigarette into the pond; it snuffed out with a tiny *pfft*. "No, my name is Helger, property administrator. Do you have any idea where you're going?"

Nikolai struggled for an answer and finally admitted, "Not really."

Helger smiled compassionately. "No, of course not. All you know is that the Germans just took over the country, and you're on the run."

"Are they here?" Nikolai asked in an urgent whisper. It was the moment of faith.

Helger understood. "Don't worry. They're not here," he said. "In fact, the Baron just kicked out the commanding officer of all SS troops in Latvia." He shared a glance with the other man.

Nikolai could sense the depth of their satisfaction. He felt better, but he was still cautious. "Kicked him out?"

"Told him to get the hell out! My pardon, miss. But he's a man to be reckoned with, our Baron! If you look out there, past the three hills, between the hills and the lake ... see the road? See those three cars? That's the famous SS general, with his SS tail between his legs!"

"I'm sorry, I didn't know we were trespassing," Nikolai said.

"The Baron is not concerned about this," said Helger. "He noticed you from the veranda. He thought you might need help."

Katya could not contain herself. The world had become so implacably cruel in the past two days that a sob of relief bubbled out of her throat. They followed Helger and the other man up a winding path that led to the manor house.

The entrance hall was paneled in dark wood that shone with oil. There were the usual ancestral portraits of stiffly posed aristocrats, punctuated by white marble busts of Frederick the Great and Bismarck, of Goethe and Heinrich Heine. This formal display gave way to long panels comprising patterns of slatted oak. Still further along, six fluted columns of mahogany were arrayed to one side of the hall; they were oddly out of place, like abstract trophies of some distant war, yet they were pleasing to the eye.

The rooms they passed through had the same effect—a mad, eclectic decor that somehow delighted the eye and lifted an essentially somber architecture to playful levels. Above all, there was a sense of warmth, heightened by flowers brightening the dimmest corners.

Helger brought the young couple into the study and deferentially retreated. Hundreds of bound volumes reinforced the ambient air of the manor. The Baron, behind a desk topped in bright red leather, studied them with an expression of intense curiosity. Suddenly, he rose with a smile. His face radiated delight: an old friend renewing a relationship. "What beautiful young people!"

He paused, and his face took its characteristically somber expression. "The situation in our little country is not cheerful, is it? Well, we must carry on as best we can."

Nikolai and Katya felt more like tramps than refugees in front of the Baron, but they might have felt the same way under any circumstance, and in any case, the Baron fluttered his hand, dismissing their apologies. He announced that they would be his guests this evening. When they told him that they were not married, not even sweethearts, just second cousins, the Baron summoned a servant, who showed them to separate guest rooms.

It was dark but still early for dinner when Katya tapped at Nikolai's door and entered. Both looked scrubbed and alive again. They had soaked in luxuriant baths. Fresh clothing had been provided. "Can you believe it?" she said. "Think of it, Nikolai! A real Baron! And he's so wonderful!"

"He's taking a chance," Nikolai said. "For one thing, we're not popular with the Germans, and for another thing, neither is he."

"But there is something about him," she said. "He's not afraid of them."

"You're in love."

"Of course not! He's not even good-looking. Except in a mean way," she said, grinning. "My favorite type."

"Your favorite type? You're only seventeen."

"I'm eighteen."

"Okay, eighteen. For girls, that's still Baron-on-the-brain time."

"He's not the first Baron I've ever met," she said. "I met two Barons in Sweden."

"The one I met barked. That's a nice dress."

"You don't look bad either. But that's what I like about him. You don't have to ask. It's just there."

"Baroness Katya. I see the whole thing."

"I'm not above luxury," she said royally. "I wonder if he's married."

"Chances are you're wearing her dress."

"Good God, Nikolai, you think a lady with a title would wear something like this?" She picked up the hem and ruffled the dress. "It's been laundered a hundred times."

There was a pause, and he said, "Katya, I really don't even recognize you."

"What you really mean is, look how big you're getting on top."

He grinned. "What have you been learning in Sweden?"

"Everything a girl needs to know," she said impishly. Then: "Nikolai, what happened?"

"What happened is, the roof fell in."

"Nothing will ever be the same again, will it?"

"No."

"Tati's gone. So is Papi. I know that. They kill everything."

She was drifting, spiraling down, and Nikolai said brightly, "What we have to do is get across the Baltic to Sweden."

She glanced over, musing, "I still have my return ticket."

"Regular shipping's out," he said, "but there must be a million fishing boats."

Caught up in his words, she swung around, bright-eyed. "Nikolai, the Baron will help us. I'm sure of it."

"Don't be, Katya. He's still a kraut."

"But he hates the Nazis. I know he'll help us!"

Soothingly, he said, "Okay, but don't say too much, and don't expect too much."

She nodded. It made sense, but she didn't want to make sense of anything. Her mind swirled with images of blood and the ballet-like death flight of the two young brothers.

They went downstairs and joined the Baron in a sitting room. Katya, slowly emerging from her despondency, brightened in the warmth of the Baron's smile. An attendant poured champagne and offered hors d'oeuvres of caviar, herring, sprats, and various cheeses from France. The Baron turned the label of the bottle of champagne to his guests and said he hoped they liked it: a 1932 Bollard blanc de blanc.

It was difficult not to fall into a pleasant sense of belonging. Nikolai began to suspect he was being paranoid. The Baron's reserve had given way to an open manner. Perhaps it was the champagne, but he was jaunty and talkative. He described the Russians and the Germans as two sides of the same coin: plagues.

Of the two plagues, he suspected that the German plague was the worst, particularly with the beer-hall clown Hitler at the helm. There were times when one resented one's own lineage. On the other hand—straight faced and unpredictably droll now—he rather liked the haughtiness that came with Prussian rank, but what good was position and a large estate when one was subject to the vagaries of war and a horde of insects?

He passed on these zigzag thoughts in a burst, the flow of his words accelerating toward the end, and his delivery was so adroit and naturally comic that when he broke into a braying laugh, his guests laughed too, then laughed even harder when the Baron let out a high-pitched giggle.

Over dinner, served by two uniformed servants, he learned that Nikolai's mother was the renowned actress Tatiana Ulanova. He visibly saddened at the news of her death. He had always adored her—a superb actress. He proposed a toast, and with it, conversation slowed, and the mood darkened. Then logs in the fireplace shifted, sparks flew, and the fire flared up and crackled merrily. "Shall we forget the war?" the Baron suggested. They agreed, and good spirits returned.

The Baron used a thin, platinum cigarette case. On it was inscribed a crest with a black Maltese cross superimposed against an eagle; across the top of the crest in script was the family name, Hartigens-Hesse; at the bottom, the family motto, *"Ehre bis zum Tod."*

Another bottle of champagne was opened—Nikolai thought it was the fifth—and the Baron proposed another toast: "To beauty! Beauty is everything!" He put his hand over Nikolai's and said, "You are my beautiful boy, aren't you?"

The champagne dissipated in a blink. Nikolai looked at Katya, but there was a soft, oblivious smile on her face, and her eyes were half-closed. Nikolai realized that the Baron was waiting for some sort of answer. He shook his head, as though to clear it.

"Too much champagne," he slurred.

"I think you heard me," said the Baron. "And I think you know what I mean."

"Sorry?" Nikolai stalled, grinning foolishly.

The Baron examined Nikolai. "We need music," the Baron said, sounding almost flighty again.

Nikolai was encouraged. The Baron seemed to have changed course. "Mu-sic!" said Nikolai, dividing the syllables.

The Baron rose, waving his champagne glass. "To the music room!"

Nikolai worked at rising and managed to sway upright. "Sorry! Not going to make it!" he intoned tunefully.

"Of course you'll make it. I count on you, my beautiful boy." Nikolai's heart sank. The Baron was focused and intent. "What a shame," he said. "She's falling asleep."

"I think we'd better get to bed," Nikolai muttered.

"Now, that is perfect nonsense," said the Baron cheerfully. "Helger, help the young lady."

Nikolai whirled. Out of nowhere, Helger had appeared. He was gently tugging Katya to her feet. Her eyelids fluttered, then she made out Helger and smiled. She caught Nikolai's worried expression and said, "Think I drank too much." Helger had taken her elbow and was guiding her. "Where are we going?" she asked Nikolai.

"Music," Hartigens-Hesse called over. "Do you like to dance, young Miss Katya?"

"I think I'm too tired," she said pleasantly.

"Beautiful young people are never too tired," said the Baron. He headed out of the room, with Helger steering Katya right behind him.

"Hold on a second," Nikolai said, but neither the Baron nor Helger paid attention. Katya again noticed Nikolai's expression, and this time she connected it to Helger's sturdy grip and the Baron's determined step, and she stopped short and pulled free.

The Baron turned and came back to her. "What seems to be the problem?"

"I don't want to go."

"Let her alone," Nikolai said, coming up and taking Katya's arm.

"You said you were friends, nothing more."

"She doesn't want to go with you. I'm not going either."

The Baron made a show of bewilderment. "I take pride in my hospitality. But I do not like it abused."

Helger, with no further pretext of civility, pulled Katya free and propelled her toward a door. She stumbled, trying to keep up, and Helger unceremoniously pushed her through into the next room.

"What the hell do you think you're doing?" Nikolai shouted, barreling in pursuit. The Baron, with a strange smile, held the door open for him, and Nikolai brushed past. He found himself in a large music room. It was very softly lit with two or three electric candelabra on the walls. There were more busts and more paintings: Mozart, Beethoven, Bach, Handel. The walls were covered in tapestries, dark and moody, evoking the sixteenth and seventeenth centuries; the ceiling was a dazzling yellow collage of flute-playing satyrs. This formality was relieved by a scattering of old, comfortable furniture, including two large sofas, deep-set lounge chairs, and an exotically curved chaise longue.

Katya, now seated in a chair, gripped the arms with a dazed look. But Helger had moved away from her. His hands were piously clasped before him, and he wore an eager look of expectation. The Baron entered the room and paused to pluck a cigarette from his case. While he lit it, Nikolai said, "This is crazy! What's going on?"

The Baron responded puckishly, raising his finger to his lips and shushing him. Still sporting a loopy smile, he crossed to the piano. His gait was stiff, and his feet barely skimmed the carpet. He bowed and sat down. His fingers fluttered: a limbering exercise.

"Ladies and gentlemen, I promised you music, and for your patience, I thank you."

Helger politely applauded. The Baron began to play. He had a light touch and a deft hand, which was somehow not surprising, but his choice of music took Nikolai aback. It was a Gershwin medley: "Love Walked In," "Embraceable You," and "Our Love Is Here to Stay." Cigarette smoke drifted up to his eyes, and he closed them rapturously.

By now, Katya was more curious than frightened. She was beginning to think that the Baron's performance, like his showy entrance into the music room, was stagecraft rather than malice. As for Helger, his thuggish conduct seemed more like a joke now; he was tapping a toe to the music.

The Baron finished with a flourish and a flash of teeth. Helger applauded and looked over exhortingly. Katya dropped all concern and joined in.

"Helger!" the Baron called. In an instant, Helger, who had produced a small leather kit, was at his side. The Baron let his jacket fall to the floor and rolled up his sleeve. Helger took out a needle and a vial and slipped the needle into the Baron's arm with remarkable speed.

Nikolai was too surprised to do anything but watch with clinical interest. Then he felt foolish, as logic flooded his brain and cleared away the fog. In London, he had briefly known the pampered son of a Harley Street physician who smoked, swallowed, and stabbed himself with any form of morphine-based drug he could steal from his father. The pampered son and the exotic Baron were two peas in the same deranged pod.

Katya's eyes were wide again. Nikolai moved to her and took her arm. "That's it. Let's go."

She rose quickly, and they started out. But Helger cut across to the door and turned a key. He stuck the key in his pocket and faced the couple. "Open it," Nikolai commanded.

"I don't think so," said the Baron, who approached, rolling down his sleeve. "Helger," he said.

Nikolai caught a flash of metal. Helger was holding a Luger. "Be nice," said the Baron. "In this house, we are all friends."

Helger waved them toward a sofa. With his gun barrel, he made another gesture. The Baron impatiently clarified, saying, "Off, off, off."

They stared over, frozen. "Do it now," Helger snarled. Nikolai's hand floated up to his shirt, but Katya kept staring, and Helger, without bothering to change his expression, pulled her ear out of a tangle of long hair and pressed the muzzle of the Luger against it. He fired.

Blood spattered on Katya's dress and on her face and hair, and her mouth dropped open in astonishment. The bullet ripped off her earlobe and left a jagged residue of mangled flesh. The gasp that came from her mouth was a scream she could not form.

Nikolai roared and shot forward, but Helger was too fast, too accustomed to brawling; he brought the butt of the gun down on Nikolai's neck and sent him spinning. The Baron ignored Nikolai; he stuck his angry face into Katya's and bawled, "Off! Off! Off!" But she was in shock. Her hand went up to touch her ear, but she could not summon the will to do so.

Seething, the Baron began to tear at her clothes. Katya did not move. She observed his furious clawing and tearing as though from a distance; she watched the strange twists and turns of his mouth, heard his wordless rage, and felt his angry spittle, but she was embedded in stone.

"Stay on your knees," Helger commanded Nikolai. "Now, off. Everything."

Nikolai's head was throbbing, but there was nothing he could do. He unbuttoned his shirt and took it off. Through a cloudy prism of pain, he could see the Baron's frantic fingers strip Katya's upper body. Her solid breasts altered the Baron's mercurial mood. "Ooh!" he said in adulation, tweaking her nipples. "Look, Helger."

Helger, keeping the gun trained on Nikolai, leaned over and pinched. Katya cried out in pain. Jolted from her stupor, she flailed her hands. The Baron grinned. "What a delicious bitch you are!" He cracked her face with the back of his hand, and her head flew back. He hit her again. "Now, you take off the rest, or he gets a bullet!"

Shaking, Katya peeled off what was left of her clothes. Helger kicked Nikolai sharply in the side. "Hurry it up, pig!" Crouching on the carpet, Nikolai painfully pulled off the rest of his clothing. "Back on your knees, and keep your head down," Helger ordered. The Baron looked on keenly while Nikolai inched up to his hands and knees.

"I think, Helger, on the ottoman."

Helger whacked the back of Nikolai's neck again, not hard enough to send him reeling this time, but just enough to cloud his brain. Helger moved to a large ottoman done in leather triangles of black and white; with his foot, he slid it in front of Nikolai.

"Up, up," he ordered. Dizzy, Nikolai dragged himself to the ottoman, his stomach flat against the leather and his head drooped to the floor.

"Butter his bum," said the Baron. The numbed Nikolai tried to raise his head in protest, and once again Helger brought the Luger down on his neck. Nikolai went limp with a soft groan, and while Helger moved to a sideboard, the Baron turned Katya roughly around and said, "Bend."

Her response was slow, and the Baron shouted, "Bend!" She did so, and he nodded with satisfaction.

At the sideboard, Helger uncovered what turned out to be a butter dish; it was filled with dinner-size cubes that were soft but not yet melted. He picked up a wooden rod and dipped and turned it in the butter dish until the rod was slathered. He returned to the prostrate Nikolai and unceremoniously shoved in the rod. He turned it a few times, jabbing it back and forth, then threw the wooden rod into a wastebasket, like a busy doctor with a tongue depressor.

"Ready," he announced to the Baron.

"Thank you, Helger," the Baron said with a cavalier wave. Almost ritualistically, they changed places.

The Baron dropped to his knees and unbuttoned his trousers. With a gasp of anticipation, he slid into Nikolai. Nikolai's sense of what was happening was vague; his will had been systematically weakened in the manner of a Spanish bull debilitated by banderilleros. Helger, with the smile of an aficionado, shouted, "Olé!"

He turned his attention to Katya. He motioned for her to lie back on the sofa. Her mouth was open, and she was breathing hard. She shook her head, and Helger hit her face with the heel of his hand. She fell back to the sofa, and he placed a hard knee in her groin while he fumbled with buttons. He opened her legs with a brusque motion of his hands, as though opening a coconut, and plunged into her. He kept driving, then sensed a sticky, lava-like flow within her. "Look!" he called over to the Baron. He had pulled out and was exhibiting his blood-stained penis.

"Bravo," said the Baron, but his voice was tense. Katya's virginity did not interest him. The fact was that he could not maintain his stroke. He had shriveled and recoiled. He was dangling, limp and small. Indignation swelled. "Open up! Open up!" he ordered Nikolai. He tried again, but the muscle hung like a rotting vine.

Helger had returned to his rape of Katya. He was big and hard, and he noted with delight her squeals of pain. He was not a subtle man, and he soon poured into her, bellowing his triumph. When he pushed to his feet, the Baron was staring at him in anger. Helger recognized his pique—when the Baron failed, he fumed at Helger. The scenario varied only in the butterflies they trapped.

Empathetically, Helger said, "They close up, that type."

"You have to use dynamite," the Baron said. It was familiar, but Helger laughed.

He slapped Katya's rump. "Try this one. Tender and juicy."

The Baron considered the proposition, It began to appeal to him. In a sudden flush of enthusiasm, he said, "Get him off."

Helger moved to Nikolai's limp form and kicked him in the ribs. Helger thought he heard a crack, the snap of a bone, as Nikolai tumbled from the ottoman and sprawled across the floor. Helger followed up with a short, hard kick to the groin. Nikolai's head rolled over, and his eyes snapped shut.

Helger moved back to Katya. He grabbed a handful of her hair and jerked her off the sofa—he had clutched the side of her head where her ear had been partly shot away, and she screamed wildly. Helger dumped her across the ottoman, face down. With his boot, he prodded her thighs apart and elevated her rear end.

"Slippery-smooth," instructed the Baron. Helger glanced at him like an overworked housekeeper and retrieved the wooden rod. It was still moist, and he rammed it deep into her violently quivering body, withdrew the rod, and waved it like a baton. "Ready, your highness," he said with a sneer.

As always during such moments, the Baron, busy juggling his pounding complexes, did not pick up on this daring note of scorn. His eyes were riveted on the target; he felt a renewed stirring in his loins, inched toward her, and began to inch into her. But then his world collapsed, and once again he was hopelessly soft.

He roared in anger. Then he called out, "Helger!" Helger, the deity.

Helger knew just what to do. "Use this," he said. He handed over the Luger. The Baron's eyes popped open. Of course! He thrust the gun barrel into Katya's anus. It slid in smoothly and remained inflexibly stiff and hard. It was perfect. The Baron trembled with a new sense of excitement.

He began to thicken and rise. But he would not trust himself to alien confines; he tightened his grip on the butt of the gun and redoubled his piston-like efforts. With his free hand, he stroked himself. In a rare and wondrous moment, he soared, and it was magic. In the same second, he pulled the trigger.

CHAPTER 3

▼

Fresh off the crosstown Manhattan bus, Leo clomped up the stairs to Heinz Baumann's apartment door, faded corduroy jacket pulled aside to reveal a photograph of Hitler, a page he had torn out of *Look* magazine. Dueling Checker cabs out on the street honked their horns as Leo waggled the photo like a porno dealer. "*Gute geburtstag!*" he said to Heinz, who for a split second wondered how Leo, though no great brain, could place Hitler's birthday in February instead of April.

Heinz Baumann was a stocky man with thick black hair and piercing, close-set eyes. He was in his mid-forties but looked younger. Suddenly, he remembered that it was his own birthday. Only that morning, in fact, Anna had tossed off a "Happy birthday, Papa" when she left the house, but it was low-key and little more than a whisper, because they were fighting, and as usual, Anna went quiet and Heinz sullen when they argued. So he had brusquely shoved aside her greeting, to the point of barely remembering it.

Anna was a growing puzzle. The charm of her innocence seemed to have disappeared over the past few years. The paradox was that people kept telling him how beautiful she was, even more beautiful now that she had flowered out of her teens into womanhood, but all Heinz could see in her womanhood was the hard edge that came with it, the loss of obedience, the streaks of independence that reminded him of her mother, the thought of whom made him bristle, even after all these years.

He felt a pang because the photograph of Hitler failed to arouse him, as it once would have had. His beliefs were as strong as ever—stronger—and his fealty unquestionable. But he had outgrown the Pavlovian responses of the old days.

The old days of the *Bund*, of uniformed marches and the Horst Wessel till their throats were raw: those days were gone. In their place was a quieter, even deeper dedication, solemnized by the clandestine life he now led.

"Where's Anna?" Leo asked, entering the apartment as Heinz hastily closed the door.

"Work," Heinz said impatiently, with the tone of a man forced to repeat the obvious ad nauseam.

"Work?" Leo said, slapping his forehead. "Of course!" He held up the photograph of Hitler, creased and a little stained—coffee, or butter from a roll. "You got a tack? We could put it up."

Drooping an eyebrow, Heinz said, "What else should I do? Hang a swastika out the window?"

Leo's eyes blinked. He was something of a fool, but so staunch that he understood everything, given enough time. "No, Heinz, no. I don't mean for serious put it up. I meant just for now, before somebody, she comes home."

"I ain't putting up no photographs just to look at for five minutes and then you flush it down," Heinz said. He could see that Leo, with the brittle sensitivity of a scorned woman, was a little downcast, so he added, "Thanks anyway."

Leo perked up, but he went through the usual gradations of recovery. "I should've brought a real present."

"Since when? I ever ask you for a present? Who wants a present?"

"I should've brought. What's a paper picture from a magazine? Even Hitler."

The last was a hissed sacrament, but Heinz looked over sharply. "And don't use names open. You know better."

"No more," Leo agreed. He was curiously satisfied; taking orders from Heinz wove him back into the fold.

Heinz frowned. He gestured at the photo, still clutched in Leo's sweaty hand. "Dumb walking around with something like that anyway."

Leo nodded grimly. As always, when he reflected on his clumsy ways, he clicked his tongue: *Shame on myself!* His first impulse was to tear the photo of Hitler into dozens of pieces, but he could not bear the thought, and he folded the thin paper until it was the size of a postage stamp and slid it into a jacket pocket.

He pointed to a crumpled *New York Daily News* on a chair. "You see the war?" he said, mouth widening to the good news, two teeth missing, the rest yellow-gray. "Halfway through Russia."

"Halfway, but now they got winter," Heinz said glumly.

"Far as Rosenfelt and his gang coming in the war," Leo grandly assured him, "they got *scheiss* in the pants."

"Got *scheiss* because they know better," Heinz said.

"You saw it in the paper too?" Leo said excitedly. "How we got secret stuff in the works?"

"Maybe," Heinz said.

Leo studied him. "Didn't even see it in the papers! You knew!"

"Didn't say I knew," Heinz said. "Just said maybe."

"And maybe you hear things special!" Leo said brightly. Heinz let it go, and Leo, sensing humility, grinned.

The moment passed, and Leo wiped his brow. "You mind I let the water run cold?"

"So take a beer," Heinz said.

Leo scampered into the kitchen. In all the time they had known each other, he had never been able to ask for something like a beer, so it was always the indirect approach, the ritual playing itself out with Heinz frowning at being put upon, but accepting the imposition as normal, even requisite to the relationship.

"You want one?" Leo asked, plucking out two bottles.

"*Ja*," Heinz said.

Leo opened the bottles and returned to the cramped living room. It had a love seat, two chairs, a couple of tall lamps, and two tables with doilies. Anna hated the doilies; she said they were corny and smelled like wet dogs, but Heinz had brought them back from his trip to his home village in the old Sudetenland three years ago, at the tail end of his hegira to Berlin. They did smell, but they smelled more like hops to him.

They sat in their familiar way, sucking moodily at their beers. The time was habitual too—Heinz had just closed his shop, and Leo was on the night shift, selling tickets at an IRT booth under 96th Street.

"How's it going downstairs?" Leo asked.

"Downstairs" was Heinz's electrical shop a block over, the tiny store he had opened over twenty years ago.

"Same."

"I was thinking," Leo said. "Everybody's making money from business, so how about us?"

It had all changed since the old days, except that Leo still came up with cock-eyed schemes, even if they were less flamboyant than his proposal to open a ham-burger stand in Brooklyn's predominantly Jewish Prospect Park area and mix ground pork with the hamburgers, or to telephone Harlem residents with the news that they had won fifty dollars to be picked up in Africa. "How about us what?" Heinz asked.

"You know what I saw one block east on 91st, walking home yesterday?"

"Listening."

"Empty store," Leo said enthusiastically.

"Empty store. What for?"

"Open another place," Leo said. "Everybody's busy like hell from the war, right? Am I right? So you open another store, and you make twice as much."

"Where's 'us'?" Heinz innocently asked. "You an electrician now?"

"I got a few bucks put away," Leo said. "I could put in with you. Partners."

"On thirty-two bucks a week's salary, you got put away?" Heinz said.

"Thirty-six fifty," Leo protested. "We got a raise. Anyway, I got three hundred bucks for investment money, if you want to know."

"All right, all right," Heinz said, backing off, giving Leo a dollop of dignity. Heinz sighed. As always with Leo, the thought was there, but not the thinking. "Let me give you the problems."

He swallowed some beer and wiped his mouth with two fingers facing in, an old habit. "First problem is, where do you get help these days for electrical? In New York? You could look till you're blue in the face. Next problem—" He leaned forward intimately. "Next problem is, Leo, what don't I want the most?"

Abstract questions bewildered Leo. He stared at his beer bottle, brain racing but fogged.

"I'll tell you," said Heinz. "What I don't want is stand out like a sore thumb. The more people I see, the more I stand out. You understand?"

"Yeah, but what are we talking? Another little store."

"Let me tell you how it is with one little store. Maybe not so many people come in anymore, but the ones that come in, most of them I never seen before. They buy a plug, they got a shorted-out lamp, they need a wall plate. Never seen them before, so how do I know who they are? Maybe from the cops, from the FBI—how do I know? I don't. I'm taking my chances. New people every day. Now you want two stores, twice as many people to point the finger. Don't make sense."

Leo moved in and whispered, "You think they're still looking?"

"How do I know they ain't?" Heinz said, hard and impatient now.

Boldly, Leo said, "If you ask what I think, that whole thing's dead as a door-nail. Not one cop ever came by with a question. Am I right? So that means, as far as they're concerned, they don't know you from Adam about that whole thing."

Heinz grunted a maybe.

"Son of a bitch," Leo hissed. "Should've cut his balls off, that Ebell."

Even though it was hushed, Heinz cautioned, "Use your brain!" But then, uncharacteristically waggish, he said, "Don't worry. The balls went flying, with the rest."

Leo rocked back, then roared with laughter. When it subsided, they sat and sipped and stared into nothing. Then Leo said, "Wish we could start up something again." Heinz nodded. It was silly, beyond foolish, but he felt the same.

"What if we did?" Leo offered, bold again.

"With what?" Heinz said. "With three hundred dollars?"

Leo was batting his eyes again, as always expecting more for meaning well than Heinz was prepared to give.

"It ain't the old days, is the point," Heinz said. "What you can forget is, 'This is a free country.' It ain't free for us. For us, this country is a prisoner of war camp, so you can't just go out and start up another *Bund*. And you can't run around telling about the Third Reich no more, because you're telling that to the enemy. *Verstehst?*"

It was simplification to the point of insult, but Leo nodded sagely. Then he sighed hugely and said, "I wish we could do something."

It was so plaintive that Heinz said, "Who don't?" He sucked out from between his teeth a string of boiled beef left over from lunch. There was another silence, and Heinz finally said, "Well."

It was the signal for Leo's departure; he checked the time on a battered one-dollar pocket watch. "Better go make some dough, hey?" It was an old joke left over from his bakery days. He emptied his bottle and paused, the vacillation that sometimes produced another beer, but not this time.

"Well," he said. "So, what time she gets home? Anna?"

"Don't know."

"How's the job?"

"Okay, far as I know."

"I never see her. Maybe I'll stay for once to say hello."

"She'll be tired," Heinz said.

"Too tired to get a kiss hello from her own godfather, Uncle Leo?" burbled Leo.

"Godfather" rankled Heinz, first because it was a title that Leo had awarded himself when Anna was still a child, and second because it implied a sharing that Heinz would never surrender to anyone.

The subtleties of temperament eluded Leo, so he had no idea he was making it worse now, saying, "Another thing I been thinking, Heinz. One of these days, our little Anna, she's gonna find somebody, and just like that, she'll be gone."

He was as glum as he could be, too distracted to notice Heinz glaring at him, dark-faced.

"Time to go," said Heinz in a choked voice. Leo looked up. He registered mild perplexity, wondering what he had done wrong. Nothing, he decided; Heinz too was unsettled at the prospect of losing Anna. Leo moved to the door, and in the crisp tone of someone who knows when to leave, he said, "Well, going," and left.

Heinz listened to Leo's off-balance, arthritic descent of the stairs, the distant echo of his work shoes hitting the tiny marble floor of the foyer, then the big door locking into place like the sound of a truck door.

Street noises seeped into the apartment, but Heinz strained them out. What was left was an intense silence that had a rhythm all its own, one in which time was curiously suspended. Lately, Heinz was given to reverie. *Like an old man,* he thought. But he was frozen in the present, so where else could he go but the past?

The *Bund* kept popping up in his thoughts, and fat-ass *Bundesführer* Fritz Kuhn, whom he had once worshipped, and who was now in jail. And even though it was American law that had put him there, Heinz felt nothing but satisfaction. The short-sighted Kuhn had killed *Die Lanze*, Heinz's proposal for a special action group within the organization.

There had been plenty of social activities in those days: beer fests and baseball games at Camp Siegfried on Long Island, uniformed marches with a noisy band in lederhosen keeping time. There had been a certain amount of political action too: flyers tacked to telephone poles, pamphlets handed out at street corners, and the periodic rallies, though none surpassing the one at Madison Square Garden a few months before the war, a golden night of nights with twenty thousand people screaming for the triumph of national socialism in America. From that evening on, it was not enough to carry a standard on parade or prance around in a uniform that would never see battle.

When Kuhn rejected *Die Lanze*, Heinz had quit the *Bund* and formed his own squad of activists. There were six of them, and they were dedicated to harassing the enemies of national socialism. But there were problems from the start. Dues were a modest one dollar per week, but there were always holdouts and excuses; Heinz kept feeding the kitty in order to maintain some semblance of a treasury.

Heinz had put his foot down, but discipline was shabby, at best. They were a rowdy bunch, given to anarchy. No sooner would Heinz propose a plan of action when an outcry would go up. For example, he once proposed sneaking into the offices of the *Communist Daily Worker* and pouring molasses into the printing presses. Metzger, a cabbie, said, "Who the hell cares about a bunch of commies?

The ones we should go after is the wops. They stink from garlic and they're the worst tippers."

Freitag wanted to hit the *Schwarzes*, and the brothers Haas, Oskar, and Gregor were indignant because they thought there should be one target and only one: the Jews. "If our money don't go for the Jews," Gregor had said indignantly, despite the fact that he and Oskar were two weeks in arrears, "then what are we here for?"

Worst was Ebell, a rodent-faced short-order diner cook. He challenged Heinz's authority in general, "Who made you the *Führer?*" And he objected to Heinz's plans because they missed the point. He had expected a big-time approach. They should be knocking over businesses, gas stations, upscale apartments, anything worth a buck; the proceeds would fuel a real treasury, not "this penny-ante shit." He said it using the snide tone that infuriated Heinz and made him want to kill Ebell, which he eventually did.

Die Lanze broke up soon enough, but Heinz never stopped. With Leo's help, he attacked small, select targets. Thomas E. Dewey was a special irritant, so Heinz slipped into the courthouse garage, waited until Dewey's chauffeur walked off to lunch, then set fire to the district attorney's Buick. When the fire was attributed to vandals—the note left under the windshield wiper apparently having been destroyed along with the rest of the car—Heinz decided that his next effort would have to bring more notoriety to the cause.

He pondered the problem for days before hitting on an ingenious idea, and on the following Sunday, he and Leo snuck into radio station WNYC. With Leo on guard, Heinz ranged through the corridors until he found the studio where Fiorello LaGuardia was reading the funnies over the air, a Sunday morning innovation during the newspaper strike. Heinz had burst into the studio, grabbed the microphone from the astonished mayor, and shouted, "Here is Special Unit KG! We interrupt to bring you the truth about this famous Mayor LaGuardia! He is a friend only of the communists and Jews! Do not listen to his lies! Long live national socialism! Long live our glorious *Führer*, Adolf Hitler!"

All the while, LaGuardia and his engineer on the other side of the glass were frozen in shock, along with several hundred thousand listeners. Heinz had successfully fled the building, with Leo pounding behind him.

The city buzzed with the incident, but its political implications were dismissed as the work of a crackpot.

More frustrated than ever, Heinz realized that nothing could be done without influence. Influence required power, and power required money, and he had none of those things. He began to think. If these things were unobtainable where he was because of who he was, then he must go elsewhere to acquire the mantle of power that would change his life and empower his mission.

He juggled these ideas until the answer fell into place. He must go to Berlin. He must persuade someone in the hierarchy of German government to bless his cause—which, after all, was their cause. How could they refuse?

Leo was stunned at the audacity of his plan. "To Berlin? To talk to Hitler himself?"

"Maybe not Hitler himself," Heinz had corrected.

Leo repeated, "Hitler himself!" Even Heinz was caught up in the exhilaration of the moment, but it soon devolved to grim reality. Where would the money come from?

The problem seemed insoluble but turned out to be no problem at all, and the LaGuardia escapade had done the trick. It was the next night, and Heinz and Leo were sitting over steins and bratwurst when Helga Schmidt came in. Tall and lean with a long, angular face, she was the widow of a man who had done well in the wholesale food business; she was cynical and hard-edged, yet she was considered quite a catch. Men probed for a key to her affection, or at least the easier life she could provide, but Helga, content in her upscale independence, easily fended them off.

Earlier, Leo had introduced her to Heinz in the hope of financing *Die Lanze*. Her politics were solidly national socialist, and she had been attracted to the gruff, no-nonsense Heinz but had silently branded him small-time, and Heinz, perceiving her scorn, had told her to go to hell. Now, these many months later, she had slid into his booth at the Stuttgartenkeller, ordered a beer, lit a cigarette, and smiled broadly. "Baumann, you are one gutsy son of a bitch."

She had recognized his voice on the radio. She never had thought much of nuisance activities like burning Dewey's car, or harassing Jews by breaking windows, but the LaGuardia stunt showed not only audacity but also imagination, and more importantly, it was a propaganda triumph. It was big-time.

Leo eventually went home, and Helga brought Heinz back to her apartment, which was large and handsomely furnished. They drank and talked with growing fervor about Hitler and the Third Reich. Eventually they succumbed to the Wagnerian circumstances and made love, an enterprise that Heinz viewed queasily; it was her aid he sought, not her body. But he realized that the two were inextricably meshed, and when it was over, Helga sat naked at a secretary, small-breasted and lean-shanked, and scribbled out a check for five hundred dollars so Heinz could go to Berlin.

Heinz had taken the Bremen and exulted through eight days of stormy weather as she trembled in the Atlantic trough. Nothing mattered, because Berlin was at the other end, and when he reached it at last—the holy city—tears filled his eyes. For the next few days, he was rapturously lost. The buildings were stately, the streets intimate; there were open-air cafés and cobblestone paths along the winding river Spree. The people were confident; they radiated purpose. And banners and flags of red, white, and black draped with swastikas were everywhere. Berlin fairly vibrated with the excitement of the new order. In this city, which he had never seen before, he was home.

But fidelity to the homeland did not ease his task. Heinz went from one ministry to another, propelled by sacred duty, and everywhere, he was treated with indifference and sometimes with contempt. Heinz saw their point. He had come with no credentials, and the fact that he had been born in Germany did not make him less of an alien in their eyes. He was also forced to admit that bureaucrats were bureaucrats, even in this superior society.

Butting his head against a stone wall was rankling; he began to lose his temper. Returning for the fifth time to the Ministry of Propaganda, where he had worked his way up to a plump, low-grade clerk named Frau Kobler, Heinz once again repeated his story: He needed support to reinvigorate the Nazi movement in the United States, the German-American *Bund* was worthless, and he had come all the way from America to discuss this vital matter with the proper authority— such as *Reichsführer* Goebbels, he hinted again.

Like the four clerks before her, Frau Kobler, her little eyes buried like raisins in a bun, had looked up with a smirk. An appointment to see the *Reichsführer* had to be supported by proper credentials, references, and recommendations, none of which Heinz possessed. He was welcome to return and resubmit an application when such criteria were met. If all was then in order, Heinz might possibly gain an audience with one of the *Reichsführer*'s deputy advisors. "As to a personal meeting with the *Reichsführer* himself," Frau Kobler had added, with unmistakable disdain, "I suggest you dismiss such a notion from your mind."

So dripping was the woman's condescension that Heinz had exploded, bending over her desk and sputtering his rage two inches from her face. Frau Kobler's cry had brought two uniformed guards racing over. They had each grabbed an arm and were starting to cart him off when a tall, slim man of about thirty appeared before them. He had just come out of an office and had overheard a bit of the exchange between Heinz and Frau Kobler. Now he flexed a finger, whereupon the two guards instantly released Heinz.

Perhaps he could be of some service, the man had said, graciously enough. One thing led to another, and soon Heinz found himself at a café near the ministry, drinking beer and pouring his heart out. The man's name was Maximilian Siebert. He worked for the government; he had been visiting a friend in the propaganda ministry when he became aware of Heinz's problem. Siebert had recognized an American accent and intervened. The German virtue of hospitality must be maintained, new Reich or old. In any case, he had remarked with a smile, Heinz, a native German, hardly qualified as an *Ausländer*.

Siebert had listened patiently, and he was so sympathetic and straightforward that Heinz began to sense that he had found the important ally he needed. But in this he was disappointed. Siebert bluntly told him that his trip to Germany was a waste of time.

"But with the help of an important person, it can succeed!" Heinz had interrupted.

Siebert shook his head, accepting the mantle of "important person" and dismissing it all in the same breath. He explained that the world was about to change. Germany would soon be at war. Inevitably, America would be drawn in, and her sympathies would lie with England and France. National socialism in America was doomed to failure. Heinz argued that the *Führer* was too shrewd to start a war. And why should he? Everything was falling into his lap!

Two SS officers passed, crisply dressed in black uniforms of high rank, polished black boots synchronously clicking against the marble floor. They knew Siebert and nodded. Siebert nodded back. But the exchange was not quite equal: Siebert's nod was less deferential. Suddenly, Heinz felt foolish. This man Siebert obviously understood the workings of the government and the party and had a clear insight into its foreign policy. Who was he, Heinz, to argue his penny-ante politics with this authoritative insider?

He stammered an apology; he regretted taking up Siebert's time. His objective had been to, in some small way, advance the German state; in a confession that was as rare as it was heartfelt, Heinz admitted that he had not always gone about this in the best way. Siebert smiled warmly. He extended a hand.

When Heinz took it, Siebert remarked that men like Heinz were invaluable: they breathed passion into the cause. Siebert had not yet relinquished his grip when he said, "Tell me, Herr Baumann, would you do *anything* for our country?"

"Anything!" Heinz had replied.

"Then such a moment may come, *mein Herr*," Siebert said. And then he had walked off.

CHAPTER 4

▼

When the harbor came into view, passengers scrambled up out of the bowels of the ship and claimed places at the railing. It had been a rough winter crossing of nine days, and the *Kungsholm* glistened with an icy coating. One day out of Malmo came the news that the Japanese had bombed Pearl Harbor. Two days later, America and Germany had declared war, and the torpedo-wary captain of the *Kungsholm* steered a zigzag course that took them into the vortex of a North Atlantic storm system.

Everyone became sick, but the foul weather had its advantages—churning seas minimized submarine attacks. At last, on the final day of the journey, the turbulent waters calmed, and the old ship sailed past the lighthouse as the skyline poked through the fog. Nikolai and a Czech named Stefan Razek pushed up to the railing. Out of the silence, the usual mystical quiet that attended arrival from across the sea, an incredulous voice shouted, "Where is Statue of Liberty?"

"You stupid," came an impatient reply in the same accent. "Here is Boston. Statue of Liberty, New York."

"Oh," said the first voice, amid much laughter. Stefan was a barrel-chested young man with thin curls of reddish hair. He had taken to chewing gum several months before, a habit made possible by innumerable trips to the American embassy in Stockholm and the indulgence of a State Department clerk, a young woman who liked his flirting. Stefan's features were too pronounced and somewhat oddly placed, but he generated so much bonhomie that women sniffed around like dogs. He had a theory: women liked enterprising men; they were good providers. The fact that he had been a thief in Prague and had twice been jailed did not alter his theory.

Nikolai had met Stefan at the embassy. Out of the welter of languages being spoken there, the two men had discovered a common ground in English. So many hundreds had stood in line there that day that a permanent detail of Swedish police had been assigned to keep order. Adding to the frenzy was the fact that many of the refugees did not have proper documentation, They came from conquered countries all across Europe on anything that would float, and those who made it arrived exhausted and empty-handed. Neutral Sweden could not absorb them all, and most arrivals were only granted short-term visas. But even refugees who could stay in Sweden wanted to move on. America was the golden goal.

The two young men stood in the lines every day, and every day brought rumors. One day, the rumors had it that no further applications for visas would be accepted. The next day, rumors restored the applications but sharply reduced the quota. And the day after that, word went up and down the lines that petitions from several countries, including Latvia and Czechoslovakia, were now permanently excluded.

Nikolai had escaped Latvia with nothing more than the clothing on his back and the Baron's platinum cigarette case. In normal times, the case would have been worth a great deal, but now there were so many refugee baubles floating around that the market was flooded. Not that it mattered to Nikolai; he would never part with the cigarette case.

Nikolai eased it out of his pocket and read the inscriptions aloud "*Hartigens-Hesse*", and "*Ehre Bis Zum Tod.*","*Honor to the death* It was his only tangible souvenir of that night's madness.

There were also flashes of memory, such as his rocket-like bicycle ride down the bumpy path that descended from the rear of the house to the cataracts and the cold pool into which they had dipped their feet. His wild ride had taken place in the thin light of dawn.

Staggering, he had made his way through dark rooms, bouncing off furniture, crashing to the floor, swiping at the walls for support, and leaving bloody swaths wherever he went. Had the staff not been separately housed, he would have been discovered within a minute. But the only two people who could have heard his painfully labored exit were nakedly intertwined, drugged, and drunken.

The bicycle was parked just outside the kitchen. He had no idea how he had managed to elevate himself to the seat, or how, after crashing twice, he had managed to return to it. That he'd stayed in the seat at all was nothing short of astounding. His ribs were broken, and the pain was excruciating. He tried desperately to concentrate on balancing the bicycle, but he kept drifting in and out of consciousness. The woods went by in a blur. He recognized the cascades, the pool

… realized he was off the path and cutting through the woods … then he was back on the path and the woods were thinning, the ground leveling, the bicycle slowing through a mossy meadow … slowing to a dreamlike pace, and he was tumbling into a mattress of thick grass.

When he awakened, he was bouncing again, but this time down a pitted road in the back of a rickety truck with four mistiming cylinders and spent springs. Each jolt was pure torture, a stab in the side with a red-hot sword. At one point, his eyes rolled open and took in blue skies and puffy June clouds. He was taken with the thought that his journey was the stuff of Christ, but could Christ have made his big trip in June?

In and out, in and out, and the next time he was in he thought, *How could it be June if he rose in April?* He began to think that he was floating upward—Nikolai Is Risen. In a few seconds, he would touch the clouds.

There was another period of oblivion and resurrection; then he was in a high bed with a headboard in a comfortable bedroom, with three people looking on. A man in a dark vest was bending over him, turning him, and taping his ribs. Nikolai's eyes flew open wide, and he gasped in pain. The man in the dark vest, a doctor, was saying, "How does that feel?"

Nikolai wanted to say that his ribs hurt like hell; but his mouth was stuck.

One of the other people, a woman with a motherly smile, held a glass of water to his lips. He sipped and felt better.

"The pain will ease in a few days," said the doctor. He gestured to the third person standing before the bed, a sturdy, red-cheeked man. "Lucky he found you.."

"My husband, Mr. Malgins," the motherly woman said. "He brought you here in his truck"

"Thank you … all," Nikolai wheezed.

"We have a son your age," said.Malgins. "Already captured. His entire regiment."

"They beat you to hell," the doctor said. "How many?"

"Just two," Nikolai told him.

"There's nothing worse than a German," Malgins said, "unless it's two Germans." The doctor and Malgins shared a small laugh, but when Nikolai tried, the sword sliced between his ribs again.

Malgins approached with a bottle of plum brandy and looked toward the doctor. The doctor shrugged, as if to say, *If it doesn't kill him, why not?* Malgins handed the bottle to Nikolai, then helped him hold it to his lips. Swallowing cost more pain, but the brandy kicked his body back to life.

Malgins and his wife tended him for two weeks. Then they took him down to the piers, and Nikolai was hustled aboard a coaler en route to Göteborg.

Katya. He remembered how, in a millisecond of horrendous insight, his eyes had drifted open in the very instant that Hartigens-Hesse had pulled the trigger. And then he was out again. When consciousness returned, he could not move. He could focus, but he was as helpless as a torn animal. His mouth was open, sipping air so he would not have to inhale it through his nose, and he had remained in the same position for hours, staring at the bloody rag doll that had been Katya. Through the endless night, he had slipped back and forth, in and out of a nightmare vision that he could not escape: her bullet-ripped body, the spattered wall of blood and flesh.

When, toward dawn, he had found the strength to agonizingly crawl from the room, he had discovered them in an adjacent bedroom, sprawled and entwined. Wavering at the door, he had searched the room with his eyes for the Luger, so he could kill them both, but it had been nowhere in sight.

He had felt himself toppling and leaned against the door. It creaked, and Helgers snorted but sank back into his drunken coma. Nikolai's head swirled, but he held on to the door handle with all his strength; gradually, the dizziness eased, and he opened the door and dragged himself down the long hallway to the kitchen.

That had been almost six months ago. Since then, the German drive into Russia had taken the Wehrmacht to the gates of Stalingrad, but here, the assault had slowed, and the Russians had stiffened all along the wintry fifteen-hundred-mile front.

Meanwhile, Nikolai had lived in a Red Cross hostel until his new friend, Stefan, had triumphantly connected with the American clerk in the embassy. Within a week, their visas had been granted, and they were on the high seas.

And now, about to disembark, Nikolai realized how sharp was the divide between past and present. The months in Sweden had been a buffer zone in time, and a new life was beginning. But when his fingers touched the cold, platinum cigarette case in his pocket, he knew that he would never be able to erase the old life. It was coiled up inside his guts, dark as death.

Nikolai found the richly textured Old World/New World city of Boston appealing; searching for work, he explored it restlessly and soon found a night job at a bakery. He slept during the day and rarely saw Stefan, who jumped from job to job in the daytime and from girl to girl at night. In, fact, menial jobs were easy to find. America was girding for the struggle, and tens of thousands of people flowed into the armed forces and war industry each month, leaving tens of thousands of low-level openings, no questions asked.

They found a one-bedroom apartment on the edge of Chinatown. Rents were cheap, and so were the restaurants, and the noisy streets were filled with servicemen and Bostonians day and night. One Friday night, they met at Wah Yen's on Tyler Street, and Stefan noisily discussed his latest adventure, meeting a girl with a big bed; the girl had a girlfriend with a car, and the four of them could take a ride this Sunday.

Nikolai wondered where the gas coupons would come from, and Stefan grinned. "No problem. I got."

Nikolai scowled, aware of Stefan's growing connection to the black market. "You're crazy. You're going to end up in jail."

"Ain't gonna work all night in bakery."

"That's for now. Soon as I can, I'm going in the army."

"Talk about crazy! You ain't even American."

"All I have to do is prove I lived in England. Residency."

Stefan shrugged. "Only stupids go to war."

Several times a week, still bleached with flour from his graveyard shift at the bakery, Nikolai made his way to the British consulate in Post Office Square to check the inquiries window. He was waiting for a copy of his proof of residency from London, but each time, he came away empty-handed, the clerks clucking about the war and how long things took.

On a cool day in early June, almost a year since he had fled Latvia, Nikolai reported to the consulate and discovered that a copy of his residency permit had been mailed from London twelve weeks ago. The clerk shook his head. "Terribly sorry," he said. "Much too long."

"You mean, you think the ship was sunk."

"We don't actually know that for sure, do we?" said the clerk, who was as sure as sure could be.

And he had even worse news: the annex building of Records Section had been bombed and burned to the ground. This meant that all evidence of Nikolai's residency permit was now gone.

Morosely wandering back to the apartment, Nikolai was greeted by a jubilant Stefan. "Going into tires, buddy boy!" He noticed Nikolai's face. "Didn't come through? The paper?"

To cheer him up, Stefan sprang for lunch: fried clams at Durgin-Park. He talked about his new business—tires were big! Then he worked up to a proposition—come in with him! He and his new partners could use another man! "Why walk around splotched with flour for fifteen stinking dollars a week? Hey, you listening?"

Actually, Nikolai was looking off dreamily. He hadn't heard a word. An idea was taking shape. "I know how to do it," he said absently.

"Do what? What you talking?"

"Get in the army," Nikolai said.

He said nothing more, knowing how foolish it would sound; it even sounded foolish to him. The odds were respectable, but hardly certain, that the army would send him to Western Europe instead of the Pacific or Alaska or the Panama Canal—but what were the odds that a vague proximity to Latvia would allow him, an ordinary American soldier, to find a Prussian Baron in the middle of the chaos of war?

Laughable. But the very existence of odds was enough.

CHAPTER 5

▼

A sound punctured his daydream, and Heinz broke out of the past with a small cry. Someone was on the stairs. Anna? No, too heavy a step and too slow—old lady Gruss down the hall. He sagged back. Max Siebert. It was strange, this business of Siebert. He had talked to the man no more than ten minutes and had never seen or heard from him again. That was four years ago, but Siebert was still indelibly etched in his mind.

Perhaps because everything Siebert had predicted had come to pass. Twenty-four hours after they had parted, Germany had invaded Poland. England and France had plunged into the war. And Heinz, returning to New York, had immediately sensed a tightening political atmosphere.

But that was only the beginning. Once America was in the war, the last vestiges of tolerance for things and people German disappeared. Yorkville's *Gemütlichkeit* metamorphosed into Yankee Doodle Dandy. The *Bund* vanished, along with the Yankee Freemen, the Christian Mobilizers, the American Destiny Party, the Nationalist Party, the Gray Shirts, the Paul Revere Sentinels, the Anglo-Saxon Federation of America, and the Committee of One Million, which had never achieved a membership of more than a few hundred. Dissident right-wingers, their citizenship revoked, were scooped up by the FBI and thrown into camps three hundred miles from the coast.

But they had never caught up with Heinz, not for the Ebell business, not for his membership in the *Bund*, and not for his nuisance activities outside it. He did nothing to attract attention to himself, but he did not bother to hide, either. More than once, he had looked into a mirror and thought, *Born of good German blood. Born at the right time. Born to make a difference!* And lately, he had begun to view this proud heritage as something even more: a mantle of invulnerability. *Fick* the FBI.

Still, when the entrance door reverberated downstairs, he strained for the first footfall and rocked forward, ready to spring up and grab the .32-caliber automatic hidden in the hall closet. But the tread on the stairs was familiar. It was Anna's light bounce, and he settled back in the chair, brightening as he always did when she was near. But then he remembered their morning squabble and knew they would be at it again, the same silly business, and this time, he would put his foot down. *No two ways.*

The key grated in the lock, and she came in, pink-cheeked from the wind. She did not clutch at anger as Heinz did, like some fierce animal; their morning spat had diluted into resentment. "Hi," she said, but flatly.

"Yeah. So," he said.

She ignored this reminder of his unbending will by ignoring him on her way to the kitchen. There, she opened the refrigerator and took a long drink of cold milk, not bothering with a glass.

Heinz bounded up, piqued at her high-handed attitude. Midstream, he changed strategy, sidling over to the refrigerator and taking a beer. He opened it and took a satisfying slurp.

"So," he said again, somewhat less combatively.

"How was your day?" Anna asked.

"Usual."

"Good."

"You look like you got something to talk. Maybe your day, how it went?"

Anna sat on a chair at the kitchen table. The chairs were maple, flat-seated, and not all that comfortable; the year before, Anna had painted them a lime color, which was now fading. Heinz settled across from her.

"Listening," he encouraged, with mock tolerance. Anna was staring down at the table top, which was made of soft wood unlike the chairs. It was nicked, scuffed, and scraped, all by Heinz, during a hundred temper tantrums. When she failed to answer, his feigned good nature dropped away. "I said, listening."

"Look, Papa," Anna finally said, "we can't have a discussion if we can't talk about things."

"Who said no?" Heinz was irritated. "Who sat down to talk if it ain't me?"

"You know what I mean."

"No, I don't know. All I know is, you're the one came in, and I'm still waiting for a hello."

"I said hi. And that's not the point. The point is, this is left over from this morning, and I think we should talk about it."

"Said I'm listening. How much more you need?"

Heinz was rather enjoying the exchange. He knew it was a high-wire balancing act, but at the moment, he was studying her with an old satisfaction, even wonderment. Where had she come from, this delicately featured child with her almost saintly beauty? He preferred this over the reality: Maria, drunk and florid-faced, her hair hanging in tangled knots over vacant eyes. An image fourteen years in the burying. How could such a creature have given birth to Anna?

"I need to be able to talk about things in a normal conversation. What good is it if you always blow up?"

"You want to talk? Talk," Heinz said. "But one thing, let's get straight so everybody understands. You ain't taking no apartment."

"Well, I'm glad we got to discuss it," she said bitingly.

"No point beating the bush. What I said this morning—no girl of mine moves into somebody's apartment—that goes double."

"'Somebody's apartment'? It's Jenny Capuletto's apartment! She's my oldest friend. I've known her since the fifth grade, and so have you. Anyway, women my age don't live at home anymore. They work in defense plants, and they live with friends all over the country."

Her mention of defense plants nettled Heinz—wrong country. No less galling was Anna's easy alignment with America. "Settled," he hissed.

"For God's sake, Papa, I thought just once we could work out a problem like grown-ups. Because I'm not a child anymore, you know, no matter what you think."

"I can hear you ain't a child from the way you talk," he chided. "Even use 'God' these days."

"That's a hot one," she said. "All of a sudden, you're sanctimonious, and you haven't been in a church since I've known you, which is day one."

"Didn't keep you out, did I? And don't bother with big words, because I heard that one, big shot!"

"No, you didn't keep me out, but you tried. Every time I went with Jenny or anybody else, you told me it was silly stuff. Garbage on Sunday."

"That's what it is, all right."

She lowered her voice. "Of course it is, because that's what your friends, the Nazis, told you."

Gravely, Heinz said, "Don't talk over your head, Anna."

"Well, I'm sorry to tread on such delicate ground, Papa, but that dumb Nazi business was exactly that. Dumb."

The bile rose in his throat, but Heinz reined himself in. He knew that she was deliberately taunting him, working him up so that he would expose loyalties set aside—which was to say, concealed—since Pearl Harbor. Occasionally, she would needle him, about the *Bund*, the party, his trip to Berlin: tactical invocations meant to weaken his grip on her, as now.

It was incredible! What had happened to his little Anna? So soft and sweet. *Ach!* he thought. *It's what happens.* And the truth was that he had never understood her. Yes, she was compliant, but there was a stubborn streak too. His own stubborn streak, he reflected, with a trace of pride. *It's okay when they are kids,* he thought for the thousandth time, *but when they start getting a mind of their own, watch out.* From that time on, nothing had been the same; one day, running around like normal, and the next, lying in bed with a sour face; and he had scolded, *Stomachache, heh? That's what you get for eating too much candy, I bet!*

It's cramps, she had replied, and when he looked confused, she had said, *It's a girl thing, Papa.* And when he still looked blank, she had whispered, *Period.*

The memory made him recoil even now. The female functions had always confused him, and pubescence was as alien as little green men on Mars. Once, when she had used the word "menstruation," he had bellowed, *Don't have to hear that in my house!*

Now, across the kitchen table, he said somberly, "Maybe you ought to think before you talk these days, *meine Tochter.*"

"Same old thing except the subject matter," Anna said dourly.

"What's the subject matter? That a girl still ain't ready for the outside world should live away from home like some bum?

Quietly, she said, "Don't you see, Papa? I'll always be a little girl, and if I do anything normal, like live away from home, then I'm a bum."

"Didn't raise you to be no bum," he said.

"For God's sake, I'm not a bum," she said tartly.

Slit-eyed, Heinz said, "When you're around bums, that's what you get to be."

Anna's mouth opened. She groped for words, and then they angrily poured out. "Are you trying to say Jenny's a bum? Is that what you're getting at?"

"Word to the wise is what I'm getting at. Take it or leave it."

"But that's absolutely preposterous! For your information, Jenny doesn't do anything, and she never has!"

"Didn't ask for no personal rundown!" Heinz objected, now drawn, against his will, into intimate territory.

"Well, what else are you talking about, if it isn't sex?" she demanded.

The word "sex," coming from Anna, splashed over him like a nasty wave, but he shook free and said, "All I know is, people like her, they ain't too particular. So maybe she's okay for a soda or the movies, but that don't mean you should move in with her!"

"In other words, you still think she's a little loose. Isn't that it?"

"You said it, not me."

"Where did you come up with things like that?"

"Where I came up with is, she's a wop Italian, and that's what they do. So you ain't moving in with no Jenny Caputo!"

She took it in stride, more amused than ever. "Well, here's a new one. It used to be the Jews. Now it's the Italians."

"Still the Jews!" Heinz said, a bit too vehemently for someone who was supposed to have renounced his old calling, but he abandoned caution and plunged on. "Wops are almost as bad, if you ask me. Bunch of crooks you can't trust, and the ladies are the same."

"Poor Jenny," Anna lamented.

Shifting into shrewd mode, Heinz said, "Maybe she ain't so innocent like you think, 'poor Jenny'."

"I know Jenny," Anna said sweetly. "We're good friends, and we talk about things."

"She know you too?" Heinz said, and now Anna understood where he was going.

"You mean, what have I told Jenny about me? My sex life?"

He hadn't expected this directness, and he slammed down the bottle, beer slopping out of the neck. But he was even more curious than angry, so he prodded, "You got something to tell me, go ahead and tell."

"If you want to know, Jenny's innocent, but that doesn't mean everybody is." The line came with a brazen thrust of the chin, stagy and unreal, none of which Heinz caught. All he picked up was her allusion to the unspeakable, and he was stunned; his mouth sagged.

"You ain't never!"

"Why not?" she said, all but flouncing. "It happens to every woman, sooner or later."

Shattered, Heinz stumbled through a righteous litany: "Who? When? Where is he?"

"Where is he? He's in Europe, in the infantry, fighting the Nazis."

Only now, in his apoplectic stare, did she realize she had gone too far. She discarded her brazen pose and said, "For God's sake, Papa, I wasn't serious."

His black rage dissipated, he smiled fearfully. "So now it's only a joke," he said. "That's all?"

"If you don't want to believe me, don't," she said.

"If it's the truth, I'll know. Tell me again."

"I don't have to be treated like this!" she said.

He shook his head and said gravely, in formal indictment, "Don't believe you."

"I don't care what you believe!"

"Then maybe you believe this," Heinz said, the words solemnized by their finality. "Go move in with your friend, the tramp. I don't want you in my house no more."

His spine stiff in virtue, he walked out of the room.

CHAPTER 6

▼

Nikolai told the grumbling Greek who owned the bakery that he would have to take Saturday off. Of course, the Greek grumbled, but Nikolai kept going, threw a few things into an overnight bag with a broken zipper, and headed for South Station.

The train was crowded—they all were. Everybody seemed to be waving a newspaper: "Big Victory at Midway," read a headline, "Navy Flyers Sock Japs!" On the Russian front, the German advance had been stopped cold. In North Africa, the British had routed the Italians and Rommel. It was June 1942, and there was a creeping sense of turnabout in the war. Looming over all was the inescapable immensity of American might. Nikolai was beginning to worry that it would be over too soon.

It was less than five hundred miles from Boston to Washington, but by the time they rolled through New York, in a series of stops and starts and shuntings that typified rail travel all over the country, he had spotted a dozen or more huge freight trains carrying military supplies. On a siding in New Jersey, he counted 138 freight cars loaded with tanks and trucks and tarpaulin-covered heavy machinery.

Nikolai's car was crammed. The aisles were filled, and uniforms dominated. Near his seat, a noisy bunch of savvy-looking sailors were bent over a poker game, and every once in a while, he would catch a glance: *healthy-looking guy faking it.* He wasn't the only young, male civilian around, but it troubled him not to belong when he so ardently wanted to. He avoided eye contact. Finally, he gave up his seat and pushed into the vestibule. He smoked, looked through the sliding floor plates at the racing ties and listened to the clacking tracks all the way into Union Station.

By the time he arrived, it was one o'clock in the morning. He found a bed in the YMCA and spent the morning looking around Washington. It was a majestic city, patriotically charged, filled with the color and resolve of war. It made Nikolai wonder why he had come. All around him were people who belonged to something, who were not grains of sand on a foreign shore. Still, he could not help but study the faces, dozens and then hundreds of faces, seeking the impossible miracle that would be Hartigens-Hesse.

He started to walk back to the station. Then he stopped right in the middle of the street. An angry policeman blew a whistle. He had come for something; he had to see it through.

He wondered whether to telephone first. No, an impersonal call could defeat him before he started. He made inquiries and boarded a bus that took him to Georgetown. Then he walked five blocks and found himself before a handsome brick town house. The elaborate entrance featured a glossy black door set off by shiny brass fixtures.

He rang the doorbell, and the door opened to reveal a short, boxy woman in a starched gray uniform. She looked at him suspiciously. "Is this the Granger house?" he asked.

"Who should I say?"

"Nikolai Granger."

She digested the fact that he had the same last name and invited him in. Then she advised him to wait in a spare room off the foyer. She went off, and some minutes later, Lionel's new wife swept in, straight-backed and imperious, a woman in her fifties who was all hard angles. "You are?" she asked.

"Nikolai Granger."

"And you are here to see?"

"Lionel Granger."

"May I ask the nature of your call?"

"He was my stepfather for some years. In Latvia."

"In Latvia," she repeated.

"Is he here?"

"He is, but he's rather busy at the moment. I would not want to disturb him unless it is important."

Nikolai studied her teeth. They were forbiddingly large and reminded him of a picket fence. He said, "Yes, it's rather important."

Lionel Granger himself appeared, looking, in his dumb surprise, like Nigel Bruce as Dr. Watson.

He seemed older, beyond the half-dozen years or so since Nikolai had last seen him. He was the sort who aged in stages of gray, not so much his hair, which had indeed grayed, but in the darkening gray of his silver-sallow skin. He brushed at his gray mustache with a forefinger, an old and suddenly familiar habit.

"Well, well, well," Lionel said. "Well, well, well, well." This was just as familiar as the mustache trick. "How are you, young man?"

"Fine, sir. I'm in the United States now."

"Excellent. And how is your mother?"

"She's dead."

That diverted the river of pleasantries. Lionel was taken aback. "May I ask how it happened?"

"Shrapnel."

Lionel looked confused, as though wondering if she had been fighting in the front lines.

"They shelled the city."

"Ah!" Lionel said. "I assume you have met my—" He paused at the indelicacy of it. "I remarried three years ago."

Nikolai and the new Mrs. Granger nodded like pecking chickens.

"You now live in Washington, is that it?" Lionel asked.

"I live in Boston."

"You came from London?"

"From Riga. To Sweden. And then Boston in December."

"Ah. I see." There was a pause while Lionel, befuddled, juggled his obligation.

The new Mrs. Granger stepped in. "We were about to have lunch. Perhaps you would join us."

Lionel was startled, and then he seemed to understand. "Yes, yes, of course. What an excellent idea, Eunice."

Nikolai was no less startled. The new Mrs. Granger, who had taken pains to make him feel unwelcome, rang a small glass bell with a tiny brass ringer. The boxy maid shuffled in. She too looked surprised, having expected Nikolai to be gone. She took instructions and left. Eunice herself led the way to a sunroom in the rear, where a table had been set for lunch, the maid already having added another plate.

When they had settled (a particularly noisy affair of scraping chairs in the dead silence), Lionel poured sherry and said, "To your mother." It eerily evoked the last toast Nikolai had heard to Tati, from Hartigens-Hesse.

The memorial concluded, Eunice steered the conversation into practical areas. "Is there some way we can help you?"

It was a miracle of timing, saving Nikolai the embarrassment of launching his plea. He described his problem. Lionel stroked and stroked his mustache, and then summed things up. "In brief, you require some sort of confirmation of residency."

"Yes," Nikolai said eagerly.

Lionel looked at Eunice, who looked embalmed.

"Quite a conundrum," said Lionel. "Let's think about it, shall we?"

While he was doing so, Nikolai politely glanced about in appreciation of a patterned wallpaper that gave the effect of thousands of insects, then ran his eye over an assemblage of bric-a-brac tastelessly arranged on a lowboy. One of the items seemed to leap from the marble top and stab his memory.

He rose abruptly, drawing shocked expressions from Lionel and Eunice, then moved to the lowboy and picked up a medal set in a dark wooden frame. The medal was of a dull, pewter-colored silver; the ribbon attached to it had once been multicolored, possibly blue and red, but the colors had faded to a homogeneously bland gray.

"Old medal," Lionel explained, puzzled by Nikolai's interest. "Just an old military decoration."

"Yes," Nikolai said, holding the medal and staring at it.

Lionel blinked his way to a new level of comprehension and said, "Oh. Yes. Your mother's." And then, clarifying, "Gave it to me."

"I'm glad it's in the family," Nikolai said.

The maid arrived with lunch, a tray of cold meats and a salad bowl. Lionel heaped food on his plate but looked thoughtful, apparently dedicated to Nikolai's problem. Eunice began to eat with tiny, rhythmic bites, her lips forming a pout—nutrition was a chore. Lionel was more robust, but he chewed so thoroughly that the crunching of food in his mouth reverberated around the room. Eunice broke the silence with crisp questions about Boston, on the assumption that, despite his refugee status, Nikolai mingled with the bluebloods.

At last, the moment came. Lionel was fluffing his mustache again. Nikolai could not help it. He leaned anxiously forward.

"You would like to enter the army."

"Yes, sir."

"But you lack the requisite documentation."

"Well, yes, sir," Nikolai said, all but clawing at the air in his impatience.

Lionel said, "I see, I see." A thoughtful moment passed. "You have tried the immigration authorities, have you?"

Nikolai had the sudden sense of going backwards. "I've tried everything."

"I'm not sure how I can help you," Lionel said, rather baldly.

"I thought you might be able to intervene," Nikolai said. His distinctly sharper tone widened Lionel's eyes even as Eunice narrowed hers.

"I beg your pardon," said Lionel.

"You're with the State Department. I thought you might know people who could help in something like this."

Eunice looked over at Lionel; her eyes were slits of instruction.

"I'm afraid that's easier said than done," said Lionel.

Nikolai tried to be jovial. "I'm not trying to rob a bank. I'm just trying to get in the army."

"That is indeed admirable, Nikolai." It was the first time he had used the name, and he did so now as though juggling eggs. "But the war itself, you see, mitigates against you."

"Mitigates. How is that?"

"Well! The aliens law makes it much more difficult these days."

"Limb," Eunice interjected.

Lionel looked over uncertainly. Her narrow lips carefully formed the word again, "Limb. Limb."

The floodgates opened, and Lionel said, "Ah! Right! Right!" He turned back to Nikolai. "In normal times, one could go out on a limb. But these are not normal times. There is a war on."

"Look, Lionel," Nikolai said, an intimacy that rather stunned his hosts. "Let's forget pulling strings. All I need is some sort of proof of residency in England over the last few years. A letter from you, to whom it may concern, stating that I was a student at the London School of Economics for three years. Apparently, Records Section in London was destroyed in a bombing raid, but I'm sure the army would accept your word in the matter."

"Yes, I see," said Lionel. "But this letter you suggest—I'm afraid there's a problem."

"A problem?"

"Indeed, yes. You see, when we parted—that is to say, your mother and I— you were attending school in Switzerland. And planned to attend the London School of Economics in the fall?"

"Yes, that's right. What would be the problem?"

"I'm afraid I cannot attest to something outside my personal knowledge."

Nikolai just stared for a moment.

"Something of a conundrum," said Lionel, thoughtfully.

"We do wish you good luck," said Eunice, rising. Nikolai rose too. Stabbing into his consciousness now was the reason for Eunice's sudden about-face, from icy matron to accommodating hostess. She had calculated that two hours surrounding an ascetic lunch would adequately discharge all obligations. It was the moral equivalent of morality.

Nikolai started out, then turned and said, "Tati was right. She said you were a fucking idiot."

✳   ✳   ✳   ✳

The failure of his mission brought a certain release. He sensed that it had to do with activating his mother's memory in a shared antipathy for Lionel. He could not help but wonder how his mother, with her almost frightening insight, had selected Lionel out of a pack of millions.

He plucked a Lucky Strike from its package and made his way back to Union Station, where the next train to Boston was the Merchants Limited. It was fast, comfortable, and required a premium-fare ticket, which Nikolai did not have. He boarded it anyway.

His careless mood took him into the soft-lit club car, where he spotted an empty chair across from a young woman scribbling on a pad. When Nikolai eased toward the chair, the young woman looked up. Nikolai noticed only her eyes, which flared at his approach. They flashed rebuke. She would not brook contact. The usual social amenities that came with the mating contract were out of the question.

Nikolai swung past her, theatrically whispering, "I too wish to be alone." He padded down the carpeted aisle to the next car, found another seat, and was asleep by the time the train rolled out of the station. The conductor assumed that Nikolai was a weary serviceman whose ticket was in his pocket and let him sleep all the way to Boston.

Somewhere between dreams and memories, he was five or six or seven, peeking past the door into Tati's boudoir, where she was seated naked before her mirror. When she saw him, pale and apprehensive but bright-eyed with curiosity, she smiled and beckoned to him in the mirror. He approached timidly, because Tati, regally posed before her mirror, had become not simply an asexual playmate but a sensual creature.

He went over, and she stroked the thick mass of black curls above his pale face and said, "Do you know who you are? You are my beautiful boy. You are my perfect one." And she took him into her arms and pressed his face to her small, perfectly rounded breasts, where he drank in the perfume of her soft flesh until his head swam and he thought about the actors who often toppled in a dead faint on the stage at the National Theater.

"You like your mama, don't you?" she said, stroking his face. She placed his fingers around a dark, thick, hard nipple. "Here, touch Mama. Rub with your fingers, my beauty. Rub hard. Now harder, harder. Does that feel good? Does that feel good? Do you know why? Because you took milk from that little spout.

"And down here, you see this soft hair, dark red. You see what it covers. It covers where you came from. You see that place, that opening. You came out when you were tired of sleeping in my belly, and you said, 'Here I am, world! You can see me now!'"

She rubbed his fingers over the mossy down of the secret world they had shared, and Nikolai could remember his wonderment as a sense of pleasurable comfort swept over him.

∗   ∗   ∗   ∗

Along with the tire business, Stefan and his partners had bought into a small auto repair shop in Cambridge, and once again, they approached Nikolai with an offer: to work in the garage. Nikolai balked; he knew very little about automobiles. "So what?" Stefan countered. All Nikolai had to do was listen and learn, and the pay was forty-five dollars a week.

At first, he did odd jobs, and he was still dirty at the end of the work day, but now it was with grease, not flour. Gradually, he took on minor repairs, changing oil, greasing chassis, and flushing radiators. He suspected that a small storehouse at the rear of the property was stuffed with tires, new and used, but he kept his distance.

An article in the *Boston Traveler* mentioned free advice for aliens, and one day, on his lunch hour, Nikolai took the streetcar to Scollay Square from Cambridge. The legal aid department was hidden in a rabbit warren of offices on the second floor of a gray-black pile that had been taken over by the federal government at the start of the war. Dozens of people jammed the anteroom, and the wait was agonizing.

"Granger!" a clerk finally called. Nikolai followed the signal to one of the office doors. A good-looking girl with the glaze of overwork was seated behind a small desk. Without looking up, she waved him to the chair across from her. Nikolai sat, and their heads swiveled to shocked recognition. It was the girl from the train, the one to whom he had acidly whispered, "I too wish to be alone."

She glowered and said, "Look, if you don't want a scene, get out of here now."

"Hold it. Wait a minute." His protest sounded truncated; to his exasperation, he realized he did not know her name.

"I'm not up to games, okay?" she said. "So just take off."

"I didn't come for a goddamn date, lady," he said, before he could stop.

She bristled, but she was uncertain too. "Weren't you the one on the train?"

"Yes, I was on the train, but I was looking for a seat, not you, and I wasn't looking for you today, either." He saw her surprise and inwardly fumed. What would this get him? Forcing himself to be calm, he said, "I didn't know it was you. I just came for legal advice."

She looked him over skeptically, factoring in the dirty hands and grease-stained face that went with low-class come-ons. "Legal advice," she repeated, with everything but the *hmph*.

"If that's what you do," he said. "Otherwise, I'll go somewhere else." *The hell with it. The hell with her,* he was thinking, tensing to rise and go; but she was looking at him curiously now, head a little cocked, because she had picked up an accent.

"Are you English?"

"I'm Latvian."

"But you went to English schools?"

"Switzerland. England."

He could see that admitting to being Latvian had lowered his status but that Switzerland and England had brought him back up, though not all the way, because her lips were tightening again. "What sort of legal advice were you seeking?" she asked.

"I want to get in the army."

"Oh," she said, not exactly warmly, but with a hint of approval.

He told her most things, but not everything. He included an explanation for his grease-stained appearance, and she nodded; his story and his straits had brought her to the brink of compassion, and she commented approvingly that most educated aliens would resist taking on a low-level job.

It was meant to smooth their tricky course, but it did not come out quite right, prompting Nikolai to remark that elbow grease was the American way. They looked politely at each other, aware that the honeymoon was over.

"I'll do what I can," she said, his case already distant. She shoved over a form. "Fill out the application, and the office will contact you." He started to work on the form, and she said, "You'll have to do that outside."

He rose but did not move.

She looked up. "Yes?"

"Might I ask something personal?"

She was about to say that under no circumstances would she consider a drink, a coffee, or a Coke, but he surprised her by asking, "Are you really a lawyer?"

He was looking across at the diploma from Yale. She said, "Yes, I am. Is that so unusual?"

"In Latvia, yes."

"I hope you approve, Mr. Granger," she said.

"I do approve," he said. He turned and left, leaving her suddenly curious, wondering who and what he was.

CHAPTER 7

▼

Business was so slow that Heinz decided to close for the weekend. *Not slow for others,* he thought bitterly. *They have their war.*

Over the past year or so, Heinz had grown even more distant from his neighbors and his neighborhood. Shopkeepers frowned when he went by. At one time, he had been tolerated as an object of quiet derision, but this had evolved into outright hostility. His was the only shop on the street without a flag or tricolor bunting. There were no patriotic posters in his shop window, no urging to buy war bonds or "Keep 'em flying!" Twice, his windows had been smashed, but that had been earlier in the war, when its course was still in doubt. There was no longer any doubt; the Russians were at Germany's eastern borders; the Western invasion forces were smashing through France and the low countries.

These neighbors, just as German as he was in the beginning, had abandoned Germany. Heinz despised them. He had long stopped speaking to them, and they, adopting the virtue that came with their new contempt, had stopped snickering at his appearance in the streets. He was unworthy of their attention.

But they had efficiently spread the word; good Americans no longer patronized his little electrical shop. His income had fallen to the point where he could barely keep up with the rent. He had saved a few thousand dollars, but it was going fast. If things did not change, he would be out of business in six to eight months. Oddly enough, this did not prey on his mind. He had too much anger to brook depression; he channeled his emotions into an almost rapturous pleasure in his loathing of the Judases who surrounded him and the situation that was closing in on him.

But he could not escape the fact that his life was ebbing away in the meaning-lessness of his existence. How could a man survive without being part of a cause? It was not enough to cheer at a distance, as though for a team of athletes. To serve the fatherland, he would plunge into the fires of hell.

He turned his key in the lock, automatically tried the door, then absently moved off. He wandered toward the park, oblivious of people, of traffic, of the crisp autumn air. Suddenly, he was plunged into the green anonymity of Central Park. He followed a twisting path and found a bench.

In no time at all, he was drifting again, this time into the great triumph of his life, his spectacular return to Krasbach, his hometown, in the summer of 1939. That was the summer he had undertaken his crusade to Germany. It had ended in rejection upon rejection, and it would have ended in disaster if he had not changed his plans at the last moment and postponed his return to the United States by three days.

Up until the year before, the town had been Crsbacki, a town of two thousand bordering the Ore mountains in Czechoslovakia. The people were farmers, all of German stock, and they were still celebrating Hitler's takeover of the border-lands, the Sudetenland, when Heinz got off a creaking bus in the cobblestone Karlplatz, the heart of the tiny village.

Almost thirty years had passed, but he was astonished by how little it had changed. At the south end of the *Platz*, water still flowed from the mouths of small stone dogs into the octagon-shaped fountain. Above the heads of the dogs rose a centerpiece filled with brightly colored flowers.

All around him, life moved at the same slow pace he remembered. The town was a magic reincarnation. He was a child again. He crossed the little bridge over the deep-gorged Ikro River, and he passed the same solid, three-story buildings of stone with white-curtained windows flanked by blue shutters and set off by flower boxes. He passed the city hall, heavyset and authoritarian, made more so these days by a rippling Nazi flag.

If his first steps were tentative, Heinz soon took on a cosmopolitan air. These were simple country people; they did not recognize him except to note that he was obviously a person of stature, dressed as he was in a vested suit topped by the hat he had bought in Berlin only days before, worn Hitler-style, with both brims down.

Down Neumarktstrasse he went, past the same butcher shop where, so many years before, soup bones had cascaded out of the flimsy shopping bag his mother had provided; soup bones, the shameful badge of the destitute, scattered across the straw-covered floor as snickering neighbors looked on. The plight of the poverty-stricken Baumann family, on view.

He stopped before the butcher shop and looked in the window. With the detachment of an art gallery patron, he studied a piglet hanging by its tail. He went inside. The butcher's son, once a skinny redhead, now a gray-haired sausage of a man, came to the doorway with a shopkeeper's smile. Heinz had known him as a schoolboy: a taunter, like most of the others.

Failing to recognize Heinz, he swayed to a half-bow, declaring, "It's a fine piglet!"

"Wrap it," Heinz had replied imperially.

The butcher's son had done so, staring at Heinz and peering back into time until he had discovered their past, then exclaiming in wonderment, "Heinz Baumann!"

Heinz wandered through the narrow streets for the next two hours, buying things he did not need and did not want, while the townspeople studied him and recognition flooded across their faces. By the time he had crisscrossed the little village, knots of people had gathered to discuss his return. The prodigal son, enriching them through his casual purchases. A bold few worked up the courage to speak to him directly. They recalled his parents, good people remembered with fondness; they asked after his sister, a sunny, bright-eyed little girl; they wondered, with appropriate delicacy, how Heinz had surmounted all obstacles and made it to the top.

Heinz did not tell them that his parents had died the way they had left the town, in poverty; he did not inform them that his sister, closer now to hag-like than sunny, was married to a dirty wop.

As for himself, well, yes, he had managed to prosper. Good German hard work had done the trick, had built his flourishing electrical contracting business. Not the biggest in New York, he had murmured modestly, which could be taken to mean the second or perhaps the third biggest in New York.

When he started back across the bridge toward the Karlplatz, where his bus was now waiting, Heinz was trailing villagers like the Pied Piper. An eager simpleton the townspeople called Bismarck was pushing a heavy cart loaded with the things Heinz had bought; it contained the piglet, sausages, a bottle of milk, tomatoes, a bottle of wine, breads and cake, a pair of sandals, a pair of scissors, a pair of lederhosen, souvenirs, a mouthwash, a newspaper—something from almost every shop in town.

By now he had spent most of his money; he had only the bus ticket back to Terpitz, the train ticket back through Dresden to Hamburg, and his North Lloyd

German Line ticket aboard the *Europa* back to New York. He would have to scrounge his way through the return journey, but it was worth it.

Halfway across the bridge, with onlookers following but maintaining a respectful distance, Heinz stopped. Bismarck brought the cart to a halt and waited with a loony grin while Heinz looked over the stone railing of the bridge at the racing waters of the Ikro in the gorge far below.

The townspeople could only gape while everything piled onto the cart was thrown into the river—all except the piglet, and this Heinz and Bismarck did together, swinging it over the railing and watching it splash into the river.

"Is your name Baumann?"

Heinz was shocked to discover that he had been lost in dreams again. He was back in Central Park. Two squirrels were squabbling over an acorn just across the pathway. Alongside the bench, two men in their forties were leaning over him.

Heinz squinted, looking into the sun, looking them over. He said nothing.

"I asked, is your name Baumann?" the man said. He was the plumper of the two, his expanded waist hiking up his pants to reveal white socks.

"Yeah, it's Baumann," Heinz said. "So, who wants to know?"

The other man, with a wart on his nose and a drooping mouth, checked a piece of paper and said, "You mind coming with us?" He had taken out an identification badge of some sort. Heinz did not bother to examine it. He rose from the bench, squelching the urge to ask what this was all about. He knew without asking what it was all about. It was about Ebell.

Just before the war, Heinz and Leo and several others had established yet another dissident pro-Nazi organization, this one called the American Warriors. It was a tiny cell and little more than a political discussion group until such time as monthly dues would allow the purchase of guns. It took a year to amass the necessary money, at which point disaster struck. The entire treasury of four hundred and ten dollars, kept by Leo Muller in a shoe box, was stolen from his apartment. The American Warriors promptly fell apart.

Heinz, shattered and infuriated, had been determined to track down the thief, certain that the man was one of their own, an arrogant, ferret-faced twenty-five-year-old named Wally Ebell. From the beginning, Ebell had been looked upon as an oddball and none too bright; he had proposed that they concentrate their future sabotage on burning down all the Army & Navy stores in the New York area; it was his understanding that the stores were actually owned and run by the army and the navy.

Heinz soon discovered that Ebell, who never worked regularly and always had trouble scraping up his dues, had suddenly acquired a used Ford convertible and new clothes, including a zoot suit with a gold chain so long that he could swing it like a lasso.

The confrontation took place in Ebell's one-room apartment. He had just greased down his hair, primping himself for the evening, when Heinz burst in, Leo trailing. Ebell had denied the charge until Heinz kicked him in the testicles; squirming along the floor, Ebell had moaned his confession. Heinz sat astride his chest and methodically slugged Ebell's face. Heinz could hear Leo calling his name and feel him tugging at his shirt from behind, but Heinz kept smashing his fists into Ebell's face.

His death failed to make the *Daily News* or any other Manhattan newspaper. A Newark weekly, anxious to dilute the city's current crime problems, ran a small squib under the heading, "Another New York Zoot Suit Murder."

Heinz had always expected to be caught, but after two and a half years, he was comfortably ahead of the game, so he accompanied the two plainclothesmen without protest. Jail was better than doing nothing, he thought.

But the policemen turned out not to be policemen at all. They were federal officers working with the New York City draft boards. The draft board for the Yorkville area had dispatched them on a tip. Heinz was accused of draft evasion.

"Let's see your draft card," said a new face, a member of the draft board.

"Ain't got no draft card," Heinz said warily. What did a draft card have to do with Wally Ebell?

"Everybody's got a draft card, buddy," said the plump federal officer. "There's a war on."

"Don't have nothing to do with me," Heinz said defiantly.

"Sons-a-bitch krauts," the draft board man murmured. "You get them like that around here."

"So you never got a draft notice. That it?" said the man with the wart on his nose.

The instinct for self-immolation was fading. Heinz began to realize that the situation, through some cockeyed mistake, had nothing to do with Ebell. "Nope, never got one," he said. He was beginning to enjoy himself.

"This your name?" said the draft board man. He shoved a piece of paper before Heinz.

Heinz looked it over. "Baumann, yeah," he said.

"Yeah, well, this is a draft notice, Mr. Baumann, and what's going on here is a very serious charge of draft evasion, punishable by a prison term of no less than five years. Are you aware of that?"

"You say, so I am," Heinz said indifferently.

The plump man said, "You a wiseass, Baumann?"

The draft board man said, "This your signature, or isn't it?"

"Nope," Heinz said.

All three smiled. The man with the wart said, "It's not your signature."

"Nope."

"Your name is Hans Baumann, but that's not your signature," the draft board man said.

"Nope. Name ain't Hans Baumann," Heinz said.

"Now it's not his name," said the plump man.

"Name's Baumann, but it ain't Hans. It's Heinz. Heinz Baumann."

They studied the copy of the draft notice. "This is for Hans," the draft board man said.

"I thought it was the same name. Heinz and Hans," the plump man said.

Heinz produced his social security card. When it was checked against a thick register, the man with the draft board said glumly, "Address is different. Age is different. Wrong guy."

Heinz started off, then turned to say cuttingly, "Thought this was America, land of the free. Next time maybe you dumbasses check better, before you go around bothering people." The incident put him on an upbeat course. *Still ahead of the game.* His invulnerability validated his actions; killing Ebell had been solidly right. He headed for the Beer Garden on 78th, where they still called them knockwurst, not "big dogs" or "fat dogs" like the Jew delis on Broadway.

Suddenly, the seesaw day took a downturn. He saw a young woman walking a dog, her face alive with recognition. The small, jumping dog was yapping at his feet. He wanted to kick it, but the girl said, "Margie Potter, Mr. Baumann. How's Anna?"

"In a hurry," Heinz said. He rushed off. The whole thing was over in a flash, but it had left him enveloped in a cloud of unease. Anna!

Resolutely, he crossed Second Avenue against traffic, daring the trucks, the C Sticker sons-a-bitch Chevys and Fords, and the stinking cabbies, not even bothering to wave a fist, just glaring his way across the lanes.

The Beer Garden was all soothing, dark wood, gray cigarette clouds, and the damp smell of beer. Of course, the music was carefully neutered these days: jolly polkas with an American tint, for the most part.

Leo was waiting for him in a booth, one end of which was a truck-size beer barrel bottom. *Keller* decor. "You got early," he said, surprised.

Heinz shrugged. He could close his shop whenever he wanted.

The waiter, Old Felix, a little man with a rolling walk made for a sailing ship, brought Heinz a stein of pilsner. Heinz slurped and frowned. "Tastes like piss these days," he said.

"The good stuff goes to the war, is what they say," sneered Leo, "but what I heard from my nephew Walter—that's Freda's sister's kid—he's in the artillery—what they get beer is worse than piss, it's so thin." He leaned forward intimately. "What do you hear?"

"What do I hear from what?" Heinz said, immediately irked.

"You know," Leo said. "Don't hear."

Leo knew better than to peck at his intransigence like a scab. But if it was true that Heinz was the dynamic sort who executed big ideas, it was also true that such people needed the sage counsel of people like himself.

"Heinz, we been good friends a long time, is why I say … Anna, she's my own goddaughter. Close to me like a real daughter, am I right?"

"So?" Heinz said

"Maybe I'm stepping off turn a little," Leo admitted, mitigating now because he could see that Heinz, for all his outward calm, was quaking with rage, the precise point at which Leo had shrewdly retreated a thousand times before; but he was skidding, plunging over the abyss, and he blurted, in words so heartfelt they tugged at him like a violin strain, "Heinz, I think you should talk to her."

He waited, following the countdown in his mind, but Heinz did not blow. Instead, he said, "Get the hell out of here, Leo."

Leo grinned, or pretended to grin, smarting at his rejection, refusing to accept it. He joked, "All right, you don't want my advice. Maybe comes too cheap!"

"Get out. Beat it," Heinz said.

Leo shifted. Volcanic eruptions from Heinz were as common as slugs in the subway, but never had he heard such a tone, such solemnity, such finality. Leo made an elaborate point of looking around for Old Felix, then slid out of the booth, clutching his stein. He held it up and tapped it with a forefinger. "Get another beer," he said and winked, serving notice that he rejected his dismissal by Heinz. Then he shot off for the bar.

Heinz had no intention of waiting for Leo's soppy return; he was through with Leo, and the hell with everything. Enough. He emptied his stein and prepared to slip out of the booth, but in rising, he glanced into the gloom of the long bar, and saw that Leo was talking to someone. A woman. Leo was blocking the view, but there was something vaguely familiar about her to Heinz, and this moment of curiosity cost him his departure: the bartender handed Leo three steins of beer, and Leo and the woman were heading for the booth.

Even so, Heinz prepared to head off, and if they saw him, who cared? But now her face was coming into focus, and it held him.

Her name was Antonia Graf—Toni. She was one of the core group of five who had formed the American Warriors, and he hadn't seen her in over three years.

Awkwardly poised, still ready to run but now intrigued, Heinz nodded in recognition and tried to negate what must look like a cavalier gesture (politely standing at her approach) by settling in the booth again.

"Heinz, look what I found!" Leo exclaimed.

Leo and Toni Graf sat across from Heinz, who said, "Long time."

Toni was severely handsome rather than pretty, with short, dark-blonde hair, a rather broad nose, and narrow, gray eyes. She was slim-chested and slim-bodied, with long legs.

"So, how you been?" she said in her indifferent way. She lit a cigarette.

"So-so," he said. It was what he had liked about her: her cold detachment. And she had guts. She had come to him when the group was first formed and had announced that she wanted to join. Heinz had rejected her out of hand, but Toni had told him flatly that he would need her, dispassionately adding that the rest of his Warriors were either crazy or half-assed and that she had more guts than any three of them put together. Besides which, he might be interested to know that Hitler's personal pilot was a woman named Hanna Reistch.

Heinz had been taken aback by her boldness and her crude language, but then he had thought, *Well, why not a woman? Somebody with balls.*

Leo pushed a beer across to Heinz: a peace offering. "Just like the good old days, eh?" he whispered, grinning broadly. "*Prosit!*"

"Hell, they weren't that good," Toni said, dryly enough to draw a thin smile from Heinz.

"You still got that shop?" she asked.

"Still," he acknowledged.

"Me, I'm still underground, like a coal miner," Leo said cheerfully, unheard.

"So, I guess you ain't working Deutsche Bibliothek these days," Heinz said—a joke.

"Went the way of the Russian front," Toni said, a jarring irreverence that brought Heinz's chin out of his beer; but then he realized that was her persona, rough as a frozen corncob up the ass, as the old country farmers used to say.

"Where you working?" Heinz asked.

"You know, places around. See anybody?"

"Like who?"

"Like who else?" she said impatiently.

"Never seen one. You're the first."

"Except me," Leo chirped, still busy restoring ties.

"Only one I ran into was about a year ago," she said. "Necker, the one with the short leg." She took a big drag from her cigarette, then added, "Selling ladies stuff. Handbags. Still a jerk."

Of course, she was right about Necker, a crybaby, a destined loser who never should have been admitted to the American Warriors' ranks, but it was somehow grating to bring it up now, almost a personal affront inasmuch as Heinz had been tasked with approving each and every member.

"Needed dues. Didn't have time to pick and choose so careful," Heinz said as a counterweight.

Toni took a man-size swallow of beer. "You know what that son of a bitch tried to do, first meeting? Tried to feel me up. Ran his hand all over my ass."

The tension fell away. Heinz grunted, almost a snigger, and Leo, following, earnestly rasped, "You should've let him feel. Would've got free handbags."

He laughed anew, trying to drag in Heinz, and he was rewarded with an amused wheeze, a normalization of relations. Leo seemed to gauge it as an apogee; ruddy-glowed with good feeling, he jumped up. "Think I say hello to Kohler! Stay and talk. I come back."

He left, and Old Felix shuffled over. "You want?" he said. Beer was automatic; he meant food.

"Wurst," Heinz said. "You?"

"Same," Toni told Old Felix. He moved off.

"Kind of rough these days, huh?" Toni said after a moment.

Heinz bristled. "What's that mean, 'rough'?"

Toni did not back off. She was lighting another cigarette. "What I hear, business is off."

"Where you get that from?" he rasped. He fired a death-ray glare across the room to Leo, who was bobbing and bubbling at Ferdie Kohler's table.

"Hey, don't take it out on Leo. The poor slob worries about you."

"Nobody asked him!" Heinz said.

"Take it easy, Baumann. Did it ever occur to you that you don't have to explode every time you open your mouth?"

"I see you ain't changed," he snarled.

Easily, she said, "Hey, Heinzie, you're wrong. That's what it's all about. You go with the flow. Maybe that's your trouble. You don't know when to bend."

The first time she had called him Heinzie, he had gasped at her gall. His mother had called him Heinzie, but no one else, ever. But his sputter of outrage had been muffled by a groan; they were in her bed, and the sound had come from Heinz himself as Toni, laughing, had circled his penis with her lips—another audacity: no one had ever done that before. She was still laughing, trying not to laugh, but forced to disengage her mouth, letting his foreskin slide back over the nub, then peeling it back and flicking her tongue like a snake, laughter subsiding, caught up in the emotional surge at hand.

They were unlikely lovers. Love and lovemaking were strange to Heinz, not so much exotic as a despoiled business that was better left in the barnyard. But to his consternation, an odd moment of desire rose from time to time; the occasion would surface, the opportunity would arise, and the outcome, unsought and unplanned, always came as a surprise.

As for Toni, whose tastes were more eclectic, exploration itself was her life-style, and satisfaction came at the end of curiosity, which manifested itself in companions of either sex, group sex, and three marriages, all disastrous. Abandoning formal union, she was attracted to Heinz, a poor man's Führer, down to his lackluster performance—which was only hearsay, of course, but perfectly understandable in the complex Führer personality.

In any case, Heinz, eyes already dilated when Toni mounted him backwards and giggled into his genitalia, was even wider-eyed when Toni's bedroom door opened to reveal what turned out to be her roommate, Flo, another free-swinger, who promptly discarded her clothes and jumped into bed. Heinz, already drawn into a social cauldron beyond his ken, had huffily left the party when the roommates went to work on each other.

That had been their one and only intimate contact. From that moment on, it was business, pure and simple. He had pushed the occasion itself so far back past memory that it had taken the jarring "Heinzie" to dredge it up. It did not help his flustered state to read her knowing smile; she was reading his mind, remembering with obvious amusement every grubby detail of their squalid evening.

"Here's to the good old days," she said, lifting her stein.

He avoided her face, sensing facetiousness, but then was not so sure when he glanced up. It was more like a "one of the boys" expression; she was not laughing at him after all, only sharing. Well, to give the devil her due, she had turned out to be what she had claimed: the best of the bunch.

"So you haven't run into any of the old gang, right?" she said.

Heinz looked over sharply. There was something in her voice, an inflection that was less curious than inquisitorial.

"Nobody," he said evenly, waiting.

"How about Ebell?" she said.

"Ebell?" he asked, cold as ice.

"Wally Ebell. Remember him?"

Heinz took his time. "Yeah, I remember him."

"But you haven't seen him around."

"No, I don't see nobody around from the bunch. Includes Ebell," he said.

She took her time—a puff, a swill of beer, the cigarette again. Heinz bent toward her. "What's on your mind?"

"Nothing much. Little Wally." Another drag. A smile. "You put him away, didn't you?"

"You got a point, maybe you make it now."

"Don't get the idea Leo told me something. He didn't. I figured it out for myself a long time ago."

"Don't know what you're talking about."

"Yes, you do. You knew he stole the money, so you killed him."

"Still ain't heard the point," he said.

Theatrically, she dropped her jaw and stared at him, open-mouthed. "Hey, you're looking for a shakedown or something. Hell, if you didn't kill that little fucker, I would have."

Heinz cautiously said, "That so?"

"I'll tell you the truth, Heinzie," she said. "When it comes to doing what has to be done, you got big ones. I wanted to tell you that all this time—that I knew—but I stayed away. I figured maybe the cops had somebody tailing us— maybe me, maybe you, maybe all of us—and I didn't want to spread us around, you know?"

Heinz said nothing. He waved a hand, thinning her smoke.

"You don't believe me," she said.

"Just here listening," he said good-naturedly.

"I'll tell you one thing. You are one lucky son of a bitch. I mean, far as the cops go. Am I right?"

He would not be drawn in. He upturned a palm: still listening.

Her voice dropped a notch, a confidential monotone. "Look, all I'm saying is you did the right thing, and I'm glad you got away with it."

He made an ambiguous gesture: more or less, thanks.

"You know something?" Toni said. "Those were crazy times."

After a moment, Heinz nostalgically responded, "*Ja.* Didn't sit around. Did things."

"Crazy things. Especially you. Everything kind of slam-bang in those days, right?"

"Better than sitting around with a thumb," Heinz said, venturing into pseudo-profanity.

"Well, I'll tell you, Heinzie, that was then, this is now. Who the hell cares?"

Heinz stiffened. "Who cares?"

"You got to be crazy to be political these days. I mean, *that* kind of political."

"What kind of political you talking?" he asked.

"Oh, come on. *Das Vaterland, der Führer,* Thousand-Year Reich, all that bullshit."

"You think that's what it is?"

"Are you kidding? You still sopping up that crap?" she said.

"Never thought it was crap," Heinz said solemnly.

"Hey, Heinzie, come into the twentieth century," she said. "Let me bring you up to date. *Das Vaterland* is down *die Toilette.*"

"Ain't true," Heinz spat out.

"Come on, get with it," she said, almost entreatingly, as though to a confused child. "It's all gone. Germany's finished. Hitler's finished. The Nazis are finished. Read the newspapers. You know where I work now? Republic, out on Long Island. You know what they make? Fighter planes. You getting the message? If you can't lick 'em, join 'em."

"I don't want to hear no more," Heinz said. His blood was churning, a fierce storm raging; but he was in control, surprisingly so, surprising himself.

"Hey, Heinzie, sorry to bring the bad news," she joked, "but what is, is, and you can't change it."

"It's a free country," he joked back. "Think whatever you want."

"Come on, it's just dumb politics. Let's forget it."

"Sure."

She smiled, something close to coy. "I'm still in the same place. Fixed it up. Living alone, these days. Why don't you come visit? Tell you what—make it tonight. Bring your toothbrush."

"Lady, wouldn't come near you with a ten-foot pole."

She took it in good grace, finishing off her stein, then slid out of the booth and walked away.

Two minutes later, Leo returned, looking anxious. "What happened?"

"What happened what?" Heinz said.

"I saw she went all of a sudden. Something happen?"

"Nothing happened. She turned American, is all."

CHAPTER 8

▼

Minutes before the doors closed, Nikolai moved past a protesting guard into the Federal Building. A clerk, scurrying off, said Mr. Fennelly was gone, so Nikolai continued into the large waiting room. It was empty of supplicants. But from a familiar office at one end, he heard a chair scrape, and Nikolai pushed past the door.

She was in the process of propping her long legs on the desk and rapturously sucking in the first drag of a cigarette, but when she saw him, her legs crashed down, and cigarette smoke caught in her throat.

She coughed, and her face turned red. Nikolai stood before her, calmly await-ing her return to normal. At last, the spasm ceased. She ground out her cigarette with ill-concealed resentment. "Office hours are over," she said, half sputtering, concealing the fact that she had failed to recognize him. Not only had two months passed, but Nikolai was scrubbed and wore a new jacket and slacks.

Nikolai waved a penny postcard. "This came, from somebody named Fen-nelly, but he's gone for the weekend. I need some help."

She glanced at the postcard, and her nose twitched in regret; the situation was beyond her bureaucratic pale. She handed back the postcard.

"There must be something I can do," he said. He waved the postcard. "This is a blank wall."

She stared for a moment, off-guard, impressed once again at his accent, remembering him now but recalling nothing of his situation. Nikolai caught her vacant look. "It was about trying to get into the army."

"Yes, I remember," she said tautly, remembering only in that second. Carefully, she said, "This was a question of no papers, wasn't it? And, something about ... school, in London?"

"London School of Economics, residency papers, bombing raid, records destroyed," he summed up.

"Yes." She churned it over for a moment. "There is one possibility and one option. The possibility, though slight, is that the law will be eased in the near future for temporary visa DPs, such as yourself. The option is that you find an American wife."

"Will you marry me?"

She gaped. Nikolai laughed, startled at his own spontaneity. She smiled, then grinned, then sobered. "Look, I'm sorry about this. I know it's not really funny to you."

In deference to his troubles, she closed up and walked out with him. Her name was Maureen Eliot. When they reached the sidewalk, she pointed toward the Commons, the direction she would be walking. "I've got to be running along. And I really am sorry. I wish you the best of luck." She walked off, swaying primly, and Nikolai watched her. His interest was not in the least personal.

That evening, he visited Stefan, who now lived in a two-bedroom apartment near Fenway Park. "I need a girl. Somebody to marry," he explained.

Puffing a cigar and sipping scotch, Stefan looked away, as though lost in soaring thought, before pronouncing the idea half-witted.

"Can you find me a girl or not?" Nikolai said.

"Your funeral," Stefan finally agreed.

*   *   *   *

It was another late Friday afternoon. Nikolai sat on a bench in the Commons, drinking in the air. A soft, silky June breeze fluffed his hair. He was thinking about the nuances of life in the new land. How formal and structured European society was; how loose and irreverent America was. Particularly after England, America's brashness had been jolting. And yet he had came to realize that for all its coarseness, this great, heaving, vibrant nation would become the model for God knew how many future empires.

Was that to the good? He didn't know, but he was coming to like the new land. In the beginning, the tiny apartment off Tyler Street had been like penance and perversity, but living alone had not only expanded his living space but also transformed the raucousness of the street, the clanging of kitchens, the high-pitched jabber of cooks, and the odors of soy and ginger and sesame oil from frying woks; no longer annoyances, they were exotic prisms to new worlds.

He made her out now, approaching along the path; in back of her, the state house dome glinted a dull gold. When she passed him and walked into the sun, light poured through her flimsy dress and outlined her legs beneath a short slip.

"Miss Eliot?" Nikolai called.

She turned and focused, taking in the casual spread of his arms along the top of the bench. "Well, aren't you comfortable?" she said. (Too comfortable for someone trying to get to know her, she thought.)

But she was glad to see him too. Behind her reproving glance at his audacious behavior, she allowed a thin smile. Nikolai rose and tossed his jacket back over his shoulder as he joined her.

"I just happened to be sitting in the park," he said.

"What a coincidence."

"I thought you might want to hear the latest developments."

They walked slowly along now, and she said, "I'm not sure I should."

"Your idea," he said.

"That's why I don't want to hear about it."

"I'm to meet her tomorrow evening."

She stopped short. "Really?"

"Her name is Iris McCorkle. Twenty-two years old. The rest is a riddle wrapped in a mystery inside an enigma."

"Churchill," she muttered. Then she added, "Well, one thing's not a mystery. Boston Irish." She thought about it. "Why don't you know any more?"

"Actually, that's the reason I wanted to talk to you. Would you have a drink?"

"I'm afraid not," she blurted. "It's been a hellish week, and I'm dog tired."

"Could I walk you home? No business talk?"

She hesitated. "I suppose that would be all right."

As they walked, Nikolai airily told immigration tales: his experiences in Sweden, waiting to get to America, his bumpy voyage across the ocean.

Somewhat later, she said, "Actually, I live on the next block, but I'm a little concerned about your lady friend. Maybe we'd better have that drink."

They glided into a bar on Newbury Street and settled at a window table, watching the night take over in a series of soft, dark shades. The lights of Boston came up. Maureen ordered a manhattan and Nikolai did the same; it was his first.

"Regarding your bride-to-be, I would suggest you limit her to an allotment."

"That's the arrangement, unless she gets playful."

"Don't let her," she said, with a lawyer's edge. "What does she look like?"

Nikolai took an envelope from his jacket and handed it over. Maureen slid out the photo. It revealed a girl with a pretty teenage face and a coy expression. Maureen was impressed. "Very nice."

Nikolai took the photo and examined it, as though for the first time. "Yes, I suppose she is."

"What about the ceremony?" Maureen asked, brisk again.

"I don't know. Civil, I guess."

"Make sure it is. Religious ceremonies add complications. For example, when you get around to undoing it."

"That's mainly what I want to talk about. Is there any way I can protect myself?"

"Good God, no. That's precisely the problem of entering into a relationship like this one. It's not only unholy, but basically amoral. She's doing you a favor, you're doing her a favor, but the pact has nothing to do with the legal definition of marriage, so there's nothing to protect either of you. In actual fact, she'll be holding the cards, which is in the nature of the marriage contract, so you have to be particularly careful."

"Might I call you Maureen?"

She was taken aback but said, "Yes, I suppose so. Why not?" She paused. "There's another possible consequence that should be examined. What if there's a child?"

"That's impossible."

"Why is it impossible?"

"There will be no honeymoon. There will be no connubial bliss. What I want from her is legal access to the army."

Maureen drained her manhattan and impishly said, "What if she wants more?"

"That's not part of the bargain."

Bemused, Maureen said, "She may spring it on you—sort of a marital surprise."

Nikolai finished his drink and signaled the waiter for two more.

"There's another possibility," she persisted.

"What's that?"

"You might grow fond of her. After all, relationships are a mystery. She could turn out to be the girl of your dreams." Maureen's eyes sparkled with interest. She had been dragged into the situation but was now enjoying this.

"I don't think so," he said.

"How can you be so sure?"

"I'm not looking for a mate."

She dismissed this with a wave. "Everybody's looking for a mate. That's what it's all about."

"Are you looking for a mate?"

"Not at the moment," she conceded. "But that's a specific, and I'm speaking in the abstract."

"I'm not sure what that means," he said, as the waiter brought the new drinks. "Does it mean that you've been looking for a mate and will soon be looking again, but that in the meantime, you're resting?"

He spilled it out so smoothly and with such a straight face that it took her a moment to laugh. And when she did, it was a surprisingly throaty rattle. He acknowledged it with a huge smile.

He said, "I had no idea."

"That I laughed?"

"Like that," he said approvingly.

After a moment, she said, "You're really quite different, Mr. Nikolai Granger, with your Old World manners and your patriotic passion. Granger—were your parents English, then?"

"My father was Russian." He paused, allowing her to fill in the vagaries of his beginnings. "So was my mother. She was quite marvelous. She was a well-known actress in her part of the world. For a while, she was married to a man named Granger. She was beautiful, too."

"Then she's not alive."

"No."

"Was it recent?"

"When the Germans came in."

"Oh," she said apologetically. "How did it happen?"

"It happened," he said.

"Sorry." Flustered, she took a gulp of her drink. "I should be going." She gathered her things and stood up.

"Don't go."

"I really must."

"Would you be a witness?"

"A what?"

"To the wedding, if there is one."

"Well, I don't know. I'm awfully busy. I think you know that firsthand."

"Actually, I don't know anything about you."

Slowly, she sank back to her chair. She picked up her drink and made a stab at resurrecting the mood. "What did you want to know?"

"First, why you aren't married."

"And second?"

"Everything else."

"All right, let's start with everything else. My parents are alive and well, quite prosperous, not terribly emotional. I'm an only child. You are too, aren't you?" He nodded, and she went on. "I'm from New Britain, Connecticut, and my father is a lawyer, so I wanted to be one too. No other reason, just a passing interest in the law."

"And the rest?"

"Why am I not married? Well, I was engaged. In fact, I was engaged twice. I broke them off."

"Why?"

"I don't really know," she said slowly and thoughtfully. "They were both terrific … but missing something. And I still have no idea what it was. And now, Mr. Nikolai Granger," she said, with sudden animation, "what about you?"

"Nothing. Nobody and nothing."

"Nobody? Back in England, or the old country?"

"No."

"But even if there was …" She paused before going on. "Even if there was somebody, she wouldn't be important right now, would she?"

"I guess not."

"Getting in the army is everything."

"Yes."

"Here's the interesting thing. Both of the young men I was engaged to were like that, and yet entirely different."

"What do you mean?"

"They were both gung ho. They couldn't wait to get in. One of them went into the navy just before we were engaged, and the other one went into the air force just after. They just bubbled with patriotism. But that's not you, is it?"

"No." He emptied his glass. "One more?"

"I don't think so," she said. In the beginning he had been engagingly correct, and now she realized there was more, that he was quirkily independent too, and this she liked in him. But he was also maddeningly uncommunicative. It upset the balance of power, and she was accustomed to control. "I've got to go," she said.

He rose and extended his hand. "Thanks for everything. Thanks for your help." She shook it and forced a smile.

CHAPTER 9

▼

Iris McCorkle spoke in short, machine-gun-like bursts, as though conserving ammunition. She was as pretty as her picture, except for her teeth; now that her mouth was no longer clamped shut, he could see that her teeth were long, chipped, and a vague color that wasn't white.

They had rendezvoused in a corner drug store on Hanover Street, not far from St. Stevens Church. Maureen Eliot's whimsical notion that the prospective bride might have a romantic soul turned out to be ill-founded.

"Let's get one thing straight right now," said Iris breathlessly. "There ain't gonna be no fooling around."

"Fine," Nikolai said.

This was too facile an agreement for Iris. "Hey, I mean it. This is strictly a business proposition. I don't just jump in bed with every Tom and Harry," she said, conveying, by omission, her virtue.

"I admire that," said Nikolai.

Mollified, Iris said, "Okay, that's better."

They discussed the time and place of the ceremony (next week, City Hall) and her uneasiness about the mechanics of the allotment. "What if you try to hold out on me?" she asked, pouting in advance.

"I checked. The legally married spouse of a serviceman cannot be denied her military allotment."

Iris lit a cigarette. She favored Chesterfields. New to the habit, she came close to setting her nose on fire. She took a dainty bite of smoke, coughed, and said, "Okay, we're down to the nitty-gritty."

"I beg your pardon?"

"The advance. The two-fifty."

"What two-fifty? I don't know anything about two-fifty."

"You trying to tell me he didn't tell you two-fifty up front, in advance?" Her face was reddening. She slurped her dregs of Coke.

"This is the first I've heard of it."

"Well, that's a hot one," she said disbelievingly. She slurped on the ice again and took another agitated puff. "Anyway, that's what it is. That's the deal."

Nikolai knew it was a shakedown. He said, "I don't have two hundred and fifty dollars." He showed her his wallet. "Look, this is the treasury." He opened the wallet and showed her his money. "Forty-two bucks, and that's forty-two over the deal."

"Not from where I sit," said Iris.

"Well, what is it you want me to do?"

"Hey, you're the one wants to get married. Get it someplace."

"Suppose I give you an IOU for two hundred and eight dollars and pay it out on time. As soon as I get in."

"Pay it out on time?" she scoffed. "On thirty-two bucks a month? I'll tell you what I'll do." She plucked the money from the wallet and squashed it in her fist. "I'll hold this for a down payment. You meet me in front of Filene's on the Milk Street side at twelve o'clock noon tomorrow. Pay me the balance, and we keep going right to City Hall."

"I can't get that kind of money by tomorrow."

"Well, that's the way it goes," she said, and as though the deal were dead and buried but the commission for her troubles was forty-two dollars, she shoved the money into her purse.

"I want that back," Nikolai said. She started to rise, but Nikolai grabbed her arm and pulled her down with such force that her thump was closer to a crash.

His eyes radiated malevolence, and she gasped. His grip was painful. When he released her, she recoiled in fear. "Take your stinking money, you goddamn foreigner!" she bawled, then dropped the forty-two dollars on the table and bolted.

Stefan, out of town during the fiasco with Iris, returned in a frenzy of activity. The last thing on his mind was finding another girl to marry Nikolai. He had deals all over the place—tires, second-hand cars, and gasoline coupons, a thick wad of which he waved in agitation.

"Good Christ, where'd you get all these?" Nikolai asked.

"Don't get so excited. They ain't even real."

"Fakes? You're crazy."

"You listen, Mr. Goody Two Shoes. You want something, you take chance! You don't sit around, play game. You do something!" This was not the usual bantering. Stefan was angry.

"Go ahead and say it," Nikolai invited.

"You want army? Takes balls! That's how you get into army!"

"Like what?"

Like right here!" Stefan shouted, waving the sheaf of coupons in Nikolai's face. "Stop pussyfoot around with wife business! You need papers for army? Make papers!"

Nikolai blinked. It was suddenly simple. He had wrapped himself in a spiderweb of ethics, but where had his cherished ethics gotten him?

"Do you know anybody?"

Stefan smiled. "My treat, buddy boy."

The forger's name was Frederick Pinosh, but Nikolai, detecting a vaguely Turkish accent, suspected that the man was himself forged. He conducted his business without showing himself, wearing dark glasses and floppy hats. He worked from a modest photo studio, which served to cover less legitimate activities.

Pinosh was swamped with work. He could not promise a delivery date for the new identity, and Nikolai spent the next few weeks chafing. At last, the call came, and Nikolai ran through the twisting streets of Boston to Pinosh's rundown studio. Frederick Pinosh was not a man of false modesty; he handed the envelope over with a toothy smile. Creating a brand-new human being from scratch gave him a sense of the divine. God was in the details.

In fact, Pinosh was talented. The various licenses, certificates, accreditations, diplomas, and references were properly aged, the ink correctly was faded, and seals and signatures had been masterfully reproduced.

Delighted, Nikolai immersed himself in the details of his new self. He would be John Martin Henley, of 162 Fuller Street, Brookline, Massachusetts, the only child of Reginald and Pauline Henley, who had emigrated from London, England, in 1919, at which time John Martin had been born, an automatic American citizen. Both parents were now deceased.

Within hours, Nikolai put his new identity to the test. He was standing in front of an army recruiting sergeant. The sergeant, a square-shaped man with thick features and a bass growl, kept looking from one document to another. "What I can't figure out, John," he said, "is how you could have graduated high school in 1929, when you were ten years old." He looked over, slack-mouthed.

"What?" Nikolai said, attempting disbelief and indignation.

"Right here," said the sergeant, handing over a diploma. "If you were born in 1919, that makes you ten years old coming out of high school."

Nikolai looked at the offending document. His heart was sinking. How could he have been so foolish? He hadn't even bothered checking the diploma, or anything else, for that matter. Pinosh's huge, triumphant smile had been enough. *Idiot.*

Even worse, under the sergeant's baleful eye, all he could think of to say was: "That's got to be a mistake."

"Unless you were a boy genius," said the sergeant.

"It's got to be a typographical error," Nikolai said. He was holding down his English accent and praying. "I graduated high school in '39."

The sergeant took back the diploma. He studied it. "You're right. That's what must have happened."

The rest was easy. Nikolai sailed through the psychological test and physical exam, neither of which would have kept out a deranged dwarf. He reflected that the sergeant hadn't been fussy either.

He was told that he would be notified as to where and when to report for assignment to a basic training camp; such notification would arrive sometime next week.

Like a schoolboy, Nikolai whooped and skipped and jumped all the way back to his apartment, then met Stefan at Wah Yen's. Throughout the meal, Nikolai waved at every serviceman in the restaurant.

When they were finished, Stefan lowered his voice and said, "Listen good. I put some money away for you. Bank book coming in post office mail."

"What for?"

"To buy candy bar and cigarettes, stupid."

Nikolai smiled. "Thanks."

Notification from the army arrived three days later. He was to report to Fort Devens, in Ayre, Massachusetts, the following Tuesday. A bus ticket and meal coupons were enclosed. On his last day, he worked until closing time, then went into the washroom and ritualistically scrubbed himself until he was as pale as worn marble.

He lit up a cigarette and started for the corner. Then he saw Maureen standing under a streetlight. It wasn't exactly a Lili Marlene pose; she was holding her small purse in both hands, as though waiting for the collection box to be passed.

She moved forward to meet him and said, "How did it go?"

He was totally confused for a moment. Then he said, "Oh, God, you're talking about the wedding."

"Of course."

"It never happened. But I got in the army anyway."

"That's great. When do you leave?"

"Tuesday."

"I'm glad for you. It's what you want."

They started walking, but then she stopped abruptly. "Are you busy? I mean, tonight."

"I'm incredibly free."

"Would you like to ride down to the Cape?" She saw his expression. "You've never been there."

"No."

"Come on."

She guided him to a dark blue Mercury convertible. Its chrome nose was aggressively poised. He took note of her status with a nod and a word: "Spiffy."

They slid in, and Maureen powered down the top and eased into traffic. Effortlessly, she snaked through Boston and out to the Cape road. The wind cut down conversation, and Nikolai closed his eyes. The tires thumped a rhythm, and in his mind, he filled it in with a jingle: *Twice as much for a nickel too! Pepsi-Cola is the drink for you!* It kept going, over and over, until he floated into a serene, pleasant sleep.

When he awoke, it was twilight. The Mercury was parked in a lot overlooking the Cape Cod Canal. The great Sagamore Bridge loomed ahead, lights glimmering, so close that it looked surreal in the dusk.

Maureen was standing at a guard rail. Nikolai joined her, and they watched as a small passenger liner slowly slid under the bridge and cruised away majestically. Caught up in the beauty of the moment and the cathedral-like silence of the coming night, they watched the boat move into the distance before Maureen broke the spell. "That's the St. John, on the way to Halifax." A cold breeze came up, and she rubbed her hands together and warmed her shoulders.

Nikolai said, "There are submarines out there, no more than a few miles."

"How very romantic, Mr. Granger," she said. "Let's go. I'm starving."

They ate at the Falmouth Inn, an eclectic union of Colonial, Federal, and Georgian architecture with a saltbox entrance. It was sprawling and endlessly charming, with small rooms and roaring fireplaces and the glint of pewter and old plate set off by an army of candles.

Nikolai watched her. The fire backlit her hair, and the right side of her face reflected a reddish gold. He suddenly realized that she was quite beautiful and said so.

She said, "My goodness. How extravagant! Now, what brought that on?"

"You wanted me to say it."

She paused. "Fair enough. But you certainly do take your time."

He seemed to notice her for the first time. "Are you being forward?"

"Forward as hell. But it's an act."

"Yes, I know."

"You know. So you think you know me."

"I know you' re spoiled."

She was taken aback.

"And I know you're a snob," he said.

"Ouch."

"And you like things your way."

She smiled. "Yes, I do. So you're right. I'm spoiled. Latvia," she said suddenly, tilting her head quizzically. "What's it like?"

"Small. Quiet, self-conscious. Comes from being occupied most of the time."

"I feel so ignorant. I don't even know what they eat."

"*Cūku pupas* is a specialty."

"It sounds terrible. Is it?"

"Not at all."

Her fork was suspended. "I don't trust you. I'm sure it's disgusting."

"Not at all."

"Go ahead. I'm not that delicate."

"You sure?"

"Go ahead."

"Broad beans in butter sauce."

"You tricked me!"

"You tricked yourself. Anyway, here's a Latvian joke for you. This bull is roaming around, looking for a little romance, and he comes across a pretty spotted lady cow and says, 'How would you like the biggest organ you've ever seen?' And the lady cow says, 'Where would I keep an organ in my stall?'"

She grinned and said, "That's a Latvian joke?"

"I didn't say it was a good joke."

"And if I'm so snobby, why, pray, do I truck with the likes of you?"

He mimed her café society tone perfectly, saying, "So you can say things like 'truck with the likes of you' and be understood."

"I was thinking about you. How mysterious you are."

"In what way?"

"You hide things."

"Such as?"

"Love affairs. You said they didn't exist. Is that true?"

"Of course."

"Oh, brother," she said, in dismissal.

"Why don't you believe it?"

"I don't know. I look at you, and I think something's smoldering."

"Zmoldering?" he said, breaking it into Germanic syllables.

The deep-throated laugh floated up again. "I have a new theory. You were on the stage. Maybe with your mother?"

"Never."

"How about school? Amateur production?"

"I played the village idiot in a Tolstoy play. I was very good."

She smiled. "You like to amuse without giving yourself away, don't you?"

The waitress came and cleared away their dishes. They ordered coffee and lit their cigarettes.

"Tell me about her," Maureen said.

"Who?"

"Your mother."

He hesitated before saying, "She was a woman of many passions. She was always in love. She lived many lives, and when she was bored, she moved on to a new one."

She looked over uncertainly. "That sounded like a memorial service."

He nodded, and after a moment, he brightened with memory. "When I was about eight or nine, she took on a lover named Arturen Murgos. He was a prominent doctor, an internist. He was very somber—dealing with people's guts, I guess. He had a spade beard. He played the cello, too, so I had to call him Uncle Arturo. I didn't like him. I don't think my mother liked him that much either, but they had a busy love life, so it lasted a couple of years. When she ended it, Arturen blamed me. He said I poisoned her mind. Around this time, I had a breathing problem, and to get even, Arturen told me the problem was a hole in the heart. He knew the symptoms. He said I'd be dead inside of five years."

"Oh, my god!"

"My mother found out and put me through a week of examinations. I was okay—no hole in the heart. But there's more. She was doing a play, something about the Black Plague, very cheery, and she's nine months gone, about to produce the last hope for this dying peasant village. I was in the audience that night, and of all people, so was Arturen. By now, his wife had died, and he was remarried, to a very prominent lady with timber mills. And the reason he's there, of course—third row, center—is to show her off to Tati.

"End of the play. Curtain calls. Tati comes out and quiets the audience. She's still got this big nine-month bulge. And she says, 'Ladies and gentlemen, my son, Nikolai.' I hated things like that, but I got up and bowed. Then she says, 'I am happy to announce that drama and life are one and the same.' She pats her big, fat stomach. 'Soon, my son will have a brother or a sister.' Big applause.

"'I am also happy to announce that the father is here with us tonight—the eminent physician, Arturen Murgos!'

Maureen laughed but shook her head. "That can't be true."

"Famous story. True," he assured her. "She was an actress, you know. There was life, and larger than life, and stagecraft, and fairy tales."

"You loved her," Maureen said.

When they got in the car, she said, "I want to show you something."

She drove out of Falmouth and followed the winding road along the coast to Old Silver Beach. She turned sharply into a narrow driveway and went up a short rise to a cottage that looked out over a moon-soaked expanse of hard-packed sand and receding tide.

It was her parents' place, she said, producing a key. He looked uncertain. "Come on," she prodded.

It was functionally but pleasantly furnished in a rattan motif. Maureen dug into closet drawers and came out with two beach towels. "Let's go swimming."

They stripped to underwear in separate rooms, then wrapped themselves in the towels and walked across the sand.

Maureen saucily tossed aside her towel. "Ready?"

It would have been tasteless excess to pose, so she did nothing, waiting for him to look over. He did, at last, staring briefly. She was majestic in the light of the moon. A simultaneous impulse prompted them to strip off the rest of their clothes. Maureen stretched out her hand, he took it, and they ran into the sea.

The water was cold and briny; it needled their skin. And then the water was perfect, and they splashed and swam. Maureen came up behind and jumped on his shoulders, then rode him until he flung her off with a huge splash. She came back and enveloped him in a bear hug, then slipped an ankle behind his and shoved. Off balance, he fell, but he grabbed her going down, and they both fell with another splash. Locked together, they wrestled, twisting and wriggling only inches beneath the surface of the water until they came up, gasping for breath.

They sat laughing, sprayed by soft waves. Maureen's breasts were so balanced on the surface that they seemed to be floating on the water.

Chilled, they ran out onto the sand, draped on the towels, picked up their clothing, and headed back into the house. Maureen found a bottle of her father's scotch, and they warmed up, looking like Indians wrapped in their towels. She rose suddenly and headed into a bedroom, calling back, "Bring the bottle."

By the time he appeared at the door, she was under the covers, and when he hesitated, she growled, as though to a backward child, "Come to bed, Nikolai." He let the towel fall and slipped between the sheets.

She rolled against him. Her body was still chilled, but a magical warmth sprang up in the instant of contact. With a single gentle finger, she turned his face to her lips and softly kissed him. She opened her eyes and scanned his impassive face. She kissed him again and let out a soft moan. She squirmed, and her hands moved across his body.

She inched down and took him between her lips. Her tongue ran across his penis and glazed the tip. She was incredibly gentle and endlessly patient, but at last, her head came up. "What is it?"

He failed to answer, and she lay back next to him. "It's okay."

"No, it's not."

"Can't you tell me?"

"Maureen, don't."

"It's because I like you, you know."

"I know."

"Is there somebody else?"

"It's not somebody else. I think we'd better go."

They drove back to Boston at breakneck speed. Maureen ignored the speed limit and every traffic light along the way. Even with the roar of the wind, the silence was intense. At three o'clock in the morning, she screeched to a stop at the corner of Tyler Street, and Nikolai got out and watched her race away.

He lit a cigarette and walked the half-block to his building; the walk was no less dreary in the early hours of morning than any other time. A faint light shone above the door, and he slipped the key into the lock. At the rasp of the tumbler, a voice said, "Are you John Henley?"

Nikolai whirled. He was facing two beefy men in drab suits. A third man was standing alongside a dark sedan. Vaguely, Nikolai wondered why he hadn't noticed them.

"Keep your hands where we can see them," said the second man.

The first man revealed a tarnished gold badge. "John Martin Henley, you are under arrest."

CHAPTER 10

▼

There were two charges. The first was counterfeiting: *Whereas the defendant has employed fraudulent means of reproduction for the purpose of gaining acceptance into the ranks of the United State Army.* The second charge: *Criminal activities in regard to the manufacture of bogus gasoline certificates for the purpose of illicit profit.*

Two more charges were waiting in the wings, one more serious than all the others put together: the question of treason, a suspicion based on the defendant's assumption of a fictitious personage with the possible intent of engaging in seditious and disloyal activities against the United States of America. Also to be determined by investigation was the extent of the defendant's involvement in the black-market tire business at 237 Hope Street in Cambridge, Massachusetts.

Earlier that evening, the FBI had swooped down and arrested twenty-six members of the "gang," as they were referred to in the official indictment. Along with ringleaders Stefan Razek and his two partners, various confidants, runners, salespeople, and buyers were caught in the net, as well as employees of the Hope Street Auto Repair Shop and a printer named Frederick Pinosh.

The trial was swift, punishment was even swifter, and the sentences were severe: they ran from two years in prison up to twelve, with Nikolai at the high end. Stefan got eight years. The judge banged the gavel twice, and the miscreants were bundled off in handcuffs. Within moments, Nikolai and Stefan, isolated by the technicality of their alien entry in the country, were in a paddy wagon en route to Charlestown State Prison. Ironically, it was not that far from the Hope Street Garage in Cambridge.

"See what can happen in a free country?" Stefan cheerily commented. "You're the only one ain't a real crook, but you got the most."

Nikolai smiled mirthlessly.

They were assigned to the same cell, and then to the same kitchen detail. Weeks went by, and when they became months, Nikolai began to understand the true nature of prison: it was a faucet from which life and vengeance slowly dripped.

A new kitchen-mate named Dancer Rhodes brought spice into their lives. He was a limber little man in his thirties with a Midwestern twang that sometimes gave way to a faint Irish brogue. There was a pixie-like quality to him; people said he resembled Fred Astaire. In fact, he had hoofed it in vaudeville as "The Dancing Fool." Apparently, he wasn't bad, but he wasn't that good, either, because he had turned from stage work to robbing movie box offices.

He had served two minor terms, but this one was five to eight. And yet, he was an upbeat presence; in the kitchen, he would break into song-and-dance routines, buck and wing and soft shoe, sounding quite authentic on the gritty kitchen floor. Dancer's routines were labored, but he bubbled, and even the guards were amused. Life in prison was constriction, depression, and humility, and Dancer brightened the agony of time.

Stefan, ever flexible, staked out a commercial niche, selling smuggled-in merchandise to his fellow convicts. The market was there, and the guards could be bribed, but there was a problem: the commonwealth had located and attached his bank accounts. He was broke.

He came to Nikolai with a wan smile, a five-thousand-dollar smile—the money he had deposited in Nikolai's name when Nikolai was joining the army. Through contacts, Stefan had learned that the account was still intact.

Nikolai squirmed, because the only person who could get the money for him was Maureen, and Maureen was the last person in the world he wanted to see. She had no idea he was in prison. Stefan smiled again, wanly.

Three weeks later, she arrived, along with a small flood of visitors. The room was prison-movie perfect: long and gray and windowless, with rusty radiators at both ends. Three heavy tables and three dozen heavy chairs formed three rows; everything was heavy, so it could not be thrown.

The prisoners were seated when the visitors arrived in an anteroom in which gift packages were examined. Then a guard flung open the anteroom door, and the visitors piled into the room, and the prisoners scraped back their chairs and jumped up amidst a babel of greetings while the guards admonished them to sit down.

Eventually, everyone sat, and the room vibrated with conversation. Maureen had sauntered in acting like a sociologist on Mars, eyes taking in the colorful occupants of the zoo. She was wearing a Sunday outfit with a big white collar and big shoulders; something that was meant to evoke a skimmer sat back on her head. She looked so determinedly smart that the women, who were interested only in seeing their men, nonetheless looked her up and down, and the men, loins aching, gave her a once-over before settling across from their women.

She placed a small package before him; it obviously had been torn open and examined. "I wanted to bring you something, and all I could think of was socks. Was that all right?"

"Of course. Thanks."

"For God's sake, Nikolai, what are you doing here?"

He told her, and she stared back, appalled. "But you were only trying to get in the service."

"How are you?"

"Why didn't you let me know?" she said, suddenly angry. "That was eight months ago."

He looked her over. In this drab room of pinched and pasty faces, she was stunningly out of place. Self-conscious, she fluffed her big collar.

"What about the money?"

"I transferred it into his account." Her voice fell to a whisper. "You're not going to use it to do something dumb, are you?"

"Like break out? Of course not."

She smiled. "I think I've seen too many movies. Can you smoke in here?" she asked, then noticed one of the stern No Smoking signs. She took a breath. "What's it like?"

"It's fun."

"Sorry. That was stupid," she said.

"How's it going?"

"Okay. Office is thinning out. Everybody's getting drafted. My dad's an air-raid warden. He's got a helmet and a little badge, and my mother says he sleeps with them."

"And you?" he said, studying her.

She deliberated. "I'm getting married," He nodded, and she said, "You're not surprised, are you?"

He shook his head. "That's the business I'm in now. I'm not surprised at anything."

She studied a nearby couple, who had been squabbling since the woman had sat down, greeted by her husband saying, "You look like crap."

"Nikolai, was that real? In the letter, you said twelve years."

Her hand reached out to touch his. A guard lightly thumped the end of the table, and Maureen withdrew her hand as though it were on a spring.

"Oh, Nikolai," she said. In that hopeless and irreconcilable moment, her voice snagging and breaking, she had surrendered all artifice. Her eyes flashed, and she leaned in. "Why didn't you do it? Why didn't you make love to me?"

"Let it go, okay?"

"No, goddamnit. It's not okay." Her outrage gave way to a tight-lipped pout. "Don't you even want to know what he's like?"

"Of course."

"He's navy. His name is Douglas. He's on a cruiser—communications officer. I've known him since I was a kid. You know, families."

She heard the sound of her own smugness: "families," as in "good families," and added, "We're not sure about anything. It was just an impulse. He's going out soon."

For a moment, every other voice in the room sliced through, like dozens of overlapping telephone lines. Then she said, "I'm overdressed." She reached back, took out the hairpin, and removed her hat. It freed her. She looked over saucily. "I have a theory. Want to hear it?"

"Sure."

She caught herself and pulled back. "Forget it."

"Go on."

"No. All right. I think maybe it's about your mother."

"You mean … faithful to the memory of my mother makes me a lousy lover?"

"God, I don't know. I don't even know what I'm saying."

"It's not that crazy," he said thoughtfully. "When I was a kid, I'd crawl into her bed at night and wish I could be part of the things I heard, all that moaning and groaning with Arturo and the rest of them."

"Nikolai, what I'm trying to say is … I understand, and it doesn't matter."

She radiated empathy, and he smiled in gratitude and let it go at that. A few minutes later, the guards announced that visiting time was over. They scraped back their chairs and rose, and she said, "What can I do? How can I help?"

He shook his head. "Thanks for coming." She looked over uncertainly, but he was already turning away, and they headed for opposite doors.

Over the excruciating months that followed, filled with endless reflection, Nikolai drifted through stages of surreal disbelief. How had he come to this? What was he doing in a prison? What part of him belonged to this United States of America? How much guilt should he attach to his status as pariah?

The fact was that he felt no guilt. His intent had been to kill the enemies of America; how could its legal institutions fail to recognize his moral imperative? What good were laws which punished virtue?

From time to time he seethed, fashioning himself a wartime casualty for wanting to go to war. But in other, more reasonable moments, he brushed aside his indignation for what it was: the weakness of anarchy. Because if he was not accountable for lawlessness, no matter the motivation, then Hartigens-Hesse was not accountable for anything he had done, and Nikolai would have no reasonable grounds to judge him.

In the silence of his lonely nights, he thought much about the Baron. In a strange, way, Hartigens-Hesse exerted a fascination that went beyond the driving engine of revenge. It had to do, he suspected, with the Baron's patrician standing—a perversity stemming from his childhood, from Tati's whispered incantations that they were special, that they sprang from royal blood and must never descend to pedestrian level.

She had never elaborated, and much later, he came to realize that it was a game she had played with herself, taught to her son to make him strong. He had forgotten the game, but in an odd way, it had come back to serve him. He was more than an equal to Hartigens-Hesse; he would survive everything and destroy this consummate evil.

So went the delicious world of his dreams, shattered by the sure knowledge that the day of reckoning was as far away as the Earth from the moon. He must overcome prison, an intervening war, the geography of ocean, and even the Baron's death; because if Hartigens-Hesse should somehow die in the war, Nikolai would be the clear loser. These thoughts stabbed at his brain, but he shook them off. Fantasy was his reality.

Stefan's new business was a rousing success until the arrival of two new prisoners. Their names were Joseph Schenck and Otto Kleist, and they would change everything.

According to Dancer, the two men were old-time Nazis out of the German-American *Bund*. They had been picked up following an aborted attempt to rob the First New England bank of Somerville.

They were big men, on the order of thugs, overbearing and intimidating. Nikolai easily slotted them in the pantheon of bad Germans in B movies. They postured brazenly, but it was more than theatrics; at the core of their arrogance was fearlessness. Like most brutes, they exulted in hard contact. The bank job, for example, had included the stabbing of a guard and the deliberate breaking of a female teller's arm. In the few weeks since their arrival, they were suspected of gouging out an eye and chopping off a thumb in run-ins with two prisoners.

Kleist, in the classical manner of the villain, had a perpetual scowl as the result of a knife slash that ran across his upper lip and lower cheek. He had come to the United States from Darmstadt only five years earlier, and his accent was bold and unapologetic. He had rippling muscles and displayed them like trophies.

Schenck, born in Wisconsin of solidly rooted farmers (two generations removed from the fatherland), despised the United States. Along with its politics, he was chagrined at dozens of other social indignities that came with living in America, such as the fact that you couldn't get a decent loaf of bread in the whole country. He was brighter than Kleist, quieter, more ominous. While Kleist's bravado came with a Germanic chortle, Schenck never laughed.

They made no friends, but there were the usual hangers-on, lapping up leftover power like dogs at the king's table. Dancer had warned Stefan that sooner or later, they would be trouble, and the day came with surprising swiftness. The Germans had been exercising in the yard, and they boxed Stefan in with their thick, sweat-stained arms.

"So we talk, heh, pig face?" said Kleist. He lifted an elbow, waving a rank, wet, mop of underarm hair in Stefan's face, and announced that they were taking over the business. There was more laughter from the back row.

"What do I get out of it?" Stefan brazenly said.

"Maybe you get to live."

"You can kiss my ass!" Stefan said, loud enough to be heard by almost everyone in the courtyard.

Swaggering past Nikolai and Dancer, who were looking astonished, Stefan flashed a big smile.

"He's out of his mind," Nikolai said.

"They'll take him apart."

"No other way. Got to do it," Nikolai suddenly hissed. His mouth strangely twisted.

"What?" Dancer said.

"We have to do it. We have to kill them." The words tumbled out in a bitter burst.

"Whoa, boy. What're you talking about?"

Fiercely, Nikolai said, "We take them out, then we vouch for each other— don't know anything, didn't see it. Who's going to care? The warden? The guards? They don't want the krauts here fucking up their prison."

Dancer was studying him with a surprised smile. "Am I hearing you for real?"

"What the hell's so funny?"

"I'm just a little taken aback, kid," Dancer said, still amused. "I never thought of you as warlike."

"I didn't plan it."

"You really think you could take those guys out cold-ass?"

For the first time, Nikolai examined the idea. "Yes."

"Well, I hate to leave you in the lurch, pal, but that's not my cup of tea. You're on your own."

They went back to mulling over the situation, and the hours passed. To their surprise, the crisis failed to materialize. The next day in the yard, the krauts kept to themselves, while everyone else waited for them to attack Stefan. Nikolai and Dancer kept an eye out, and the guards seemed to be on the alert, but nothing happened.

Stefan, who had begun to acknowledge the true nature of his peril, reverted to bravado, saying, "Told you I scared them!" Despite warnings from Nikolai and Dancer not to stir things up, Stefan took to wider and wider forays across the yard, swooping past the krauts with choice provocations. "*Deutschland über alles!*" and "*Sieg heil,* boys!" he'd say, animatedly goose-stepping past them.

The goose-stepping did the trick. Kleist reached out, caught his foot, and brought Stefan crashing to the ground. He began to kick him methodically— groin, kidneys, ribs—but now Nikolai hurtled in, head smashing into the small of Kleist's back.

Kleist was forty pounds heavier, but Nikolai had the momentum and never let up; knees astride the belly-down Kleist, he jerked his head up by the hair and slammed it into the concrete courtyard. Kleist's smashed nose spurted a fountain of blood. Schenck grabbed a rock, but Dancer was rushing in too, and then the guards, waving rifles and clubs.

The yard chief, a heavyset man named Girardi, shook a finger at all four, refusing to categorize winners or losers, right or wrong. "One week in the hole!"

As it happened, a benevolent decree from the governor's office—ironically based on a little-used Puritan holiday—freed the miscreants in three days. Returning to his cell, Nikolai found an envelope waiting, ivory-hued and vellum-soft. Within it, protected by a small rectangle of patterned tissue, was a handsomely engraved wedding invitation. The bridegroom's full name was Douglas Bryson Enderhall. The wedding was only a few Sundays off. They were to be married in Hyannis. The reception would take place at the Falmouth Inn.

Nikolai smiled, suspecting that the Falmouth Inn was a personal stick in the eye. He thought of that night, the candlelight, and calling her a snob, and her lazy, easy response: *Why, you dirty dog.*

What did it mean? *Maureen and Douglas Bryson Enderhall.* He stared into space dispassionately. He juggled the off-key elements, Maureen against the mosaic. How much did he care? Did she belong in the steaming stew of his fragmented life, along with dead Tati and dead Katya and prison and the delicious obsession that was Reinhard Ernst von Hartigens-Hesse? Quite possibly, he and Maureen had never been destined for a lifetime, only minutes—something less than sleek ships passing in the night, more like tugboats tooting hello and good-bye.

At the sum of all sums, everything was gray, from his feelings and his senses to the air he breathed, to the walls that surrounded him, to the sky through the rectangular slit in his cell. Gray thoughts caught up in gray rivers of time, gray conversations with gray people in gray clothing. He ate gray food and slept on a gray mattress, twisting endlessly through the night in a series of foggy, gray dreams.

CHAPTER 11

▼

Most of the inmates were in the mess hall, which was now converted to its twice-a-month movie function. The projection screen had ripped during a fight one night, and a large sheet served in its place, tautly fastened to one wall. Tables had been shoved aside, benches lined up.

The movie was *Back to Bataan*. Overrun by rapacious Japanese, the hopelessly outnumbered American troops were retreating and dying. The crash of battle onscreen was matched by the clamor from the kitchen. The prisoners watched tensely, caught up in patriotic fervor. "Kill them yellow motherfuckers!" someone shouted.

Stefan entered the room and slid alongside Nikolai. Onscreen, the action tapered off, the Americans sprawling to light up, waiting for the next assault while they talked about home.

"You see Dancer?" Nikolai said.

"Still in the library, I guess." Stefan, his body in constant motion, kept looking around. Then he jumped up.

"What are you doing?"

Stefan said quietly, "Check the storeroom."

"For what?" Nikolai said impatiently, but he knew what, and for that matter, Stefan was already gone.

Coming out of the hole, Stefan had launched a crusade to nail Schenck and Kleist. He followed them whenever he could, convinced that the pair were involved in peddling drugs. Drug peddling was only a hunch, but it made sense. Back in the yard, before the fight, the krauts had been furtive and oddly slow to provoke, from which Stefan concluded they were hiding something big, and what was bigger inside the can than drugs?

His attention had come to focus on a storeroom just off the kitchen. Twice, he had seen the krauts go in and come out of the room—but always empty-handed. It was a mystery. If they were hiding drugs in the storeroom, why wouldn't they add or take away from their stock? One possible answer came to him sitting next to Nikolai, which was why he had jumped up and left the movie so abruptly. The krauts could not operate without bribing the guards, but the guards couldn't be trusted not to steal the merchandise!

It made so much sense that Stefan grinned hugely. He had been right all along! The drug-peddling theory was on the button, and the drugs were hidden in the storeroom, which he had searched once, but too hurriedly and carelessly.

He slipped quietly along the corridor past the kitchen and peeked around the corner. Nobody was there. He moved to a broom closet and plucked a ring with two keys off a hook. Then he padded to the storeroom door and let himself in. He closed the door quietly and pushed a wall button. The room lit up.

Stefan looked around the big room with a curious pang of possession: the storeroom was to be his storeroom. He had bribed the guards for this space—space taken from him by the krauts, along with the business itself. For the first time, he truly understood his mercantile passion, not simply the making of money in the exchange of goods, but the joy of ownership.

He could sense a future of legitimacy and propriety. In an almost religious sense, he felt cleansed, almost virtuous. They were prisoners in the same prison, but he had nothing in common with the krauts. His euphoria began to fade when he opened carton after carton and failed to discover anything related to the drug trade.

The door handle turned with a rasp, and Stefan ducked below a stack of cartons as Charlie Dugan barreled in on a beeline. Stefan closed his eyes, waiting to be hauled off, but Dugan had scraped to a stop. He tugged open a small carton and pulled out packs of gum, tore open several wrappers, shoved the gum in his mouth and the packs in his jacket, and left the room.

Stefan slowly straightened, relief whistling through his teeth. He started out, but his eyes fell on a large shopping bag that seemed to have fallen behind the stacks. He picked it up; it was soft to the touch. He opened the bag and peered in: clothing. Slowly, he pulled out the top garment. It was a jumpsuit, blue-gray in color, rumpled and stained. Stefan pulled out the rest of the clothing: two more jumpsuits.

Perplexed, he stared at the jumpsuits. They were somehow familiar, but why? And then he remembered the jumpsuits worn by city sanitation workers.

A shockwave of sound froze him—three blasts from the big horns of the garbage truck, coming through the east gate. He hurried to the door and looked out along the corridor. It was clear, and he started toward the kitchen area. A figure was striding toward him, obscure in the uneven light at first, but then unmistakable: Dugan again. Stefan retreated quickly, finally pulling aside just short of Dugan's station, into the shadows of an unused pantry area.

Dugan strode past purposefully, heading toward the barred gate that led down the long corridor to the loading platform. He opened the gate, then abruptly turned and started briskly back toward the kitchen. Before reaching it, he disappeared down another corridor.

Stefan blinked in astonishment. Could he have imagined it? That Dugan had unlocked the gate and gone off? It defied all reason, to the point that Stefan at first didn't notice the scurrying figures, three men emerging from the very corridor Dugan had taken.

Stefan again pulled back into the shadows. The figures materialized, the two in front easily identifiable by size and gait: Schenck and Kleist. For a moment, they hid the third man. And then he swung into the clear, and Stefan's mouth dropped open. The third man was Dancer.

The three men headed for the storeroom. The lock was opened, and they disappeared inside. Stefan dared not breathe. He stared at the storeroom door, listening to his heart thump inside his body.

"What the hell are you doing here?"

Stefan recoiled sharply, banging the back of his head against the pantry wall. Nikolai was standing before him, irritated. "The movie's over. We're into ten-minute grace. Let's go."

"Jesus, Nikolai! Jesus!" Stefan wheezed.

"What the hell's the matter with you? What've you been doing?"

Stefan pointed to the storeroom. "Nikolai, it's the krauts! They're making a break! Dancer's with them."

"Dancer?" Nikolai looked disbelievingly toward the storeroom. "They're in there?"

"One minute ago. Just before you came." Unevenly, he blurted out his discovery of the uniforms and the fact that Charlie Dugan was in on the break. "They're going out on the garbage truck!" he said, inching back and forth like a spooked horse. He plucked at Nikolai's arm. "We got to do something!"

"Like what?"

"I don't know! Dancer—he'll get himself killed!"

"If he's with them, he's the one worked it out," Nikolai reasoned. But he was surprised. *Dancer breaking out. Dancer throwing in with the krauts.*

The storeroom door eased open. Kleist inched out, checking the area. In back of him were Schenck and Dancer. All three were now dressed in jumpsuits. They moved toward the guard station and the gate, which was closed but unlocked.

Stefan kept jerking forward, and Nikolai restrained him, whispering, "Don't be stupid!" But he was torn, sharing Stefan's concern that Dancer was in way over his head. The moment was insane; he knew that. There was a madness in this tableau of action and inaction, of the trio of escapees starting to push through the gate, of Stefan and himself frozen in the shadows.

And then Stefan shot out of his grip and bounded ahead.

"Dancer!"

The three figures wheeled around. "Steffo!" Dancer shouted. "Get out of here!"

But Stefan rushed up to him, glaring at Schenck and Kleist as though they were two neighborhood kids corrupting his ward. "Don't do it! Don't go with them!"

"For God's sake, Stefan," Dancer pleaded.

"What goes on here?" Schenck said, whirling to face Dancer, his voice grating like sandpaper.

"I don't know!" Dancer said angrily. "Go on, get going. I'll follow," he told the Germans.

"I don't like that idea," Schenck said

He flicked a finger, and Kleist grabbed Dancer and spun him around, pulling his left arm up behind his back. Kleist's right arm circled Dancer's neck.

"You trying to pull something here, little man?" Schenck said.

"Don't be crazy!" Dancer said in a half-choked voice. "I didn't know he was going to be here!"

"What about that one?" asked Schenck; Nikolai was emerging into the uneven light.

"Oh, shit," Dancer said.

"Okay, let him go," Nikolai said. He was moving quickly toward the group, and his aggressiveness was unexpected, because he did not stop and confront the Germans. Instead, he went right up to Dancer and Kleist, who were pressed tightly together. In one swift motion, as though kicking a soccer ball, Nikolai kicked Kleist in the shins. His heavy shoe found the mark with a sharp thunk. Kleist tumbled back with a howl.

Dancer was free, and he grabbed Nikolai's arms and whispered in his right ear, "Stay out of this!" He was small but sinewy, and his right fist came up out of nowhere and caught Nikolai in the face. Nikolai slumped to one knee, and for a moment, his head raced in circles, and pain shot across his jaw.

From the rear yard, three more horn blasts sounded; they were closer now. The garbage truck had backed into the loading bay.

Dancer turned to Schenck. "Let's go."

"Who you with?" Schenck asked sharply.

"What do you think?" Dancer said, motioning. He moved to help Kleist to his feet. The two pushed through the barred door, into the corridor leading to the loading platform.

"Dancer!" Stefan called plaintively.

Schenck moved before him. His thick hand clutched Stefan's shirt at the neck. "Don't stick your nose next time, Czechko." His right hand swiped across Stefan's face like a hasty blessing.

He turned and hastened after Kleist and Dancer as Stefan, wild-eyed, stared after him. But then he collapsed, falling in soft turns like a leaf. Nikolai, still on one knee, was trying to bring Stefan into focus. There was something odd in the rag-doll slump of his body and the twist of his head, something that reminded him of Tati in the soft light of the apartment in Riga.

Like Tati, Stefan's neck was awash in blood, blood pumping from the arteries in his neck, from the jagged razor-cut slash across his throat—Schenck's benediction. Stefan's head was so thinly attached that, beneath the seething fount of blood, ragged ends of bone and gristle could be seen.

Stefan's wide eyes seemed about to drop from his face. He opened his mouth in one last, frantic effort. Mindless words bubbled out with streams of blood. Then his eyes froze, and he was dead.

Nikolai stared, helplessly drawn. A voice blared at him, but he could make no sense of it. Then rough hands jerked him to his feet. He heard the voice again, a wave of sound crashing in his ear: "What the hell did you do? What'd you do, Granger?"

It was Charlie Dugan, outraged, his eyes taking in the great burgundy stain on the floor, and Stefan's pasty-white face, and the terrible eyes, and the ring of red that was his cut throat. Dugan took out a whistle and blew it fiercely.

"Jesus, Mary," Dugan said. In all his years at Charlestown, he had never seen anything like this. By now, a pattern of logic was sifting through his brain, and the impulse to blame Nikolai had shifted to a more likely unfolding of events.

Two guards came running up, shoes squealing as they braked and stared.

"Holy Christ," the first guard said. He looked over at Nikolai. "He do it?"

The second guard roughly frisked Nikolai. "Nothing. I don't see no knife."

Dugan looked around sharply as the garbage truck sounded again, its frog-like horns more distant now, coming from the muffled confines of the north gate as the truck left the prison.

Nikolai's head was a kaleidoscope filled with questions that touched on riddles that led only to mysteries. One of them was the open door at Dugan's station. As though reading his thoughts, Dugan moved to the gate and locked it, pretending to check it. Dugan caught Nikolai's eyes on him. He hurried back to the group.

"Better get him out of here," he said, and Nikolai suddenly realized that the tone was a message—that he was to keep his mouth shut.

CHAPTER 12

▼

Moving down the dank corridor, the two guards kicked him and threw in odd punches; it seemed the thing to do, even without finding the murder weapon. They descended to basement level and reached solitary, a short row of window-less cells. They opened a big steel door and flung Nikolai into musty darkness; the guards had not bothered to switch on the light.

Nikolai felt along the cold wall until he came to a steel cot. He sprawled out at full length and lay there for hours, imponderables poking through his brain. Exhaustion closed his eyes, and he fell asleep. Moments later, or so it seemed, the door squeaked open, and the overhead bulb came on, splashing a drab light across the tiny cell. Three men were at the door: a guard Nikolai had never seen before and two men, obviously from the outside, dressed in drab suits.

The guard moved forward and rapped Nikolai's bunk with his club. "Okay, let's go, Granger," he snapped.

Nikolai blinked, unwound stiff legs, and swung them to the floor.

"Move it," the guard said.

Nikolai walked out of the cell and down the hall, flanked by the trio. From the cells they passed, he heard occasional domestic sounds: prisoners scraping metal food trays or banging on walls, and one plaintively singing "Stardust."

His escorts never spoke. The guard, now leading the way up a stairway, then down a corridor toward the south end, was tight-lipped and bored; the two men in civvies were tight-lipped and grim.

To Nikolai's surprise, they were pushing out a door into the light of day; it was a gray, early morning sky, Nikolai suddenly realized. They were in a small courtyard in which half a dozen passenger cars were parked, and just beyond them, a small van.

It was the van they were heading for, and now one of the suited men opened the rear loading door and signaled for Nikolai to get in. Nikolai balked, out of curiosity; he wanted to ask where he was going.

The guard came up behind him and gave him an angry shove. "Get the hell in there, you son of a bitch," he said.

Nikolai boosted himself and slid into the back of the van. The door slammed behind him, and he pulled himself up to a bench that ran along one side. The back of the van was windowless and empty. *Another isolation cell,* he thought whimsically. The vehicle lurched into motion, rattled ahead, then came to a grinding halt. Nikolai could hear the dynamo hum of big gates opening, and he was pinned back as the van shot out of the courtyard and out of the prison onto the cobbled Charlestown streets.

They drove for hours, over ruts and rails and cracked roads, then hit smoother going and highway speed—obviously heading out of Boston, Nikolai guessed. But where? It was a cold day, and he was lightly dressed. He curled into a ball on the narrow bench, bounced on top of the axle, and wondered what was happening.

At one point, careening from one side of the truck to the other, he pounded angrily on the divider wall to the cab. There was no answer. The van surged on, and then on and on.

At last it slowed, cut to one side, and stopped. Nikolai heard voices, metal clanging against metal, the sound of a pump. They were in a gas station. The door opened just a few inches. One of the two suited men, thin-faced, a gum chewer, threw in a paper bag that slid along the metal floor and stopped at Nikolai's feet.

He was holding an automatic, but loosely, not clenching it. "No noise. Keep your mouth zipped. And don't bang again, you dumbfuck," the man said. He slammed the door into place. A minute later, the van started to roll again.

Nikolai heard the whoosh of the wind and the whine of the tires. "Fuck you," he said aloud, staring at the brown paper bag. He stretched out again. The stiff-springed van bounced him along. He sat up again and opened the paper bag. Inside was a thin ham sandwich, a small carton of milk, and an apple. He ate.

An image shot into his mind, like a flash of lightning: Stefan, throat cut, puppet head dangling on a thread.

The van rolled on and on. Nikolai tried the floor, went back to the bench, and finally floated off to sleep. When he awoke, it was out of a fragmented dream in which he was rowing on the Thames but going nowhere, not so much as a ripple; Tati was on the shore, smiling benignly despite the fact that he needed some sort of help. His eyes opened, and now he understood the urgency of the dream. He filled the milk carton and put it back in the paper bag.

Just then, the van slowed, and Nikolai realized they were in a city again. Back to Boston, for some weird, irrational reason? No, the echo effects were more diluted: wider streets, more space between the buildings. They rolled deeper into the city. Horns blew. The van stopped in traffic: obviously, a light. The light changed, and the van surged on, straight as an arrow for a mile or so. Then they were taking a tight turn, slowing, coming to a stop. The cab door slammed. Then again. Then casual voices. The rear door opened.

Again, time surprised Nikolai. Despite his endless journey in the dark, he had expected light, but the sky was an inky black. They were at the back of a large building, and now his traveling companions were just outside, warily looking in.

"Okay, buster," said the gum chewer who had tossed him his lunch. "End of the line."

"You mind telling me where we are?" Nikolai said. When his words had formed somewhere in his brain, they had seemed hard and indignant, but what came out was reedy and weak.

"Let's go," the other man said. The tone was not quite indulgent, but it brooked minor grousing. Nikolai slid out of the van and planted shaky legs. He sipped the warm spring air and looked over his two escorts, bland faces in double-breasted suits, the gum chewer still chewing, the other man, with a squat nose and bullish shoulders, pulling out cigarettes and lighting one.

The gum chewer hooked one of his arms, the one with the squat nose guided with a fat palm on the shoulder, and they moved toward a rear entrance. *Always the back way,* Nikolai thought. He swiveled and glanced past his escorts at a sliver of the city and the shadowy lights of monuments. The wartime lights of Washington.

The men walked into the building and went down an antiseptic-gray corridor. It was a basement, with thick overhead pipes. They followed the pipes to a stairway and mounted two floors. Nikolai suddenly found himself in a small room, ascetically furnished with waiting-room chairs, a small, hard sofa, and a refrigerator.

The escorts locked the door and moved straight to the refrigerator. Inside were cold drinks. They each took a Coke and uncapped the bottles.

"You want a Coke, take a Coke," said the gum chewer.

Nikolai moved to the refrigerator and took a bottle. For a moment, the three of them guzzled Cokes, an odd tableau of contentment, considering their disharmonious journey. Then Squat Nose moved to a door and opened it. It was a walk-in closet that held suits, jackets, and other items of men's clothing, all of excellent quality.

"Find something fits. Clean up first," said Squat Nose. He motioned to another door, and Gum Chewer opened it in invitation: a bathroom.

Gum Chewer said, "Mr. G. likes clean, so work yourself up."

Nikolai struggled with these senseless words, but they still fell within the purview of benevolent change. As though he understood everything that was going on, he looked over the clothes in the closet, selected a shirt, a jacket, a pair of slacks, and a pair of shoes, set them aside, then edged into the bathroom.

"Get in there. The works," said the gum chewer. He was pointing to the shower.

The works, Nikolai thought, and then he had a wild vision: they were dressing him so he could be taken out and executed by a firing squad.

It satisfied the negative side of him, but it also made no sense, and he leaned into the mechanical motions of taking a shower, going so far as to pull the plastic curtain around him, since his wards seemed not to care.

He toweled himself, worked over his hair with a comb and brush he found on the sink, then noticed undershorts and socks on a bathroom chair and pulled them on. Then he put the rest on, and the two men looked him over.

"Where's the fucking tie?" said the gum chewer.

Squat Nose burrowed into the closet and came up with a green plaid tie.

"That's it?" the gun chewer asked critically.

"Whaddaya want, Saks Fifth Avenue?" said the other man, with a twisted smile. He tossed the tie over to Nikolai.

The gum chewer said doubtfully, "You know how to tie a tie?"

"I guess," Nikolai muttered. He went back into the bathroom and faced himself in the mirror, and to his astonishment, he felt jittery. Here was the first tangible challenge of the day, and he was not sure he could meet it. Far more smoothly than he expected, he executed a rather neat Windsor.

He focused on himself. He was shocked. He looked thinner, harder, older—but he was dressed up, a vanity he had not practiced for a long time. He was passable.

"Okay, Snow White," the gum chewer said from the doorway to the bathroom. "Let's shake it."

They exited the room and moved through a door out of the service area. They were in a marbled hallway, moving to a bank of elevators. The escorts stayed close but no longer guided him physically. While the elevator whisked them up, Nikolai noticed them primping. Squat Nose tugged shirtsleeves out of his jacket; Gum Chewer toyed with his collar.

The doors opened at the top floor. The lighting was subdued, but the marble shone with more luster here. There was thick carpeting on the floor. They entered the outer office of a suite. There were two secretarial desks but no secretaries.

Squat Nose brought up a knuckle and paused before knocking, an exquisitely frozen moment that flashed Nikolai back to his childhood and the portentous lulls that accompanied melodrama on the Riga stage.

Squat Nose rapped delicately. A muffled something came from within, a grunt or a growl, or maybe a throat-clearing. Squat Nose opened the door and entered, and the gum chewer waved Nikolai ahead of him.

Nikolai entered. His escorts flanked him. The three men were facing a huge desk and the heavyset man behind it. His face was a series of shadows and ruts, a very round, grimacing, unhappy, unpleasant face that was part bulldog and part frog, with thick, sensuous lips and large, protruding eyes. The thin overhead lighting was barely noticeable; two brass lamps topped by green plastic shades cast a brilliant oasis of light across the desk and its occupant. The walls were coated with patterns and designs from the two lamps.

The man behind the desk took out a cigar. It was long but not thick. Using a kitchen match, he took his time lighting it. The tip glowed.

"Your name is Granger."

It was not a question; it was a statement, as though Nikolai had been waiting years for this revelation.

The room was large, and now Nikolai could see that it was handsomely appointed, with English Regency furniture and languorous landscapes across the walls. There was a large tapestry on the wall behind the desk: dogs tearing out the throats of two deer.

"How was your trip?" the man asked. It was not a pleasantry; he wanted an evaluation.

"No problems, sir," said Squat Nose.

"No problems, sir," Gum Chewer chimed in.

"I believe we have discussed this," the man behind the desk said sharply. No one but the gum chewer understood; he feverishly plucked the gum from his mouth and dropped it in a wastebasket.

"Empty it, and stay out," the man behind the desk ordered. The gum chewer picked up the offending receptacle, and he and Squat Nose smartly retreated.

Now a side door to the office opened and a figure entered, a tall, thin man with a pronounced limp. He was dressed in a blue serge three-piece suit with a gold chain across the vest. He took a deferential position behind and to one side of the man behind the desk and puffed on a long-stemmed pipe.

"Give me your name, your age, the crime for which you were convicted," the squat, frog-faced man said. His voice had a basso growl, like the rumbling of a distant tropical storm.

Nikolai recited the requisite details.

"There's a trace left," the man behind the desk said, without turning his head.

"But nothing pronounced," said the man in the three-piece suit. "It could be Harvard." Interestingly enough, he himself carried a faint Scottish burr.

"Do you know me?" asked the man behind the desk.

"No," Nikolai said.

"Sir."

Nikolai paused. "Sir."

"Sir," the man said again quickly.

"Sir," Nikolai said, filling in the pause this time.

"My name is Guthrie. This is Mr. McKennan. What do you suppose you're doing here?"

"I don't know. Sir."

"You are here because you now have the opportunity to serve this department. And to thereby serve yourself."

Nikolai found himself poised, not simply with the interest that the situation deserved, but with the electric awareness that he was standing once again on the razor's edge of precipitous change, a cannon shot into the unknown.

"What I suggest is that you may be able to pay your debt to society in a different coin of the realm, so to speak." Guthrie spoke the words in distinct, raspy little clusters. His voice lowered to an ominous bass. "This is not to say that I condone your infractions under any circumstance. I am contemptuous of your breed, Mr. Granger. I do not tolerate those who violate the law. Is that clear?"

"Yes, sir."

"If you cross me in any way—in the slightest manner, in the smallest detail—I will feed your balls to my dogs. Understood?"

"Yes, sir. But …"

Guthrie's tiny mouth parted. Nikolai could see an uneven row of small teeth waiting. "But?"

"I was sent to prison because I tried to get into the army," Nikolai said.

Guthrie tipped his large executive chair forward, and his palms slapped the red leather-topped desk.

"I know why you went to prison, Mr. Granger." A trickle of spittle, a tiny stream of outrage, sluiced out of the side of his mouth. "It was because you broke the law. The law!"

"Does that make me a criminal?! Wanting to fight the Germans?"

"Do not speak!" Guthrie shouted. "And above all, do not confuse your virtue with the law."

"I'll try not to," Nikolai said. "Sir."

"Channel your virtue into honor."

"Yes, sir."

With that, the door at the rear of the office opened again, and a new figure slid into the room. Nikolai gaped. It was Dancer.

CHAPTER 13

▼

Lights flickered wildly as the subway car plunged through the bowels of the city. This was an express, and the train lurched through the 66th Street station with an awesome roar, wheels screeching like hoarse banshees on the turn. On the platform, two dozen forlorn faces looked into the dark tunnel from which the express train had just exploded, searching for the local.

Within the second car, Heinz cursed at the swaying train, at the annoying pulse of the lights, at the sweating carcasses that slammed into him. Pigs, *Schweinehunde*, all of them, with their elbows and their big feet, and always the garlic and the gum and the spray of spit from their city stories of deprivation from the war, which bore no relation to sacrifice. Germany, fighting for its very life, was the standard-bearer of sacrifice.

The train shrieked and careened through a ninety-degree arc, and the passengers teetered into each other—for the most part, with good-natured cries at the adventure of it.

Somewhat less carefree, Heinz growled at a woman wearing a hat that looked left over from World War I. Centrifugal force had flung her at him, a huge sack of potatoes with a bust that smothered his face, and for all his resolve to yield to nothing and no one, he lost his grip on the support pole and crashed back, landing in the lap of a coffee-skinned man in his sixties; the man's glasses were knocked comically askew.

"What the hell you think you're doing?" the man said.

The accent was Mexican or something, Heinz thought, not one of the homegrown ones, but the man's surliness deserved a riposte, and his skin was dark. Heinz, detaching himself, hissed, "*Schwarze.*"

The train ground to a stop at 42nd Street, and people charged in and out of the car. The heavy woman who had sent him flying stepped out, and Heinz thought about following (he had words for her too), but she was suddenly gone. The doors slammed into place, and Heinz watched with a scowl as she disappeared in the scrambling river of ants shooting up the stairs.

More bodies piled around him. The train staggered off again. Heinz was blaming himself for making this foolish trip down to the Battery. Then it was Leo's turn, for persuading him to make the trip at all. "Heinz, you got to meet me!" Leo had said, but he had refused to tell him why.

The train half-emptied at 23rd Street, and Heinz settled into a seat with a grunt. "Idiots," he muttered. He thrust his hands in his pockets, and his eyelid drooped, betraying surprise as his right hand struck something. He was sure that the pocket had been empty, but his fingers were now clutching an object that was small, hard, and cylindrical.

What could it be? Not something he had put in the pocket—of this, he was sure. Slowly, he brought out his hand and uncoiled his fingers. In his palm lay a package of Lifesavers. For one crazy moment, he wondered if he could have bought them. But that was impossible. He was not the sort to chew or suck on things or to puff at weed burning in his mouth. He stared at the package of Lifesavers as though they had just arrived from another planet.

Only then did he notice something unusual: some of the white wrapper was fluttering loose. He took it between his fingers and gently tugged. On the underside of the wrapper, a scribbled message sprang into focus: *Take 12:35 Staten Island ferry. Destroy.*

He blinked his bewilderment, then sat back. His mind was a tangle. He could not grasp exactly what was happening, but something … something. His pulse raced.

He shoved the message into a pocket; he would take care of it later. Only now did the Lifesavers come into their own, ingenious in their innocence. He had unwrapped a roll of candy. In case anybody was watching, he slipped a Lifesaver into his mouth, for the first time in his life.

Heinz arrived at the ferry docks with twenty minutes to spare. He looked down at the rainbow-oily water and allowed the shredded remains of the note to scatter on the windy surface. Leo, of course, was nowhere to be seen. But this was no surprise. Everything was different now.

Heinz had sorted through a hundred names and faces from the old days, but he could not imagine who had slipped the note into his pocket. For one jarring second, he thought it was a trap—the police, at long last catching up with him for Ebell.

But that was ridiculous, of course. Why would they bother to plant a note? And the even more ridiculous "destroy." No, they simply would have arrested him.

Another uneasy thought occurred to him: one of the old gang, one of his American Warriors, setting him up. For what reason? A friend of Ebell's getting even? It made no sense. Who liked Ebell? No one.

The ferry churned out of its slip and struck through choppy waves and foam toward Staten Island. Heinz made his way to the stern rail and waited. He refused to look around, to draw attention. Whoever it was would appreciate this professionalism. But then, watching the Manhattan skyline recede into a mesmerizing mist, a pang of anguish cut through him. All this exuberance and anticipation, this turn-of-fortune excitement, based on what? The old days were gone, the war was going worse than ever; it was craziness itself to hold on to the old dream of an American insurrection. And yet he was here, out in the middle of the Hudson River, foolishly clinging to a toothpick of hope, because that dream would not go away.

Staten Island was emerging in the distant mist. His heart sank, because it now occurred to him that he was involved in a charade. Again he summoned the old faces. He did it with less fear but equal rancor—some son of a bitch maybe playing a dirty trick on him. Who? Only one—that bitch with the balls, Toni Graf!

Craftily, he reconstructed the subway scene, the jarring, the swaying; he searched for faces, searching for hers. He was now sure that she was the one who had slipped the note into his coat pocket. She must be there, somewhere in the film of memory.

But he could not call her to mind. He kept remembering faces, from 86th Street to Bowling Green, but she would not materialize. There was the moment of jostling by that hippo of a woman who had sent him flying, but no Toni Graf. And no one else that he knew.

So he let himself drift with the frothing water, until his ire turned into yet another theory, this one pathetically benign: the note in the pocket was an accident, a joke. Kids, playing spy.

In a bittersweet mood, he realized how far he had come—Baumann, the old firebrand. The passion was still there, but it had to be lit these days.. Perhaps he was wiser now. Wisdom came from clinging to the things that were worthwhile in this world; in this, he was tenacious. He would never abandon his hope.

The bittersweet moment was punctuated by a pleasant voice saying, "Quite a sight, isn't it? The Statue of Liberty?"

The figure that had so quietly slipped alongside him was slight in build. The face was lean and clean-cut, partially obscured by a shallow growth of salt-and-pepper beard. The man wore glasses, a long raincoat, and a rakishly tilted fedora.

The man was totally unfamiliar, yet there was a touch of mystery to him, like one of those crazy paintings with the eyes and ears and nose scattered across a canvas like a puzzle, and somewhere in the back of the mind was an answer.

Low, scudding clouds made a backdrop for the Statue of Liberty. Heinz thought it ugly, but of course he did not express this opinion. Cautiously, in response to his companion's comment, he nodded.

"When I leave, when we arrive at Staten Island," said the man, his voice still pleasant and unhurried, "remain here at the railing. Do not look back. Understood?"

The man's voice had yielded the trace of an accent; his pronunciation was almost perfect, but there was a fine nuance, indicating Germany, education, breeding.

For a moment, it was silent, except for the slapping of waves and the cry of seagulls wheeling in the wake of the ferry. It struck Heinz that something was expected of him, something properly wary but circumspect, a countersign of sorts.

"I don't know you," he said cagily.

After a moment, the man said, "Look again."

Heinz looked. The man's face was still in profile, but ever so slowly, he turned to face Heinz. Heinz stared, and suddenly, the dissonant components of his features came together, and the realization struck him like a cold wave.

"*Mein Gott*," he whispered. "Max Siebert." Siebert, whom he had last seen in Berlin just before the war. That was five years ago. "It's you!" Heinz said. He sucked in air, drowning in excitement.

"Easy," Siebert said softly.

"Yes," Heinz said, realizing the need. "Yes."

"Are you still ready?"

Everything came back now: Siebert's last words, like a sacred invocation: *Would you do* anything *for your country?*

Anything! Heinz had pledged. "I am ready," he fervently whispered now.

"It will not be easy."

"I don't care about that," Heinz dismissed.

"Good."

Max Siebert was genuinely admiring. How many still cared? Maybe it had something to do with inverse distances to the fatherland. Flecks of doubt occasionally crept into his brain, but a strange metamorphosis had turned the old skepticism around. The more Germany descended into its spiral of disaster, the more he began to believe that it would survive and triumph.

"I want you to listen carefully," Siebert said. "Time is important. Obedience is important. The iron will of obedience."

"You have my word."

"Did you know that the FBI follows you?" Siebert said.

Heinz gasped his surprise. He started to swing his head around.

"No," Siebert instructed. Heinz corrected his impulse, and Siebert eased his concern. "They are not here." He lit a cigarette.

"You will leave New York. Simply hang up the 'Closed' sign inside your door. Leave it there. You will leave your apartment in the same manner—with no fanfare, nothing to draw attention. Spread the word—a neighbor, maybe two. You have decided to look for a job outside the city."

"Where?"

"Leave that for the moment. There is another point. You will take your daughter."

At this, Heinz snapped his head around hard. "Impossible," he said.

Siebert studied him, a harsh judgment that did not require words.

"I'm sorry," Heinz gasped.

"She is important to you," Siebert said, a pragmatic, unemotional statement.

"She won't go," Heinz said, his voice wavering.

"Because you don't want her," Siebert said.

Heinz felt himself being torn apart. Everything he wanted was butting up against everything he did not want. And there was the ludicrousness of arguing about something that was so personal and intimate. They had no right advising him how to deal with Anna. Anna was his.

"You would do *anything* for your country," Siebert said. He had not forgotten either. Nor was he gentle. His voice was icy. It put things into perspective. *Germany. Germany.*

"I understand," Heinz said.

"Do you understand?"

"Yes. Yes." said Heinz. Siebert stared straight ahead in silence, waiting. "I swear on my sacred honor."

"Either turn your tail and run—and there are Germans who do that now—or never, ever again, question your solemn duty."

"I swear it."

To Heinz, the harshness of the moment hung in the air; the air itself seemed to smart with his rank failure. How could greatness come from such weakness?

Siebert seemed to understand this. He touched Heinz on the arm, a contact of such solicitous depth that Heinz blinked in open surprise. "You are a good man, Baumann. You believe. Now I want you to believe this."

He made sure that Heinz caught his eye, so that he would truly hear Siebert's messianic message: "You have an opportunity that few men have ever had. You have the opportunity to help change the history of this world on behalf of our beloved fatherland. You are not a meaningless cog in the great machine. You are one of the few, the special few, who can help bring us our victory."

Heinz had evolved; the beating of drums no longer had its old effect. But this was far beyond anything he had ever heard before, and it struck him with a force far beyond anything he had ever felt before. His eyes were damp when he looked at Siebert, and to his astonishment, he saw the same dampness in Siebert's eyes.

When Siebert found his voice again, it was functionally cold, and his instructions were explicit. To everything, Heinz agreed without question.

As the ferry bumped into the fenders alongside the Staten Island slip, Siebert evaporated with the stealth that had marked his arrival. Heinz stayed at the railing, staring into the brackish water.

Had it really happened?

✳　　　✳　　　✳　　　✳

The kosher emblem in the window stopped Heinz in his tracks. A gigantic plastic corned beef sandwich, dripping bright yellow mustard, stuck out of the mouth of a cardboard American soldier. Another display showed foot-long salamis piled up in the open freight cars of a toy train. A sign read: VICTORY TRAIN.

Heinz was standing in front of Wolfe Bros. Deli on 49th Street near Eighth Avenue. It had never occurred to him that "Wolfe" could be anything but German.

Two men came out of the restaurant, wielding toothpicks. They wore suits and smacked of contentment. Heinz used their passing to delay his own entrance. Inside was a land as alien as the Congo. His feet would not move. But how long could he stand in full view outside this place? He gritted his teeth and went into the deli.

It was filled with shouted conversations and clattering plates. Bustling waitresses crisscrossed the room. The walls were crammed with framed photographs of minor celebrities, with and without the Wolfe brothers (apparently there were three). A bulky waitress with two warts on her nose loomed in front of Heinz. "You want?" she demanded.

Heinz was slow to respond, so she soared on, scooped up some plates from a small, empty table in the rear, and disappeared. He decided that she had offered him the small table, so he made his way to it and sat down. Almost immediately, she was back, scowling. Heinz noticed that the warts seemed to brighten with her displeasure. "I asked if you want," she said. She glared, as though ordering him off, but when he started to rise, she relented. "All right, stay." She whipped out a pencil and said, "You know, or not?"

"Tea?" he suggested at last.

"That's it?" she said. "Tea?"

"Tea," he said.

The wart-nosed waitress flashed her disapproval and clomped off.

Now that he belonged, Heinz glanced around. He was looking for Anna, and she appeared suddenly at the far end, bringing a tray of plates to a table. She put down the plates and disappeared into the kitchen again.

The waitress with the warts roared up to Heinz with a pot of tea. "Sure you don't want marble with that?"

When Heinz hesitated, she slapped down a check and rushed off. (Heinz never saw her again.) He sipped tea, a few drops at a time, waiting for the crowd to thin out.

It did so almost all at once. There were empty tables now, and waitresses altered their frenzied pace, as though responding to silent music. They tossed off irreverent fragments and cackled across the room.

Heinz looked up, sensing a presence. It was Anna, standing in front of his table.

"What are you doing here?" she demanded.

"Came to visit," he said, with an almost jolly smile.

"That's very nice, but I don't think we have much to talk about."

"Used to talk plenty in the old days," he said, still jovial.

"I'm busy, Papa. If you don't mind, I have work to do."

"Tell you what," he said, hastily unfolding the menu. "How about a corned beef sandwich?"

It was so bizarre, coming from him, that she stared in shock. "You want a corned beef sandwich?"

"Sure, why not?" he said grandly, the apostle of reclamation.

She shook her head in wonderment. For all her rage at him, the crease of a smile appeared at her mouth. "This, I don't believe."

"Why not? What's so wrong, a corned beef sandwich?"

"Nothing, except you wanting one," she said.

"You ever heard, things change?" he asked.

She shook her head again, this time tightly, like a quiver. "I don't believe you."

"Well, don't blame you," he said. It had a brave sound to it, that of a man come to an awareness that he himself could not understand.

"Why did you come here, Papa?"

"To talk to you. To talk to my daughter."

"About what?"

"Things that people with the same blood, maybe they should talk about."

There was a pause, and she said, "Are you all right?"

"In my head?" he joked. "Or the health?"

"You know what I mean."

"Never felt better," he said heartily.

"Then what?"

"Can we talk here? Or maybe someplace else?"

"I'm not off until three o'clock."

"I can wait," he said warmly.

She bit her lip, thinking it over. Then she said, "I have an apartment with another girl. 344 West 55th, five-A. I have some shopping. If you want, we can meet there at four."

"Four is good."

"Well, then." She turned and walked off. She was quite a woman these days, he disapprovingly noticed. Her uniform was too tight, and her behind stuck out too much.

He was at the door of her apartment at exactly four o'clock. He was holding something awkwardly behind his back when she opened the door, still in her waitress uniform.

"Brought a little something," he said, whipping a paper bag into view. "Open. Go ahead."

Anna opened the bag and brought out a charlotte russe. It was a treat from childhood, and she was unable to conceal her delight. "My god," she said.

"Ain't easy to come by these days, Charlie Russe," he said, a modest paean to his perseverance. Shyly, he added, "All right to come in, maybe?"

She opened the door wider, and he entered, but he did not presume to proceed further. "It's okay. You can come in," she said.

The apartment was small and cluttered, the apartment of two working girls, neither fanatically neat. Nonetheless, Heinz looked around with approval.

"Looks okay," he said.

"It's too small, but you can't get anything these days."

"So, this is with another girl you share?"

"Yes. She works until eight. We kind of overlap, but it's not bad."

"This is your friend, I guess," he said. The voice, intended as casual, was measured and careful.

Anna's face darkened. "If you mean my friend Jenny, it's not her."

"Didn't know who," Heinz parried, all innocence.

"That's exactly who you thought it was," Anna said. Despite this high moral ground, and the fact that Heinz looked uneasy, it was Anna who now gave in. "I'm sorry."

Surprised, Heinz said, "Don't have to be." He had no idea why she was sorry.

Anna bustled about. She turned on a lamp, then turned it off. She tugged an easy chair of frayed damask closer to a small table and indicated the chair. "Go ahead, sit down."

Heinz nodded appreciatively. He settled in the chair with an almost dainty bounce, then nodded again. "Feels good."

"It's only secondhand."

He bounced again. "Better than mine. My chair, it's four-hand by now." He smiled at his own joke.

"Would you like something to drink?"

"Why not?" said Heinz, the convivial guest.

"Beer?"

His eyes opened. "You got beer?"

"Yes, sure," she said.

"Girls these days, living alone, they keep beer?" he said, but not disapprovingly.

She smiled tolerantly. "Yes, they keep beer for the boys."

"Oh!" Heinz said, as though he had just been propelled into the world of the avant-garde.

Anna went into a small kitchen alcove. Heinz heard a cap pop free, and she returned with a bottle of Schlitz, still foaming at the neck.

"Favorite!" Heinz said.

"Do you want a glass?"

"Don't need," Heinz assured. He took a healthy swig and smacked his lips in satisfaction. "So, how long you been working this job?"

"A couple of months."

"What happened to the old?"

"Macy's? I don't know. I got bored."

"But now you're not bored?" he asked, smiling to cover the question.

"It's not a career," she said pointedly.

"It's still waiting on tables."

"I don't mind," she said. "You meet people. Sometimes they're interesting."

"They're interesting?"

She understood. "You mean, being around all those Jews?"

"Just asking," he said.

"As it happens, the people I work for are very nice. They treat me very well, and the customers are nice too."

She expressed herself dispassionately, but Heinz recognized her irritation. He smiled a clumsy smile, the smile of a man who means well, bumbling his way through alien territory. "I ain't going to lie they're my favorites," he conceded. "Same with the wop Italians and the *Schwarzen*. But maybe there comes a time you have to say, enough, it's stupid. You can't change the world, so maybe you better take for what it is."

She knew better than to accept this at face value, but it was like the dog in the joke, who could speak, but the accent was terrible. Maybe Heinz was trying.

"Who's the new one?" he asked politely.

"Her name's Connie."

"Also a waitress?"

"No. She's a copywriter at an ad agency." Anna could not help blurting, "She's getting me an interview."

"Ad agency?

"Yes," Anna said.

"Sounds good."

Anna went back into the kitchen and came back with a glass of orange juice. She sat in a high-backed rocking chair. She rocked for a moment, then said softly, "You were right about Jenny."

"Oh?"

She looked over, exposed and vulnerable but undaunted. "The truth is, she turned out to be exactly what you thought."

"Zo?" Heinz said. He sat back expectantly, extending his hands along the arms of the chair.

"Actually, I'd just as soon not go into it."

But it was not that easy for him; the reflex of domination was too strong. Razor-sharp, he said, "Maybe should have listened before you ran away."

"I don't think so," she said.

It was chilly enough to sober him up. He inched out of his lordly stance and folded his hands on his lap. Then, all at once, he stood up. "You think I blame you? What's the matter with me? Anna, do me a favor. Kick me in the behind out of here, where I deserve. What am I talking, you should have listened? Listened to *me?* The biggest fool you ever met. I came to you because there was something to talk, things to tell you. But why should you listen?"

He started for the door.

"Where are you going?" she said, rising.

He turned and said, "I never deserved you, *Schatzi.*" He reached for the door.

"Papa, wait."

He froze.

"Sit down. Please."

He did so, staring ahead with the expression of the undeserving.

"What things, Papa? You said there were things to tell me."

"Well, to tell the truth," he said somewhat sheepishly, a man caught in an unfamiliar net of virtue, "been thinking about changing things."

"What do you mean?"

He shrugged his thick shoulders. "Maybe close the shop, do something different." Again he paused, awkward, embarrassed. "Maybe take a plant job."

Anna searched his face. Almost incredulous, she said, "You mean, defense plant?"

"Why not?" he said quickly.

"Oh, Papa," Anna said.

Ingenuously, Heinz said, "What I hear, they pay good, the plants."

Anna smiled, then grinned at the thought of Heinz, the sensible burgher, the political neuter, casually shifting lifestyles and immutable prejudices for a better-paying job.

He saw the humor of it and said, "Don't think such things can happen, is that it? Well, maybe you stick around long enough, you see everything, heh?"

"Papa, it's so incredible."

"Even to me," he said: a serious joke.

"It's so hard to believe. What happened?"

"What happened is, people change. One day, you look in a mirror and you wonder, what for? Don't make no sense." He blinked his bewilderment.

"I just can't believe it," she said. Heinz looked up sharply, to gauge the degree of her skepticism, then realized that she wasn't skeptical at all, merely unable to get past her shock.

In whispered homage, he said, "Miracles happen."

"Papa, I'm so proud."

"Nothing to be proud. Been stupid too long." He brightened. "What I got to thinking …" He paused awkwardly, and the alien charm of it filled her with joy.

"Tell me," she encouraged.

"Maybe if I go, you would come too," he spilled out.

"Come with you? But where are you going?"

"Don't know. Someplace else. Plenty of places—it's a big country. Don't have to be New York. They got factories all over. I looked in the papers. They run ads from plants all over the country, pay to get there, pay for everything. So, what I thought, we could maybe go together."

Heinz snuck several optimistic glances, more guileless charm, but to his alarm, Anna's reaction was somber silence.

"What I thought, to be together," he said, uncertainly.

At last, she said, "I want to." Her voice was pained. "I would like that."

"Then what?"

"Papa," she said.

"Go ahead, say what you want." He modified this to fit his new, softer image. "You got a problem, maybe I can help."

"It's not easy to talk about," Anna said.

"Go ahead, talk," he encouraged warmly.

Anna took in a breath. She looked around, as though seeking help. Then she said, "I met this boy. We made love."

Heinz blinked. That was it? "You told me," he said: absolution with a smile.

"You don't understand," she said, with a bite of impatience.

"That fellow you told me about," he insisted. "You told me."

"It wasn't him."

"Oh? There's more? Somebody else?" Tolerance was flowing out of him like liquid through a sieve. "So, what you got to tell me is, another soldier, after the first."

"Yes," she said sharply, her humiliation fading along with his restraint.

"That don't encourage me to hear," he said.

"We spent ten days together. Ten wonderful days. I even thought …"

"You even thought?" he bellowed.

"Don't worry, it didn't happen."

"Didn't happen?" he said, springing to his feet, throwing off his new persona like a filthy cloak. "But could've happened!"

"Well, now you know you were right," she said. "Just another tramp. You did the right thing when you threw me out."

"What kind of a crazy world?" Heinz roared. "A world full of tramps!" This burst of vitriol collided with the character he had so assiduously structured; he strove to repair the damage. "How did it happen?" he asked. Then realized how asinine it sounded, and he mumbled, "Don't mean 'how' that way. Tell me, this boy."

Anna accepted this reversion from a kinder, benevolent Heinz to the old Heinz and back again with a certain equanimity. She had waited for this revolution of the soul all her life; she understood that he could not easily surrender the brute he had always been.

She told him about the young man, a Malcolm Caine, from Wisconsin. He was quiet, gentle, intelligent. He wrote poetry. He planned to go to law school when the war was over. And then they would plan their future. But that was finished now.

Heinz knowingly clucked. "Promises. That's what they do. They promise."

"He would have kept it," Anna said. She raised her hand to display a school ring, loose on her middle finger. "This was his."

"What happened?" Heinz asked, suddenly aware.

"He was killed on his second mission. He was a gunner. B-17s, England."

Heinz summoned tight-lipped commiseration, and Anna dissolved into tears. She came into his arms, and he stroked her hair. "Maybe we start over," he soothed. "Just you and me again, like the old days.

CHAPTER 14

▼

Nikolai's eyes flickered as he attempted to assimilate the incredibly out-of-place figure before him: Dancer, flashing a sly and capricious smile, prison uniform shucked for a well-cut dark-blue suit and a solid maroon tie. Not a supplicant like himself, and hardly a stranger to the imperial figure behind the desk.

"You miserable son of a bitch," Nikolai whispered.

"I don't like that," Guthrie said.

Dancer's arm shot out, and his sharp knuckles sank into Nikolai's stomach. Nikolai folded, as though in slow motion, to his knees, holding his belly.

"Get up," Guthrie said. Dancer moved to help him, but Guthrie waved him off.

"In this department, Mr. Granger, we do not use foul language. Is that clear?"

Nikolai caught Dancer's eye. There was no animus, only a signal. Nikolai himself was flaring. This was the second time Dancer had hit him. He sucked in enough air to address Guthrie. "Yes, sir."

"You will wonder who I am and what we are, Mr. Granger. These are the offices of the Special Assessment Unit. Do you know what that means?"

"No, sir."

"No. The fact is, very few people in this country have heard of this organization. Perhaps no more than ten or twelve people in this city. And this discretion will be maintained. Are you paying attention, Mr. Granger?" he said acidly, prompted by Nikolai's shifting stance.

"Look, I just spent five hundred miles locked up in a bouncing box," Nikolai said sharply. "And if you don't like my fucking manners, send me back."

Ironically, it was not Guthrie's wrath that surprised him, but his own street voice. The appalled expression on Dancer's face said, *All wrong, idiot!*

For his part, Guthrie was inching out of his chair in a rising tide of indignation.

Dancer whirled and shouted to Nikolai, "This is about the krauts!"

Everything stopped. Guthrie's bulging eyes froze, watching Nikolai, waiting for his response.

"What do you mean?" Nikolai finally asked.

Dancer gave way to Guthrie, as graceful in descent as in rising. He wove his fingers together, faultlessly manicured nails gleaming in the light of the twin desktop lamps.

"Do they interest you?" Guthrie asked. It was hard to pin down, but something had changed, a civility somehow based on common interest. Guthrie continued, "I speak of your colleagues in Charlestown, Otto Schenck and Wilhelm Kleist."

"Otto Schenck and Wilhelm Kleist," Nikolai repeated, the rhythm of it suddenly evoking Jack and Jill, Mutt and Jeff, Laurel and Hardy. "Interested in what way? Sir. Yes, I'm interested in them. They slaughtered a very good friend."

He looked at Dancer. "His good friend too." And then, speaking directly to Dancer, he said, "What happened? You went out with them. Where are they?"

"We split up. But their location is known."

Nikolai was thinking, *Dancer. And something called the Special Assessment Unit.* And the federalese: *"Their location is known."*

"I don't understand," Nikolai said, turning back to Guthrie. "You know where they are. You obviously have the legal means to grab them. Where do I come in?"

"I have said that you may be helpful. The question is, would such an opportunity appeal to you?" And then he said, with an amused look, "Arliss."

Nikolai swiveled sharply. No one in America even knew his middle name—he had never used it—and here was this odd-looking little man calling him "Arliss." He refused to show surprise. "Yes, it would appeal to me."

"Good."

"I'd like to know a little more."

"What would you like to know?" Guthrie said, quite amiable now.

"Where does all this lead?"

"Where do you think it should lead?"

Nikolai thought about it and said carefully, "Assuming I satisfactorily complete whatever you have in mind, what sort of return can I hope for?"

Guthrie took time to examine the delicacy of the wording. He said, "This office does not, as the commies do, subscribe to a cult of personality. Therefore, you would be working not for me, but for the Special Assessment Unit."

A silence followed, as though he had forgotten the original thread. Nikolai stayed quiet, bland-faced, expectant.

Guthrie said, "I have already mentioned the possibility that you might be able to pay your debt to society through useful service."

Nikolai dutifully pounced. "Does that mean a pardon?"

"There is that prospect, or something like it."

"Something like it? Something like what? Sir."

Guthrie's face was dark again. "Something like anything that it pleases this office to give you."

"I would like something a little more concrete."

Guthrie's brief excursion into good nature disappeared. "I can have you shot full of holes and dumped in the Potomac. I don't need you, Mr. Granger."

"I'm counting on the fact that you do, sir," Nikolai said with a smile, as though counting on Guthrie's famous sense of humor. He caught Dancer's wide, alarmed eyes.

"Well, Mr. Granger," Guthrie said, "you are a spunky fucker."

"Thank you, sir," Nikolai agreed.

"If you handle yourself competently," Guthrie said, "there will be no need for a pardon."

"Why is that, sir?"

"I think you can guess the reason, Mr. Granger."

"You're talking about a new identity."

"Perhaps."

"Would some sort of guarantee come with this arrangement, sir?"

This time, Guthrie settled for a frown. "Don't stretch it, Mr. Granger," he said.

"Get him settled in, sir?" Dancer tactfully suggested.

"Nine o'clock tomorrow morning," Guthrie said, with a wave of dismissal.

They exited the room, Dancer tight-lipped as a turnkey, and took an elevator that let them off near another side entrance to the building, this one at street level. Dancer forged swiftly ahead, turning onto 15th Street.

"Why don't I just take off?" Nikolai asked, not seriously.

"Because you know it would be stupid. Let's get out of here," Dancer said, as though the very sidewalks were bugged.

Uniforms dotted the streets. They came across a knot of noisy sailors trying to figure out which way to go, one of whom sang out, "Draft dodgers!" Dancer sliced through and led the way to a taxi stand. A taxi arrived, and Dancer opened the back door just as a pair of bird colonels (Army Corps of Engineers) came huffing up.

"Afraid we're going to have to commandeer this," the shorter colonel said assertively but good-naturedly. "*C'est la guerre.*" He was about to push his way into the cab, but Dancer pulled him back by the collar of his shirt..

"Hey!" the second colonel hissed fiercely. The sailors, five or six of them, were drifting by.

"What do you think you're doing?" the first colonel shouted into Dancer's face. The sailors took in the commotion and charged toward the cab, bonded in patriotism.

"Back off!" Dancer said to the sailors. He was flashing an identification of some sort; the sailors could not see it, but one of the colonels made it out.

"Okay, fellows," the colonel said to the sailors. He signaled his colleague, and just as suddenly as they had all descended, they were gone. Dancer said something to the cabbie and jumped into the back seat. Nikolai sat beside him, and the cab lurched off.

"What was that ID?" Nikolai said.

"Not now," replied Dancer.

Nikolai swallowed a thousand questions and let his head flop back, suddenly weary. His bones ached from the long ride, and if he closed his eyes, he would sleep. But he kept them open, watching a cavalcade of buildings slide by. He drifted off for a few seconds, then was jolted awake as the cab stopped before a low brick building. It looked familiar, and Nikolai recognized the neighborhood: Lionel and Eunice, Georgetown.

They got out, and Dancer handed some money to the driver, then said to Nikolai, "Got a single?"

"We don't carry money around in the jug," Nikolai said. Dancer put together some change, and the cab drove off.

Dancer led the way through a front entrance and then into a small, very comfortable apartment on the second floor. He double-bolted the door, and from a sideboard, he produced scotch, bourbon, and gin.

"What's your pleasure, kid?"

"A beer, then scotch."

"Beer's in the kitchen," Dancer said, pouring scotch. Nikolai took a beer from the refrigerator and drained it in two giant gulps. He joined Dancer in a cozy living room area furnished with a leather sofa and large club chairs.

"Now?"

"Shoot."

"Who the hell are you?"

Dancer smiled. "Yeah, I can understand that. Here you go." He handed Nikolai a glass of scotch. "Well, I guess you can say I work with the man."

"I figured that part out. What were you doing in prison?"

Dancer smiled again. "Watching the krauts."

"Jesus Christ! You volunteered to sit in Charlestown for almost five months?"

"It was a little more complicated than that," Dancer conceded.

"You broke them out?"

"That was part of it, yes."

"Why?"

"To find out where they would go."

"What happened?"

"We found out."

"Where did I come in? Accident? Stumbled into it, saw too much, had to get me out of the way?"

"No."

"What does he want me to do? Why would he want me in the first place? I'm being recruited, I guess," he muttered, "but for what?"

"One thing at a time. Stefan's the one stumbled into it. He wasn't part of anything. The krauts are fucking animals, you know. No telling what they're going to do, and Stefan got the bad end."

"In other words, you're responsible for killing him."

"I'm responsible for my job, period. End of story," Dancer said sharply.

"God almighty, another guy responsible for his job, and the last person on earth I would have expected."

"If you want to piss on me for the whole thing, piss away. But I couldn't control everything. The krauts were wildcards. I liked Stefan."

Nikolai swallowed half a glass of scotch in a gulp. It was single malt, smoky and velvety trickling down. He let himself go, no longer weary, just floating. He scanned the apartment—good furniture, tastefully decorated, a warm, cozy cocoon. In this place, in this minute, everything was so orderly, and everything else was chaos. He couldn't even remember the movie in the mess hall the night before.

Dancer, legs crossed and one foot bouncing, lit a cigarette and slid the pack across the coffee table. It was difficult to reconcile the streetwise loser Nikolai had known back in Charlestown with the urbane gentleman across the coffee table.

Nikolai took a cigarette and lit it, and Dancer motioned to the pack. "Take them," he said. There was a strange sparkle in his eye, and he suddenly produced a cigarette case: Nikolai's cigarette case, carefully hoarded and hidden all these months—the platinum case with the Maltese cross.

"Where'd you get that!" Nikolai jack-knifed forward, relieved, but abashed too, because he hadn't even remembered he had it left behind, hidden in his cell.

"Thought you might want it back," Dancer said.

Nikolai's mouth fell open. Dancer's bland face conceded no significance in the cigarette case, but the association was inescapable. Eventually, Nikolai asked, "How did Guthrie know my middle name?"

"I have no idea," Dancer said. "But you don't want to underestimate Simon Guthrie."

"Another thing—why the hell did you hit me?"

"Because you were beginning to ruffle him."

"Well, fuck him. I do not give a rat's ass about Mr. Guthrie."

"How about that?" Dancer said affably. "A few months in the can, and our puppy dog turns into a rottweiler."

"Fuck you too."

"Freshen your drink?" Dancer sang pleasantly.

"In other words, when people talk up, your job is to slap them down."

"Not at all. It's just that I know the man. I know his tolerance level, and you were getting there."

"Am I supposed to thank you for shutting me up?" he suggested.

"Maybe," Dancer said.

"Because he fills people full of holes and dumps them in the Potomac?" Nikolai snidely offered.

"This is America, son. We don't do things like that."

They dragged on cigarettes and sipped scotch.

"How did you get involved?"

"I was Army CIC. Counterintelligence. Got bored. Moved over."

"What about him?"

"Guthrie? Well, our Mr. Guthrie is a mystery man."

"And that's it."

"I heard he was a cop somewhere, got thrown out for overzealous performance. I heard he was a Marine officer, ran a brig, ran it too tight. I heard he ran strikebreaking for Ford. I heard he drank blood for breakfast. Just stories, but I believe them all."

"He doesn't use names," Nikolai mused. "He's into depersonalizing—the animal treatment. And that reminds me. What the hell is your name?"

"Rhodes. Dancer's good. Keeps it simple."

"And Mr. Guthrie likes it simple," Nikolai recited. "What about this Special Assessment Unit? Who's it under?"

"Can't tell you,"

"Can't tell me, or you don't know?"

"Don't know."

"Who signs your checks?"

Dancer grinned. "Department of the Interior."

This did not satisfy Nikolai. Looking skeptical, he said, "FBI?"

Dancer grinned. "I don't think so."

"Why?"

"Guthrie despises J. Edgar Hoover. They look alike, you know. The story is that they're twins—the product of a jackass and a jackass."

This brought a smile, but not satisfaction. "Okay. But what do you do?"

"There's a war on. People wander around where they shouldn't, do things they shouldn't, work against the best interests of the United States. We try to keep tabs on them. Keep them in check, so to speak."

"But that is FBI. You're not under the FBI, but you're doing exactly the same thing?"

"Not really. We handle very special cases. The FBI doesn't get involved with our stuff."

Nikolai still looked skeptical. Then he said, "Where do I fit in?"

Dancer deliberated. "That's going to depend on you."

Nikolai worked up a smile. "You sure you're not the Special Silver-Tongue Unit? Let me try a direct question. What do I have to do?"

"Let me put it this way. Initially, it will involve surveillance."

"Surveillance. Are we still talking about Schenck and Kleist?"

"Yes."

"Out of curiosity, what are my peculiar qualifications for this honor?"

"For one thing, you don't suffer the enemy gladly."

"Okay, so I hate Germans. It's a popular business these days."

"You're bright, and you're educated. Mr. Guthrie likes people with that kind of mix."

"Hell of an exotic mix. Includes jailbirds."

The provocation hung in the air, and Dancer gave it a moment's reflection. "Bottom line is, he trusts my judgment."

"That's not answering the question."

"Listen to me. 'Special,' as in Special Assessment Unit, means special as hell. The job calls for a certain personality, a kind of special loyalty. I think you have it."

"I still don't get it. You talk about a special personality that calls for a special loyalty. You talk about special cases—so special, the FBI not only doesn't handle them but doesn't even know about them. The whole thing's so hugger-mugger special, it comes out oddball." Nikolai added, "Don't hesitate to stop me if I sound a little confused."

Dancer smiled. He emptied his glass and poured another. "That's one of the reasons I recommended you—that irksome intellectual curiosity. Hey, that's a stupid waste, spending a big chunk of the good years inside a cell."

Nikolai looked over, trying to read Dancer's face. "What's another reason?"

There was a pause. "I think you can handle tight situations."

"That's news to me," Nikolai said edgily. "And how tight?" He leaned forward. "What are we really talking about?"

"We're talking about justice."

"Keep going."

Evenly, Dancer said, "People like Otto Schenck and Wilhelm Kleist do not play by the rules."

It was a stunning cliché, but neither man laughed. Nikolai said, "So the Special Assessment Unit doesn't play by the rules either. I kind of figured that out, but there's more, isn't there?"

"There are people on the loose in this country who are so dangerous to national security that the implementation of special procedures is required to neutralize them."

"Now that is a fucking mouthful. And I believe I heard 'special' again. Okay, here at good old SAU, we speak a strange and mystical tongue. But let me see if I've picked up the gist of it. You got the krauts out, figuring they'd lead you somewhere, which they did, and now you're ready to pick everybody up."

Dancer nodded equably.

Nikolai said, "Trouble is, in a democracy, things grind too slow. When a war comes along, the law cannot keep up with the needs of the state. Expedition becomes a priority. Special cases call for special action. Next thing you know, a special department is born, like the Special Assessment Unit. It does away with messy things like arraignments, indictments, courts, and trials. My hunch is that the Herren Schenck and Kleist fall into this category."

"Very good," Dancer said.

"My next guess is that a very special place has been set aside for these very special people, something like the camps they put the Japs in, only a little more on the order of a max-security prison. Probably use the army to run it."

Dancer nodded thoughtfully, as though he were grading Nikolai and Nikolai had done well.

"What else is there?" Nikolai persisted.

"That's about it." Dancer held up his glass and downed his drink with a smile.

Nikolai did the same and added cheerily, "I still don't know what I'm doing here."

Listening to his words, a little wooden, a little slurred, he balanced their performances and realized that he was almost drunk but that Dancer, who had downed a good deal more, was not. "What does surveillance mean?" he asked.

"It means that we go out, and we survey. We're a team, kid. Tomorrow, we get you some clothes. Mr. Guthrie likes his people nicely dressed. The budget is generous in this regard. You'll stay here with me, because I've got an extra bedroom, and he doesn't care where his people stay, just what they look like. You've got that dumb look on your face. What's on your mind?"

"Nothing. Except I still don't get it. What qualifies me for this super-secret stuff? I'm a convict. I don't have a police background, military background, government background, but here I am."

"I told you—you're here because I picked you out, and I sold you."

"But what did you sell? What's my talent for the spy business, or whatever it is? Why would Guthrie take in an amateur like me?"

"You're a pain in the ass, you know that? Twenty-four hours ago, you were wearing a number."

"Twenty-four hours ago, I knew you, Dancer," Nikolai said, riled. "I knew you were a friend. Now I don't know."

"You fucking ingrate. I'm the one who gave you back your life."

"I owe you for that," Nikolai said. "But this thing is one big, thick fog, so if you don't mind, I'm curious."

"Okay, but get it straight—you're only a prospect, sweetheart. They're willing to take a chance, and if it doesn't work, it doesn't work."

"What happens tomorrow?"

"We go up to New York, and we look around. Your job is to stick close to me and do everything I tell you."

"You said they've already been contacted. What happens now?"

"The krauts went straight to an empty apartment in the Bronx. Trick now is to find out who their contact is. Won't be that easy—they'll lie low for awhile."

"Why are those two goons so important?"

"It's not them—it's their connections. When the war broke out, some of the extremo assholes went underground and formed a new organization, the True American National Patriots. They haven't done much yet, mostly handbills and hand-churned propaganda, but what we hear is they're working up a new docket, like sabotage. And it could be the money's coming from German intelligence."

"The *Abwehr?*"

Dancer looked over sharply, and Nikolai, smiling, said, "Don't be so impressed. I got it from a movie." He paused. "You really think German intelligence would tie up with guys like Schenck and Kleist?"

Drily, Dancer said, "We brought you in, didn't we?"

Nikolai shrugged. *Fair enough.*

"They're big believers—that's the point. And Schenck isn't all that dumb in the first place."

"Who worked out the escape?"

"Me. The krauts were itching to get out. I figured they had something going on the outside, so I came up with the sanitation truck, got the warden's okay, got the krauts to put up the money, and here we are."

"What about Dugan?"

"He got five grand for looking the other way." Dancer grinned. "Warden made him give it back."

"What happened after you broke out?"

"Dropped off near South Station."

"You dropped off first," Nikolai suggested.

"Sure. Didn't want the boys to think I was watching them, right?"

"One of your guys was driving the truck?" Nikolai guessed again.

"Driving the truck, and a gray Ford trailing," Dancer said. "The krauts were cute, though. They got off in Milton, took a couple of trolley cars, took a bus to Providence. Car picked them up and nosed down the Merritt Parkway to New York."

They sipped scotch, filling the room with thoughtful silence.

Nikolai said, "What about me?"

"Give it a month. If it works out, you get thrown into an eight-week crash course. Four weeks Marine base at Quantico, four weeks army intelligence. They start you out at the equivalent of grade twelve—around ten grand. If there's a next year, grade fourteen. No official status. You'll be on independent contract with the department. Second Security Bank of Virginia will handle your money." He refilled Nikolai's glass. "You got any more fucking questions?"

"You got something to eat?"

Dancer jumped up and nimbly padded to the kitchen. He was back a moment later with a tray of cold cuts, several beers, mustard, and sliced rye bread.

They exchanged not a single word for the next fifteen minutes. They made sandwiches, opened beers, and ate and drank in silence.

Finally, Nikolai said, "Who knows about all this?"

"Nobody."

"How many people in SAU?"

"It's compartmented—can't be sure. Couple dozen, maybe. Half in the field."

"In the field. How does it work, teams?"

"Teams," Dancer confirmed.

"Two to a team?"

"Right."

"Where's your old partner?"

"That was Larry. Larry didn't have it. Wanted out. Guthrie let him out."

"Just like that?"

"In a way. Larry wanted back in the military, so Guthrie had him shipped off to Alaska."

"I guess he lets you know if he's not pleased," Nikolai said, working up a smile. He yawned.

"Back bedroom," Dancer said. "I'll get you up at seven."

CHAPTER 15

▼

They reported in at nine o'clock the next morning, Guthrie looking Nikolai over in surprise, obviously uncertain who he was.

"Nikolai Granger, sir," Dancer prompted, with a distinct military snap.

Guthrie, studying Nikolai anew, said, "Brown is not his color."

He wiggled a stubby finger in dismissal, and Dancer hauled Nikolai out of the room as Guthrie answered a ringing phone with a bark: "What?"

Out in the hall, stunned at the brevity of the meeting, Nikolai looked down at his gray tweed jacket. "The son of a bitch is color-blind," he said.

"We're none of us perfect," Dancer said, pushing him into the elevator.

Dancer took him to Carrolton & Wilton, the Georgetown haberdashers, who outfitted Nikolai in two suits, two jackets, half a dozen shirts, conservative ties, dark slacks, and three pairs of sensible shoes. The quality was prewar, which was generally unavailable. The service, despite the hard times, was impeccable.

It occurred to Nikolai that, in all his years of schooling in Switzerland and England, he had never wondered where the money had come from—maybe Tati on stage, or maybe Tati borrowing money from people like Arturen Murgos. Or even Tati, Tati the survivor, exchanging charm for subsistence. They were strange thoughts. Tati had always been so untouchable, so clean and removed from the dirty world, and now she was one of the gang, part of the passing parade.

The purchases were sent to Dancer's apartment, with the exception of clothing for the trip. Nikolai picked up an overnight bag five doors down, and they sliced along Connecticut Avenue toward Union Station. He saw himself striding by in a store window, looking elegant, buoyant, and free, and wondered how long it would last.

They pushed through a swirling mob dominated by uniforms and boarded the train with only seconds to spare. There were no seats, only the usual cursing about a war going on, but Dancer had strolled to an office hidden under a stairway and flashed his ID, and now they were being ushered into a small compartment, from which a scowling businessman was being evicted.

The train inched into motion, ground to a stop, then lurched forward again. Nikolai thought of his last exodus from Washington following his disastrous encounter with Lionel and the latter-day Mrs. Granger. His reverie was punctuated by half a dozen aviation cadets in the hallway, who were jiggling the compartment's locked door, just for the hell of it.

Dancer opened his overnight bag, rummaged in it, and brought out a fresh bottle of scotch: single malt again. He rang for the porter, who arrived twenty minutes later, already flustered—and they weren't even halfway to Baltimore. Dancer ordered ice and sandwiches. He had not yet opened the bottle, a note of civilized restraint, which he passed on to the porter with a gesture along with a ten-dollar bill. Galvanized, the porter saluted and hurried off.

The train settled into its rhythm, and Dancer impishly toe-tapped along to the clicks and clacks of their progress.

"That part's not a fake, is it?"

"The dancing? No. I hoofed a little. Depression. Everybody did everything."

"But you don't really have a record."

"No. That was strictly for the krauts."

"What about family?"

"In that, we share. We are both orphans, kid. My father was a hardware king. He owned three stores. My mother painted. Nothing but still lifes. She had a tiny studio in the attic, and she never came out of it the whole time I was growing up, except for meals, and we had a maid did that. A succession of maids. My old man plunked them one and all, and when he got tired of one, he would bring in another. He was a good drinker, too. I never took to hardware, but when I tried the sauce, he said, 'Keep up the good work. Here's mud, kid.'"

"When did they die?"

"About fifteen years ago, a few months apart. She died—who knows from what?—and the old man piled into a gas station one night, crocked. Boom! I quit third year college, Ohio State. Went into the peacetime army."

"Lord, that was a long time ago," Nikolai whispered. He was clutching for memories: the good life, the normal life, convention locked into place, the smooth unknown ahead.

"Good old London School of Economics," Dancer said, putting on a fair upper-crust accent. "Not your first drawer, of course, but good enough for trade folk, I suspect. By the by, whatever happened to her?"

He caught Nikolai flat-footed. "What?"

"That girl," Dancer said, back to the twang. "The one who came to visit you." He smiled into Nikolai's wide-eyed face. "Maureen Eliot, I believe."

"You son of a bitch."

"What's the surprise? It was my job to know everything about you, *nicht wahr?*"

He said the German words so easily. Nikolai asked warily, "What in the hell did you do in the army?"

"Same thing," Dancer said, smiling disarmingly. "Just a bit broader."

"Like languages?"

"German and French," Dancer conceded, almost shyly pleased. "How about you?"

"Same."

"Plus a few more."

Nikolai smiled. "Why do you ask, if you already know?"

"That's the game. You give nothing away. You ingest, but you give back nothing."

"Good advice," Nikolai said, reaching for a chicken salad sandwich.

"You haven't answered the question."

"Maureen," he said, briefly lost. "The answer is, I don't know."

"Would you like to know?"

"Go ahead."

"After the wedding, they moved out to the coast. Lieutenant, senior grade, Enderhall is sailing a desk in San Diego these days."

"Jesus, you actually steamed open the invitation," Nikolai said.

"She's pretty," Dancer noted absently.

"I'm glad you approve."

"Where's it at?"

"Where's what at? She's married."

"You still care?"

"What is this, advice to the lovelorn?"

"I want to know if you're moony-eyed."

"So Guthrie can get his jollies?"

"He wouldn't give a damn. I'm curious."

Nikolai paused before saying, "Nothing there."

"You're better off," Dancer said.

"Tell me something. Do you happen to know how we met?"

"You and Maureen? No, I don't." Nikolai's big smile mystified him, and he said, "What?"

"You don't know everything."

"Such as?"

"On this very train, last year."

"I'll be damned." Dancer said, as though struck by the limits of Man's reach. "That must have been after your visit."

Nikolai looked over charily.

"To Lionel Granger, in Georgetown," Dancer said, eyebrows dancing. "I believe he served as your foster father for a few years, when he was attached to the embassy in Riga?"

Nikolai threw up his hands in disgust.

They arrived as darkness washed over the city. Nikolai was taken aback by New York. It was a starburst of excitement, pulsing and bright, even under a brownout. From Pennsylvania station, they took a cab to a modest apartment building on 85th Street just off First Avenue. Dancer rang a bell on the second floor, and a round-faced man with thinning black hair opened the door.

The apartment was skimpily furnished; it looked like a low-end motel, except for the artillery-spotter binoculars set up on a tripod behind the living-room curtains. The man's name was Willard Poole. His face was flushed with urgency, and his big eyes blinked rapidly. He shot his thumb toward the apartment building across the street. "They went out about twenty minutes ago."

"Went out where?" Dancer said, cold but edgy. "Where's Fry?"

"It's okay, it's okay," Poole hastily placated. "He's on it. He tailed them to a bar, couple streets over."

"They traveling?"

"No bags. Came out of the building clean."

"Okay, let's move," Dancer said.

They covered the two blocks in minutes, Poole trooping behind with drumbeat-fast steps to keep up. He pointed to a neon sign just down the block: the Red, White & Blue Bar, formerly the Municher Garten.

He gestured again, at a Plymouth sedan parked beyond the bar. They moved to it and piled in. Gus Fry, small, thin-faced, hawk-nosed, was behind the wheel.

Greetings were less than perfunctory. "You sure they're still in there?" Dancer asked.

Fry nodded. "I just checked."

"They alone?"

Fry nodded. "Last booth on the right."

"What about the back door?"

"There isn't any." He pointed down the street. "Pickups and deliveries go through that side door."

"They got to be dumb as turkeys to waltz around in the open," Poole said.

"They wouldn't come out just for a beer," Dancer said. "They went in there to meet somebody." He glanced at Poole. "Go in and buy a pack of cigarettes. Light one up."

Poole jumped out of the car and sauntered toward the bar.

"What are you thinking?" Nikolai asked. He was self-conscious, because he was not only the new boy, but the new boy on probation, as much a jailbird as Schenck and Kleist.

Dancer said, "You've got to figure the Germans want them back. They may not be Einsteins, but they know a lot of general shit. Plus, there's the pride of getting them back."

"How?"

"Well, I wouldn't say these two are worth a submarine pickup, especially since the *Abwehr* tried that last year and got burned, all eight guys. It's got to be Mexico, and that's a trip, so they need money and IDs."

"Do the Germans still have that much organization here?"

"Damn right. It's not big, but it's there, and it's dangerous." He stabbed a finger toward the bar. "You make out any contacts, Gus?"

"Nope. Not that I stayed that long. One quick beer."

"Place loaded, empty, what?"

"Halfway," Fry said. "Twenty, twenty-five people, mostly old-line Yorkville."

A few minutes later, Poole emerged from the bar, cigarette dangling from his mouth. He turned right, moving down the street away from the Plymouth—obviously a procedural caution. Dancer and Fry watched the entrance to the Red, White & Blue, but no one came out. Fry shoved the car into gear and eased down the block to the corner. He turned it and braked for Poole, who jumped back in.

While Fry made a U-turn and brought the Plymouth back into observational position, Poole said, "They're still alone, but just when I started out, this guy at the bar gets up and goes to the men's. Wears glasses. The minute he disappears, so does Schenck—follows him in. I thought about taking a leak, but I figured if that's the contact, I might spook them."

A few minutes later, a middle-aged man and woman came out of the Red, White & Blue; arguing, they wandered down the street. Five more minutes passed, and another figure appeared. A man, wearing glasses. "That's him," Poole said.

"Okay, we split," Dancer instructed. "You two cover the krauts. We'll tag this guy."

"What if they take off?" Fry asked.

"Then you stick with them," Dancer said. "Even if they just get their marching orders, they're not going anywhere tonight. Too risky. Stick out like sore thumbs." He glanced over; the man with the glasses was just turning the corner. He nudged Nikolai, and they jumped out of the Plymouth and headed down the street.

Tailing the man with the glasses turned out to be absurdly simple; he was anything but devious and lived only three blocks away. Dancer and Nikolai watched him descend half a dozen steps to the basement apartment of a shabby building. On his door, resting under a grimy alcove, was a small sign with a name: LEO MULLER.

Dancer was pensive as they walked back toward 85th.

"You don't think he's one of the big boys, do you?" Nikolai speculated.

"Do you?" Dancer asked, with a provocative tilt of his head.

Nikolai shook his head. "Not that I know what I'm talking about, but my guess would be delivery boy."

"My guess too. And if he was their contact, he's either bottom rung or paid to meet the krauts in the bar and hand over documents and money."

"Either way, the name's right," Nikolai mused. "Leo Muller."

"This whole part of New York's named Leo Muller. It's Krautland."

While they walked, leather soles slapping the pavement, Nikolai dryly mused that America was a wonderful place: less than two days ago, he and Dancer and the krauts had been in prison. Along with Stefan, and now Stefan was dead, and he and Dancer were trailing his killers. They ducked into a coffee shop for half an hour, then Dancer called the apartment. Fry answered; Schenck and Kleist were back in their apartment; Poole was on the binoculars, keeping tabs.

Dancer led the way through a rear entrance and up the stairs to the kitchen door. Fry opened up and said, "They're drinking. Take a look."

They moved through the apartment and joined Poole at the front window. He moved aside, and Nikolai took over the binoculars. They were focused on a living-room window across the street, first floor. The shades were drawn, but narrow slices of the apartment were visible.. Through subdued light, Nikolai could make out a bottle of liquor on a table. It looked like a still-life. At one point, Kleist hurried past, talking anxiously; a moment later, it was Schenck, listening.

Dancer and Nikolai took the first watch; then Poole and Fry took over. Dancer poured two drinks from a bottle of scotch in his overnight bag and went to sleep. Nikolai stretched out on the twin bed and stared at the ceiling. When he rose, black night was giving way to a thick, gray sky.

Fry stuck his head in the bedroom, "They're up." Dancer jumped up and moved to the window, yawning.

"Car down there," Nikolai said. "Maybe a Buick."

Dancer studied the car. "Oh, shit," he said. He turned to Fry, now alongside him. "Does FBI local have one of those?"

"They use anything these days. Could be."

In the living room, Dancer pushed Poole aside and took over the binoculars. "Jesus H. Christ," he said. "Hoover's goddamn stiffs, all right." His brain was churning. "Okay. Fuck. Okay. We've got to move."

He spat out instructions, and within moments, all four had exited the apartment through the kitchen. Fry and Poole cut through an alley and circled half a block. They turned the corner and eased along a building wall, kneeling behind garbage cans some distance short of the tail-end of the Buick.

They drew their guns and fired several shots. Two bullets hit the back tires and sank the back of the car with a one-two *whoosh!* The two FBI men came out cursing, guns drawn, but there was no one in sight. The FBI men made their way toward the corner in a series of cover moves. Low and slow, they moved past the garbage cans and inched their way to the intersection.

There was nothing there. Their assailants had disappeared. They exchanged sudden, dire glances and raced back along the street. They bounded up the steps and pushed into the building, unceremoniously shot the lock off the entrance to apartment 137, and crashed through the door.

Otto Schenck and Wilhelm Kleist were gone.

Their quarry had, of course, fled at the first sound of gunfire, out the back way and down the back alley and several more alleys until they had found a hack stand on 79th Street. They had jumped into a taxi and were let off at the West Side bus terminal on 42nd Street. Twenty minutes later, they were rolling through the Holland Tunnel on a Greyhound bus bound for Nashville.

CHAPTER 16

▼

Trailing in the Plymouth, Nikolai turned sharply at the corners and kept catching up to the bus before hitting the brakes to drop back again. "What the hell are you doing?" Dancer complained. "Haven't you ever driven a car before?"

"Once," Nikolai admitted. "I was about fourteen. By the way, I don't have a license."

"Jesus." Dancer sighed. "Remind me when we get back. We've got a guy for that stuff."

"Real ones, or does he make his own?" Nikolai said.

"Makes his own," Dancer said, not joking. He feigned paying attention to the road for a while but finally dozed off.

When he woke, half an hour later, Nikolai said, "What about the FBI?"

Dancer dipped into the bag for a wake-up nip, then said, "What about them?"

"Are they going to buy into this thing—a bunch of Nazi cowboys pulled it off?"

Dancer smiled tolerantly. "They're fogeyish but not that dumb."

"In other words, they already know you did it."

"You're not so dumb either," Dancer said, grinning. "You're one of the boys now."

"But aren't they annoyed? From their point of view, you screwed up an arrest, you shot up their car, and you let the krauts take off."

"They have no point of view," Dancer said. "We put out a special stay-the-fuck-away at least two months ago. But you have to know old 'Teeny Nuts' Hoover—he hates Guthrie. Hell, everybody hates *both* of them. But I can tell you what happened. Hoover figured, screw us, he'll just go ahead and nail the krauts and chalk up a big one and then blame the whole thing on a mixup."

"How cute. A private little war."

"Boys will be boys."

"Especially when they're both untouchable," Nikolai said, thinking that omniscience was a pleasant state to live in. "But I still don't understand something. Why are we following them? I thought the idea was to give them slack until they were contacted. It worked. Somebody contacted them, and now you know who he is and where he is. So why do you want them on the loose again? Why are we following them?"

After a brief pause, Dancer said, "Leo Muller was their New York contact, but you never know. There could be somebody else along the way."

There was nothing wrong with his logic, but his delivery was a trifle studied.

Nikolai asked, "Does that mean we follow them all the way to Mexico?"

"I doubt it," Dancer said. "Stay back, but don't lose them," He closed his eyes.

It was nine-thirty when the bus pulled into the Nashville terminal. Unlubricated joints creaked and stretched as the passengers piled out. Schenck and Kleist went straight to a window and bought tickets from a waxy-skinned man with an odd streak of white hair. Their destination was El Paso, Texas. The bus would be leaving at 1:15 AM. It would drive through the night, across Arkansas and the vast subcontinent of Texas, to reach its westernmost destination on the Mexican border in approximately twenty-two hours.

Dancer chattered with the ticket clerk and returned to the Plymouth. Ten minutes later, Schenck and Kleist exited the terminal building and wandered off. With this first and most dangerous leg of their journey complete without incident, they regained their old, insouciant swagger and went into a quiet bar at the far end of the dark street.

Watching them from the car, Nikolai said, "Do we pick them up now?"

"In a manner of speaking," Dancer said.

Nikolai tried to peer through the murk that Dancer generated. "Jesus Christ! Say something straight once, will you?"

"Come on, kid," Dancer said amiably, and Nikolai knew that they had crossed into new territory.

Nikolai said, "There is no special prison, is there?"

"No."

"Why didn't you tell me?"

"I didn't know if you were ready. I still don't."

"Does that mean I have an option?"

Dancer hesitated. "Not really."

Out of nowhere, a memory flashed, and Nikolai found himself replaying the moment in the yard when he had melodramatically said, *"We've got to kill them!"* and Dancer, in coy restraint, answering, *"Not my cup of tea, kid."*

The moment passed. Dancer said, "Look, you don't do anything. Just be there for me." Nikolai was staring, and Dancer misinterpreted. "It's okay if you sit it out. Just stay in the car."

Surprised, Nikolai said, "Why would I stay in the car?"

Dancer said, "Let's get something straight. If this thing goes off the track, there might be a temptation to take off. Don't."

Nikolai smiled. "You mean you'll have to shoot me."

"I'm a sweet prick, but that's the way it is."

"Hey, wow, what a tough bunch."

Dancer reappraised him. "Are you jerking me around?"

"I'm jerking you around."

Dancer frowned uncertainly. "You're ready?"

"I'm ready."

Skeptically, Dancer said, "Ever shoot a gun?"

"Military school."

Dancer opened the glove compartment. In its recessed gloom, a .38 automatic glinted blue-black. "Ever use one of these?"

"Revolver. Target practice."

Dancer indicated the pistol. "How were you?"

"Not great."

Dancer took a breath and said, "Doesn't matter. Your job is to stay here. Do nothing—not a fucking thing." He closed the glove compartment.

There was remarkably little traffic, pedestrian or vehicular, and even this eased as the hours passed. Parked at the top of the street, between the bar and the terminal, Nikolai and Dancer listened to the radio: Glenn Miller, Artie Shaw, the Andrews Sisters. At midnight, a newscast came on, then Benny Goodman.

At twelve-thirty, Dancer turned off the radio and checked the gun in his pocket. He looked over. "You okay? You look a little white around the gills."

"I'm good," Nikolai said.

Two minutes later, Schenck and Kleist came out of the bar, but so did another man, sloshed and angry. He waved a fist and shouted. When the krauts moved off, he followed like a terrier, words nipping at their heels. Finally, Kleist turned him around and booted him. The man slunk off.

Loose but not quite drunk, Schenck and Kleist moved up the block. Dancer glanced at Nikolai, then got out of the car. He leaned back against it.

Shadows so engulfed Dancer's lean form that Schenck and Kleist did not see him until he was close, almost face to face.

Everything happened lightning-fast. Schenck and Kleist suddenly realized their danger. Both men reached for guns as a voice called out, "Schenck!" Schenck, swiveling from surprise to surprise, saw Nikolai standing on the other side of the car. Dancer pulled the trigger and pumped two bullets into Kleist, who crashed down like a fallen tree. Schenck, frenziedly tugging out his gun, spun around with a bullet just above his clavicle and fell to the sidewalk, clutching his throat, then kicked his legs and died.

Dancer jumped into the car, and Nikolai put it into gear, headlights still doused.

Dancer was fuming. "You dumbfuck!" he said. Then, checking the mirror, he said, "Slow down. Hold it."

Nikolai pulled over and hit the brakes as Dancer turned around. Headlights appeared behind them at the top of the street.

"What's going on?" Nikolai asked.

"Sweepers," Dancer muttered. On seeing Nikolai's expression, he added, "Clean-up, for Christ's sake. Okay, move. And turn the goddamn lights on."

Once they were out of the city, Dancer suddenly bawled, "Who the hell do you think you are—Wyatt Earp?"

"Looked to me like he might get a shot off."

"That is solid bullshit! I had them lined up one-two, guns weren't halfway out, but here comes big-time Granger, the get-even kid! You couldn't wait to blow that fucker away!"

"Must have been first-time jitters."

"From now on, you do what you're told. Period."

"Right," Nikolai said. He gestured behind them. "Sweepers?"

"They follow. They sweep," Dancer said simply.

Nikolai suddenly understood. "Fry and Poole. They followed us down. They clean it up with the police."

Dancer frowned. His pupil was too precocious for this time of night. He grabbed the bottle of scotch from under his seat and drank deeply. "I don't know if you're a cool cat or a nutcase," he said. "You just knocked somebody off, and you're twinkling."

"I'm feeling good," Nikolai acknowledged.

They drove through the night and wearily piled into the apartment as the sun rose. Dancer phoned the duty officer, and they flopped into bed. Three hours later, a jangling phone awakened them. It was Guthrie. He wanted a report. His voice grated in disapproval; his people did not sleep until noon.

They showered and dressed, Nikolai barely recognizing himself in the mirror—his new clothes had been delivered from Carrolton & Wilton. Then they made their way through bustling midday Washington to the nondescript building that housed the Special Assessment Unit.

When they arrived, the unpredictable Guthrie was out of the office. A pockmarked, German-accented assistant named Stecker put them in a small anteroom and suggested they not leave. One never knew when Herr Guthrie would return, and he would want to see them immediately.

When they were alone, Nikolai said, "What's this 'Herr' business?"

"Mr. Guthrie likes the alien touch. Gives it a wartime atmosphere."

"Mr. Guthrie is as nutty as a fruitcake," Nikolai said.

Guthrie returned some two hours later. He told Nikolai to wait and took Dancer into his office.

Thirty minutes later, exiting the building, Dancer said. "The man is pleased. He thinks you did good."

"Thanks," Nikolai said, but he thought airily, *Hey, good things come to those who kill.*

"You're a complicated clock, Granger," Dancer was saying. "Want to tell me about that cigarette case?"

"Nothing to tell." Dancer kept up the pressure with his eyes, and Nikolai sweetly said, "I don't think that's any of your fucking business."

"On the other hand, it is," Dancer said. "We're not just business partners, kid. We're dependent on each other. I don't want to worry about your problems."

They were crossing a park square, watching cars, people, blinking traffic lights, and the colorful swirl of uniforms. They sat down at a bench.

After a moment, Nikolai said, "There was a man back in Latvia, a German, a Prussian, an estate owner, a big man in a little country. I was with my cousin, a girl, eighteen. We were trying to escape. This man killed her. He did a lot of things, but he ended up killing her."

Dancer nodded slowly, a piece of the puzzle sliding into place. "So that's where it is."

"That's where it is."

"Look at it this way. Everybody else is stuck with patriotism. You've got revenge."

Nikolai bristled, then realized it was not irreverence, but a sustaining truth.

*   *   *   *

Processing turned out to be a piecemeal affair. Nikolai took a physical at Fort Meade and a psychological test at the Pentagon; identification and documentation happened at a small office located in the Treasury Department. There was no connection between the procedures; in all cases, different numbers for the various locations were substituted for Nikolai's name, and the numbers transliterated to names other than his own. The object was not only to provide him with pseudonyms but also to maintain his anonymity within the government itself.

Despite the fact that it was outside the pale (or perhaps because it was), the covert world had a bureaucratic silliness all its own. Clerks spoke in monosyllables, squinted in suspicion, and were dutifully unfriendly.

When it was over, fully poked, prodded, jabbed, photographed, and documented, Nikolai made his way back to the apartment. It was still light but almost seven o'clock, and Nikolai was feeling a little giddy, like walking home alone from school the first time. He stopped for a newspaper, then stopped for a shine, his very first.

As it turned out, indulgence was the order of the day. Dancer was waiting with a feast, a great deal of liquor, and two girls. Their names were Doris and Pauline. The girls got drunk quickly, and when Nikolai disappeared, they wobbled into the bedroom with Dancer.

*   *   *   *

Emerging from the building, Nikolai sniffed moist, warm air. It had rained during the early evening, and the sidewalks and streets glistened. Wandering, he found himself near Union Station; something clicked, and he went into the terminal. Even now, toward midnight, the station was crowded. People went by in a blur.

Something clicked again, and he went to one of the telephone stations scattered around the terminal and began the exhausting process of locating a new telephone number in San Diego. Then he remembered his new ID. Within minutes, the operators had made the connection, and somebody said, "Hello?" It was the wrong voice, a man's voice, but he plunged ahead and asked for Maureen.

When she came on, he was suddenly speechless. Then said softly, "Nikolai?"

"Yes. Sorry."

"That wasn't Doug. Just a friend, visiting. For God's sake, how are you?"

"Good."

"Are you still …?"

"No," he said quickly. "I'm out."

"That's fantastic. How did it happen?"

"Long story."

"Where are you?"

"Tell me how you are," he said.

"I'm fine. It's crazy. I mean, the war, the navy, the whole thing. Are you all right?"

"Yes. I shouldn't have called. It was a wild, wild impulse. Is it going all right?"

"Am I a happily married young woman? I guess so. It's too fast to think about. And Doug's going to be shipped out soon, he thinks, so we're up in the air, but that's the way it is. I'm going to have to run. Call again." There was a pause, and she said, "Good-bye, Nikolai."

Heading back to the apartment, he told himself that she was irretrievably gone, no more or less than he had expected. There was something clean and virtuous about this ending, as though he had honorably concluded their relationship. And yet his step was lighter, something made his pulse beat faster, and he knew that it was not over.

The long night brought a terrifying dream: a bicycle crashing down a rocky path to the valley floor, weaving off the trail through thick brush and forested glen before bouncing back onto the path again. The figure perched on the bicycle should have been his, but it was not. It was the ghoulishly taunting face of Baron von Hartigens-Hesse.

END PART ONE

PART II

▼

THE PROJECT

CHAPTER 17

▼

Buffeting winds across the mesa tossed around the plane like a leaf. They were headed for Santa Fe, riding a bucket-seat Air Transport Command C-47. The plane was filled with uniforms, mostly army, mostly officers. The civilian exceptions were Nikolai and Dancer and a chattering cluster of five rumpled-suited men. Oblivious of the turbulence, they strained forward against their seatbelts, attempting intimate conversation amid the howl of the engines.

It was Nikolai's first flight, but the rough air reminded him of an amusement park ride. Dancer, pea-green and miserable, stared at nothing, Nikolai watched in fascination as snow-capped mountains slid by below. Then clouds covered his view, and he became aware of distorted bits and pieces of conversations from the five civilians across the aisle. "Mostly European," he remarked to Dancer.

"Who gives a shit?" Dancer mumbled.

"Three of them are German. I think the thin one with the slouch hat is American." Dancer failed to answer. and Nikolai said, "You're not much of a flyer, are you?"

"Go fuck yourself."

The trip to Santa Fe had followed a strange period of relative inactivity. There was no official problem. but the unofficial truth involved an investigation by the Justice Department. Rumors were rife of a Byzantine battle at the highest levels, having less to do, of course, with scruples than suzerainty. Guthrie and Hoover were squabbling again.

Ironically, Nikolai had completed his training at Quantico and Fort Meade just as SAU, out of business for two months, was reactivated. Forty-eight hours after that, Nikolai and Dancer were on their way to New Mexico.

For Nikolai, it was all different, even exciting, but somewhere over Kentucky, a huge and familiar and icy truth swept over him: he was moving sideways. His manic, unrealistic pursuit of Hartigens-Hesse was skewed beyond retrieval. Integration into SAU had brought him an odd, albeit amoral legitimacy; but it had also taken him on an exotic detour from his goal. Somewhere over Kentucky, he wondered why he could not simply move past his obsession. Somewhere over Arkansas, he shouted, into the roar of the engines and the creaking fuselage and the *whoosh* of the wind, "Because it's an *obsession,* stupid!"

They landed in a short series of updrafts and gusts. Inside the terminal, which was serviceable but primitive, Dancer wobbled to a men's room and came out smartly braced by two stiff drinks. They moved outside into the late-summer dry heat. The sun was white, starting its descent into the horizon. Nikolai smiled and thought, *This is the Old West.*

A khaki-colored staff car picked them up, and the driver, an MP sergeant, leaned out. "You gents Department of State?"

Nikolai and Dancer showed their IDs and climbed into the car, which nosed out of the airport, heading north. The sky opened to a breathtaking panorama of darkening blue against purple mountains as they crossed thirty miles of high desert and winding mountain road, heading up toward the twinkling lights of a city.

A wind whistled across the butte as the car slowed, moving down the main street of a hastily constructed military installation. And yet, Nikolai noted, there were just as many civilians as uniforms, and no less unusual, entire families of civilians: mothers and fathers tugging kids. And there was something else—an odd reclusiveness about the place. It was not simply ascetic, but withdrawn—an entire city in hiding. The place exuded secrecy. Every other road had a gated entry manned by guards, and even past the gates, many buildings were marked: OFF LIMITS WITHOUT SPECIAL PERMIT.

The buildings themselves were still so new that tar paper flapped along their sides, as though vying for attention. There were barracks for the military, double-size barracks chopped into small apartments for the civilians, and even larger frame structures housing a PX, a commissary, a movie theater, dining halls, laundry facilities, and warehouses.

The car stopped before a barracks, and the driver, Sgt. Rivera, dropped their bags. "Visitors' BOQ," he explained. "Captain Lomax, he'll be picking you up in about an hour, sirs." He saluted and drove away.

Settled in their bare-bones room, Nikolai stared out to the intensely purple line on the horizon that was the sunset and said, "Where the hell are we?"

"A place called Los Alamos."

"Those civvies on the plane were scientists. One of them was talking about critical mass."

"What's critical mass?" Dancer asked.

"I think it has to do with atomic fission—releasing energy."

"Atomic fission," Dancer said, lost. He took a bottle out of his bag. Sipping drinks, they studied the photograph of a man named Donald Winters, who was more than likely an Austrian national named Dieter Krone. The photograph had been taken sometime in 1936; he would be in his mid-forties by now.

Krone's last known association had been with the SS. Before that, he had acquired a German criminal record dating back to 1924: three sentences for armed robbery and one for manslaughter. His membership in the Nazi Party went back to 1927, when he had joined the brownshirts. He had switched over to the SS in 1935, become SS liaison to the *Abwehr*, then made his way to America as a refugee. Here in Los Alamos, he worked as a machinist in the ordnance lab.

Nikolai said, "How come the FBI isn't onto this guy?"

"Looks like they missed him."

There was a knock at the door, and Nikolai opened it to a short, stocky captain. "Bill Lomax," he said heartily. "CID." He did everything with a kind of nervous rhythm, as though run by a metronome. Dancer showed his papers. (He was Craig Morrison; Nikolai was Ted Adams.)

"Time for a drink?" Dancer invited.

"I'm running a little late," Lomax said. "Let's go get you a look. We can socialize later, if you want."

They went out into the night and jumped into Lomax's jeep. He drove it hard, sure of himself. Five minutes later, they were in front of an innocuous framed building.

Still behind the wheel, Lomax said, "If this is your man, what happens to him?"

"Take him back for questioning," Dancer said.

"Could I ask what it's about?"

"Criminal charges involving false entry and suspected affiliations."

Lomax smiled broadly—a compadre-in-the-same-business smile. He led them into the building and up a back stairway to a small, bare room with a window overlooking dozens of men working rows of milling machines. The din was awesome, and the building shook.

Lomax singled out a man filing a tool at one of the machines. "That's Winters."

Nikolai caught Dancer's eye. Winters was twenty pounds heavier than Dieter Krone. He wore glasses, had a lot more hair, and wore a mustache. Back in Washington, Guthrie had been smugly sure of Winters' real identity; according to rumor, Guthrie had acquired a high-ranking *Abwehr* officer, who was now singing exclusively to SAU. Further rumor had the officer liberated from Allen Dulles and the OSS.

Guthrie was proud of his *Abwehr* canary; the man had proven reliable. But Nikolai and Dancer, studying Donald Winters, were not sure.

Outside the building, the three men arranged to meet at the officers' club in an hour. Dancer and Nikolai decided to walk, and Lomax, heading off on errands, called back, "If you get there first, ask for Corporal Gilbert."

Watching the jeep sputter off, Dancer unfolded a housing map. He said, "G-141."

Occasional traffic roared by, lights stabbing into the darkness. Jeeps, weapons carriers, six-by-sixes, and occasional staff cars, all in khaki uniform.

"Some things are the same," Nikolai said. "Height, eye color, right-handed."

"What about the Dumbo ears?"

"*Abwehr* could have pinned them back. Clark Gable had Dumbo ears. They pinned them back."

"How do you know that? You're a fucking foreigner."

They walked along in the darkness under an inky sky, then it cleared and was filled with a million flickering stars. They were seventy-five hundred feet up, so there was a nip in the air, and the infrequent strollers moved by at a brisk pace.

Dancer, maintaining his silky glide, said, "A man could freeze his ass off out here."

They located G-141, climbed the stairs, and listened to the rhythm of the building. There was virtually no soundproofing, and the place fairly rocked with domestic life, including at least two screaming children and a crying baby. People laughed and shouted; radios fought each other up and down the hallways.

Dancer took out a multipurpose tool and wiggled it in the lock. The tumbler rasped, and they went into a small one-bedroom apartment. Within moments, Dancer found a jar of spirit gum. "Whew," he said, sniffing. "Toupee shit."

A few minutes later, Nikolai delicately lifted a mop of hair from a hook in the closet. "Here's the one he's not wearing."

Dancer was certain now. "That's our boy. Let's go." Passing a window, he jerked back. "Shit."

Nikolai discreetly joined him. There was a jeep below, with Sergeant Rivera behind the wheel. Rivera threw a cigarette butt out the window and eased the jeep into gear.

Almost amused, Dancer said, "How about that son of a bitch Lomax? He's keeping tabs on us."

The officer's club was bright and cheery, filled with jukebox music and early-evening revelers. The furniture was functional: the chairs were cushionless and the tabletops knotted, and the room, which was the size of a basketball court, still smelled of the forest.

The place was filled with a mixed bag of base personnel. There was only one officers' club, and military and civilians of all grades and brackets noisily mingled.

Nikolai and Dancer wove their way to the bar and found Corporal Gilbert, who pulled out a bottle of Jack Daniel's from under the bar and poured.

The two men settled at an empty table. Nikolai looked around and said, "Guess who's here?"

Dancer turned and saw Dieter Krone with two men in a booth across the room. Krone, idly chatting, flashed a silver tooth. He was sipping beer and puffing a cigarette in quick bursts.

Nikolai said, "Watching that son of a bitch have a good time bothers me."

Straight-faced, Dancer said, "Well, then, why don't we kill him?"

With one eye on Krone, they soaked up the setting, a convivial atmosphere in a babel of tongues that somehow exuded frontier and sophistication at once.

Dancer was saying, "Did I ever tell you my old man started out as an undertaker? That was before the hardware business. My grandmother told him he needed a trade, so he went into a local parlor and got a job." Dancer, finishing his third drink, was already into what Nikolai called his sweet and lowdown stage. "Even without the undertaking, he was a melancholy bird," he said. "He taught me to drink. He said nothing good on Earth ever came from the reality of things, only in the escape of them."

Nikolai surprised himself by saying, "My mother said mine was executed by a Bolshevik firing squad, but I don't think she really knew. I think that was her idea of glamour."

"Bolsheviks? That has to be way back."

"It was 1917. They weren't married. They were together two weeks."

Dancer leaned in. His smile was avaricious; a revelation was around the corner. "What about the cigarette case?"

"What about it?" Nikolai said, suddenly impenetrable.

"Listen," Dancer said, "I clammed up all my life, and it never did a thing for me."

"What's the point?" Nikolai said, unamused.

"Is it the girl?"

"What girl?"

"The one he killed. That girl."

"Go fuck yourself." Nikolai slammed down his glass and jumped up. Heads turned.

"Sit the fuck down," Dancer ordered. "I asked you if it's the girl, your cousin. The one you tried to get away with, maybe the one you still feel responsible for, and sometimes you can't help it—it eats you up. That girl."

Nikolai slowly settled back in his seat. "it's still none of your fucking business."

"You in love with her?"

It took Nikolai a minute. "Not that way."

They drank. Dancer said, "There's ways to love somebody besides sticking a dick in them."

"I didn't take care of her. He killed her. I mean, that fucking animal just pulled the trigger and blew her apart, the way you'd split something up in a slaughterhouse."

"And it's your fault. You couldn't do a thing about it in this world, but it's your fault. You've got a life to live, son. Keep her inside, but let her out. Here's to her."

Nikolai hesitated. Finally he raised his glass to a soft clink.

At that same moment, Captain Lomax barreled into the club. He settled at their table with a jar. He had something on his mind and was loath to hide it. He jerked a thumb toward Krone. "You figure on taking him when, tomorrow morning?"

"That's right," Dancer said warily. "Is there a problem?"

"Matter of fact, there is," Lomax said, registering concern but enjoying himself. "This friend of mine in the State Department says you fellows didn't come up on a single personnel list. Not one."

"I think you know why, captain," Dancer said smoothly.

"Yeah, I get the picture," Lomax said, "You fellows are covert, which is all well and good. Except I don't like people strutting in here from Washington, thinking they own the place. Like sneaking around this post on their own."

"I beg your pardon?" Dancer said.

"I call it breaking and entering, mister!" Lomax said, red-faced now. "I don't go for Mickey Mouse stuff. Donald Winters stays right here until you guys come up with a bona fide authorization. Try to fuck me over again, and I slam you into the stockade. Understood?" He strode off, the stagy exit of a gunslinger.

"Well, Stanley," Dancer said, "here's another fine mess you've gotten us into."

They stared after the captain. Then Nikolai said, "Dancer? Thanks."

Dancer understood, but shrugged it off.

"Anyway, it's not a mess," Nikolai said.

"It's not a mess?" Dancer shifted forward in interest. "Why isn't it a mess?"

"Because I found something in Dieter's closet, in a jacket," Nikolai said, oddly sanguine. He pulled out a slip of paper and read, "One three three E eight eight, four nine one nine four four."

"What the hell's that mean?"

"One thirty-three East 88th Street, April 9, 1944."

"That night in New York!"

"Right. Outside the Red, White & Blue, that kraut bar they turned into God bless America."

"Leo Muller," Dancer remembered.

Nikolai said, "Check the date, Dancer. That was only three months ago."

"Jesus Christ," Dancer whispered, surprised. "They've still got an operation working."

"The question is, how big an operation?"

"Probably small. Maybe just the two of them."

"Maybe a little bigger," Nikolai speculated. "Remember Leo Muller's file? He was a messenger boy. Would they use him as sole contact to Dieter Krone? The one and only *Abwehr* agent working a secret installation? What makes sense is Leo Muller as a know-nothing mail drop for Krone and maybe for three or four more agents."

Dancer nodded slowly. "You're right."

Thoughtfully, Nikolai said, "Try this. We chose not take Krone out because we uncovered something bigger—Krone getting his orders through Leo Muller, the very same man we tracked down in New York."

"Which means there's an active *Abwehr* operation in the works," Dancer said, warming up to it. "Probably big-time out of Mexico, passing orders on to low-level Leo Muller in New York, who pipelines the stuff to Dieter Krone, *Abwehr* agent in place in Los Alamos."

The excitement was contagious, and Nikolai said, "We bust up a spy ring, Guthrie aces Hoover, Roosevelt invites us to the White House for cocktails."

They drank to it, drinking in the excitement until the seconds ticked it all away.

"He'll never buy it," Nikolai said.

"Not in a million years," Dancer said.

CHAPTER 18

▼

Incredibly, Guthrie bought it with nothing so much as a dubious look. He had paced behind his desk with a fearsome smile, as though trailing Hoover's cortege. "Good work, good work," he kept saying.

No less amazingly, they heard nothing more for the next three weeks, but now they were sitting in McKennan's office, awaiting what they assumed would be some sort of proxy account of progress on the case. With McKennan rambling on about the need for discipline at every level, Nikolai's mind was on the three teenage soldiers who had passed him on Pennsylvania Avenue a few days earlier, one of whom had been wearing a sharpshooter's medal. And in that strange way that the brain generates unfathomable mysteries and then, just as neatly, solves them, Nikolai realized what had been quietly gnawing at him for the past year and a half, since his visit to Lionel Granger, in Georgetown.

His face showed his distance, and McKennan said, "Am I boring you, lad?"

"No more than usual, Mr. McKennan," Nikolai said, with just a suggestion of a burr.

McKennan twisted his mouth into a smile. He and Nikolai had developed an easy rapport over the months. The Scotsman's nicely honed sense of humor had come as something of a surprise. For his part, though gloomy by nature, McKennan had a strain of the romantic, and Nikolai somehow suggested Scots virtue.

McKennan had been a headmaster at a private school in Edinburgh before the war. He had joined British intelligence in 1939, been wounded in a German bombing raid on London in 1942, been posted to Washington shortly thereafter, and was on some sort of cross-collateral leave to SAU, the intricacies of which he had never sorted out.

Dancer kept shifting in his chair. "What's up, Mac?" he said.

McKennan glanced over disapprovingly, and the pipe clamped between his teeth drooped. He did not like Dancer calling him "Mac," and he did not like Irish Catholic drunks, which, in his lexicon, came to one word. He was also aware that Dancer had dubbed him McKennan, the Peggy-Legged Prick.

"Gentlemen, in regard to your recent trip to New Mexico, Mr. Guthrie and I agree that a piece of luck has presented itself and must not be squandered. Therefore, a decision has been made to pursue the operation as a cooperative venture." Less affably, he added, "I expect an attitude consistent with departmental loyalty."

Nikolai and Dancer looked over sharply, and McKennan said, "You will be working field duty out of New York City."

"New York City?" said Nikolai, taken aback.

Uneasy, Dancer rasped, "What does 'cooperative' mean?"

Nikolai was studying McKennan, learning little but speculating much. "It means the FBI, doesn't it?"

"It does," McKennan acknowledged.

"Jesus H. Christ," said Dancer.

"It's not that queer, gentlemen," McKennan said. "We are, after all, on the same side."

"First time I've heard about it," Nikolai said, and McKennan's leathery face loosened, but only briefly.

"Does the FBI know about this?" Dancer asked.

"They have been briefed," said McKennan. "Look, lads. When you discovered the connection between Los Alamos and New York, you sensed an opportunity, did you not?"

"For SAU," Nikolai conceded, "not the FBI."

"Unfortunately, Mr. Granger, we are faced with problems that threaten our very existence. In this spirit, Mr. Guthrie has made an accommodation with Mr. Hoover. For the foreseeable future, we shall, when it is mutually beneficial, share certain assignments with the FBI. This means we work harmoniously for the good of all, gentlemen. Is that clear?"

It was clear, but it was not easy to take. Dancer and Nikolai argued with McKennan, until McKennan shouted, "If Simon Guthrie can agree to work with J. Edgar Hoover, then, by the head of William Wallace, so can you!"

It was also clear that Guthrie, attempting to expand SAU's mandate, had not only lost the battle, but also the war: SAU would eventually be swallowed by the FBI.

Still grumbling, Dancer said, "Do they know about Dieter Krone?"

"They do," McKennan said.

"What about Krone?" Nikolai asked.

"The FBI has him under surveillance but will hang back and allow the situation to develop out of New York. That's where you two come in."

"Doing what?" Dancer said.

"Cooperating with the FBI, damn it."

Nikolai said, "Who have they got so far?"

"Leo Muller—the man you followed in the Yorkville area—a man named Heinz Baumann, and a woman named Antonia Graf. Graf's probably a waste of time—apparently quit the Nazi business when the *Bund* went bust. And one other—a rather shadowy figure, a man named Raymond Harris. If there is a cell and it is connected to Los Alamos, this Harris is probably pulling the strings."

"Is he in New York?" Nikolai asked.

"The FBI doesn't know where he is," McKennan admitted, "or even who he is. The one thing they do know is that Raymond Harris deposited fifty thousand dollars in the New York Mercantile Bank last month."

"What's the tie between Raymond Harris and the New York people?" Nikolai asked.

"That's the triangle squared, so to speak," said McKennan. "Once we concluded our arrangement with the Bureau, they started reading Dieter Krone's mail. Almost immediately, they came across a letter out of Mexico, from an old acquaintance named Hector Ruiz, and Ruiz made a passing reference to a mutual friend, R. Harris."

"Does the Bureau have anything on this friend, Hector Ruiz?" Nikolai asked.

McKennan nodded. "In the letter, Ruiz talked about the old days. It seems he and Krone worked together as engineers in the late thirties, at a machine-tool factory in Hamburg, Germany."

"Did you see this letter?" Dancer asked.

"A copy, yes. And the FBI was able to verify the machine-tool company—Kleindorff GMBH—along with the existence of Hector Oswaldo Ruiz, born in Mexico City in July 1907, graduate of the Institute of Technology, Mexico City, 1932."

"How could Hector Ruiz in Mexico know Dieter Krone's address in the middle of a war?" Nikolai said.

"Apparently, he didn't. He sent the letter to Krone's last known address in Germany, and the *Abwehr* obviously managed to forward it to Krone's post office box in Santa Fe."

"Was the FBI able to locate Ruiz?" Dancer asked.

"Not yet. He's off on a mining job somewhere in the Yucatan. But—" He paused for effect. "Mr. Guthrie suspected a link, and so we checked the handwriting of the letter and the deposit slip made out by Raymond Harris at New York Mercantile. Hector Luiz and Raymond Harris are one and the same."

"If the deposit slip is more recent than the letter," Nikolai mused, "then Raymond Harris—Hector Luiz—is probably in New York right now."

"That is a reasonable assumption," McKennan said.

"What does the Bureau know about this guy Baumann?" Dancer asked.

"Heavy German-American *Bund* involvement before the war. On the order of a fanatic."

"Still a fanatic?" Nikolai asked.

McKennan sucked on his pipe. "They think so … but toned down."

Dancer coughed again, and Nikolai said quietly, "Jesus, put it out."

Dancer ignored him and waved his cigarette, as though looping it through his thoughts. "What makes the Bureau so sure Berlin's even involved? It sounds small—could be on the amateur side—so maybe it's just local. New York is headquarters, Los Alamos is the action."

"We think not," McKennan said carefully. "We're quite confident about our information."

Not mincing words, Nikolai said, "Is that because we have a special source?"

Tolerantly, McKennan said, "We have any number of sources, Mr. Granger."

"The rumor is that SAU has a private feed," Nikolai persisted. "Somebody pretty high up. Military defector." The tone avoided provocation: he was simply passing on gossip.

McKennan trotted out an officious smile. "I am sorry, but I cannot help you."

"They say this guy is stashed somewhere in Virginia," Dancer chimed in.

"Is that what they say?" McKennan, amused, relit his pipe and puffed up an aromatic cloud. "That's a nice stab in the dark, lads. But as we say in the hills of Aberdeen, when you poke into the waste pile, you're bound to come up with a wee bit of shit."

"Then we don't own such a person?" Nikolai said, trying one more time.

"No comment," McKennan said, puffing.

Nikolai shifted gears. "What about this bank account? Who's got access?"

"Only one person—Raymond Harris. The account is untouched to this date, but it's new. One assumes they'll get around to using it."

There was a silence, and Nikolai, filling the off-guard moment, said, "What's going on in Los Alamos?"

McKennan hesitated, and Dancer said, "Come on, Mac, don't be such a tightass."

McKennan frowned—Scots stern, steaming with censure—but Nikolai quietly deflected him. "Mac, I'll bet the FBI knows. Which makes us a pair of idiots when we get up there."

"You've got a big mouth," McKennan chided Dancer. To both, he added, "But you've got a point. Los Alamos is part of a very, very large operation called the Manhattan Project. What they're doing is working on a bomb. An atomic bomb. If they come up with it, it could immediately end the war."

"Jesus H. Christ," Dancer said.

"Where are the Germans?"

"Neck and neck."

"What you're saying is, fifty-fifty they can win this war."

"Fifty-fifty, if they come up with a delivery system."

"You mean long-range bombers," Dancer said.

"Right," McKennan said.

Nikolai said, "They've got factories turning out everything from battleships to mousetraps, so what's the big deal about a rush program for a few long-range bombers? And that's all they need—a few. And back to Los Alamos—if the place is that important, maybe the *Abwehr* has got a regiment of Dieter Krone's in place."

"I think not," McKennan replied, so easily that Nikolai and Dancer realized that the rumored oracle was very much in place.

"What's their next move?" Nikolai asked.

"That's anybody's guess," McKennan admitted. "We'll have to wait until they start tapping into that bank account. Meanwhile, go up to New York, familiarize yourselves with the situation. Observe, but do not intrude. Above all," he said, adding a dramatic flair of the nostrils, "cooperate."

He handed a manila envelope to Dancer. "These are your New York arrangements, background on the people in question, and the names and suggested times of contact with the FBI. As always, memorize and eliminate." Nikolai and Dancer rose and turned to exit, but McKennan gestured to the connecting door to the next office. "Mr. Guthrie would like a few words."

They entered and stood before Guthrie. "Sit," he said. He was staring toward a window that showed a narrow slice of the Lincoln Memorial.

They sat.

"You may smoke."

The invitation was unprecedented; the two men lit up from one match, exchanging glances. It seemed to take an eternity, but Guthrie, churlishness nowhere evident, seemed not to notice.

Finally, he said, "You have been updated?"

"Yes, sir," Dancer said.

Slowly, his unseen small feet tapping out his progress, Guthrie swung around, the chair emitting an eerie screech, the legendary screech that, it was said, Guthrie refused to oil out because of its unsettling effect.

"Gentlemen," he said, "the nature of our function is changing. War is a period of adjustment."

The adjustment—which was, of course, his forced pact with Hoover—was killing him. He looked awkward and out of place, immersed in feelings only a man without feeling could feel. He was a man who did not suffer clichés, not even his own, yet "war was a period of adjustment." And there was more. "Where the benefit is mutual, where the cause may be advanced by alliance, then we must merge our forces for the common good."

It was prime pap, unworthy of a benevolent despot, leave alone a merciless tyrant. Nikolai and Dancer squirmed, and their embarrassment at his weakness broke the silence. Suddenly, Guthrie said, "Cooperate, but do not capitulate!"

The line pleased him. It served as a slogan, a declaration, a mantra. He opened his palm and slashed the air, sweeping them out of the room.

Dancer rose and started for the door to the outer office, but Nikolai remained in his chair. "I'd like to talk to you, sir."

Dancer completed his withdrawal and closed the door. Guthrie stared through Nikolai and said, "What?"

"Some time back, you suggested we could discuss my situation."

"What situation is that?" Guthrie asked.

"A pardon," Nikolai said.

"A pardon?" Guthrie looked puzzled. He could have been a stranger, stopped on the street.

"I've earned it."

Guthrie seemed to shift gears, as though accepting the subject matter after all; but now he temporized, something he could do with his thick eyebrows alone. He said, "Not from my vantage point, Mr. Granger."

With a gush of anger, Nikolai said, "At your bidding, I have been involved in a number of cleansing operations on behalf of the state. I would appreciate knowing the quota expected of me in order to gain your blessing."

Guthrie dug his knuckles into the desk; the room fairly pulsed with his intensity. "Insolence!" roared Guthrie, straight out of Dickens. "Do you know what you are, Mr. Granger? Who do you think you are? You are a slimy convict! You have no rights!"

The irony was too tempting to resist. "I seem to have the right to kill, Mr. Guthrie."

Guthrie did not fail to turn these words over carefully. "Are you attempting to blackmail me, Mr. Granger?"

"I was wondering the same thing about you, sir."

Perhaps because it was so true, Guthrie said nothing. He screwed himself up to an Olympian perch and said, though he seemed somewhat diminished, "Insolent."

"I'm attempting to point out my work record, sir."

"The record that counts is the one that sent you to prison."

"It's the same record that brought me here, sir. It's a record that you indicated could be absolved by the degree of my competency in this department, and I believe I have performed well."

"What you have done is called self-preservation, Mr. Granger."

"Yes, sir, like any soldier in the field."

"The difference is honor. A soldier fights with honor."

"I have been that soldier."

"The capacity to kill does not automatically reflect honor, any more than it reflects loyalty or patriotism. You are, I believe, a Latvian."

Perhaps for the first time, Nikolai understood Guthrie's elementary prejudice. It was not simply his criminal record; it was his alien status. No, more than that, it was his lineage. Guthrie's America had no room for non-Americans. Non-Americans could not become Americans. Immigrants were not Americans. Aliens who fought against America's enemies were not Americans. Nikolai was not and never could be an American.

So Guthrie's promise of absolution counted for nothing. Nikolai was a pawn who could never be more than a pawn. And it followed that the reason Guthrie did not throw him out on his ass for demanding his due was this very hearing; his reward for satisfactory performance was the privilege of audience. His dossier would never be altered. His criminal record would never be expunged. When he was no longer useful, his existence would be ended.

Nikolai rose. Almost jauntily, he said, "Perhaps we could talk again sometime, sir."

With the grace of a sun king, Guthrie said, "Yes, of course. Why not?"

Outside the building, Nikolai felt curiously free. He flagged down a cab, and for no reason in the world, he had the driver take him to Arlington Cemetery. He drifted through rows of monuments and memorials to presidents and ordinary soldiers and wondered, sometimes aloud, what he was doing there. He thought of cemeteries as an extension of pagan ritual: gone was gone, and what did a chunk of inscribed stone have to do with unreachable memory? But he could not escape the thick air of reverence that filtered through the afternoon light, and he realized why he had come. It was for Tati and Katya, who were part of the same earth and therefore shared the same reverence.

When he returned to the apartment, Dancer was embryonically coiled up on the sofa, his head hot, his face red and glistening. He was clutching an empty bottle and said, "I'll be okay…. Get me another bottle."

But his eyes closed, and he was asleep by the time Nikolai covered him with a blanket. Travel was out of the question. Nikolai made a decision. He packed an overnight bag and scribbled a note. Out on the street, his strides were long and purposeful. The wartime hordes had receded for the weekend, and traffic was light. Only now did he sense the languor of the city, encased in soft, humid September air.

He stopped in his tracks, taken by a sudden thought. It was foolish enough to warn him off and intriguing enough to disregard the warning. Nikolai spun around, headed for Georgetown.

The house was apparently empty, and the curtains were drawn. He made sure by climbing the stairs to the solemn door with its brass knocker. He rang the bell as a short, stocky couple marched by, Georgetown aristos, their tiny steps and bulky silhouettes perfectly synchronized. They disappeared around the corner as Nikolai used the knocker to thump at the door. Silence.

He descended the stairs and lifted a latch on the arrow-topped iron fence that led to the back. A faded red-brick path followed the side of the house, and he moved past the west-facing sunroom, where he had been wined and dined by Lionel and Eunice prior to being dumped back out in the street.

Nikolai checked the fuse box on the wall outside the kitchen; it was straightforward, with no add-on alarm wire, no other gimmicks. He cut off the main switch and moved to the kitchen door. Then he took out the Baron's platinum cigarette case; within it, Nikolai now kept a miniature pick set, a gift from Dancer.

Within seconds, he was in the house, and the rest of it was absurdly simple. He pocketed his father's medal from the lowboy in the sunroom and retreated through the kitchen, grabbing an apple on the way out.

Forty minutes later, he was in Union Station, with time enough to look over an art exhibition on the air war over Europe. Then he bought a magazine and crossed the cavernous terminal to track 17, where the *Gotham* was poised for departure.

Nikolai pushed through the usual thicket of bodies and made his way to car C, compartment 9. Inside, a harried porter was still clearing the residue of the incoming trip—a lively gala, by all accounts, since dozens of empty bottles and a carpet of cigarette butts, potato chip crumbs, and other garbage, along with one sodden, leftover Air Corps lieutenant, were scattered around. The apologetic porter opened the bar car ten minutes early, and Nikolai settled quietly at a small table.

Now the train was sliding past the skeletal supports of the track sheds and gingerly picking its way across a spaghetti tangle of rails. It picked up speed and was soon boring its way through the outskirts of Washington, the tracks beneath now clicking like typewriter keys.

By then, Nikolai was nursing a drink, and the bar car was swarming with travelers small-talking against the roar of the train.

Out of the welter, one voice suddenly cut through: "Nikolai?" Her voice was incredulous. He turned to look: her eyes registered shock. Nikolai too was stunned.

"Is it you?" she said.

He shook his head, smiled, and touched her hand. They sank across from each other at the little table just as a porter skidded by. "You folks, somethin'?"

"My God, yes," Maureen muttered.

"Two manhattans," Nikolai said.

Common sense invaded, and she whispered, "What are you doing here?"

"It's okay," he said. "I'm not being chased."

She blinked, bewilderment returning. "You're not?"

"No. All settled. On the up-and-up."

"That's wonderful," she said skeptically.

"Now you."

"Me? Oh, well, things didn't work out. We're getting a divorce. The hell with me! How come you look so good, sleek, expensively dressed, and—" she leaned closer and whispered, "cocky as hell, if you don't mind my saying so?"

"I don't mind," he said.

The porter popped out of a huddle of soldiers and approached. "Compartment's ready when you are, sir."

Nikolai slipped him a bill. "Can we get a couple of glasses? Some ice?"

"My pleasure, sir!" The porter moved off, balancing himself smartly with a Chaplinesque skitter as the train went into a turn.

"Okay with you?" Nikolai asked, rising.

"Good God in heaven, how did you get a compartment? Nobody gets compartments. I almost had to offer my body just to get a ticket."

They picked their way through the car and then through the next one, to Nikolai's compartment. Almost on their heels, the porter arrived with glasses and a bucket of ice. Eventually, Nikolai produced a bottle of scotch and poured it over ice. They clicked glasses.

"I can't quite believe this," she said. "Among other things, this is how we met. On a train. Out of Washington."

"I know."

"It's all too much."

"Fate," he said lightly.

"Maybe that's true," she said.

He sipped. "Maybe."

"But it's not desperate any more, is it?" she said.

"It's …" He searched for a word. "Tempered."

"That's certainly romantic," she said.

He grinned. "You still have to knock them dead, don't you?"

She sighed theatrically. "It's not supposed to be that obvious. What's that?"

Nikolai looked down in surprise. He could not remember taking the medal out of his pocket, but it was in his left hand, and with the fingers of his right hand, he was rubbing the frayed threads of the faded cloth attached to the medallion itself.

"It's old, isn't it? May I?"

He handed it over. She examined it, focusing on the inscribed words, which she could make out but could not understand. "What does it say?"

"Same thing they all say. 'For the honor and glory of the country.'"

Her eyes widened. "Is that what you stole?"

"Yes."

"Is it worth that much?"

"That depends. Maybe ten dollars in a pawn shop."

"Then why?"

"It was my father's."

"You stole your father's medal?"

"That's right."

"Now I'm really confused," Maureen said. "That's not exactly the kind of thief I had in mind."

"Has it occurred to you that I'm not a thief."

"Not for a moment. But I'm willing to listen."

H said nothing, just showed the edge of a smile that was harder than anything she could remember. She tinkled the ice in her glass. "Maybe I'll just settle for another drink."

He poured. They watched the sun slip out of sight as the train plunged into the darkness of a tunnel with a whooshing explosion of sound. Ten seconds, and it was out in the clear again, twilight filtering through the trees.

They had been sitting across from each other, but now she jumped up and plunked down beside him in one swift swooping motion, glass neatly balanced, not a drop spilled. "Lord, I don't know what I'm doing here."

"Welcome to the club."

"You're the last person I ever expected to see again." Absently, she squeezed his hand. "When you called, I kept thinking, why in God's name is he calling? What can we possibly say?"

The wonder of it, the irrevocably alien nature of it, brought her to a dazed pause. He slid a hand behind her neck and gently drew her lips to his. It was a sad sort of kiss, a little dry, as though parched by time. But when they kissed again, it was warm and moist and deep.

Suddenly, the moment was on fire. Maureen jumped up and shut off the overhead lights; in the same second, she was tearing at her clothes, and he was helping her. They laughed and fumbled with buttons and zippers, and she seemed to burst into nakedness, and she pulled his shirt over his head. He flung the rest of his clothes aside, and she slipped to her knees, and her tongue slid over him, licked his flushing skin, the penis thick and erect as she moaned like a distant banshee over his painfully muted voice.

The interruption was classic, a comic-opera hard-knuckled rap at the door. Maureen, attached to him like an abstract piece of plumbing, looked up to him like a faithful dog.

"Got a telegraph message here, sir!" the porter shouted.

"Just slip it under the door," Nikolai gargled out.

There was a brief silence marking the licentious images now tumbling through the porter's mind. "Sorry. Got to sign, sir."

"I'll sign it later," Nikolai said impatiently.

There was a faint against-the-rules mumble, then the envelope appeared under the door.

Maureen detached herself and sat back against the high-backed velveteen bench seat, her long-legged body a coppery glow in the off-light. She closed her eyes. It was an awkward interim, of course, but somehow erotic in its own right, the cold air from the overhead vent languidly brushing her body, wafting across her breasts, stiffening her nipples.

She felt Nikolai settle next to her, tugging the message from an envelope. He unfolded it and broke into a smile.

She took it from his fingers and, warding off his hand, read aloud, "Solo, I'm sick, but you're crazy. Liquid helping. Defend the faith." Maureen looked over. "What does it mean?"

"Bon voyage," he said.

"You look kind of cute, just sitting there with everything hanging out."

"So do you," he said. The breeze from the air conditioning had parted her blouse, and a blonde cockscomb poked out between her legs.

"How long will you be in New York?"

"I'm not sure."

"Will I be able to call you?"

"Afraid not."

What she heard was less regret than indifference, and her face tightened. She set her drink aside and swiftly dressed. "Lord, I never understood us, and now it's worse."

Nikolai dressed, while Maureen poured herself another drink. They stared out at nighttime America, an endless parade of racing lights.

When they pulled into Penn Station, she left a scrap of paper and said, "If you want to get in touch with me, this is my new address. If you haven't got time, that's all right too."

Mechanically, he took note of the address, but his mind was already fastened on something else: his New York contact, an FBI agent named Wilbur Menzies.

CHAPTER 19

▼

They were in the Oyster Bar at the Roosevelt Hotel: Nikolai, Wilbur Menzies, and Lyle Boettinger. The bony-faced Menzies, age thirty-eight, chopped at the air with his fork when he talked, a habit picked up from his father, who had been a Baptist preacher. Long removed from bayou provincialism, Menzies was on the stylish side: double-breasted suits and solid knit ties from Bray Bros. on Lexington Avenue.

Boettinger, was in his early forties, an ample-sized man in a rumpled suit. He slid a mint back and forth in his mouth while he stabbed at a plate of fried shrimp and french fries. He had long ago traded ambition for easy-does-it; he was vaguely popular for his irreverence but generally unwanted as a partner. Hoover himself had once reported him for dirty shoes. But Menzies, a shrewd rocket of ambition, had hooked up with Boettinger at the first opportunity, calculating how good he would look in contrast.

Nikolai, who had just arrived and was still standing, politely waited while Menzies picked at a crab cake with a two-tined fork. At last, he dabbed the corner of his mouth with a starched white napkin and looked up. "Frankly, Mr. Granger, I would have appreciated some sort of notification."

"It was last minute," Nikolai said. "It was either cancel the meeting or go up without him."

"He's ill, you say."

"He's got a fever."

"It would have been a lot more convenient if we had heard before rearranging our schedule to come here," said Menzies.

"I can well understand that," Nikolai said, watching the put-upon Menzies empty his glass and signal for another whiskey sour.

Menzies carefully chewed the crab cake; there was a delicacy and a tentativeness in his munching that reminded Nikolai of a king's taster. Menzies again looked up. "What did you say your name was?"

"My name is Nikolai Granger," he said, "and I'll tell you what. If you prefer to wait for Mr. Rhodes to join the discussion, I can head back, and we can set something up again when he's feeling better."

It so dripped with sarcasm that Menzies looked surprised, and Lyle Boettinger opened his mouth to reveal a fresh mint between his teeth.

Menzies came up with a Bureau smile. "No need for that. It's just that I know who Rhodes is, but I don't know you."

"Then we're both starting from scratch, because I don't know you either."

Finally, as though in grudging concession to the new reality, Menzies said, "Where're you staying?"

"Commodore."

Menzies nodded, indicating his approval; he approved of it because of its convenience. He chopped the air, inviting Nikolai to join them. "You eat?" he asked,

"I ate."

Slowly, the dust settled, and they talked about the weather, the food at the Roosevelt, the progress of the war. Nikolai ordered a drink, and Menzies offered a cigarette. With rapport now sanctioned, Boettinger commented about some oysters at the next table: "They look like lungers."

"Thank you, Lyle," Menzies said, but it was more in the nature of a tolerant parent. He would never be lovable, not even likeable, but he was dedicated. Rising abruptly, he said, "Let's get to business."

He led the way out of the Roosevelt, and they piled into an FBI car illegally parked in front of the Yale Club. The New York policeman watching over the car saluted, and Menzies hatchet-chopped a return. He, who had worked his way through the Beauregard Chilton Law School in New Orleans, did not mind tweaking the establishment. They drove to 79th street and parked in the middle of the block.

"That's where Baumann lives," Menzies said. He was pointing to a grimy, ocher-colored building; the alley side of it was an erector-set tangle of rusty fire escapes.

"Where's the shop?"

"Next block."

"Is that one of your people?" Nikolai was pointing to a man reading a newspaper behind the wheel of a black Chevrolet.

Menzies frowned. He hadn't expected a rookie from an organization as crude as SAU to zero right in on an FBI stakeout. "Hickey," Boettinger spontaneously noted, drawing a glare from Menzies.

"There he is," Menzies said.

Heinz was coming out of the building, angled against the autumn wind like the figurehead on a whaling ship.

"Where's he going?" Nikolai asked.

"Probably the Beer Garden, on 74th," Boettinger said. "Usually suds up around this time."

"With Leo Muller?" Nikolai guessed. Menzies nodded, and Nikolai said, "The question is, who gives them orders?"

"We'll find out sooner or later," Menzies said, bristling at what he took to be a needle. "We've got a twenty-four-hour watch on Muller."

When Heinz turned the corner, Menzies gestured, and Boettinger signaled Hickey with his lights: he was to stay where he was. They would follow Baumann.

Twenty-five minutes later, the three men took a booth at the rear of the Beer Garden. Menzies had crawled through traffic and double-parked twice, waiting for Heinz to arrive. By now, Heinz had settled in across from Leo Muller and had already launched an argument.

"Old Leo's a perfect pal," Nikolai said off-handedly. "He just sits and takes it."

"You know him? Muller?"

"Saw him once. About a year ago."

Menzies' eyes narrowed. "I hadn't realized SAU was involved that far back."

"They weren't. It was in connection with another case."

"Might I ask the circumstances?"

Politely, Nikolai said, "I'm afraid not."

"Let me suggest something," said Menzies. "We are in the same boat, friend. You can trust me, and you can trust the FBI."

In that minute, it occurred to Nikolai that the unsmiling Menzies classified himself as personable and intimate; in the mirror of his mind, he was wearing a smile.

"I'm sure that's true," Nikolai said warmly.

"Then wouldn't it be better for all parties concerned if we showed mutual trust?"

"Absolutely."

"May I rephrase the question?" Menzies said, mustering intimacy.

"I think we'd be better off moving on," Nikolai said pleasantly. "Tell me something about the woman, Toni Graf."

Menzies simmered, dignity trampled; but Boettinger, who was not one to follow the nuances of temperament, blithely volunteered, "She's out of it. That was in the report to your guy …?"

"McKennan."

"That's him."

"She's in war production these days," Menzies said "You can forget her."

"Pretty good cover for a German agent," Nikolai suggested lightly.

"It would be good cover if there was something there," Menzies said, "but there's not. With the exception of a single accidental meeting, the lady in question has had absolutely no contact with either Muller or Baumann for well over two years."

"Accidental meeting?"

"Right here in the Garden," Boettinger chirped. He pointed to Baumann and Muller. "The two of them were alone, same booth, when she came in."

"But what makes you think it was accidental?"

Menzies said, "Because Baumann doesn't get along with Graf. The moment he saw her, he tried to duck. I realize you don't know him, but we do, and he's not what you call a subtle man. His face tells you what's going on, and he was not happy to see her." He said this carefully, as though to a stubborn child.

"Muller's the one spotted her," Boettinger remembered. "He jumps up and brings her over, and Baumann's stuck. They talk for maybe five or ten minutes, fake-polite, you know, then she gets up and takes off."

"In a huff," Menzies said emphatically.

Nikolai shrugged an acceptance. Menzies looked satisfied.

"What's she like?" Nikolai asked.

"Skinny broad," Boettinger said. "No knockers."

Patiently, Nikolai said, "I mean, going back a few years, how political? Mad-dog-crazy Nazi, or just along for the ride?"

"I think I can help you on that," Menzies interjected. He paused and set about lighting a cigarette with some deliberation, but the operation went awry, matches sputtering out, and Menzies finally said, "Give me a fucking match."

For all his appreciation of the off-color, Menzies rarely cursed; though taken aback, Boettinger hastily handed over a matchbook.

Menzies recovered his poise with a sip of beer. "The thing is, she was a good, solid kraut, but not one of your crazies. When the war went bad, she got practical, like most of them."

"You don't think she's anything more than she appears to be?" Nikolai wondered.

In spite of himself, Menzies bristled again. It sounded like a trap. He was wondering if the SAU had information that he didn't have. He worked up a supercilious smile. "Are you suggesting she's the ringleader?"

"Not at all," said Nikolai quietly. "I was just wondering if Graf is lying low, waiting for a signal."

"Oh," Menzies said. It was so reasonable that he gushed out, "Well, yes, you've got a point, of course." The sounds that had burbled from his lips were now resonating in his brain. They did not satisfy him. A chill washed through him—he had lost the momentum. It rankled him, because he was FBI, the investigatory arm of federal jurisprudence. Yet this snot-nose from a fuck-all department was taking over.

He strained, silently reconstituting himself. "Look, Granger," he said, "the lady's been checked out left and right. She's out of the loop, period. End of story."

"Fair enough," said Nikolai. "Anybody else we should be looking at?"

Menzies shook his head decisively, but Boettinger, with a distant, carnal smile, said, "The one I'd like to be looking at is Baumann's daughter. That is one good-looking piece of ass."

Despite the bawdy nature of the remark, Menzies shared an impious smile with Boettinger—two against one.

That evening, the three men met in Scaletti's in Little Italy. Its reputation rested on purported killings in the twenties, but the food was good, and the restaurant was only rarely visited by mafia members these days. Its popularity had suffered during the halcyon days of the Axis, but Mussolini and the *fascisti* were long gone, along with the vague taboo on patronizing Italian restaurants.

Menzies had climbed up and down a stairway of moods since the afternoon and now paraded a mellow side. Its by-product was a spirit of cooperation. Self-consciously, he alluded to operational pressures that had made him edgy the past few weeks.

"My wife says I'm a bear lately," he said, with a flighty grin. "Imagine that! A sweetheart like me?"

Much wine had been consumed, and they laughed, even Nikolai. Menzies proposed a toast to teamwork, and Boettinger ushered in the new era by asking

Angie, their waitress, to bend over just a little more so he could check out "Mount Twin-Boobs."

Later, and in quieter tones, they discussed the "ring," such as it was. Menzies and Boettinger were smoking twisted stogies and drinking Italian brandy. Nikolai had stuck with the wine.

"Tell me about this Raymond Harris bank account," Nikolai said. "How was it opened?"

"Could have been a three-penny stamp, for all we know," Menzies said. "All it takes to open a bank account these days is an application form from the bank. You fill it out, send a check for deposit, and you're in business."

"Was it a certified check?"

Menzies nodded.

"Where was it drawn on?"

"Second National Bank, Dallas, Texas."

"You checked them out?" Nikolai said.

"Hell, we went down there," Boettinger told him. He began to cough; his cheroot had backed up in black smoke.

"Wasted trip," Menzies said. "Dallas was a weigh station."

"In other words, Dallas was only one among a number of banks?"

"Right. Harris sends a fee, along with instructions, from bank to bank. Each bank follows orders and issues a new certified check in the name of Raymond Harris to the next bank, and so on."

"Shit," Boettinger said, finally stubbing out the ratty remains of the cheroot. "Even if he made the first deposit in person, what would we have? You think this guy is going to walk into a bank wearing his regular face?"

"Bottom line is, we've got nothing until somebody goes into that account," Menzies said.

At the next table, two middle-aged couples were clinking glasses and shouting back and forth in Italian. They misinterpreted Menzies' rebuking eye and toasted the trio in another stream of Italian.

"Bunch of drunk dagos," Menzies side-mouthed.

"They're celebrating," Nikolai said. "They say the Fifth Army just took Florence."

"Oh? You speak it?" Menzies said.

"Me too!" Boettinger said. He waved to the next table and shouted over, "Hey paisano, spaghetti, macaroni!"

The couples waved back and retreated to noisy privacy.

Menzies brushed a few crumbs from the table, clearing the way for serious discussion. Discreetly, he said, "What about the Los Alamos end?"

"Not the slickest operation in the world."

"As we understand it, just the one operative, Dieter Krone?"

"That's as far as we got."

"What's your take on him?" Menzies asked.

"Low-level."

"No surprise there. The Germans are scraping the bottom of the barrel these days. But if there is more to him," Menzies said, with a trill suggesting the savior role of the FBI, "we'll certainly dig it out."

Absently, Boettinger said, "Can't see it. One guy covering a place like that."

"Nobody said he's all alone, Lyle," Menzies corrected. "Just that he's second-rate."

"On the other hand," Nikolai mused, "he *could* be working alone."

Menzies and Boettinger looked over in surprise. Bordering on snide, Menzies said, "In all honesty, Nikolai—" He paused abruptly. "Is that right? Nikolai?" he asked, with all the subtlety of an Ellis Island inspector.

"That's right," Nikolai assured him.

Menzies breezed right along, "The thing is, we're talking about Los Alamos. Does it make sense to you that the Germans would plant a single second-rate agent—your description—in the most important installation in the United States?"

"It might. Under certain circumstances."

Menzies and Boettinger again looked lost. Menzies said, "Explain."

"We've got three people possibly connected to an espionage ring—Dieter Krone in Los Alamos, Leo Muller, and a buddy named Heinz Baumann in New York. The common denominator seems to be a mysterious Raymond Harris, who also doubles as Hector Ruiz. Raymond Harris deposited fifty thousand dollars in an account here in New York. But nobody's touched the money. Is that right?"

"That's right," Menzies said.

"Why not?" Nikolai wondered.

Taken by surprise, Menzies paused. Then he said, "Simple. They're not ready to move."

"What do you think the money's for?"

Toying with a spoon, Menzies said, "That's pretty obvious, isn't it? They need people to support Krone in Los Alamos. People cost money, whether they slip them into the country or recruit a few locals."

"It'd have to be somebody better than the two guys they got," Boettinger said, plucking a bread stick from a container. "Leo Muller's a harebrain, and Heinz Baumann's your basic night-club bouncer."

"Of course not them," Menzies snapped. He was becoming irritable. He turned to Nikolai. "Why don't you tell us how one man alone makes sense?"

"Maybe Los Alamos isn't the target. Maybe Dieter Krone is nothing more than a decoy."

"That's a little bit on the wild side, isn't it, Nikolai?"

"Decoy for what?" Boettinger said. "What could be more important than a bomb to win the war?"

"I'm not sure yet," Nikolai said.

"And there's the matter of the fifty thousand," Menzies said, with scathing patience. "If it's not going for Los Alamos, what would it be for?"

"To confuse us. So we concentrate on a phantom named Raymond Harris."

"Are you saying there is no Raymond Harris?"

"Oh, there's somebody, all right—Raymond Harris, or whatever the name is—but I don't think he's ever going to show. And I don't think the fifty thousand will ever be touched."

"So," Menzies said elaborately, "Muller and Baumann are decoys, and Dieter Krone is a decoy, and the fifty grand is a decoy—to cover something more important than the bomb. But there is nothing more important than the bomb. So where does that leave your little theory, Nikolai?"

For the moment, Nikolai decided to let it go; in fact, he had little more faith in his theory than Menzies. He shrugged capitulation.

Menzies, racking up an empiric victory, smiled and said, "Case closed."

They parted outside Scaletti's just before midnight. Nikolai turned up his jacket collar against the crisp East River wind and headed uptown. Traffic was light at this hour. A pair of zoot-suiters crossed the street and ambled along in his wake, laughing too loud. Nikolai turned to face them, looking displeased. They stopped, as though reconsidering their plans; then one of them noticed a car hanging back about a block, so they abruptly peeled off and cut down an alley, their donkey-like braying echoing off the walls.

The car that had inadvertently assisted Nikolai slowly made its way up the street behind him, then turned off. It got colder, but Nikolai kept plugging along, cutting west here and there, until the traffic thickened and Grand Central Station loomed up, and then the Commodore. He crossed the lobby and took the elevator to the fourteenth floor.

Here, things took an unexpected turn. When he flicked on the lights in his room, Maureen's squint-eyed face rolled out from under the covers. She put a hand up to block out the light and said, "Nikolai."

Her valise was open on a stand. Clothes were strewn around the bed, and her shoes, for some odd reason, were separated by the length of the room.

Nikolai sat alongside her. She took his hand and smiled. "Hi," she said, her voice sultry with sleep.

"Maureen," he said.

"What?" she asked, her voice sounding all sweetness and innocence.

"Maureen, what are you doing here?"

She flopped her head a little, looking around. She yawned, coming to life, then patted the pillow, propped it up, and raised her head. "Lord, what time is it?"

"After one o'clock. How did you get in?"

"Oh, well, I told them I was your wife, and they let me in."

"Weren't you on your way to Newport?"

"I think I was. Yes."

"How did you know I was here?"

"How? Well, let me see. Oh, I followed you when we left the train. Do you have a cigarette?"

"Why did you follow me?" He brought out his Lucky Strikes in the white package (the green package was now at war).

"To tell you the truth, Nikolai, I really don't know. Yes, I do. I followed you because I know you care for me. You know what? I'm really up now. Do you think the bar's still open?"

She stubbed out the cigarette and jumped out of bed. In a flash, she was half-dressed and signaling for her shoes. She ran a brush through copper-tinged hair and dabbed on some lipstick. Within moments, they were sipping martinis and listening to a pianist doing Rodgers and Hart. He played mostly with one hand; the other was in a cast and occasionally came down too hard.

They were on their second martini before either spoke. Then Maureen said, "Are you mad at me?"

He shook his head.

"For a love affair that had everything, we sure screwed things up, didn't we?" she said.

"You're not the one who went to prison," he said.

"No, I'm the one who deserted you."

"You did the right thing—you got out while the getting was good."

Nikolai ordered more drinks, and they sipped in silence, drifting pleasurably.

"What are you thinking?" she asked.

"About love. People in love. They're not just in love. They're made for each other."

"Well, what's wrong with that?"

"Because it doesn't make sense. If they're so made for each other, why is there always somebody else?

"Is this about us or everybody?"

"Everybody."

"Good. Because when you get moody, I get nervous."

"You're not the nervous type. You're a mating queen. There would be no human race without mating queens. Mating queens keep the world going."

She shook her head in wonderment. "I've never heard you talk so much. It's wonderful. What are you looking at?"

His distraction came from the Jungle Nook, a dark-shadowed bar adjoining the lounge. Nikolai rose. "Be right back."

He crossed the room and took a left past a long, loose-woven bamboo divider. He paused, then made his way to a small table and sat down opposite a man with a thin mustache. The man, in his early thirties, was drinking a beer. He contained his surprise by continuing to drink while he stared at the new arrival, but he was not smooth about it, and a rivulet of beer found a crease in his face and reached his chin.

"Excuse me," said Nikolai. "Are you Hickey?"

Hickey lips parted. "I know you?" he asked.

"You must know me," Nikolai said. "You're following me."

"Now wait a minute—"

"One thing I'd like to know—and I ask this because you look like you're healthy as a horse—are you guys automatically deferred? Or does Edgar have to write a note to the draft board?"

"Hold it right there," said Hickey. His embarrassment at being caught red-handed had shifted to indignation. "Let's get something straight. I don't have to take this kind of crap."

"What's your first name?"

"What?"

"I was wondering what your first name was," Nikolai said, amiably enough.

Hickey hesitated. Guardedly, he said, "Elmore. That do it for you?"

"Elmore, we're in the kind of business where we just follow orders. I do what I have to do, and you do what you have to do. When I saw you in here, I said to myself, I've seen that man before. His name is Hickey. Maybe we'd better have a talk. And here I am. And here's my message. Finish your beer and take off. And if you want to tell Wilbur what happened, you can also tell him to mind his own fucking business."

Hickey hissed, "Where do you come off—?"

"But I don't think you'll tell him, because if you do that, you're going to look pretty stupid. Finish your beer, Elmore."

Hickey had never been angrier in his life, and the elixir of outrage triumphed over reason. "You son of a bitch! I happen to have a gun right here!"

"Think you could get it out that fast, Wyatt?" Nikolai said. His eyes did not move, but Hickey slowly got the message. Nikolai's stiff arms were below the table.

Hickey's eyes widened. "Are you nuts?"

Nikolai inched his hands into view. They were empty, and that made Hickey even more furious. He slammed down his beer and stormed out.

For a moment, it was funny—movie histrionics, nothing at stake but pride. Then Nikolai turned to look through the slatted bamboo wall at Maureen, a world away in the more elegant lounge. Occasionally, she turned to look toward him, looking right at him but unable to discern him, a metaphor for everything they were.

The smile was long gone. His indifference to danger had nothing to do with bravery and everything to do with a contempt for anything less than the visceral satisfaction of vengeance. But that was unachievable, so the hell with everything else.

It was all neat and simple, plodding along toward whatever. But all at once he realized that he had crossed some sort of Rubicon, the factor that was Maureen.

You care for me, she had said. And before that, he had said things like *You still look good,* and she had said, *I want to see you again,* and back and forth they had tossed little love kisses plucked from a three-million-year-old bag of mating-game clichés.

But now there was a new factor—*I know you care for me*—and with it, everything had shifted in a flash. At that moment, the joke of love had become love. Their dewy-eyed lark had somehow, through a bewildering and utterly mysterious process, become real. The burden of it jarred him. Often, he had thought about the danger to her that he represented, but it had never taken hold, because they were whimsical and detached, never so serious that they could not retreat.

But the fact was that he dealt with death. His stock in trade was murder. Where did love fit in?

He told Maureen that something urgent had come up. He would contact her as soon as possible. In her eyes, he could read her fear—justified—that he had no intention of seeing her again.

CHAPTER 20

▼

Nikolai called the apartment the minute he arrived at Union Station. It rang twice, and then a flat voice said, "Nine two nine seven."

"Cooley?" Nikolai said, in surprised recognition.

"State your purpose," said the impatient voice.

"Jesus Christ, Cooley, it's Granger. What the hell are you doing on my home line?"

"Your roomie's in the hospital with pneumonia," Cooley said.

Dancer had a private room with a single window looking north. The window was grimy, the day was leaden, and the light inside the room was faded and gloomy. His pasty skin did not brighten the ambience. He was propped up, wearing screaming red-striped pajamas. His eyes were closed, but his right leg, poked out of the covers and dangling, occasionally swung in a desultory manner. Another partially obscured object now came into view: a tumbler, apparently filled with orange juice. Dancer took a healthy slurp, smacked his lips, and opened his eyes.

"You going to live?"

"Sons of bitches. They're keeping me a week. Do I look sick?"

"Most of the time."

Dancer accepted this with another hearty swallow, and when Nikolai smiled, Dancer said, "Just a little gin for flavoring."

"You're fucking crazy, you know that?"

"What happened in New York?"

"Interesting question." Nikolai told him about Raymond Harris and the bank account.

"How was the FBI?"

"You know this guy Menzies?"

"Tight underwear," Dancer said. They laughed, Dancer with a wheeze that smoothed out with more juice.

A huge nurse entered, wearing a white uniform that looked like a moving tent. She was holding an army-style tray with compartmentalized blobs of food, the color and texture of pigeon droppings. "Lunch," she announced in her Betty Boop voice. "Eat everything. We need our strength."

She left, and they stared at the blobs. "No wonder I look like shit," Dancer said. He pondered the tray. "Have you ever been to the Old Mill?"

"Out on the Blue Hills Parkway? No."

"It's a nice place. We should go there for lunch."

"Soon as you're okay."

"I'm okay right now," Dancer said. He swung out of bed, surprisingly lithe, a display of wellness. "Be dressed in a minute." Exiting a side entrance of the hospital, Dancer tap-danced down the walk toward a waiting cab.

"You know how to keep a low profile," Nikolai said.

"The Old Mill," Dancer instructed the driver.

The cab bounced its way across the Potomac and out to the countryside. Thirty-five minutes later, they were seated alongside a bottle-glass window in the Old Mill, a woodsy tavern that reminded Nikolai of the Falmouth Inn, albeit with a view of the Blue Ridge Mountains instead of Cape Cod. A frequent guest these days, Dancer was promptly shown to a table in a rough-stone niche near a small, sputtering fireplace. Here, they could look out a window to a winter-stripped thicket of woods bisected by a small stream.

The Old Mill was a known Guthrie haunt and therefore considered out of bounds to SAU personnel. Playfully, Nikolai said, "You're feeling pretty immortal, aren't you?"

Dancer smirked back. "So are you."

The drinks came, and Nikolai toasted Guthrie. "Fuck him." When the great man failed to appear, they toasted him again.

It was a spectacularly beautiful fall day, the sun settling down to the mountains, the mountains changing colors in the haze. They ordered lunch around four o'clock, and what with having to call a cab and drive back into the city teeming with commuter traffic, it was dark by the time Dancer returned to his hospital room and peeled down to his pajamas.

The big nurse waddled in, and her eyes flew open. "You haven't touched your tray!"

"Not hungry," Dancer said.

Meanwhile, Nikolai had finally arrived at the office. Here, the situation took a different turn: McKennan thought he had been waiting all afternoon and apologized.

The debriefing took two hours. They discussed the Los Alamos-New York puzzle thoroughly. Once again, Nikolai argued his theory that the fifty thousand dollars tucked away in the bank was an elaborate feint. McKennan allowed that the idea had some merit, but he wanted to talk it over with Mr. Guthrie.

He filled his pipe, then poked it, tapped it, and lit it. "That business could erupt at any time. I want you close."

Only a few days later, McKennan called in Nikolai with news out of New York. Heinz Baumann had disappeared. So had his daughter, Anna. McKennan chewed harder on the pipe. It seemed that Wilbur Menzies had decided to push the situation along. His plan was to grab Baumann and hold him for questioning—a frightened Baumann might spill the works. If he knew anything. If there was anything to spill.

"Unfortunately for Mr. Menzies," McKennan said, highlander acid dripping from his mouth, "Baumann somehow got onto the scheme, and out of town he went before they could ask him about so much as the weather."

"Well, that's that," said Nikolai. "If there was something going out of New York, we'll never know."

"The man's an idiot and a vainglorious shit," said McKennan.

Nikolai was temporarily attached to the library, sorting through and updating enemies files. When Dancer was out of the hospital and fully recovered, the two men would be assigned back to field duty. At Nikolai's grimace, the already testy McKennan said, "There's a war on, you know."

*   *   *   *

For weeks now, Heinz had noticed the same dark-blue Chevy in front of his apartment building when he left for his shop in the morning. It stayed there all day and left early in the evening. "FBI," Heinz calmly informed Leo.

An eager ally, Leo spotted the man emerging from the Chevy one morning—gray suit, gray fedora—and watched him trail Heinz to his shop. After that, Heinz himself kept an eye on the FBI man, who, during the day, sauntered around the area, or sipped a Coke across the street, or bought a cigar at the corner store and smoked it, wandering up and down the block.

"What do you think, Heinz?" asked the anxious Leo.

"Playing games," Heinz said.

One Saturday morning at six o'clock, Leo, who was working nights, came up the back way and knocked on the kitchen door. Heinz opened it, still in his underwear but wide awake.

Leo, immersed in plot and bubbling with excitement, spewed out his news. He had decided to come by early, and guess what? The FBI Chevy was there already! "Been there all night, it looks like!" he told Heinz.

Heinz raised his hand like a traffic cop, slowing the torrent. "I know," he told Leo. He crooked a finger, and Leo followed him into the bedroom. Heinz pointed, and Leo peered down past raindrops dotting the windowpanes. There was a truck below.

"Gas man," Leo observed.

"Ain't no gas man," Heinz said.

"What do you think, Heinz?"

"Game's over," Heinz told him. "Time to move."

With Leo's help, he packed a bag for himself and one for Anna. Then Leo, wearing Heinz's coat and hat, hurried out the front entrance and down the street. Forman followed in the blue Chevy, while the agent playing gas man followed on foot. Meanwhile, Heinz rushed out the back way, a suitcase in each hand.

Anna was clearing a table in the deli when a boy approached her, holding a note. She read it and hurried out of the restaurant and around the corner, where Heinz was waiting.

"What's wrong? What is it, Papa?"

"You said you'd come with me. You still coming?"

"I don't understand. What's happening?"

"Government's after me from the old days," he said, grimly. "I'm on a list. Throwing people in jail left and right. Got to get out." Bitterly, he added, "When you try to do what's good, they don't let you."

He took a breath, a bittersweet sifting of better times. He put a fleeting hand to her cheek. "Listen, *Liebchen*, what am I doing? Why should you go? You ain't done nothing. Nothing to nobody your whole life but to be good. It's crazy you should come."

He went so far as to clasp her to him hurriedly, his churning emotion concealed in the embrace. Breathlessly, still holding her, he caught the chest-heaving rhythm of her indecision, until at last, she whispered, "I'm coming with you, Papa."

They caught the twelve o'clock train to Washington, and within fifteen minutes of its arrival, they boarded the *Dixie Flyer* to Atlanta. From there, they would take a train to Houston, another down the coast to the border, and then a bus into Mexico.

"But why do we have to leave the country?" Anna wondered. Despite the somber circumstances, a Cagney movie kept flashing into her mind, and she couldn't stop saying to herself, *We're on the lam.*

Heinz, with remarkable forbearance, replied, "Because there ain't much we can do if we stay, except hide in the woods like trapped rats. But if we get into Mexico, we can start over, and then we come right back, maybe in a week."

"Are you saying … get new identities?" She was a little shocked.

Heinz reassuringly patted her hand. "It ain't like you get your face done over with an operation. This is just new papers, which is easy to get in Mexico."

"But where would you get the money for something like that?"

"Saved up," he told her. "Got the money."

"But using false papers … isn't that a serious crime?"

"All they do if you get caught is they send you back to Mexico," he chirped. Seeing her expression of doubt, he added roguishly, "Looked it up."

"You did not," she said, grinning.

*   *   *   *

The train clacked down across the South. Broken-down shacks and cotton fields began to dot the landscape. Negroes began to pop up, on the farms, in the shanty towns adjacent to the tracks, and on the platforms of the stations they roared through. Heinz pinched his nose, then covered the gesture when Anna looked over. But he could not hide his feelings when the train stopped near a military camp and a couple of hundred negro soldiers stormed the train.

"Looks like Harlem around here," he said, his smirk meant to pass as humor.

Two high-spirited soldiers slammed down their duffel bags and slid into a seat across from Heinz and Anna. The soldiers paid no attention to their neighbors, cackling wildly at some joke or other. Heinz suddenly noticed that Anna's blouse was open, showing a sliver of white flesh, and he hissed, "Button!"

She closed the gap and whispered, "They're not even looking over here."

"They got eyes all over the place, the *Schwarzen*," he said. There was no trace of humor.

"I guess you know a lot of Mexicans are pretty dark," she said.

"Different dark," he said.

"Maybe I'll marry a Mexican," she said.

"I know what you're doing," he said, resurrecting his good nature. "Trying to get me all rileyed up." He noticed the two soldiers watching them and said, "Mind your own business."

The two soldiers were very young. They broke into giggles.

Anna leaned over and whispered, "You didn't have to be rude."

"Rude is the eyeballs falling out, which means there ain't no brains."

Anna studied him for a moment. "Papa, I think you're trying to change, but I guess it doesn't come easy."

"That's it. Don't come easy," Heinz said.

They were stiff and grimy when the train pulled into Atlanta. The soldiers had noisily departed just before dawn, clambering off the train and into a waiting procession of six-by-sixes, their lights cutting into patches of fog, here and there thinning out to the black of night.

Heinz and Anna sleepily entered the terminal, bags in hand. It was six-thirty in the morning but surprisingly busy for the hour. Heinz scoured the area, avoiding police uniforms, even steering clear of the ubiquitous MPs. They bought coffee and doughnuts, and wax-paper-wrapped sandwiches for the next leg of the trip, to Houston. It was a half-hour before departure, but a crowd was already pressed against the gate. When the gates opened, the mob surged forward wildly. Anna, her bag flapping at her side, was twice shoved outside the funnel of flesh, and twice, Heinz fought his way to her side, cursing everyone in his path.

They found two seats, but far apart. The aisles were thronged, and several babies had been placed in overhead luggage racks. Anna, with an inside seat, curled up and closed her eyes. Heinz was on the aisle, afflicted by swinging elbows and off-balance feet from a forest of limbs.

When the train reached Mobile, the cars half-emptied; Heinz and Anna found a seat together but spoke little. It was dark again, and again they drifted in and out of sleep, sometimes awakened by a rough roadbed or the train's piercing whistle, and sometimes by the pure monotony of the clacking track.

In the morning, they were in Houston, and by that afternoon, they arrived in Brownsville. They crossed into Mexico in a scarred bus that threatened to turn over as it jolted along on springless springs.

It had taken three incredibly exhausting days. Anna looked around the exotic slum that was Matamoros and cared only for a bed, even in one of the grimy hotels that looked like postcard bordellos. While she waited, Heinz was inside an office marked TELÉFONOS. It was hot, and the air was thick with dust. Not a single thing about Mexico appealed to her.

Heinz appeared at last, weariness shucked aside, a resilient bounce in his steps. "Okay, we get a hotel," he said.

To her surprise, he headed for a taxi stand. He piled into the back seat and said, "Come on."

While Anna was climbing in, Heinz handed the driver a note with an address. The taxi took off, and for the next hour, it chugged over and around rolling hills. At last, they pulled up before Rancho Internationale, an intimate, hacienda-style villa.

There were gardens with crushed-stone paths, a grove of orange and lemon trees, and a handsome Spanish-style lobby with a gleaming tile floor. Beyond the lobby were a terrace and a large swimming pool. The tiled floor radiated an intense cobalt blue.

It was the most beautiful place Anna had ever seen. She had her own room, handsomely decorated in Andalusian style. She swam every day, while Heinz watched from the terrace, more often than not sipping beer and chatting with the proprietor, a man named Johann Lindemann. Heinz said nothing, but Anna suspected Lindemann was helping with the papers.

A perfect week went by, but the moment came when Heinz announced that the papers had arrived; they were returning to the United States.

Anna stared into the distance with melancholy eyes, looking at the fruit trees and the patchwork green scrub hills beyond. "Oh, Papa, do we have to?"

"The money, it's almost gone, *Schatzi*." When Anna nodded disconsolately, Heinz said, "Tell you what—after we work and save up, we come back for a whole month. Maybe we even bring somebody along, like a new boyfriend!"

It was touchingly paternal, but even more than that, Anna realized. It was the first time Heinz had ever acknowledged the fact that she was a young woman. Again, she marveled at his transformation. If it did not quite dispel the cloud that was his erratic behavior, she had no great desire to examine it too closely.

*   *   *   *

Weeks went by, and Nikolai was still upgrading files in the library. Meanwhile, Dancer was out of the hospital, recuperating at home. His temperature was down but stubbornly remained above normal. The diagnosis was a mild liver infection. The doctors had agreed to discharge him on condition that he take it easy. Alcohol was strictly forbidden, but Dancer adjusted this edict by drinking steadily while, for the most part, staying sober.

It was a savage day in December. A fierce wind whipped snow and sleet through the canyons of Washington. In a small French restaurant just off Dupont Circle, Dancer was holding an oversized martini up to the light, looking like a mad scientist. Nikolai came in from the street, stomping off snow.

He settled at the table. Dancer took a sip and said, "This may be it." He was in a Holy Grail phase: the search for the perfect martini.

There was a martini waiting for Nikolai, and he tasted it. "It's good," he said solemnly. Dancer smiled with pride.

The storm picked up, its ferocity enhancing the coziness of the room, with its fireplace of crackling logs and the beige warmth of its Normandy landscape.

The second round arrived. They toasted Guthrie. "Fuck him," Nikolai said.

"Fuck him," said Dancer.

A telephone rang somewhere near the bar. They exchanged glances. It rang again, so harsh and grating that it chilled the air.

"*Merde*," Dancer said.

Sure enough, the waiter bustled toward them, a short man with the doomsday face of an El Greco. The call was for Nikolai. It was urgent.

Twenty minutes later, he was in McKennan's office.

"We have heard from New York," McKennan began. "You remember Mr. Baumann, of course, the man who disappeared. Apparently, our FBI brethren have located him."

"Where is he?"

McKennan did not answer, busy tapping the residue of his dead pipe into a wastebasket. Then he said, "They have come up with an interesting idea. Mr. Guthrie believes it has promise. So do I. But it will call for a wee bit of stagecraft, lad."

"We put on Macbeth for the FBI Christmas party?"

"Don't toy with me," McKennan whispered angrily.

"Sorry, Mac," said Nikolai. "I always get frisky around the holidays."

"Don't get frisky in here," McKennan warned, but with less bite. "The idea is to get close to this man Baumann. I want you to get up to New York as soon as possible."

"Baumann's back in New York?"

"No, he is not. You will contact Wilbur Menzies for further instructions."

"Further instructions?"

"That is correct."

Nikolai said, "Mr. Wilbur Menzies works for the FBI."

"I am aware of his affiliation."

"Are you saying I'm going to be working for the FBI?"

"Temporarily," said McKennan. "On detached duty, so to speak."

"Bullshit, so to speak," Nikolai said.

"I am not looking for a hard time here, Granger."

"No, you're looking for somebody you can dump on."

"I don't like that," McKennan said. He was no longer amused.

"Look, I'm only trying to point out that you yourself described Wilbur as a vainglorious idiot. And you want me to take orders from him?"

"You know the situation," said McKennan. "We are not in a primary position on this case."

"Then why are we on the case at all? Why don't we just pull out?"

"Because we cannot," McKennan snapped.

"Come on, Mac. What you mean is, Guthrie's got his nose up the FBI's ass these days. That's what he won't pull out."

"Damn your impudence!" McKennan said. "You have an obligation here!"

"Well, now, you just tell me what that obligation is. An obligation to what? It isn't patriotism, it isn't honor, it isn't loyalty, it isn't duty, and it isn't responsibility, because, as Mr. Guthrie has noted, this isn't my country, and I don't have a scrap of legitimacy. So where's the obligation, Mac?"

"Easy does it," McKennan said, in mild turn-around.

"Easy does it? What's that mean? You don't like your slaves grumpy?"

"All right, all right. You've got a point, and I've got a job to do. I'm asking you to do your job."

"Which includes the fucking threat of being sent back to prison!"

"Have you ever heard that from me?" McKennan said.

"Does that make it different?" Both leaned in, teeth bared. McKennan inched back and let the moment coast while he stuffed his pipe. Nikolai sat down and lit a cigarette.

"Kindly hear me out before you detonate again," McKennan said, lighting his pipe and sending up a blue cloud of smoke. "As it happens, Mr. Guthrie has every intention of honoring his promise."

"He told you that?"

"He mentioned it in connection with the New York case."

"He mentioned it, Mac? Mr. Guthrie, the humanitarian, brought the subject up all by himself?"

"Let us just say that the subject was discussed," McKennan said, with a skittish let's-move-on gesture.

"You brought it up. For which I thank you, Mac. But how much credence can be put on a pledge from Simon Guthrie?"

"The pledge is from me," McKennan said. "It's my word you can take in this matter. As for Mr. Guthrie, I know what he is and what he isn't, and there's more to what he is than meets the eye."

"Perhaps if I knew him better," Nikolai said, with a touch of treacle.

"Your problem, Mr. Granger, is that you are a smartass. And that goes for your erstwhile partner too."

"That reminds me, Mac. Since you're in a pleasant mood, how about bringing Dancer back in on this, semi-active? He wouldn't have to do a damn thing but go over field reports, maybe sit in on strategy with you."

"I'm sorry."

"Why not?"

"First, Mr. Guthrie wants this project restricted to three people in the organization—himself, myself, and yourself. Secondly, Rhodes is a sick man."

"He's not that sick, and he's on the mend. And you know how good he is. Why not use him?"

"Because the man simply drinks too much."

"He's bored, Mac," Nikolai said fervently. "He's got nothing else to do but go up against the doctors."

"He's a rummy. And you know it, lad. Is he in control of himself? I have no way of knowing, and that means I have no way of gauging his reliability. Nor, indeed, his further value to the organization."

Nikolai's instinct was to flail out, but he knew it was useless. A moment passed. "Listen, Mac, he can't be tossed out like some rag doll."

His burr soft, McKennan said, "He'll not be thrown aside."

Nikolai nodded, placated. Then he said, "How about a little help? Where does Mr. Guthrie's informant fit in?"

"He doesn't. Not for now."

"How come?"

"Because he's otherwise occupied," McKennan said peevishly, reduced to confidences he did not want to share.

"Okay. Could one ask where Heinz Baumann is these days?"

McKennan told him. Then he glanced at his watch and said, "May I suggest you get on with it? The next train for New York leaves in one hour."

✳   ✳   ✳   ✳

Nikolai again checked into the Commodore. A message was waiting. For this particular rendezvous, Menzies had selected Toots Shor's. It was now clear that good restaurants were his favorite method of establishing dominion. At their first meeting, of course, his jockeying for power had come to nothing, but this was different. This time, he was in charge.

Lending a properly clandestine air to the occasion, Menzies had arranged a table in the exclusive POT Room, which stood for "Pals of Toots."

"Sit down, sit down," he said genially when Nikolai was escorted to his table. Lyle Boettinger was there, and he threw a small sardonic salute over to Nikolai; it contained none of Menzies' veiled condescension, but was more of an amiable *Welcome to the "Everybody Gets Fucked Over Sooner or Later Club"* salute.

Toots Shor himself happened to be in the room, headed their way. "Like you to meet a friend, Toots," Menzies said.

In the best tradition of the business, he did not offer a name, and Shor, portly, slit-eyed, baggy-cheeked, said out of the side of his mouth, "Jeez, another god-damn G-man to feed?"

It was good for a private laugh. Nikolai managed a strained smile.

Alone now, Menzies said, "How about a drink?" The genial host did not wait for an answer and signaled a waiter.

The drink came, and Menzies said, "Here's to the new member of our team."

They drank, and Menzies said, "I have to hand it to you. You said the bank account was a decoy, and it looks like you were right on the button. How about a steak? Old Toots runs the place like vaudeville, but the food's for real."

They had steak. Menzies chatted on, the latest joke about Hoover, but not too risqué: Hoover bought an American flag to hang out in front of his house, and the flag saluted.

"Well, boys," Nikolai said when they were on their coffee, "what's the next move?"

Menzies looked ruffled. It was the intimacy of the word "boys" that bothered him. He suspected that Nikolai had tossed it out for effect. Social parity was no longer appropriate, and irregularities made him bristle. But he restrained himself. It was possible that Nikolai was still adjusting to the new order of things.

"The next move, as you call it," said Menzies, even generating a twinkle, "is to go over procedure, including details of your cover package and secure contact numbers here in New York, as well as field arrangements, such as housing and employment briefings."

He slid a manila envelope across the table. "This is a layout of the complex. It is strictly confidential. Understood?"

"Perfectly."

Menzies slid across another envelope. "These are photographs. The subject and his daughter."

Nikolai glanced at the photographs as though they were a poker hand, started to shove them back, then stared at the photo of Anna Baumann. Menzies began drumming his fingers, so Nikolai slid back the photo in the envelope.

Menzies launched a ten-minute instructional speech on Nikolai's duties, FBI parameters on handling himself in public, how to maintain a low profile, and, most importantly, how to ingratiate himself with Baumann. "Any questions?"

"No questions," Nikolai said, with just a bit too much of a courtroom chant.

Menzies rocked a little. He narrowed his nostrils, as though sniffing impropriety. "I wonder if you have a full grasp of the stakes here. We're trying to build this bomb before the Germans, and some people think they're ahead of us. This situation must be taken seriously. Understood?"

"Understood, chief."

Menzies was not pleased. He tapped a finger on the table, face locked in a frown. "Let's get something straight. The nature of our relationship demands a certain adherence to protocol. Do I make myself clear?"

"Absolutely," Nikolai said, this time sounding too dutiful.

"Look, Granger," Menzies said, "I dislike pulling rank, so to speak, but the effectiveness of an operation lies in maintaining a proper chain of command. Am I getting through?"

"Loud and clear, Wilbur," said Nikolai amiably.

"Now you listen to me, you son of a bitch," Menzies said, with the sibilance of an old radiator. "I know when I'm being jerked off, so let's get it out on the table. You don't address me on a first-name basis from now on."

Nikolai seemed taken aback. "Well, how would you like to be addressed?"

"With the dignity that goes with a leadership position. And that means a certain respect for rank. In other words, organizational discipline."

"I can understand that," Nikolai said cooperatively. "How would you like 'Special Agent Menzies'? No. Too much on the nose. Could be picked up in public."

"This is getting to be a ridiculous conversation," Menzies said.

"I know what you mean. I'm just trying to help. What if I called you 'Mr. Menzies'? No, that doesn't give you proper rank or title. Wait a minute—what does Lyle call you?"

"'Lyle' is an FBI agent. He's a colleague," Menzies said.

"Now I see. I'm not FBI, so I'm not really a colleague."

Menzies, way over his head, blurted, "Let's just forget it."

"I think you're entitled to something," Nikolai said. "What if I just called you 'sir'?"

"Are you working me over?" Menzies fumed.

"Absolutely," Nikolai said.

"This is a bullshit arrangement," Menzies hissed. "How would you like me to get in touch with McKennan?"

"Be my guest."

"How would you like me to fucking bring you up on report?!"

"Bring away, Wilbur. It's your ass on the line."

"Where do you get the gall—! The gall—! The gall—!" Menzies, caught up in an apoplectic fit, could not change the record.

"Look, Wilbur, I wouldn't mind taking orders from somebody I trust, but you just don't inspire trust. You're too busy chalking up points. So if we work together, it's got to be straight. No ass-kissing and no two-bit tyranny. How does that sound?"

Menzies rose half out of his chair and settled back down, then did it again, each time remembering that exiting Toots Shor's under the circumstances would constitute retreat.

Frustration in the form of a strange keening tore from his throat. At last it died. His breathing slowed, and he settled down. The savage gleam in his eye remained, however. "All right, you want to play games, we'll play games. I know a lot about you, Mr. Granger."

"Don't be bashful, Wilbur."

"You're nothing but a goddamn jailbird."

He waited, hawk-like, to pounce on a denial, but Nikolai said, "That's true. But working hand-in-glove with a convict says as much about the FBI as the convict—don't you think?"

Menzies dropped into stony silence.

"Here's the way I see it," said Nikolai. "We're partners. We're unlikely partners, but we're partners. Unless you want to terminate the operation right here and now, which wouldn't bother me any more than the gravy on your tie."

Appalled, Menzies looked down, almost cross-eyed, at the offensive gravy stain. Feverishly, he wet his napkin and rubbed the tie, then he made one last stab at command. "I'm sure you appreciate what's at stake here—a race against time. We must put aside petty feuds and personal feelings. I expect every cooperation and every effort. Do we understand each other?"

"Perfectly," Nikolai said, with a smile.

Back in his hotel room, Nikolai took out the photograph of Anna Baumann. He studied it in morbid attraction, so much did she remind him of Katya. Katya, too long un-grieved, covered in a blanket of time.

He stretched out on the bed and fell asleep, still remembering Katya, watching images of Katya and Anna Baumann stir in a ghostly soup.

He woke up with dawn breaking over the East River. His thoughts were no longer dreamy or abstract. By the end of the day, he would begin a new life in a place called Oak Ridge, Tennessee.

END PART TWO

PART III

▼

THE NEW WORLD

CHAPTER 21

▼

In the sprawling frontier town that was Oak Ridge, looming with massive New World structures, security was a way of life. Traffic entering the mammoth installation had to funnel through one of four main gates, where identification was carefully checked and vehicles were searched. The high and the low were equally subjected to evaluation and examination.

Admission to the general complex was the beginning of the process. Specialized areas, surrounded by barbed-wire fences and more entrance gates, still had to be negotiated, and these required different colored badges, depending on the degree of security required. Within these industrial villages, gigantic factories belched smoke night and day. Some of these complexes dwarfed the imagination; K-25, for example, with its horseshoe bend, was one mile long.

Of the tens of thousands of workers in Oak Ridge, only a handful knew that its end product was fissionable uranium.

Operating three shifts, twenty-four hours a day, seven days a week, hordes of young women labored at the huge Alpha and Beta electromagnetic plants, studied gauges, calibrated dials, and filled huge notebooks with figures that had absolutely no meaning to them. Legions of military and private security personnel manned hundreds of posts and roamed thousands of acres without the slightest idea of what they were guarding and patrolling. An armada of bulldozers and graders churned across the Tennessee landscape, uprooting trees and smoothing the land for the ever-expanding, seemingly purposeless project.

In fact, Oak Ridge, for all its immensity, was only part of an audacious undertaking known as the Manhattan Project: fissionable uranium was the magic potion that would be stirred into the manufacture of the world's first atomic bomb.

Heinz, whose birth certificate and Social Security card now read "Herbert Brenner," knew nothing more about Oak Ridge than his co-workers, but when he walked into the employment office of Skidmore, Owing, and Merrill in downtown Oak Ridge and announced that he was a carpenter, heads turned. They read his letters of recommendation as though they were biblical revelations, and he was signed up immediately. Since he would be working in non-secure areas, a detailed investigation of his credentials could wait.

In fact, Heinz had been a carpenter before he became an electrician, and as he explained to Anna, it would be better not to return to the electrical trade just yet. Now he was one of an army of construction workers who were putting up new buildings in every direction. Because he was not cleared for the restricted areas (K-25, Y-12, and X-10, for example), he was assigned to general construction and became involved in the erection of a warehouse building near Jackson Square.

Nobody seemed to know anything, but everybody guessed at the secret product under development, the manufacture of poison gas being one of the more popular theories. Another popular speculation was the development of a Buck Rogers-like death ray. The mystery was tantalizing but rarely pursued; security officers tended to visit people who guessed too much.

The irony of the situation did not evade Heinz. He was a spy for the German cause, and he had cleverly wormed his way into a super-secret American project, but he was just as ignorant of its purpose as everyone else. Siebert had said that he was not a cog, that he was one of the special few who could help to bring victory. It was a pleasing accolade (and one that he suspected should not be taken at face value), but it drove him without pause or question.

Soon enough, he had regained his old skills, discovering in the process the gratifying contact of hammer to wood and the innate satisfaction of working outdoors in raw weather. The days and weeks slid by, but his blind faith never wavered; in good time, he would be told the significance of Oak Ridge and the manner in which he would be called upon to help destroy it.

Still, there were times when he was troubled. What if the *Abwehr*'s plans came to nothing? What if Siebert should one day simply disappear, leaving Heinz, the faithful drone, still carrying lumber and banging nails up to the day Germany surrendered?

On that score, he no longer had illusions. The Russians were in Vienna. The Americans were at the borders. Disaster was in the air, but it brought a curious catharsis, a rapture that reminded him of Wagner's *Götterdämmerung*, music he had heard only once but would understand forever.

In this sense, the throbbing, humming, hammering world around him seemed quite perfect. A timeless moment of expectation stretched ahead, and for the first time he could remember, his patience was inexhaustible. Here, in the mysterious cauldron of Oak Ridge, he would wait for the secret to be unraveled—and then he would surprise the secret.

Anna too had found employment quickly. There were hundreds of openings, and she thought briefly about working in one of the Alpha or Beta plants, but the idea of spending forty-eight hours a week tracking the nervous movements of a bunch of needles did not appeal to her. She considered cafeteria and food services, thought about secretarial, and ended up taking a job as a receptionist at one of the medical facilities scattered around the complex.

Anna found Oak Ridge exciting. It was the opposite of New York, having neither the stimulation of a big city nor the constant need to adjust to different levels of sophistication. But in its vibrancy of change, its endless upheaval, and its sense of organized chaos, it offered an electric-shock therapy for daily life.

People were friendly. Everybody was in the same boat: beginners, pioneers. And the fact that Oak Ridge was a clandestine government project only added spice to their existence.

It was a brand-new life in a brand-new world, and for the most part, it was promising. The one snag was Heinz. A change had come over him since their arrival in Oak Ridge. Almost from the moment they had settled in their little apartment, Heinz had begun to discard, in bits and pieces, the trappings of his new persona, the bumbling penitent slowly giving way to the flinty callousness of the old Heinz.

He was stern all over again, suspicious of her movements, questioning of her friends, and dismissive of her needs. It was almost like the old days, except that she was tougher now and barely listened to his caustic remarks.

It was all very strange to Anna. Along with this Jekyll-and-Hyde reversion of character, he had developed a curiously sanguine attitude. Anna could not quite put her finger on it—perhaps it was nothing more than a click of the wheels-within-wheels puzzle of his personality—but she had expected him to be much more tense and uneasy about their situation. They were on the run, but Heinz seemed to take it all in comfortable stride—as though, Anna sometimes thought, he was waiting for something.

Their shifts overlapped; he worked from seven to five, and her day started at noon. The narrowed margin of time they spent together served as something of a buffer. To narrow it even further, Anna tended to introduce a frazzled note to her arrival: long, hard day, difficult people, much reading to catch up on.

"Look at this stuff," she was saying, trying to stamp the pervasive Tennessee mud from her shoes; a ragged piece of tar paper near the door served as a mat. She slipped out of the shoes, put down the books, and shucked her coat, then took a bottle of milk from the refrigerator and drank with a noisy gurgle.

Heinz had drifted over to the books. He fingered one, examined it. "What's all these?"

"Just books," she said.

"Here's one. Some book," he slyly noted.

"What book?" she asked, instantly suspicious.

She came in from the kitchen as he held it up, "This one. Got, you could say, an interesting title." He paused for effect. "*Love in a Tub.* Quite a title."

"All right, it's quite a title," she said.

"What I'm saying is, don't that sound a little dirty to you?"

"No, not at all," she said, wiping the milk from her lips.

"*Love in a Tub* don't sound dirty? To me, it sounds dirty."

"Well, it's not," she said, flashing a stubborn smile.

He dropped the pretense of patience. "What I see when I see a book like that is something maybe people shouldn't bring into a house."

"It's not a book like that, Papa," she said, with elaborate space between the words. "Maybe you ought to look at it."

"Don't need to know what's inside a dirty book with a title like that, to know it's a dirty book," he said. "All I know is, a girl that ain't even married don't need no book like that."

"She ain't even a virgin," Anna muttered sweetly.

"I heard that. What'd you say?"

"If you open the book and look just below the title, you'll see that a man named Sir George Etheridge wrote it. 'Sir' means a member of royalty. Not to mention the fact that *Love in a Tub* happens to be a play."

"Yeah, well, maybe that explains the filth," said Heinz. "I heard about some of those plays they put on Broadway. And if you try to tell me somebody from the royalty wrote it, they're always the ones mixed up in the worst dirt."

"Oh, lord. Papa," she explained with careful contempt, "this happens to be a very old English play. It goes back to the Elizabethan period."

"You think that makes it better? Because it's English, from old England? To me, it don't matter if it's a play or a funny-paper cartoon. That don't make it right."

"Why don't you read it? If you find anything you think is dirty," she said sweetly, "then you have my permission to burn it."

"Don't need no permission," he said, holding the book away from his body, as though over a fire. "If I want to burn it, I burn it."

"God, you're hopeless," she muttered.

"What? What was that you said?"

Wearily, she said, "I can't believe we're having these fights again."

Heinz, close to detonating, pulled back. "Ain't having no fight. Just having a talk. You bring the paper?"

"Under my coat," she said, She plucked it free and handed it over.

"All I'm saying, for your own good, is sometimes it's worth listening to a father that means well. I know you're a grown-up person now, so you make up your own mind. How's that? Sound fair?"

As usual, his conciliation softened her. "Okay, okay," she said. "Look, Papa, let me try to explain something, all right?"

"Sure. Go ahead."

"They're starting a new theater group, the Oak Ridge Players. Maybe you've heard of it."

He hadn't, of course, but tossed out a worldly shrug.

"They're going to use one of the storage buildings in back of the A & P for a playhouse."

"That so?"

She was angry at herself for explaining too much, but kept going. "I joined the group today."

He stared, showing not so much as a wrinkle of curiosity.

"Never mind."

"Listening," he insisted.

"Well, as it happens, *Love in a Tub* is one of the plays they're putting on," she said, patiently derisive. "In fact, there's a reading tonight, and I just might just try out for a part."

"A part in a play," he said, with excruciating care.

"Papa, would you try to understand something?"

"Maybe you could explain it," he said, his anger bubbling up again.

"The point is, we live in a tightly controlled U.S. government project. Everything that goes on here is censored. The whole place is like … Shirley Temple. They wouldn't dream of doing anything controversial, so do you really think they'd put on an obscene play in Oak Ridge?"

The logic of it was too much, so without looking defeated—more like being brushed in the face by a wet fish—he sputtered, "Never said 'obscene.'"

"That's what 'dirty' is," she said, grinding it in.

"All I know is, show business ain't for normal, decent people, and neither is that play, from a title like that. And I ain't the only one heard about show business. That's where people still too young to know everything get in trouble."

She grinned. Her face read: *Unbelievable. Preposterous.*

Irked, he said, "You think I don't know what goes on in the world with those people? They hear a hand clap, and they go crazy with sex and drugs from China. And now tell me I'm wrong."

"Poor Papa. Born into the wrong century."

He took this impassively. Anna brushed a hand through her hair and picked up her coat.

"So you're going."

She put on the mud-caked shoes and said, "I'll be back around eleven."

"I don't see you ate anything."

"I'll get a sandwich at the cafeteria. Okay?"

"Okay with me," he said.

She left, and Heinz took a beer from the refrigerator and sat down with the paper. The *Oak Ridge Journal* was twelve pages of censored news about the complex, local sports items, and a predictably tail-end heavy section on items for sale and for swap. Heinz went straight to the "For Sale" pages and scrutinized them carefully. He found nothing of interest but tossed the paper aside without agitation. All in good time.

Anna listened to the readings and thought twice about going after one of the parts. The play was not just Elizabethan but tangled in syntax and lost in time. *I'll give you this, Papa*, she thought, *Shakespeare it ain't.* She also had to admit that her fellow aspirants were not just amateurs but hokey.

She knew she had no right to be critical. She was no less an amateur, having had small parts in two high school plays, but she could not resist a certain smugness in her New York background. It did not automatically bequeath the tools of the acting trade, but it did confer a certain amount of poise and sophistication.

She frowned at herself. *Good God, not just insolent, but bitchy.* On the other hand, she liked the word "bitchy."

Actually, most of the girls were nice—home-baked and innocent as kittens. They blushed at the drop of a hat and giggled in little groups. But one or two girls she knew, brassy gum-chewers, talked about sex all the time, usually in barnyard terms like "hung like a horse" and "hard as a rock."

Anna knew she was picky, but the boys that the girls kept tittering about simply did not appeal to her. They were closer to yokels than locals. She wanted more. She wanted a man.

What was wrong with liking a little polish in people? They didn't have to be mannered society types, just intelligent with a touch of suave. *Let's face it*, she thought ruefully. *People who are not like my father.*

Anna shifted her attention to a new couple plowing through a reading. They were skinny, had regional accents, and were stiff as robots. The director was a bright-eyed man in his thirties. His hair was thin and styled into clumps. He viewed the proceedings from a chair straddled in reverse, the back of which propped up his chin.

A dozen or so hopefuls looked on. The couple reading droned on lifelessly. A large man with a beard listened without interest and stared off intelligently. *European scientist*, Anna reasoned. Americans did not have beards.

A man with a sharp jawline and a long, straight nose listened and closed his eyes from time to time. *Either sleepy or in pain*, Anna thought. She noticed that he held the cigarette a bit differently, not in the V between his fingers, but with the tips of his forefinger and thumb. Something less than exotic, yet faintly foreign. Another scientist? But he looked too young.

Heinz slid back into her mind. Why did she stay with him? The question had always been hanging out there, flashing like a neon sign. She wondered why Heinz, the intermittent despot, was concerned about her at all. Why did he protect her so savagely? Was it the need to possess her against the memory of her dead mother? What was she to him?

There were moments, but they belonged to obligation, not affection. The truth was that they had nothing in common except blood. So why was she still here? "Somebody tell me why," she said, and only when heads turned did she realize that she had said it aloud.

Aspiring actors looked over, the director spun around, and Anna let out a small, throaty laugh that no one else thought was funny, except the sharp-jawed man with the cigarette, who did not look at her but smiled nonetheless.

Later, heading home, Anna buttoned her coat against the cold night air and picked her way along the slatted sidewalks at a leisurely pace. A gauzy half-moon was out, and she thought about love.

CHAPTER 22

▼

Dr. Grodin was a morose man, the sort of doctor who people hated to go to because they sensed his addiction to mortality. A Stygian gurgle ran through his head; he had been known to bite his lip in front of a patient to indicate that time was running out.

Drawn-faced, he poked and prodded while Dancer whistled "Frenesi." He said, "You can dress now, Mr. Rhodes."

Dancer, buttoning his shirt, said, "Cheer up, Doc."

"When we treat the body well, the body returns the favor," the doctor advised. "Self-abuse is not the road to health."

"In all candor, Doc, I switched over to girls when I was twelve."

"I'm talking about your indifference to proper care," Dr. Grodin said. "You should be back in the hospital right now. This is serious business, which you don't seem to take seriously at all. Are you aware that you are still running a fever? Another thing—your blood count still shows traces of alcohol. You can't keep flouting the rules like that. You are strictly prohibited to take alcohol. I want that understood."

"Understood," Dancer said.

A nurse came in, sporting a helpful expression.

"Miss Cafferty will see you out," said Dr. Grodin.

Miss Cafferty, buck-toothed, crooked her arm to take Dancer's elbow.

"Miss Cafferty," said Dancer, "do you happen to know the tango?" He grabbed her arm, spun her in, and danced her out of the office. She went through the door open-mouthed.

Dr. Grodin, too late, said, "You can't do that!"

Outside the building, Dancer walked a sprightly heel-and-toe to the corner, turned it, leaned against a lamp pole, and looked for a cab. It took him several moments to catch his breath. He managed to light a cigarette and loosely flap an arm toward passing traffic. Eventually, a taxi skittered alongside, and Dancer lurched into the back seat.

In the comforting embrace of the Old Mill, tucked into his niche near the fireplace, Dancer could observe the flow of the midday crowd, from dark-suited civilians from Foggy Bottom to splashily uniformed officers from the Pentagon. In hazy contentment, he watched them come and go. Conversation bubbled these days; laughter rippled through the old rafters. It was the late winter of 1944, and the war was winding down.

The waiter, a man who appreciated alcohol but did his nipping in the kitchen, came over with a genteel cough and a menu: time to balance lunch. Dancer ordered trout and another double.

The trout was good, but Dancer picked at it. He had little interest in food. From some dim recess of history, he plucked out a memory: his mother railing at him to eat. He was seven when she died. Or six, or eight. He had not been sure for years.

A marine lieutenant came in with his girlfriend and settled at a nearby table. They were bright-eyed with pledges of affection and constancy. His hand never stopped stroking her shoulder; her fingers wove in and out of his.

For a moment or so, Dancer stared in wonder. He could not make out the words, only the sweet sound of overlapping promises. It was hardly a unique scene, but it struck Dancer with uncommon force. Romance was even more alien than sentiment, but now he was thrust back to a time when both had actually existed.

They had met two months after Dancer had enlisted in the army. The war was coming but still over a year off. Her name was Carrie, and she was twenty years old, out of Cincinnati, out of a home as broken as his, barely out of an eight-month marriage that had ended with the last of a series of beatings.

She was slim, almost boyish, and by the time Dancer met her, she was grittily tough. She believed in absolutely nothing but fatalism. The first time they made love, she had said to him, "You think there's anything else? Forget it." Dancer had smiled. He felt the same.

But their negatives formed an odd union. If it was not love, it was at least a symbiotic defense against the aimlessness of life. They did not expect much of each other, and when Carrie disappeared one day, Dancer had understood.

Watching the lovebirds, Dancer wondered if he and Carrie had been in love, in their own way, after all.

It was good for a derisive snort and a singeing swallow. Dancer pushed aside the trout and only then realized that, through a tangle of hanging plants, he was staring at Simon Guthrie's back. Alcohol, devilishly splashing in his brain, prompted him to tap Guthrie on the shoulder, as it would ruin the great man's lunch. He resisted the urge; it would ruin his lunch too.

There was a man seated across from Guthrie. He was middle-aged, with a sallow face and thinning black hair. The man wore glasses and was dressed in a well-cut dark suit with a high-buttoned vest. He had the nervous habit of ex-smokers: his cigarette hand occasionally flitted through the motion of holding a cigarette.

In fact, he had many nervous habits—almost tiny epileptic seizures, Dancer thought—his eyelids flickering in little bursts, his eyes rolling up, his body stiffening, then going slack. There were times, too, when his mouth opened in what could be taken for inexpressible anguish. Then he would recover, appearing quite normal and, oddly, even patrician. During these nervous intervals, Guthrie would politely pause, waiting for the apparent spasm to pass, and they would continue their conversation.

Guthrie's companion was speaking; he was in his self-possessed mode, smooth and accustomed to being heard. Dancer had the sense that he was less interested in dominating the conversation than in receiving homage.

Guthrie's companion very suddenly pulled a cigarette case from his jacket pocket, and Dancer allowed himself a small stab of satisfaction—he had been close. The man had not quite given up smoking; he was still trying.

He plucked out a cigarette, briskly tamped it, and lit it from a ceramic container of kitchen matches placed on the table. Even from this distance, Dancer could see that the cigarette case was quite out of the ordinary. The flickering match revealed an elaborate design.

In that second, Dancer was jarred by two extraordinary flashes of insight. One of them was that the man seated across from Guthrie was none other than SAU's mysterious informer.

CHAPTER 23

They ran into each other at the movies in Jackson Square. Both were alone, and Anna did not recognize him at first, because he was wearing glasses. It was the long, straight nose that brought him into focus, and she wondered, as she had at the reading of *Love in a Tub*, if it wasn't a trifle too long. Not really, she decided—it gave him a faintly aristocratic look.

He was at the cashier's window when she joined the back of the line, and perhaps he didn't see her—or didn't want to, she thought—as he disappeared into the theater. By the time she entered the lobby, he was gone again, into the darkness of the movie and a welter of music and laughter from a Bugs Bunny cartoon. Anna found a seat but couldn't find him, and she settled back for the coming attractions and, at last, the feature.

It was *Laura*, with Gene Tierney and Dana Andrews, and when it was over and the lights came on, her unknown acquaintance from the theater group was sitting just in back of her. "Hi," she said.

For a moment, he struggled, then he said, "Oh, hi."

With awkward half-steps and polite smiles, they made their way up the aisle and out to the lobby. Abandoning formality, they both grinned.

"My name's Richard Lyons," he said.

"Richard the Lyons-hearted," she responded, then thought, *God how trite!* But he didn't seem annoyed, so she said, "Anna Brenner."

He turned to go, and her hand fluttered up in muted protest. He saw it and hesitated. "What'd you think?" he asked.

"The movie? I loved it."

"Good movie," he agreed.

"She's gorgeous," Anna said.

"You're not ugly," he said.

"Oh, sorry—didn't mean to sound like I was fishing. But you know who else was terrific? Clifton Webb. He was …" She paused, searching.

"Urbane?"

"Exactly," she said, delighted. "May I ask you something?"

"Of course."

"Is that an accent? Just a little bit of English English?"

"Whatever's left. My folks came over in '32, trying to escape the depression. Guess what they found?"

"I think they want us out of here," Anna said. They were the last ones left in the lobby, and the ushers were sailing past with brooms and wastebaskets.

"How about coffee?"

"Actually, I'm starving," she said.

They talked in short-cut excitement, strangers hastily jettisoning layers of propriety. By the time they had finished their burgers, Anna was saying, "I'm glad we met. I mean, I wanted to talk to you, and I always think it's kind of sad when people hold back. All that foolish pride."

"Agreed."

"Actually, I was kind of hoping we'd get to meet last week. You know," she said, laughing, "*Love In A Tub*." He smiled back, and she said, "I'm talking too much, and I'm much too pushy, right?"

"Positively brazen," he said. He realized that her lips were fuller, her hair wavier.

She said, "You're staring, you know."

"I know. You remind me of someone."

"Is that good?"

"Yes."

"Well, since I'm making a total fool of myself anyway, I'll confess I kind of noticed you."

"I noticed you too."

She stopped chewing. "No, you didn't. Did you?"

"Yes."

She grinned. "You never looked over once."

"You run a thumb through your hair when you're smoothing it. Most girls use the first three fingers. You tap your foot when you're impatient. And you sulk when you're displeased." He mimed her sulk, and she broke into laughter.

She swallowed it and tried to look stern. "Sulk? You mean sulk, like a child?"

"Absolutely. For all I know, you could be a spoiled brat."

"I don't think so," she said.

"What are you doing here?"

"Receptionist, at the hospital. How about you?"

"I'm over at Y-12," he said

"Oh," said Anna, properly impressed. Quietly, she said, "Are you a scientist?"

"Sort of," he admitted.

"I know, I know—no questions. But what do you think is going on? Or do you know?"

"You a spy?"

"Of course not!" she giggled.

"Well, I don't know any more than you do."

"I'll bet." She studied him. "You just ... look like you know. Want to hear the latest?"

"Sure."

"Somebody told me they're building a space rocket."

"To do what?"

"I don't know. Go up around the moon and come down on Germany and Japan."

"Could be," he said.

"Okay, I'm not going to get anything out of you." She dabbed her mouth with a napkin. "What about the theater group? You going back?"

"Maybe. If they come up with something like Oscar Wilde."

"*The Importance of Being Earnest.*"

"Yes, perfect."

"Know what my father said about *Love in a Tub?*"

"What?"

She growled his authority but left out the syntax: "I don't want you involved in a filthy play like that!"

"Filthy?"

"You'd have to know my father."

"What about your mother?"

"Oh, well, she died a long time ago. I was a baby."

"Sorry. Then your dad raised you?"

"Dad—I never called him that in all our years together. Papa. I'm not even sure why."

"What does he do, your papa? That's if you can tell me."

"Nothing that secret," she said dismissively. "He's a carpenter. Housing over on Jackson Square."

"You're from New York, aren't you?"

"How did you know? Well, everybody always knows. New Yorkers. Is the accent that bad? I've been trying to get rid of it."

"It's barely detectable," he reassured her. "It's not even a New York accent—more like charmingly provincial."

"Oh, I like that. Keep lying."

They grinned, and she said, "You can call me Anna, you know."

He nodded, and quite spontaneously, their fingers touched across the table.

Like Heinz before him in somewhat similar circumstances, the irony of the moment did not escape Nikolai: a boy and a girl in a blossoming relationship, and both using false names.

✳   ✳   ✳   ✳

The words sprang from the inside back page of the *Oak Ridge Journal*. "For sale: *Encyclopedia Britannica*. One volume missing. Reasonable." Heinz slapped shut the newspaper in a burst of exuberance. Then he opened it again quickly, as though the ad might go away, and read on: "Gamble Valley Trailer Park, Row 3, P-14."

At last! The weeks of inaction, of uncertainty, of fear that the whole thing would end in a puff of dust—over! He bolted from the chair in a mindless fervor, took out a beer, opened it, put it to his lips, then put it aside; he was much too excited to drink. He opened the newspaper and read the ad again.

Should he make immediate contact or wait? But what was the point of waiting? He was on fire. He started for the closet and his coat, then froze, hearing Anna's key in the lock. He grabbed the newspaper and headed for his chair as she came in.

"What a day!" she said.

"You ain't the only one," he said. "How come so early you home?"

"Worked late last night," she reminded him. "They let me off an hour early. You want this?"

"What?" He turned and saw that she was holding the beer he had opened. "Oh. Forgot."

She handed him the beer, peeled off her coat, and went into the bathroom. She threw water on her face and ran a brush through her tangled hair. "What a mess," she muttered.

"You going somewhere?" Heinz asked.

"Theater group," she said, moving to the kitchen.

"I thought you was through with them."

"Choosing a new play."

"Because it was dirty, like I said."

"Not dirty enough," she said

He ignored this as she appeared, stuffing a mustard-streaked slice of bread into her mouth.

"You call that dinner?" he growled.

"Eat later."

She checked herself in a mirror, and he said, "All fussing up, I see. Must be this new friend."

"He might be there, Papa. So what?"

"Nothing, just a word to the smart. Don't get serious too quick."

"Thanks for the advice," she said.

Heinz came out of the building five minutes later. He checked for Anna—nowhere in sight—and hurried toward the bus stop. It started to rain, and he cursed. *More damn mud.* He cursed again, arriving at the bus stop just as an army shuttle pulled away. He plodded on, keeping to the slatted boardwalk until it ran out. The rain was cold and dripped down his neck. The wind came and went in angry howls. Another half-mile, and he turned onto the dirt road leading into the trailer park. The rain beat down harder, and he slipped in the new mud.

Infrequent oases of pale light, the color of parchment, divided the trailer camp into grids, but the row markers were difficult to make out and the trailer numbers even more so. He wandered to the end of a row, beyond which was a pitch-black thicket of trees and the somehow mysterious sound of rain dripping from thousands of branches. There was still no row sign, so he moved on to the next one and spotted a faded marker stuck into the ground at a precarious angle: *F*.

He was at the high end, and he plodded back through stinging rain turning to sleet. At last, he found himself before F-14, the marker half-hidden behind a garbage can.

The trailer was tightly curtained, the light from within a translucent yellow. Irritably, Heinz banged on the door.

"Who is it?" he heard, and he cocked his head in surprise. A woman's voice.

"Come about the books," he shouted.

The curtains rustled. A moment passed. The sleet whipped at his face.

"Get a shake on, will you?" he croaked.

The trailer door was unlatched, and Heinz thrust himself out of the weather into the trailer's dim light. It was unkempt: clothes scattered as though by the storm outside, a disheveled bed strewn with soiled pillows, dirty dishes in a tiny sink partitioned off by a rag of a curtain.

Heinz saw none of this. His disbelieving eyes were fastened on Toni Graf. Her lips were curled in amusement. She was smoking a cigarette.

"Take your coat off, Herbie. You'll get pneumonia."

He kept staring. There was something different, but what? Finally, he said, "What the hell you doing here?"

"Same as you."

"Siebert?" he whispered.

"Funny, heh?" she said. "Here, get out of that thing." With maternal concern, she helped to unbutton his coat and remove it.

For his part, Heinz could not help staring. Her hair was straw-colored now and piled up so differently that it seemed to have rearranged her face. He gaped, shook it off and said, "Thought you dropped out."

"That's the way they wanted it."

"All that time, and you even worked in that plant, Long Island."

"Republic, yeah," she said, grinning.

"I thought you went over. All that talk. How it didn't matter, we were all finished."

"Still finished. Worse every day," she said fatalistically, "but what the hell can you do?"

He was astonished—at everything, at her involvement, at her cynical detachment, at how much she sounded like Siebert, professionally disillusioned but undeterred.

Toni took a bottle from a cabinet and looked up as the sleet turned to hail and drummed on the roof. "Just listen to that." She found two glasses and poured. "Here's to us, Heinzie."

They drank, and Heinz stopped examining her, the old Toni melding into the new Toni until she was recognizably the person he had always known, except that she had a new name. "It's Dorothy Martin, these days. Dorothy Martin and Herbie Brenner, and what the hell are we doing here, right?"

He picked up on this eagerly. "You know what's going on?"

"Haven't got a clue," she said, too innocently.

"Hey, I got a right, you know. I'm here, so I got a right."

Hard as nails, the Toni he had almost forgotten spat back, "Start getting it straight. We take orders, and that means you don't know anything you don't have to know."

"What's that supposed to mean? I take orders from you?"

"That's what it means."

"I don't take no orders from you," he said, banging down the glass.

Toni moved to a small radio with a yellowing plastic grille and switched it on. Tinny jazz vibrated out of the speaker.

"Listen to me. You can't afford to be a hothead anymore. Those days are gone. This is serious stuff. You're not on your own. We all take orders."

"Didn't count on certain things," he said churlishly.

"I know. You didn't expect to take orders from a woman, but you've got to face it, Heinzie—either you're in, or you're out. If you're in, you take it the way it comes, and that's me."

They were hard words for him to accept, but what made them oddly palatable was the way she said "Heinzie," the intimacy of old, from the same person of whom he had once thought, *Why not a woman with balls?*

He picked up the drink again and lowered himself into a chair. He would be reasonable but not submissive. "How many?"

"Of us?"

"Sure, of us. How many?"

"We'll get to that," she said cagily.

"Don't want to tell me, don't tell me," he said, piqued.

"Can't yet," she said good-naturedly.

"So what am I, a donkey here?"

"Jesus, Herbie, be patient."

It was less a command than a plea. He sensed her wavering. He took a drink, then said quietly, "I'll be more patient if I know what's going on. Oak Ridge."

She stared at the scratchy-sounding radio. "I can't do that."

He said nothing. Toni finally swung around. "God damn you." She moved in closer. "They're making a bomb. Not the bomb itself, but what goes into it. Have you ever heard of atomic fission? It's what happens when atoms are split apart. They create this incredible power that's never been used before. The bottom line is something that can end the war, with one bomb."

"One bomb?" he said, his brain churning in confusion. "You mean that's what this whole place is about? To make one bomb? This whole place?" The logic of it would not settle. "It's a whole city of factories, this place."

"I said, what *goes into* the bomb. It's complicated. I don't know that much about it either. All I know is, this isn't the only place. There are two more out west, and one of them is actually going to make the bomb."

"Then it ain't happened yet."

"No, they still haven't got enough of the explosive, whatever it is."

"A place with factories the size of cities," he said in wonderment, "and they ain't made enough?"

"No, because it's the most important scientific project since the beginning of time. Look around, Herbie. Look what's going on! Don't you see? We have to move fast!"

"But to do what?"

"I told you, I don't know. When they tell me, I tell you."

Heinz thought for a moment, then said, "How about us? Germany," he clarified, prudently smothering the word. "We're working on the same thing?"

Toni nodded, unable to control her exhilaration. Heinz was beaming too. He jumped to his feet. "We got to get it first!"

She could not repress herself. "What I hear is, we're getting close. Maybe ..."

"Say it! Tell me!"

Tensely, she spat out, "Maybe inside three months! Three months!"

"*Gott in Himmel!*" His face split with joy. "Three months!"

"That's our job, Heinz! If we slow them here, we slow their bomb! If they fall behind, we beat them!"

"They got to send the orders to move!" he said. "What are they waiting for?"

"They know what they're doing, so we wait."

"But ... to do something like this! Not just two people, right?"

"I guess," she said, already uneasy about saying more than she had intended.

He picked up on her reticence and lifted his glass. Silently, they drank to success.

Casually, Toni said, "Maybe you'll stay over sometime."

With team-player exuberance, Heinz said, "Tonight!"

"No. Too soon. Tonight, we just met. Give it a chance to look natural."

"Might not get no more chances," Heinz said, with a grin.

"We've got time," Toni said, casually sage, confirming that she knew more than she let on.

"Anyway, got to be careful," he said.

She looked over perceptively. "You mean Anna?" She said it with the unfamiliarity it deserved—an outsider.

"That's right, I got a daughter, Anna. Remember?"

"Sure, I remember, but that doesn't mean you have to lock yourself up in a closet every night. Hey, Heinzie—*she* doesn't."

"What do you know?" he asked brusquely.

"I know she's got a boyfriend."

Heinz looked over sharply. He was reappraising Toni. And the organization too, for that matter—Germanically thorough, even with the problems of the war. But most of all, his back was up. "Ain't a boyfriend. Just somebody she met, a guy. Nothing serious. And it ain't your business anyway."

"Yes, it is," Toni said.

He wanted to glare her into submission but knew it would never work. She was right. He went the other way: "You know anything about him, I'm listening."

"Not much. Not yet."

"She thinks he's a scientist. Y-12." For all his condemnation, he said it with just a tinge of pride at Anna's choosiness.

"That could be right," Toni said, almost off-handedly. "That's what I've got, but I'm still checking."

"Boyfriends," he said, snarling his ancient contempt for the species. "Shouldn't be here in the first place."

"Matter of fact," Toni admitted, "I'm the one told Max she ought to come."

"You told him?" Heinz slapped his hand against the chair. "What for? What'd you tell him that for?"

"Hey, take it easy, Heinzie. There's a reason for everything."

"What do I need my own daughter in the middle of all this for?"

"Because it looks better—what do you think?"

"What I see is, it comes out the same. FBI knows we left New York together, the two of us, not just me. So if they look for me here, they look for her too!"

"No," Toni said quietly. "The FBI thinks you're both in Mexico City."

"Mexico City?"

"We knew they'd track you to Mexico, which they did. Remember Lindemann?"

"Hotel," Heinz said impatiently.

"The day before you crossed back into the States, Lindemann planted some leads with the Mexican border cops. The leads said the two of you were on the way to Mexico City."

"You think they believe?"

"No question. FBI's got the Mexico City cops running around like rabbits."

Assuaged just as swiftly as he had been irked, Heinz was suddenly struck by the complexity of the game—and just as suddenly proud of his integral part in it. But he was not foolish enough to wallow in it. "Sooner or later, they catch up."

"Sure," said Toni. She rocked forward. "But by that time, *Schatzi*, we do what we came to do."

They drank again.

Toni said, "One more thing. A few weeks where you are, then you're going to be transferred."

"Transferred where?"

"Don't know yet."

"Got to be K-25, or Y-12, or X-10," he said familiarly.

"That's pretty good."

"Don't have to be no genius. Three places everybody talks about. Also the ones got tightest security."

"You know anything that goes on?"

"Just rumors. Parts for the bombs, must be. But you said one bomb."

"One bomb," she confirmed.

"Big places to make parts for one bomb," he said, bewildered. "Especially K-25. What I hear, it's two buildings connected, half-mile each."

"That's it. Biggest in the world."

"Bigger than us, what we got?" Heinz asked pointedly.

"We don't need buildings that big," she told him. "Max says we're ahead on the technology."

Smugly, Heinz said, "Drop a German bomb on top of Washington."

Toni was grinning, but she put a finger to her lips and said, "Shh."

"How do you do that? Just like that, you can transfer me."

"It's not just like that. It takes some doing. But the thing is, I'm in a sweet position to do the doing. Personnel, for Tennessee Eastman."

"You sure you can do it? Nobody even checks?"

"They check everything. But I check everything first, before it goes to security. Got it?"

"Sure."

"You going to be okay with this?" she asked in shrewd appraisal. "I mean, this arrangement?"

"Sure, I'm okay." He shrugged. "You're the boss."

CHAPTER 24

▼

They were bickering—Heinz in his coat, on the way out, and Anna, still in her coat, newly arrived. As usual these days, the argument was about Anna's new friend. Heinz didn't know enough about him. "This Richard I keep hearing, he came out of nowhere," he charged.

To which Anna replied, "I didn't know him before we met. Where did you expect a stranger to come from?"

"All I know is you see him too much!"

"Once a week is all I've ever seen him!"

"You saw him Saturday last week and Wednesday night, which makes two times one week."

She lashed back, "How about you and your new lady friend? Three nights out in the last two weeks! And you're on the way out now, and don't tell me you're just taking a walk!"

"Don't have no lady friend!" he furiously retorted. "And where I go, it's my business!" They had come full circle.

Just then came a knock on the door.

"Who the hell's that?" Heinz said.

"Probably your lady friend," Anna said, so sweetly that Heinz feared it might indeed be Toni. Being closer to the door, and with no way out, he opened the door.

Standing before him was a tall young man with a book crooked under his arm.

"Richard!" Anna said in astonishment.

"Sorry to bother you," Nikolai said. "I just thought I'd drop this book off."

"Richard, this is my father, Mr. Brenner."

"How do you do, sir?" Nikolai said. He held out a hand. Heinz made it plain that he didn't want to take it, then he took it and gave the limpest of handshakes.

"This is a surprise," Anna heard herself trill.

"I know it's not very chic to pop by uninvited," Nikolai said, "but there are so few phones around here that it's hard not to barge in on people."

"Oh, no, I'm glad you stopped by. Oh, come on in, please."

Nikolai shook his head. "It was just to give you the book."

"What is it?"

He handed it over with a small smile. She read the title and glowed. "*The Importance of Being Earnest*! But I thought the library didn't have it!"

"I got it from New York."

"Oh, that's marvelous, Richard." Hardly surprised, Anna noted her father's glower. Reluctantly, she explained, "Papa, this is the play I told you about."

"Didn't tell me," Heinz said, clearly establishing his left-out-in-the-cold status.

"Oscar Wilde, sir," Nikolai said.

"That so?" Heinz said elaborately.

"Oh, I think it's great. We can present it to them tonight!"

"I didn't mean to interrupt any plans you might have," Nikolai said.

"Might as well strike while the iron's hot," said Anna. "That is, if you're free."

"I'm free."

"Well, give me a couple of minutes, Richard. Please, come in. Actually, my father's on the way out."

"Not leaving yet," said Heinz.

"Don't stay on my account, sir."

"Got time," Heinz said.

"Well, then, you two can talk," Anna said, a parting shot to Heinz as she put down the book and left the room.

Heinz indicated the book with a scowl. "This one another dirty play?"

"No, sir," the congenial Nikolai said. "It's not in the least off-color."

"Off-color." Heinz chewed over. "Well, just happens, last one she told me about was a dirty play."

"In all truth, Mr. Brenner, not exactly."

"*Two People in a Bathtub*," Heinz said. "That's a man and a woman, ain't it? And to me, that's dirty. End of story. So you work over at Y-12."

"Yes, sir."

"Anna says something about … you're a scientist."

"Yes, sir." He smiled. "Not exactly at the highest level."

"Where you from?"

"Boston, sir."

"Family still around?"

"Unfortunately, no. My dad passed away while I was in college, and my mother died last year."

Heinz grumbled below his breath and said, "So you went to college."

"Yes, sir. Dartmouth," Nikolai said.

"Never heard of it," Heinz challenged.

"It's in Hanover, New Hampshire, sir."

"Never heard of it," Heinz said resolutely.

Anna came in, head still half-cocked from listening to every word. "Ready?"

"All set," Nikolai said.

"Good, then all together, we leave," said Heinz.

Outside the building, where wide-spaced streetlights left the area in a grayish gloom, Heinz nodded and peeled off.

"Papa!" Anna called after him. She caught up. "You could have said good night!"

Heinz smiled malevolently. "You want to know about your boyfriend? I think he's a pansy boy."

He walked off. Anna was astonished. Nothing could be more devastating, because the same thought—though rejected out of hand—kept flitting through her mind these days.

The problem was his awkwardness with her. He was bright, articulate, and knowledgeable, and she found him good-looking and fun to be with. But the thing she had missed all her life, that she had so hoped for in him, was completely lacking.

The warmth was in his words and the romance was in his soul, but he avoided physical contact. The night they had discovered each other, over hamburgers and sophisticated banter, was also the high point of their intimacy—when their hands had spontaneously touched at the table.

Since then, he had kept his distance. He never put his arm around her, never had the need to touch her shoulder or the desire to take her in his arms, to run his lips across hers, to drink her in with the desperation of a parched lover.

She expected this, because she felt all of these cravings. She wanted him so much that if he had made the slightest move, she would have been there for the taking. But he never did. He was charming and desirable but indifferent.

How could that be? She was not ugly, she knew that, and she had certainly tried—touching, brushing, shoving her arm through his, even placing her head against his shoulder. And so, lately, she had begun to think the unthinkable: that he was indifferent because he was, well, one of those. No! She would not accept that. It could not possibly be true.

But when he left her, only two hours later, she was crushed. As they were parting in Jackson Square, under the darkness of a tree and the thin light of a cold half-moon, she had taken his hand and said, "Do you have to go? It's still early."

"I've got some work to do."

"More important than this?" she said, aware of the insipid sound of her coquetry. *The hell with it.*

He had smiled appreciatively and even patted her hand once or twice before removing it from his own. "Sorry."

With even more effrontery, feeling more and more foolish, she had closed her eyes and inched her face toward his. When she opened them, he was checking his watch. "Anna, I've really got to be going." He started off. "Call you tomorrow."

"Richard!" When he spun around, she said, "What about tomorrow night? Are we still going to the movies?"

"Oh, of course. Sorry, I forgot. Why don't we meet at the box office? Seven, right?"

Nikolai cut through Jackson Square, trying to sort things out. Anna generated an odd mix of signals. She was a job: she belonged to the gray area of the enemy camp. She was marvelously attractive and radiated femininity. She sparkled with affection, and he wanted to return it but could not; maybe because she was Katya too. Or perhaps because he was still caught up in Maureen.

He jumped on a bus heading east and got off at the Gamble Valley Trailer Park. Moments later, he had found row 3, trailer F-14—no great difficulty, since he had followed Heinz here less than a week ago.

The break had inadvertently come through Anna. "I think old Papa's got a girlfriend," she had said, with a daughter's amusement. And when Nikolai had carefully suggested that his evenings out could be something quite innocent, like the chess club, Anna had laughed.

"He's never had anything else. No interests, no hobbies—not even girlfriends, except a couple, way back. He never goes out." Nikolai saw it as a breakthrough. Heinz, suddenly social, had been contacted.

He turned it into a running joke with Anna: Heinz and his lady friend. Anna said she didn't care where he went or what he did, as long as he was preoccupied. But Nikolai, of course, cared a great deal. By now, he had followed Heinz on two occasions.

The first had ended in frustration; Heinz had guzzled beer all evening at a redneck bar outside the gates and never talked to a soul. But the second time had brought Nikolai to the trailer park, where Heinz had disappeared into F-14. Nikolai had tried to get close to the whale-shaped trailer, but kids kept running by, playing hide-and-seek, and when an MP jeep patrol drove through the area, he had discretely slipped away.

Now he was outside F-14 again, without the slightest idea whom Heinz was visiting or what they were saying, and the only thing he could do was to apply his ear to the shell of the trailer. It helped only a little; he heard a guttural male voice—Heinz—and a woman's voice, but the sound of a radio dominated.

Nikolai switched ears, which improved nothing. Just then, a row party several trailers down broke into song, and Nikolai called it a night. The smart thing to do was to requisition technical help; the FBI could ship some sort of listening device and have it in Oak Ridge in two days.

Something cut through the singing and the laughter—something that did not belong. He heard nearby voices, and one of them said, "I think I see him."

Another voice said, "Yeah, there he is."

Two flashlights were bobbing his way, coming from the opposite direction of the party. Beyond the silhouettes of two heaving figures, Nikolai could make out an MP jeep down the row path, headlights blazing.

"Hold it right there!" a voice shouted.

Nikolai was handcuffed and brought before MP Captain William Currier, who reminded him of Captain Neil Lomax of Los Alamos security. The circumstances too were similar, until Currier learned that Nikolai was registered under the auspices of a federal investigatory agency, his dossier marked NQTBA ("no questions to be asked").

In due course, the same sergeants who had apprehended him dropped him off at Y-12 security; there, he had a clerk check on Gamble Valley Trailer Park occupancy. Twenty minutes later, he had a name and a photo. The name, Dorothy Martin, was unfamiliar, but the photo gently stirred his memory. He kept staring but could not pin it down. He left with an envelope containing copies of the material, then ordered up a ride to Knoxville out of the motor pool.

He reached the L & N station by 11:00 PM and was on the train to New York when it left at five minutes past midnight.

*   *   *   *

It was pouring in New York, cold and uninhabitable. "Shitty winter," Boettinger grunted.

They were in the file room, poring over albums. Their frame of reference was the photograph Nikolai had brought from Oak Ridge, now blown up.

They had been flipping through the thick, heavy files for several hours. "When do you figure on going back?" Menzies asked.

"Noon train tomorrow," Nikolai said.

"Maybe you ought to stay a day." Menzies was pointing to the mass of files still unexamined.

"Can't," Nikolai said. "It's heating up down there."

Menzies frowned but could not think of an argument.

Nikolai went back to examining the photograph of Dorothy Martin. Something kept nagging at him. Menzies and Boettinger drifted alongside. Suddenly, Nikolai found himself blinking in discovery. Quietly, he said, "Nose is different."

"What?"

"Nose is different," he repeated. "She's bleached her hair, and maybe some other minor plastic stuff, but I think Dorothy Martin is Toni Graf."

"Naw," Boettinger said, taking the blown-up photo. "Where do you get that?"

Nikolai sorted through files, flipped through one, and came to the picture of Toni Graf. Boettinger laid down the enlarged photo next it.

"I don't see it," Menzies said. "Two different people."

But Boettinger was oddly quiet. Then he said, "He could be right."

All three bent closer, comparing the images. Finally, Nikolai said, "I think she even had her chin built up."

"Son of a bitch. I think you hit it," Boettinger said.

"It's possible," Menzies grudgingly conceded.

"God damn, how about that?" Boettinger said.

"The old gang," said Menzies.

"What's the name of the one running the *Abwehr* out of South America?" Nikolai said. He pondered. "Something Siebert."

"Maximilian!" Menzies shot out.

"That's it. Max Siebert."

"How do you know him?" Boettinger asked.

"Came across his name on the Los Alamos job. I suppose he could still be pulling the strings."

"Probably," Boettinger said. "The krauts aren't sending out replacements these days. Last thing we heard, he was working out of Mexico. Hey, maybe we can get the Mexicans to squeeze him. Bust Oak Ridge before they can get it off the ground."

"They haven't been able to find him for three years," Menzies pointed out.

"Pump up the moola might get those guys off their asses."

Menzies chided him with a cough. "Let's not wash our international laundry, Lyle, shall we?"

"What's so delicate?" Boettinger murmured. "They'd sell their underwear, if they wore underwear."

"Trouble is, by the time we find Siebert and squeeze him, it'll be too late."

Boettinger looked up. "Why don't we just close them out right now?"

It was so simple and so obvious. Menzies looked stunned.

"What are we waiting for?" Boettinger said. "If we haul them in now, we close down the operation before it starts."

"Not necessarily," Nikolai said.

Menzies, riding the same track, quickly jumped in. "I brought up Siebert," he said (although he had not), "because I do not accept the premise that an agent with his experience would go up against a place like Oak Ridge with second-raters like Heinz Baumann and Toni Graf."

"If that's all he's got," said Boettinger. "How many agents is the *Abwehr* running in North America these days? Practically zilch."

"You can't tell me they're down to two people, Lyle. A mission as important as this one?"

"I agree," Nikolai said.

"One last blow job for the *Führer*," Boettinger argued, but weakly now.

"With two buffoons from the German-American *Bund* days?" Menzies said. "I think not. My guess is … a total of six."

"I think that's about right," Nikolai said. "And if it is, figure four on the base in hiding—or four who haven't shown up yet."

"Now you've got it," Menzies said.

"I think you ought to get in touch with Oak Ridge security and push for a yellow alert."

Menzies' quills went up. "A yellow alert?"

"Start double-checking every 591 file on the base," Nikolai suggested. "All badge levels. And you might want to get the word out. All security personnel to be on the lookout for suspicious persons, unusual behavior—old-timers, newcomers, everybody. Drop the undercover business and go public."

Menzies was appalled. "Check out thirty-six thousand people? That would take months. We haven't got time for that."

"Round up one thousand agents for an emergency job, short term. Bring a hundred dogs, sniff out C-4, TNT, dynamite, everything explosive. The whole thing could be done in a week."

"That's ridiculous," said Menzies. "Do you think Mr. Hoover can spare one thousand agents for a whole week in the middle of a war?"

"If Mr. Hoover wants to win the war," Nikolai said.

While Menzies picked his way through the impossible logistics of selecting, transporting, and instructing one thousand FBI agents from all over the country, not to mention one hundred dogs, he had a flash of J. Edgar Hoover's incredulous response to such a request, the result of which would be to drum Wilbur R. Menzies out of the FBI.

While Menzies was cutting his way through this nightmare, Boettinger lit a cigarette. His idea had been blunted, but he brought it back for one last listless bid. "What I'm saying is, if we pull in Baumann and Toni Graf, whatever's left over is either going to be warned off before they can make it to Oak Ridge, or they'll sure as hell haul ass for parts unknown, pronto. Either way, the operation is dead in the water."

"You don't quite understand," Menzies said acidly. "That's exactly what I don't want. I don't want the rest of them to get away."

Nikolai and Boettinger exchanged glances. It was obvious that Menzies was driven less by the threat to Oak Ridge than the glory of rounding up its enemies.

"One more thing you could do," Nikolai said. "Bring in Dieter Krone, throw the book at him, and see if he'd like to help out."

"Dieter Krone?" Menzies said uncertainly.

"Los Alamos."

"Oh," Menzies said, with a squirm that meant *Maybe a good idea, but no point in admitting it*. "Have to think about that one," he said.

"In other words, I keep going?" Nikolai said.

"That's it," said Menzies. "You keep going. We don't raise the alarm. We don't scare the rest of the team off. We keep a close watch on Baumann and Graf. They will lead us to the others."

"What about specific targets?" Boettinger asked. "Got any favorites?"

"Sure," Nikolai said. "Y-12, the electro-magnetic plants. K-25, gaseous-diffusion. Or the graphite pile in X-10. They're all prime. But it could be they're playing with us."

"How?" Menzies asked.

"Maybe Oak Ridge is a feint," Nikolai mused. "Maybe they're after the Norris Dam—flood the whole valley, put Oak Ridge under a hundred feet of water."

Menzies was so appalled that he forgot to be skeptical. "Is that possible?"

Nikolai thought it over. "Actually, no. They'd need about a hundred krauts and fifty thousand tons of nitro."

"Of course," Menzies said. "Ridiculous."

There was a lull, and Boettinger looked over at Nikolai, "You think this bomb's for real?"

Menzies waited for his answer too. Finally, Nikolai said, "Sorry, fellows. I'm not allowed to talk about it."

For one long second, it hung there, the two FBI agents so immersed in the secrecy of Oak Ridge that they had forgotten that Nikolai was not really part of it. Then Boettinger laughed, and Menzies smiled thinly.

"What say we get out of here?" Boettinger proposed.

"I'll let you know when we close," Menzies said.

Inured and unflappable, Boettinger said, "I'll buy the first one, boss."

On the way out, Menzies said, "By the way, Nikolai, a word to the wise. You might want to sharpen your field skills. Know what I mean?"

"Not yet."

"Getting nabbed by the MPs," Menzies said, jollying the moment with a wink at Boettinger. "A little on the amateur side, wouldn't you say?"

"No question."

"Hey, go easy on the man," said Boettinger. "He's got distractions down there. Am I right?"

"You never know," Nikolai said.

"Hold it, hold it," said Boettinger. "You got something going with her?"

"With who?"

"With who? With Baumann's kid, who else?"

"Oh."

Boettinger grinned. "You popped her bloomers, didn't you?"

Nikolai shrugged, and Boettinger looked at Menzies. "He popped her bloomers, all right. The son of a bitch is dicking himself to death down there."

*   *   *   *

On the way to the hotel, Nikolai impulsively ducked into a sidewalk telephone booth. He pulled a scrap of paper from his wallet and dialed a number.

A high-pitched female voice, excited and boozy, answered the phone; there was a background of jazz music and the din of a party. "This is Chinese Chow Mein Take Out Emporium. What you likee order?"

Nikolai sucked in a tolerant breath. "Maureen. Is she there?"

"I look," said the girl. She dropped the phone, and it banged off something or other, swinging back and forth.

Eventually, Maureen's voice came on, bright, but in control.

"Me," he said.

There was a pause, and then she said, "Nikolai, you miserable son of a bitch! You lousy bastard! You dumped me in that hotel and just took off!"

This theatrical outburst was followed by laughter—hers, and that of the small audience she was playing to.

"Some other time," he said.

"Don't hang up! No! Nikolai. Are you in New York? Please, come over! Wait a minute!" There was some fumbling. She cursed and said, "Damn cord's all tangled!" He heard more noise, a thumping, a sarcastic "Would you mind?" to somebody in her way, and then, "Nikolai? Okay, I'm out of the room. I want you to come here. You have the address, don't you? Just come. Don't even think about it. Will you?"

"I don't know," he said. It was like riding a whirlwind.

"Goddamn you, Nikolai, you owe me that much."

"All right."

"Hurry!"

Dazed at his foolishness, he caught a cab, and twenty minutes later, it pulled up before a brownstone on 69th Street.

The noise of the party vibrated through the building; the glass panes of the inner door to the lobby tinkled with the music coming from the second floor.

Maureen was waiting for him. She was drunk, but covered it nicely, her leer a little less sexy than vindictive. "Come on in," she said, without ceremony.

The apartment, high-ceilinged with big rooms and bay windows, was filled with overstuffed furniture and two dozen or so raucous merrymakers. As they threaded their way through, with Maureen steering, she made offhand introductions. She jerked at his arm, indicating an important stop. They were before a girl with severe but not unattractive features, sitting in a deep armchair in the lap of an air force bombardier.

"Lorraine, this is Nikolai," Maureen said. There were several shades of woman scorned in this simple introduction, and Lorraine cocked a couple of eyebrows up to Nikolai.

"Well, well, well. The world-famous Nikolai," said Lorraine.

"Lorraine is my roommate," Maureen said.

"And this good-looking fellow under me—sometimes on top of me—is Tommy Newcomb. But don't anybody look shocked. We're going to be married."

Nikolai shook hands with Tommy Newcomb, an amiable-looking man in his mid-twenties with a boxing nose.

Lorraine rubbed a ribbon on Newcomb's chest, just under his wings. "Tommy just got back from Italy."

"I never know where Nikolai just got back from," said Maureen. She took his arm in another priority tug that brought them through a swinging door into the kitchen. It was white and spacious enough to look like an operating room. In it were two couples and a man entertaining them with a story.

Waves of charisma flowed from him. He was solidly built, gray at the temple, in his late thirties. The story was a variation on the man who kills his parents and then throws himself on the mercy of the court, pointing out that he is an orphan.

There was a burst of appreciation, and Maureen said, "Oh, I love that one!"

She withdrew her arm from Nikolai's elbow and slipped her hand into the storyteller's, pivoting slowly, almost ceremonially, to face Nikolai. More to confront him, of course. "And this is Holland Boone. We work together."

"Very much so," said Holland Boone. "How do you do?"

Nikolai nodded. They shook hands. Boone's handshake was a bone-crusher.

"Holland is a partner at Dreyfuss," said Maureen.

In that moment, Nikolai knew he had not just been foolish but neatly bamboozled. Maureen had acquired a new beau and was performing the de rigueur ritual of castrating the old one.

"How nice," Nikolai said. He looked at Maureen. "What happened to the Office of War Mobilization?"

"Oh, well, I met Holland," she said, snuggling against him, "and one thing led to another."

"Two happy little peas in a legal pod," Nikolai said, immediately sorry he had said it.

"How about you?" Boone asked.

"How about me?"

"Yes, Maureen says you're something of a mystery."

"Tell us, Nikolai," Maureen said. She swiped at Boone's lips and vamped her head against his shoulder.

"I'm a spy," Nikolai said.

His straightforward manner produced an odd, chilly silence, then a burst of laughter.

When the buzz of conversation returned, Nikolai made his way to the front rooms and out the door. Leaving the building, he heard Maureen's voice but kept going.

At the Commodore's reception desk, a clerk handed him his key along with a cryptic message: "Call Baird."

CHAPTER 25

▼

Baird, of course, was McKennan. Nikolai pulled shut the folding door of a telephone booth and gave an operator the number. McKennan answered at the top of the second ring with an expectant "Yes."

"Granger."

"He's back in D.C. Central."

"What happened?"

"He was in a restaurant. Drank too much, of course. Collapsed, had to be picked up by ambulance."

Nikolai paused. "How bad?"

"Bad." There was weight to the word, heavy even for McKennan.

"How much time?"

"Don't even think about coming down," McKennan said. "You've got a job to do. Do it. Look, lad, you won't make it."

"Are you saying tonight?"

"Yes. They're talking hours. No more than that."

"Jesus. Thanks."

McKennan clicked off. Nikolai held the receiver in the air for a moment before hanging up.

He went back to the desk. There was a milk train leaving at 1:40, arriving at Union Station at 6:15. He hurried to his room, grabbed his overnight bag, and made the train with only moments to spare.

Dawn was coming up over the Capitol dome and creeping up the east side of the Washington Monument when he entered the hospital. A nurse at the main desk told him that Mr. Rhodes was still in his room and therefore presumably "with us," but said that only family could visit, under the circumstances. Nikolai extracted the room number with a teeth-gnashing threat and padded down the corridor while the nurse called security.

Two hospital guards slid up before the door to Dancer's room just as Nikolai arrived from the opposite direction.

"You can't go in there!" one of guards shouted as Nikolai started to push past them. They tried to grab his arms, but he pulled free. Just then, the door opened, and a white-coated doctor came out, hurriedly closing the door behind him.

"You can't come in here!" he said, face red with indignation.

"Is he alive?"

"Barely alive," said the doctor, still furious.

"Who's with him?" Nikolai asked.

"No one, and no one can see him except family. You were told that."

Nikolai's first idea was to haul out his .38 and wave everybody aside. Instead, he said, "I'm his brother. Didn't they tell you that?"

"What? But there's no brother listed."

"Different fathers. And we haven't spoken in years."

That did it. The doctor ushered Nikolai in and then discreetly left.

Dancer had tubes sticking out of him, a dialysis machine alongside, and heart-monitoring equipment nearby. Nikolai dropped onto a stool next to the bed just as Dancer's eyes fluttered open.

"You look like shit," Nikolai said.

"What the hell'd you come for?"

His voice was thick, a little slow, and a little scratchy, and it seemed to Nikolai that it was not illness but the appurtenances of medical science that darkened the atmosphere.

"Just passing through," Nikolai said.

"Well, you caught me at a bad time," Dancer said, straight-faced. He looked out a window at the rising sun and broke into a narrow grin. "Fucking doctor told the nurse I wouldn't last the night."

He coughed, and Nikolai said, "Don't talk if you don't want to."

"This really stinks," Dancer said. "The one thing I never wanted was to die in bed. Especially in a hospital bed. Listen, I sent you a letter."

Nikolai absently nodded. Dancer reached out to pluck at Nikolai's sleeve, and his fingers weakly slid free. He glanced at the offending fingers. "In the old days, I could crack a walnut. Shit. Well, who cares? That's old business."

His eyes opened and closed, thin slits that wandered in and out of recognition and reality. "I wanted to die on a rubber raft in the Caribbean with a pineapple daiquiri. Just drift out to sea like a Viking. Doc?"

"It's me."

"Oh, Jesus, yeah. Fuck."

His eyes closed, and Nikolai prepared himself. But his eyes opened again. "You getting any?"

Nikolai laughed. "Not lately."

"Me either. That's another thing about kicking off. The appetite goes. Do yourself a favor, and don't die in bed. You get to be your own funeral. You're part of the ceremony, like it's somebody else, but it's you."

He paused to take in air and wheezed a little, catching up. Then he said, "What happened? Up there?"

"Not finished."

"Well, don't expect me to give a shit."

The doctor looked in, giving them a quizzical glance.

"That the dumb fucking doctor?" Dancer said. Nikolai nodded. "Tell him I'll let him know the minute I kick off."

The doctor backed out delicately. Dancer's hand slid out; it brushed Nikolai's. "Listen. You there?"

"I'm here."

"I want you to do something."

"Sure."

"Get me a bottle."

"Are you crazy?"

"I guess … make it scotch. It doesn't matter, even if it's shit. I haven't got my taste buds these days."

"I can't do that. Jesus Christ."

"Sure, you can. What's the fucking difference? Anyway, you can't deny a last request."

"That's for an execution."

"What do you think this is? God's executing me." He drifted briefly, then said, "He executes everybody, you know. Nikolai?"

"Yes."

"Take five bucks from my pants. Unless they stole my pants. Get me a pint."

"You're a lunatic," Nikolai said. He rose. "Don't make me go for nothing. You better goddamn hang in there."

"Promise," Dancer said. He crossed limp fingers.

Nikolai slipped out of the room. He told the doctor down the corridor that he was going down to his car for a paper Dancer wanted to sign.

He found a package store three blocks away; coming back, he broke into a run. The corridor was empty—ominously so, he thought—and he pushed into the room. It too was empty, except for Dancer, who was lying as he had been left, fingers crossed.

Nikolai stopped short. Then he settled on the stool again. He took the pint bottle from his pocket and unscrewed the cap. "You broke your promise, you son of a bitch," he said. Then he took a swig.

He was surprised to discover that he was crying. And he thought, *No matter what you do, the people you love keep dying.*

✳   ✳   ✳   ✳

In the lobby, Nikolai ran into Glenallen McKennan.

"Well?"

"Don't bother going up," Nikolai said.

"Did you talk to him?"

"Yes."

They stood awkwardly for a moment, then went out into the fresh, cold air. McKennan fired up his pipe, while Nikolai lit a cigarette.

"Goddamnit, I told you not to come," McKennan said. He tried to be stern, but it came out glum. "Can't say I'm surprised. I knew you'd be here," he groused. "You're not much for orders, you and your damned partner, either of you. Now how do you get back to Oak Ridge? Suppose I'll have to arrange a plane, won't I?"

He stopped to telephone in the necessary arrangements and they clambered into his car, a sporty Ford Phaeton, and headed out to the army air force base at Andrews Field.

"Anything happening up there?" asked McKennan.

"Nothing brilliant, and nothing fast," Nikolai admitted. "Whatever happened to Guthrie's famous source? Why isn't he giving us a hand?"

McKennan gave him the usual glower that meant *Who are you talking about?* Then he gave it up and said, with a disapproving snarl, "If you must know, he's had something of a breakdown. They're delicate animals, you know, these turncoats. Put him in R & R—Quantico or Greenbriar, one of those places. Well, here we are."

The car had pulled up to the entrance gate to the field operations building. They shook hands, and Nikolai presented his ID to a guard as the Ford pulled away.

He was listed on a B-24 heading for Wright-Patterson by way of Knoxville, departing in one hour. He settled in a wicker chair, roaming through his private pantheon: first Dancer, then Katya, then Tati, then Stefan, and then back to Dancer.

Then it was Helger, the estate administrator, and finally, as always, Baron von Hartigens-Hesse.

CHAPTER 26

▼

What struck Nikolai, watching Anna work her way toward his table, was the universality of the female pout—even when, as now, it was masked by the warmest of smiles as she settled across from him in excitement. "Richard!"

They had arranged to meet in one of the snack bars, earlier than usual, because it was her day off. The bright, flooding light of her presence took him by surprise. Meanwhile, she brought the pout into the open. "What happened?"

"Oh. I had to go out of town."

"Richard," she said, with a dose of indulgence, "I know scientists are absent-minded, but we were supposed to meet in front of the movies two nights ago."

"Oh, God," he lamented.

"That's not going to get you out of it," she said: a little flick of the whip.

"Did you try my office?"

"Yes. Well, they said you were out of town," she admitted. "But they were, well, so cold. I thought maybe you were transferred to Alaska."

"I'm really sorry. Tell you what. To make up, you can have dinner anywhere you want."

"Could we go off base?"

"Sure. Why not?"

"There's a place called Peppercorn, along the river. It's supposed to be nice."

"Let's try it."

"We'll have to take a shuttle to the Elda Gate, and then, I think, take the Harriman bus. Something like that."

"Too complicated," Nikolai said. "I can get a car."

"You can?"

"Once in a while," he said, deflating his importance as swiftly as he had raised it. "May take a while. Lot of red tape."

"Time for me to go home and change? You could pick me up there. Just blow the horn."

"Think Papa'll mind?"

"Stop teasing. Anyway, who cares?"

"What's going on?" Heinz said when she came in and shot past him to the bedroom.

"Going out," she said.

Heinz festered a minute, then jumped up and followed her. "What happened to the movies?"

"What movies?"

"Maybe you forgot already. We talked the movies tonight. Then you disappear to go meet him for a soda, and now you're back lick-and-split, and all of a sudden, I'm Mister Second Fiddle." Apparently this realization was traumatic—he put down his beer.

"Because he invited me to dinner, and I can't go out looking like work."

"I was all ready for the movies," Heinz said, laying down a slab of guilt thick as butter.

"You even said you might be seeing your friend," Anna reminded.

"Might. Don't mean it's a done deal. Anyway, don't even see her that much."

"You wouldn't want to go to the movies anyway," Anna said, buttoning a lavender polka-dot dress. There was a bow at the neck. She had put on new shoes and bright lipstick, and her hair shone.

"And how come?"

"Because it's the Marx Brothers."

"Never missed the Marx Brothers. Seen every one."

He was on her heels as she moved into the living room and started pulling on her coat. "I'll bet you didn't know they're Jewish,"

"Who?" he said, surprised. "Marx Brothers? Never heard that."

"Well, they are. Everybody knows it."

His face said: *Can't trust nobody. Not even the Marx Brothers.* But his actual words were: "So what if they're Jews? Still funny. Meantime, I see you're seeing him." He paused, then said, "Ever try to kiss you?"

It was so alien coming from him that she smiled. "Why, Papa!" She smiled even more sweetly.

"I'll bet 'never' is the answer."

"I'll bet 'none of your business' is the answer," she said, pulling on gloves. A horn sounded from below, and she checked the window. "Richard!"

"Got a car now," Heinz said. "Big shot."

"Nothing wrong with that," she said, reaching for the knob.

"Long as there's nothing wrong rest of it," he said as she hurried down the hall. He called out, "Not too late!"

Neither dinner nor the ride home shed new light on the problem. He was warm and amusing, but he never touched. Still, she stubbornly rejected the idea. He was really quite masculine; if he had a sensitive side, that was all to the good.

She decided that Richard was asexual, a word she had recently looked up. Perhaps he was shy with women, or even a little afraid of them ... although it was true that he seemed not the least bit afraid of her.

They pulled up in front of her building, and he said, "Good night, sweet princess. Been a great night."

She liked the reference, so typical of him, off-beat and affectionate. *Without the affection,* she thought.

"It's early," she said. "Come on up."

"How about Papa Bear?"

"He's not there. The lights are out, and he never goes to sleep this early, so he must have connected with his lady friend. Come on."

He hesitated, but only briefly, and they mounted the stairs to the apartment. Just inside, fumbling for the light, Anna thought that he was going to kiss her, but the second passed, and she found the switch.

There was a note on one of the end tables, and Anna picked it up.

"Everything okay?" he said.

"Just perfect."

She handed over the note, and he read aloud, "Might be out late. See you tomorrow. Papi."

"I have beer, if you'd like. And juice. That's about it."

"Juice is fine. Papi," he said, intrigued.

"He was born on the other side," she said.

It barely seemed to register. He was looking at her. "Don't bother," he said.

Perplexed, she pointed to the kitchen. Forget the juice? Or was he saying something else?

"Come here," Nikolai said.

She stumbled blindly into his arms. He tipped back her head and sank his lips into hers. There was no buildup, no graduation to frenzy, just the frenzy itself. And there was no staying the raging river of passion that seized them; they lurched into her bedroom, scattering clothes. He kissed her breasts, and then her lips, and then her breasts again. He sank to her belly, ran his tongue around its tiny crater, then sank further and drank in her musty moistness with his tongue.

Their naked flesh gleamed in the incandescent glow of a streetlight. He straightened and parted her thighs, then raised them and moved in. She cried out as he inched into her, exploring her depth, then he slid back and forth until she whimpered in ecstasy, and he joined her now, with a raw cry that vibrated through their clinging bodies.

A seaside languor hung over the room. The air was heavy, a sultry, briny wetness that clung to their skin. He ran a finger across her open lips. She squeezed his hand and wearily attempted a smile. They stared at the ceiling, watching the exotic shadow-patterns of the leaves of a tree.

She whispered, "I can't move."

"I know."

Moments passed. Fire banked, he said, "What about …?"

"He won't be home until morning."

"You sure?"

"When he says 'see you tomorrow,' he means it."

"The new girlfriend?" he said.

"I'd like to send her flowers," Anna said, and they laughed.

"Have you met her?" Nikolai asked.

"Oh, God, no," she said. "I offered, but he won't let me near her."

"Mating is a very private business."

"Private?" Anna scoffed. "The right word is *rare*."

"Really? I got the impression he was a ladies' man."

"My father? Not in this world. In fact, he never had girlfriends." Quietly, she said, "He's a man with very definite opinions. He doesn't like a lot of things. And the truth is, I kind of thought he disliked women too. But now I don't know. The last few weeks? Maybe he's coming around in his dotage." She looked at him self-consciously. "Is that right? I'm taking a vocabulary course."

"You know damn well it's right, don't you?"

"Yes," she said, proudly.

He traced a finger around her eyes and down her cheek. "What in the hell are we doing here?"

"I don't know, but I'm happy, Richard. Oh, Richard! I can't even tell you this. What he thought about you!"

"Go ahead."

"He called you a pansy boy." She broke into a giggle.

"Pansy boy," he said, straight-faced.

"It was my fault," she blurted. "He asked me if we were fooling around, and I said no, absolutely not, and he could see I was disappointed, so he teased me."

"Pansy boy," said Nikolai. "Has a kind of poetic ring, doesn't it?"

"If you want to know the truth—" she blurted out, and cut it short.

"You were beginning to wonder."

"Yes," she admitted, slipping her arms around him, clasping him tightly. "Because I wanted you so badly, and I was afraid." She propped herself up, her breasts tumbling against his arm. "Why didn't you make a pass? You didn't even touch me. Didn't you know how much I wanted you to?"

"Yes," he said.

"Oh, God, I didn't even ask you—are you married? Was that it?"

"No. I'm not married."

"Well, I wouldn't have cared," she proclaimed. "I wouldn't have given a damn. Are you hungry?"

"Starving."

"I am too. I'm starving for you, but let's eat first. Was that shameless?"

"I hope so," he said, pulling on pants.

She was dressed and padding out of the room before he had finished buttoning his shirt. He followed her into the kitchen. She was studying the open refrigerator.

"How about sausage and eggs?"

She worked in a dervish-like frenzy, but with remarkable efficiency. She set the table, lit the stove, stirred butter in a pan, and whipped the eggs.

She caught his eye on her and said, "What?"

"You remind me of someone."

"Your mother?"

"No."

She paused. "A girl."

"Yes."

"I saw that look once before. Were you in love with her?"

"She was my cousin."

"You could still be in love with her."

"She's dead."

"Oh. Sorry." She went back to the eggs. "But you were close."

"Yes."

"How long ago?"

"Years."

She turned back to him and said, "Know what? I don't know anything about you."

"Really?" he said, offering seductive eyes and a Hollywood smile.

She lunged forward, pan and all, and planted a kiss on his lips. The pan, held out at arm's length, stayed level.

Back at the stove, she said, "I can't help wondering. Do you think it's strictly physical?"

"It's strictly physical," he said.

"You are such a rotten person."

They ate quickly, watching each other with ethereal smiles that hid none of their hunger to return to bed.

Later, in the ennui of another state of exhaustion, she said, "If my father knew, he would call me a tramp. But I'm not. There were two boys before tonight. They weren't even men."

He sensed that she was waiting for some sort of reciprocal confession, but what could he tell her? That he was stalking her father, that he was coupling with her to stay in proximity to his target?

He knew it was not true. What had started as coincidence—Anna's remarkable resemblance to Katya—had shot off into a dimension all its own, an uncharted course across an emotional sea. And what was the depth of this emotion? Fucking?

No, but for all its seeming irreverence, it was Anna who had shattered the trauma of years. There was more to it, but how much more? In this, his helpless state of rapture, where the overpowering need was physical, how could he measure meaning?

Anna was watching him. "What are you thinking?"

"I was thinking about you. Anna, shouldn't I go?"

"You're worried."

"Not for me. For you."

"Do you know something? No—two things. I don't think I'd mind if he walked in right this minute. It would settle things once and for all. And I'd be free. And don't ask me why I'm not free, because I don't really know. Are we bound that close to our parents, Richard? Even when we don't want to be with them?"

"Maybe so."

"I'm not making sense, am I?"

"Yes, you are."

She smiled up at him. "You like to indulge me, and I like that."

"Keep talking. I like to listen."

She snuggled closer and said, "I was thinking about...."

"What?"

"Coming here. It's a long story, but we went to Mexico first, when we left New York. And that was the moment. I mean, I could have been on my own. I had the choice. I didn't really have to go, because ... well, it's another long story. I moved out about a year ago, moved in with a girlfriend in New York, but that didn't work out, and I came back home. And then he wanted to leave New York, and that's when I had the choice. And somehow, somehow, I felt I had to go with him. I felt he needed me. But now I'm beginning to wonder. Maybe it was because I needed him."

He nodded sympathetically and said, "What did you do in Mexico?"

"Nothing," she said, in a lazy voice. "We were at a hotel, not that far from the border, but it was in the hills, and so lovely."

"What's the name of the place?" he said jokingly. "Maybe I'll go there some time."

"I forget. Near Matamoros—oh! Rancho Internationale," she said, rather pleased with her pronunciation. And then she remembered the warnings from Heinz about the need for discretion. Here she was, blabbering away like an idiot. But this was Richard, and she snuggled closer.

"What's the second thing?" he asked.

"What second thing? Oh! The second thing is ... don't you wonder why something so wonderful doesn't last longer? Actually, I think I've figured it out— it's an algebra formula. Algebraic," she corrected. "The compensation for hastiness of execution is frequency of event."

"That's incredible," Nikolai said. "The soul of a nymphomaniac and the brain of a scientist. Was there some sort of message attached?"

"Yes, there was. The message is, you can't leave yet, because I'm going to want you again."

*   *   *   *

Heinz and Toni were comfortably stretched under the covers. Any contact was by chance; their proximity had more to do with body heat than intimacy. Still and all, she liked the occasional, if accidental, touch of his body. She liked the thick, black-haired matting of his chest and back, even the fusty dampness under his arms.

In this, Heinz's fourth nocturnal excursion into her bed over the past few weeks, he had settled into a pillow-propped position while Toni lay quietly alongside, lost in thought. The first of their overnight trysts had produced a small shuffling of embers that had turned into an awkward fit of lovemaking. It was New York in her apartment five years ago all over again, driven, as earlier, by little more than a confluence of events that seemed to call for an appropriate gesture. For Toni, who of course was not particular about gender and who took this sort of thing as it came, the coupling gave the routine satisfaction of her occasional cigarette, something one did once in a while by habit and without great expectations.

Heinz was studying an overview map of Oak Ridge, which depicted its various classified facilities. Guard gates and security installations were also indicated. The map was boldly marked "Confidential" at the top.

"Where'd you get this?" he asked.

"I got it," she said smoothly. She registered his frown and added, "You'd be surprised, Herbie. Personnel opens a lot of doors."

"So far, it ain't opened the big one," he complained. "What I see is, we ain't moving."

"We're moving," she said.

He lowered the map. "That where you been?"

"Been where?"

"I know you don't stay home for me," he said. "I mean, nights you go out."

"Why, Herbie! Are you jealous?"

"Ain't my business what you do."

"You're the best kind of man to have around the house," she purred.

"So we're moving. That mean you heard something, or what?"

"It means we're getting closer."

"When?"

"I'll let you know."

"Ain't the kind likes to just sit around," he grumbled.

"No kidding?" she said, smirking, but she coiled a small fist and tapped his arm, perverse approval of his badgering. She paused, dangling the next line like a carrot: "If you're a good boy, you might even get a better job."

He was immediately alert. "Listening."

"You can drive a truck, right? Not one of the big ones—small truck?"

"Sure."

"Starting Monday, you're a matériel coordinator for Webster."

"Webster? That's cement, ain't it?"

"Right. You'll go around to the different building projects, check what they need. If they're short and it's a hurry-up, you pick up stuff at the warehouse yourself, and you deliver it. That's where the truck comes in."

"Still didn't hear where," he said anxiously. She smiled, and he jack-knifed forward and guessed: "K-25!" The dislodged covers revealed his torn undershirt and her small, bare breasts.

"Hey, it's freezing," she said.

He flipped the covers across her shoulders, face glowing with the news, "So that's what we hit! K-25!"

"Maybe, or maybe not," she said cagily. "I'll let you know tomorrow. In the meantime, we're not hitting anything, and we don't talk about anything, right?"

"Sure, right," he said. Fishing, he added, "Still don't know how we do it, two people so far."

"When we get to it, we get to it," she said, her rote speech by now, and as usual, he scowled at her mulishness.

CHAPTER 27

▼

The taste of love made them insatiable. In the week that followed their marathon—spiced by the prospect of being caught—they managed to meet and make love almost every night. Nikolai had no idea what was happening, except that they were rapacious. *Two sickies,* he thought, quite contentedly: Anna, bursting the bonds of repression, and he, shooting past Freud with a vengeance.

What they did and would not dare talk about was the simple pleasure of being together. Nikolai knew he had lost his bearings but could not bring himself to abandon his blissful state. So here he was, shunting between paradise and hell, wondering if there could be such a thing as a wretched excess of pleasure.

For the most part, their trysts took place in the Briars, an unpretentious collection of faded-white cottages seven miles out of town. The motel did a land-office business, quaking as it did with illicit lovemaking from the base.

And one night, with the cottages all taken, Nikolai abandoned all prudence and spent the night in Anna's bed again, the two of them listening hard into the darkness and bucking like wild horses into the early hours of the morning.

Just before she fell asleep, Nikolai whispered, "What do you suppose we want?"

Anna did not seem surprised. She said, "Knowing that things can always stay the same."

When her eyes closed, Nikolai wondered what he needed beyond Anna. When their adolescent passion dimmed, she would still be good for him. *Knowing that everything can stay the same.*

Anna's body was molded against his. In her sweet warmth, with her breasts softly swelling against his skin, there was incredible security. It was a spell that promised an abiding future. It had to be preserved.

But he knew better. The appalling irony of the moment was that they could not exist. To carry out his mandate was to lose Anna. To abandon it would make him a fugitive again—no less than Anna, who would have traded one fugitive for another.

Out of the deathly silence of the night, he picked up a vibration, then the sound of someone on the stairs. He slipped out of bed and padded through the living room to the front door. Footsteps sounded from the landing, then stopped. Nikolai listened intently. The building gave off strange sounds, not the creaking of old wood, but the stretching of something new and not yet settled. The steps picked up again, heavily approaching along the echoing hallway.

It occurred to Nikolai now that he was comically naked. In less than three seconds, Baumann would slip the key in the lock and open the door, and he would be standing there in all his dangling helplessness. He covered himself hastily, but the footsteps, in thumping anticlimax, continued down the hall.

He went into the kitchen and glanced to the street. An oppressively gray dawn was working toward daylight. Wispy ribbons of fog clung to the hills and valleys surrounding Oak Ridge. Early-morning traffic was starting to trundle by, headlights cutting away the night. It was time to leave.

Turning out of the kitchen, Nikolai's eye fell on an envelope at the far end of the kitchen counter. Even from a distance, he recognized the bold imprint of army security. The letter had been opened, and he widened the flap and tugged out the notice within. It was addressed to Herbert Brenner and crisply noted that his transfer to Section E, Plant Facility 34, K-25, for purposes of general construction work therein, had been approved; said Herbert Brenner was now cleared by the appropriate security authority for entrance and exit to facility K-25; subject was requested to stop by the undersigned security office for purposes of obtaining his red identity badge.

The notification was dated four days earlier, and Nikolai was appalled at the extent of his bungling. He had been so caught up in the song of the forest that he had missed the trees.

He dressed quickly, then bent over Anna's sleeping form and whispered, "Have to go."

She stirred and murmured, "I love you."

*   *   *   *

Toni Graf picked out a chicken sandwich, chocolate pudding, and a glass of milk. She paid the cashier and found an empty table. There was no soundproofing, and a babble of voices bounced across the cavernous cafeteria.

"Mind if I sit down?" a man said. He was holding a tray, a plate of spaghetti, and two Coca-Colas.

"Suit yourself," Toni said.

The man was in his late forties, short, and thick through the middle. His name was Barnes. He settled at the table and hungrily attacked the spaghetti. Orange smears broke out around his mouth like a rash. From time to time, he stabbed them away with a paper napkin, which soon became grimy and stained; he ate sloppily and soon shredded the napkin.

"Here," Toni said. She handed over an extra.

"Thanks," said Barnes. He plunged back to the spaghetti and ate without pause until the plate was empty, then wiped it with bread and ate that too.

Toni did not bother to lift her head. She ate her sandwich slowly and methodically and without interest.

"I'm putting it under my plate," Barnes said. "Some of it checks out, some of it don't."

"What doesn't check out?" Toni asked.

"Schools. Can't get nothing on the schools."

"Back up. Social Security checks out? Driver's license?"

Barnes nodded. "ID checks out. Just the schools don't."

"Like what?"

"Dartmouth. Supposed to be a degree, bachelor of science. Nothing. Not there. And MIT—supposed to be a master's, but it doesn't show up."

The chocolate pudding was untouched. He eyed it. "You want it?" she said, and slid it over.

"What's it all about?" Barnes said uneasily.

"Don't worry," she said, with a dismissive grin. "It's not a security question. It's just one of my girlfriends; I guess he's taking her for a ride."

"Oh, I get it," Barnes said brightly, "He's married, she isn't, fake background. Right?"

"Right."

"What people won't do," he said, and winked.

Toni came up with a conspiratorial eyelash flutter and rose. "I'm late. See you."

Instead of returning to the office, she went to one of the mobile banks that dotted the Oak Ridge landscape and cashed a ten-dollar bill in small change. Then she entered a nearby recreation building and slid into a telephone booth.

Kitty Roderick's voice answered on the second ring. "New York Public Library, reference desk."

"Hi," Toni said.

It took Kitty a moment to bring it all together. "That you?"

"Long time," said Toni. "How's it going?"

"Not bad," Kitty said, a little tightly. She suspected that she would be asked to do something, but she didn't want to be involved. "Where are you?"

"Need a favor, Kit. Could you check something out for me?"

"Come on, Toni," Kitty rasped in protest.

"Not much of a favor. Just a little fact-checking."

"Where are you?" Kitty persisted.

"Nowhere near. Working for the war effort." They had lived together in the old days, loved together, and Toni could not resist a personal note. "You miss me?"

"I'm married," said Kitty.

"Yeah, so what's that got to do with it?" Toni said.

"I'm married, Toni, so don't even bother."

"No bother, sweetie. Besides, I'm about eight states away, and what I need is a little help—don't need that clammy old mop."

It had just enough intimacy to bring a hoarse laugh from Kitty. She said, "What have you got?"

"Just a little academic research. Kind of stuff we used to do back at the library in the old days."

At the other end, Kitty paused. In this case, "the old days" referred to their employment at the German-American Library and their dilettantish exploration of each other in the back rooms.

"Go ahead," Kitty said softly, warmed up by memory.

"The name is Richard Lyons," said Toni. Oliver Barnes had more than aroused her suspicions, but she wanted to be sure.

✳   ✳   ✳   ✳

Ironically, Nikolai was on the phone to New York at much the same time. He was in the small office he sometimes used, a windowless space that had a desk, a chair, and a telephone. It was his second call to FBI headquarters in New York in two days. The first call had reported his derelict discovery of Heinz Baumann's transfer to security-sensitive K-25.

"New problem?" Menzies asked, sarcasm dripping.

"I screwed up. Let's move on."

"It's not something to be taken lightly."

"Jesus Christ, if you can't let it go, find yourself another Boy Scout," Nikolai said.

"What was that?" said Menzies.

"What's up?" Boettinger hastily interjected.

Nikolai took a breath. "Okay. We agree Baumann couldn't have arranged a transfer by himself. He needed somebody, and that had to be Toni Graf."

"Is there a new point being made here?" Menzies asked.

"If you want to hear it."

"Go ahead," Menzies grumbled.

"It takes real leverage to shift somebody from general-classification security level to a red badge. Toni Graf is mid-level personnel. She needed help too."

Menzies took a moment to pause the flow of bile. He churned it over. Then he jumped. "They've got somebody else planted! Somebody higher up."

"I don't think so," Nikolai said.

Menzies was so excited that he plunged right past the stop signal. "Damn, I told you guys Siebert would be sending more people in!" Then, warily: "What do you mean, you don't think so?"

"I mean she's got somebody helping her, but I don't think he's a German agent." He could see Menzies' face break out in red splotches from eight hundred miles away.

"Well, then, who the hell would be helping her, mister?"

Nikolai said, "Either somebody she's paying or somebody she's screwing."

Jarred by his failure to grasp the obvious, no less than blasphemy over an army secure line, Menzies hissed, "Watch what you're saying!"

"She's putting out, is my guess," Boettinger said cheerily.

"That's because you've got a goddamn toilet bowl for a brain," Menzies said.

"I don't think it's money," Nikolai said.

"You know something?" Menzies asked cautiously.

"I know who he is."

"Who?"

"A man named Oliver Barnes. He's number two in K-25 personnel."

"Write that down," Menzies instructed Boettinger from his end of the phone. Then, back to Nikolai: "Why don't you think it's the money?"

"Because Mr. Barnes has three sons in the service and a hundred grand sitting in the bank."

"You've seen them together?"

"Twice in the last two days."

"Under what circumstances?" Menzies pressed.

"Yesterday, in one of the cafeterias. She was sitting alone. He came over with his tray. They chatted. Polite stuff. Went through the act—never saw each other before. She was smooth. He wasn't."

"Second time?"

"Last night," Nikolai said. "I followed them to a motel." And it was just as well they couldn't see his face at the moment, because Oliver Barnes, once having safely tucked Toni Graf into the front seat of his Packard, had driven straight as an arrow to Nikolai's sometime home away from home. The Briars.

Before he could stop himself, Menzies, in a gush of good will, said, "Nice work."

"Why, thank you, Wilbur."

"What do you think?"

"I think they're going to make a move in the next twenty-four to forty-eight hours."

"Why?" Menzies asked stiffly, raking over old coals.

"Because I can't see Siebert sending in more people at this late date."

"And I don't buy two amateurs hitting a heavily secured plant a mile long," said Menzies.

"You're looking for too much. What we've got out there is a couple of kraut kamikazes. What we've got to do, and I mean now, is look for explosives being smuggled into K-25."

"Damn it, we're going around in circles. That would be giving the game away, and I'm not going to do that."

Nikolai held the phone aside and stared at it. Fuming, he said, "What's your next move, chief?"

It was intended as a Circassian slash, but Menzies took it as submission. "I've already contacted Mr. Hoover with a request for emergency procedure authorization. That cover it for you?"

"Perfect," said Nikolai, in despair. He hung up.

*   *   *   *

Heinz picked her up at the Socony station, about half a mile outside the complex on the Clinton road. She was off to one side, a suitcase at her feet. She dumped the suitcase in the cab and checked the road before settling in.

When the truck moved off, she said, "Any problems?"

"No problems," he said. In fact, he had been stopped twice leaving the complex. A guard inside K-25 had pointed to the twilight sky and said, "Hey, sixty-seven, get those candles lit!" And then he had been stopped by a pair of MPs with upturned palms at the Elda Gates—Webster company trucks required special authorization to leave the complex.

It was a tricky moment, because the papers, supplied by Toni, were forged. Even more embarrassing in its way, if he had been caught, was the fact that he did not have a driver's license—a detail he had not mentioned to Toni because it would have cut him out of the operation right then and there.

"Where we going?" he asked.

"Get a sandwich. Turn right down there. Take the Maryville road."

"We go to Maryville for a sandwich?"

"Sure," she said, not listening.

"Can't get blood from a rock," Heinz groused.

"Sure you can," Toni said. She was grinning, suddenly bubbling. His mouth parted, waiting. She said, "It happens tomorrow."

His sallow eyes brightened. "So!" He looked over for more.

"One thing at a time, tiger."

Her penchant for dragging things out and reveling in the process sparked him. "Goddamn time to know things!" he bellowed.

"Hey, easy," she said.

"What's this Maryville?" he demanded.

"We're picking up goods, okay?"

Heinz grunted assent. He pointed to the valise. "What's that?"

"That's the juice, Heinzie."

He nodded, pleased now. At her direction, he parked the truck on a dark, deserted street, and she led him around the block toward a backlit storefront sign that read, SUTTER'S BBQ—BEST PULLED PORK AROUND!

An early supper crowd filled the restaurant. Toni ordered for them while fiddle-pitched conversations see-sawed back and forth. A big-boned county sheriff with a potbelly came in. He knew everybody, and there were twangy greetings all around. The goose-necked proprietor had a pickup order ready, and the sheriff passed Heinz and Toni, heading for the door.

Seconds later, their order came, the sandwiches thick and oozing a red-brown sauce. Baked beans and coleslaw filled out the plate.

They ate, and Heinz nodded. He liked the barbecue well enough, but he was restless.

"Killing time till it's dark, Herbie," Toni patiently explained.

Easing back, he ordered a second beer, gobbled the rest of his sandwich, and accepted Toni's half of a half. Finished, he looked out through a nearby window and watched the faded day graduating to night; across the street, a short-poled street lamp was sputtering to life, its globe clouded by the carcasses of dead bugs.

"Just about dark," he said,

She nodded. They took the check to an irrepressibly good ol' country boy behind a cash register, and Heinz worked a toothpick while she paid. He had no gender inhibitions on this score; if she was the boss, then small tokens of authority, such as picking up a check, went with the territory.

Back in the truck, she directed him to a country road on the other side of town. He noticed her staring and said, "What?"

"Don't you get excited?"

"Sure."

"But you don't show it. That's good."

"Don't see you chewing no nails," he said, sharing the praise.

"Damn it, Heinzie," she suddenly erupted, "this is big stuff! I mean damn big, you know?"

Heinz produced a lopsided smile.

The road was going from bad to worse, and now they were riding the ruts, but it was mercifully short, and then it became tolerably bumpy. They passed an abandoned barn and approached a sagging shack that was twenty or thirty yards off the road.

"That's it," Toni said. "Just turn around and back up."

She jumped out and played a small flashlight on a rusty lock across the doors of the shack. She inserted a key and fiddled until the lock sprung free, then removed it and tugged open the doors. "Back in," she instructed. "Go slow—it's tight."

With her help, Heinz backed most of the truck into the shed. He got out of the cab and squeezed past the length of the truck to the tail. He could make out an array of same-shape forms. Toni swung the light and illuminated dozens and dozens of gray sacks lined up in depth against the wall. They were marked CEMENT.

"You're going to have to do it," she said. "I'll be outside in case somebody comes."

Heinz went to work loading the truck. The bags of cement were not as heavy as he expected; he developed a slinging rhythm and picked up speed. Once, Toni's voice came sailing back with a warning: "Car!"

Heinz held his breath. He heard an engine chugging up the road, then heard it go past the shed and fade to silence. "Okay!" she shouted back, and Heinz resumed loading the cement.

Half an hour later, the job was done. Heinz eased the truck out of the shed, Toni locked the doors. Back on paved road, Heinz pointed to the cement bags and said, "That's it? That's all?"

"Just the ticket," Toni assured.

They kept a steady, legal pace all the way to Oak Ridge. When they approached the Elda Gates, Toni's lips went taut.

But it went off with satiny ease. Toni stayed in the truck and handed over the papers herself this time. For a woman who could take it or leave it, she had a remarkable faculty for generating lust. Her Bacall-like rasp and her sultry eyes promised pleasure that would never come to pass, but they served their purpose. The cargo looked like cement and the manifest stated that it was cement, but it was never put to the test. The MPs at the gate waved the truck through with a return smile.

Heinz maneuvered truck number 67 into the Webster & Co. lot and came to a stop in an empty space. Toni was still sitting in her seat, staring ahead.

"Problem?" he said.

"It's Anna's boyfriend."

"What about him?"

"I've been checking. Something's wrong."

"Like what?"

"I'm not sure. I don't think he's who he says he is."

The fact was that Kitty had not been able to substantiate a single thing about Richard Lyons. She had uncovered two of the same name in the Boston area, but neither matched the description given by Toni; among other things, they were fifty-seven and sixty-six years old.

Through another mutual friend living in Boston, Kitty had discovered that Richard Lyons had never lived at the address listed in his personnel folder (162 Fuller Street, in Brookline, a Boston suburb). No less damaging, there was no record of a Richard Lyons having attended any grammar school or high school in the area, and there was not a shred of evidence that he had attended either Dartmouth College or the Massachusetts Institute of Technology.

"Then what you're saying … he's with the army security, maybe even FBI."

"Yes."

Shrewdly, Heinz said, "You brought up this for a reason? Like what to do?"

"Yes," she said uneasily. "Because it might be complicated."

"How so?" Heinz asked, again with an insightful glance.

"Because the complications get personal, that's why."

"Ain't no complications I see. We got to make sure he don't interfere, whatever it takes. Am I right?"

"That's right," she said. But her voice was a little reedy.

"There's some problem?" he said.

"Heinz, yes. It's Anna."

"What about?"

"If we have to … I mean, this Richard Lyons … I know where the priorities are, so it doesn't bother me, but where your daughter's involved, that might be something else."

"Where my daughter's involved? What kind of involved? You saying she's so involved—serious—that's what you're worried?"

"Yes. Exactly."

Coldly, he said, "Whatever Anna's involved, that ain't what's important. What's important is like you said, the priorities."

"Heinz, there's something you maybe don't know—how serious she is. She's in love."

"You think I give a damn?"

"*She* will. That's the point."

"She ain't in love, even if it looks like it." He snarled, "All he is is a pansy boy."

There was a pause, then she said, "Heinz, I know that's what you think. But that's not the way it is."

At this, his eyes widened. He stared in disbelief, indignation, then rage. "You trying to tell me …!" He could not bring himself to articulate such an abomination.

"Heinz, listen to me. They're grown-ups. They're not children. You've got to expect—"

"Don't tell me what I got to expect!"

"It's going to happen, Heinz," she said doggedly. "That's what people do."

"Not mine!" he roared.

"Yes. Yours and everybody else's," she said, holding remarkably firm against the storm.

"Don't have to listen to lies!" he blared, reaching for the door handle.

"You open that door, and you're finished," she snarled. He hesitated. Quietly, she said, "You can't do two things at once, and you're not giving the orders. So if you don't want to hear any more, I'll shut up, and you keep going."

He hung there, as though poised on a razor blade. Finally, he said, "Go ahead, talk."

"The way you have to think is, anything they do, that's their business. As long as it doesn't interfere with our business. You understand what I'm saying, Heinz? Our business. In other words, we don't take care of Mr. Richard Lyons because he's making love to your daughter. It's got to be because he's in our way. Because if you focus on personal stuff, you're going to make a mistake. And we can't afford any mistakes."

It was more than reasonable; it was assuaging. Heinz removed his fingers from the door handle and stared ahead frigidly.

"Where?" he asked.

She frowned. "What's the difference?"

"In her own bed in my house," he realized.

"Does it matter?" she argued.

He let it soak in, then said, "Maybe not."

"That's the point. It doesn't really matter. It's an adult situation. It has to do with accepting the realities of life, not the geography. You know what I mean? Forget the location."

Heinz rubbed his sandpaper growth.

"I know what's on your mind," she said, "but if he turns out to be a problem, you're not going to take care of him. For two reasons, and the first one, I just told you. But the second reason is, it may not be necessary."

He took the lecture well, until this last part. He looked up slowly. "What do you mean, ain't necessary?"

"If we have to keep this man from being a problem, then we have to. But if we don't, then we're better off, because anything that draws attention to us could wreck what we're trying to do. *Verstehst?*"

His head shot up. The sudden lapse into German served as an intimacy, a peace offering, a fresh bonding. In the old seesaw battle of emotions, he was back to a clarity of thought that would have seemed impossible only a moment ago.

"Ain't going to argue the point. Get carried away sometimes. So, fair enough. But let me ask something. How do we keep from him getting in the way?"

So mildly was the question framed that Toni looked over with the glimmer of a smile, encouraged. "Okay, here's what I meant. What we're talking about is going to come up fast, very fast. But chances are, Mr. Richard Lyons doesn't know that, hasn't got a clue in this world. What I figure is, if he knew more than he knows, he would have stopped us when we came in."

He looked over with fresh admiration. "Back at the gate—you were ready, in case?"

"Sure, I was ready." Slowly, she withdrew a black .32-caliber automatic, then pushed it out of sight again.

Heinz brought his hand out of his jacket. In it was a steel-gray .38. "Me too," he said.

They were reunited. The penitent Heinz was back in the land of the rational. He respected her authority and appreciated her guidance.

But these were applications of the moment. They served to keep him functioning for the common good. Deep inside, in the core of the furnace, was a white-hot hatred for the filthy snake who had fouled Anna.

CHAPTER 28

▼

Even at this hour, almost 10:00 PM, trucks were roaring in and out of the lot. Nikolai watched from a distance as they emerged through the company gate: Graf first, headed for a shuttle stop, then Baumann, hands in pockets, head thrust low. As soon as they had cleared the area, peeling off in opposite directions, Nikolai drove up to the gate and flashed his ID at the Webster & Co. guard.

The guard waved him on, and Nikolai drove down one of the lanes, past scores of identical trucks. He found truck number 67, got out of the car, and went to the back of the truck. It was unlocked, which made sense: the more accessible, the less suspicious. He clambered into the truck and played a pen light across the musty-smelling sacks of cement. But there was an alien odor too, a dampness that went beyond unprocessed cement and hemp bags.

He cradled one of the sacks and, like Heinz before him, registered its weight: lighter than cement. With a pocket knife, he carefully punctured the sack and gently probed within; the contents were slate-gray and had a putty-like consistency.

Nikolai raced back through the truck lanes to the gate, and five minutes later, he was in his office above security headquarters, talking to Menzies and Boettinger in New York.

He described the trip to Maryville, the storage shed, and the picked-up load that was sitting in the Webster & Co. lot. "It's all coming together!" Menzies said.

Nikolai said, "Look, Wilbur. Don't you think it's time to bring in some help?"

"We're leaving here in a couple of hours."

"Air force out of Floyd Bennett," Boettinger provided.

"Don't try to be a big shot," Menzies warned. "If we reel those birds in too soon, we lose the golden goose."

"Look, I've been thinking it over," Nikolai said. "I'm not sure there is a golden goose. Sending a team up from Mexico made sense back in New York, but I'm beginning to think we were wrong."

"Tell you what, Nikolai. Why don't you let me do the thinking?"

Nikolai tamped down his rage. With a sigh, he said, "That truck's just sitting there."

"All right, I take your point," Menzies said, as though proving that civility is its own reward. "What do you want to do?"

"Surveillance."

Menzies sulked across the silence. Yes, it made sense, but it would spoil his game. "Too clumsy. If they latch on, the whole thing is blown!"

"No uniforms. Make it a repair crew," Nikolai suggested.

"Anything else?" said the put-out Menzies. "Look, you just stay the hell away from there. Baumann knows what you look like." He hung up.

Nikolai jumped back in the Chevy and floored it. He reached the lot, and through the windshield, he studied the bewildering mass of clones. He focused, counted, and zeroed in. Number 67 was where it had been left. A moment ago he hadn't cared, but now his relief was as palpable as the fear it replaced.

He chose a shadowy area to watch number 67 until security came. Again he was struck by the dizzying symmetry of the aligned trucks. In their collective bulk, they generated the image of a phantasmagoric monster—but the only monster was number 67.

Suddenly he understood what he had to do. Near the truck lot was a service garage, and he drove there at full speed and commandeered a can of paint. Moments later, he returned to the lot. He finished and was back in the Chevy and out on the cross street when a Webster & Co. repair van arrived.

Nikolai watched from a distance as three men in baggy blue denims popped out of the van and began mending a length of chain-link fence not too far from the truck they were assigned to watch.

Nikolai looked up at a near-full moon; its light filtered through a particle layer thrown up by round-the-clock smokestacks, a man-made borealis. He watched the security men play out their chain-link charade and tuned into Knoxville's all-night station.

His eye wandered across the '42 Chevy, one of the last civilian models off the assembly line before the factory had started churning out tanks; the trim was strictly Woolworth's, and it wore clumsy-looking wooden bumpers that reminded him of Dutch shoes. He closed his eyes, and when he opened them, two hours had passed, and it was 5:00 AM. The repair crew had slowed but was still at it.

Nikolai turned the key and hit the starter, quietly meshed into first, and rolled off.

*   *   *   *

At much the same time, a light went on in Anna's apartment. Heavy-lidded under the overhead bulb, she opened the refrigerator and took out a bottle of milk. She poured a glass and sat at the kitchen table.

To her surprise, Heinz came in, fully dressed and bright-eyed.

"Where're you going?"

"Busy day today coming up."

"It isn't even five o'clock."

"Up awake is up," he pronounced. "Notice you're up."

She shrugged and said, "Can't sleep."

"Must be a reason," Heinz said.

He took a beer from the refrigerator and uncapped it. Beer before breakfast! Anna shuddered at the thought. Heinz sat across from her at the table. He was staring in the long, familiar way, with a mixture of savage amusement and righteous contempt.

"What's the matter?" she said.

"Nothing the matter. Somebody say something's the matter?"

"Well, you have that look."

"That so?"

"What is it, Papa?"

"Nothing. Just wondering. Maybe why you can't sleep is you must be lonely. Not used to being alone."

His manner had prepared her for teasing, but she sensed his maliciousness, finished the milk, and rose.

"Where is he, if you're so lonely?"

"What's your point?" she said, glaring now.

"Point is, looks to me you got a problem when you ain't in bed with your boyfriend."

She braced herself. He was not bothering with insinuation; no beating around the bush. She stared back, trying to stare him down. "Am I supposed to confess to something?"

"Don't have to confess nothing."

"In other words, you know everything I do," she said, playfully probing.

"Could be," he said.

She smiled. "And that means you know without question that I've been with Richard."

"That's right."

"Well, now what?" she said. "Read me the riot act?"

Her arrogance brought him to his feet. "I know what you been doing right here in my own house! In my house!" He unfolded an arm and pointed to her bedroom. "In that bed, right there! You want to know how I know? I looked at the sheets. I looked at your dirty sheets, filthy pig!"

Anna was shocked. She had nothing to come back with. At last, she drew herself up, haughtiness gone, pride in its place. "Richard and I are in love. Can't you understand the difference?"

"In love? That's a hot one."

"Maybe because you don't know what it is."

"I know what it ain't. It ain't this—you and that dirty pig that takes you into bed, right here in my own house!"

"You don't understand! We're in love!"

"That's what you think, slut!"

"It happens to be true! If you asked him, he'd say the same thing!"

"If I ever talk to that pig, won't be about love! You want to know about love? It's something you ain't got, and you don't even know it!"

"What are you talking about?"

"This 'Richard' you're so in love with—he ain't what you think!"

"I don't even know what that means. I just know you'll say anything to keep me from being happy!"

Heinz paused. He was talking too much, but what did it matter? He was as free as he had ever been in his life. Still, he knew that he could not go much further. He settled for repeating, "He ain't what you think."

"You made the whole thing up," she said, almost lightheartedly, as though conceding some but not all. "And even if it was true, Papa, that doesn't change anything. We're in love."

"See if you're in love tomorrow."

"Tomorrow?" She laughed it off.

"You won't laugh so much," he said. "This Richard, your famous Richard, he's going to blow up like a bomb." He liked that. "Just like a bomb. And if you want to know where you got it, you got it from me."

She grew uneasy. "What are you trying to say?"

He got up, and slurping beer as he went, drained the bottle and tossed it in a garbage bag as he left the room.

Bewildered, Anna kept turning over his cryptic words. "I want to know what you mean," she bawled out suddenly, but it was too late. The front door slammed.

✳   ✳   ✳   ✳

A thin streak of dawn broke as Nikolai hit the Knoxville road. He was heading for the airport, some twenty miles off. A cloudburst dumped pellets of rain, and he had to slow down; but suddenly, it was over, and by the time he reached the airport, the sky was clearing.

Nikolai watched a C-47, running lights blinking, as it clawed for the sky and turned north. In the operations building, he discovered that the flight from New York's Floyd Bennett Field was only about ten minutes out. He returned to the Chevy and settled behind the wheel again. It had been a long night's vigil; his eyes fluttered shut.

He opened them again and caught an image in the rear-view mirror. A black sedan was now parked just behind and to the side of the Chevy. A man in a black suit and gray fedora materialized at the driver's-side window. Another man, in another dark suit and gray fedora, was stationed near the passenger-side door.

The man on the driver's side waved something. It took Nikolai a moment to realize that it was a gun. The man kept the gun leveled while he tugged open the car door.

"Okay, out. And I want to see those hands at all times," he said, gun waving.

Nikolai climbed out. He kept his hands visible. "Who're you?" the man said, leery-eyed.

"Who're you?" Nikolai said back.

"FBI," the man told him.

"Well aren't we all? Sort of," Nikolai said.

"Don't get smart. I'm still waiting."

"Granger. You want an ID?"

The FBI man had a square face with a large mole on the chin. "I want a real slow ID," he said.

Nikolai brought out his wallet in discreet stages. The FBI man took it. "What the hell's this? What's a liaison agent?"

"It's just below second-class scout. You waiting for Menzies?"

The two FBI agents turned out to be from the Knoxville office, and two more got out of the car. At the same time, another black car with Tennessee plates roared up and braked dramatically; it contained four more agents, these from the Memphis office. Meanwhile, a Beechcraft with Air Force markings was drifting down toward the runway. The wheels touched, the brake screeched, and the plane made a sharp ninety-degree turn, taxiing toward operations.

Menzies and Boettinger jumped out as the Knoxville contingent surged forward. Menzies was so pleased by this attention, albeit arranged, that he thanked the group at length for being there. From the rear of the group, Boettinger discreetly waved to Nikolai.

Menzies approached Nikolai. "What's the situation?" he asked. Boettinger drifted over too.

Nikolai said, "Truck's still there. That was thirty minutes ago."

Menzies called over to the other agents, who looked like a football huddle in the half-light. "Do we have radio phones?"

"Both cars," one of the FBI men called back.

Menzies gestured, and Boettinger got into one of the cars and called through to Oak Ridge security. All was still quiet; truck number 67 was still where it had been parked.

"Let's get on the road," Menzies said. He waved an arm like a wagon master, and the FBI groups moved like magnetized filings for their cars.

Back on the highway, Nikolai set the pace at a steady seventy-five miles per hour.

"What about Baumann and Graf?" Menzies asked.

"No sign of them since last night."

"I just hope to hell they haven't been scared off," he said. He looked over suspiciously. "You didn't do anything, did you?"

"You mean like stand in front of the truck with a spotlight on my head?"

"Just want to make sure you're straight on this," said Menzies.

"Straight as an arrow," Nikolai said.

As the cavalcade swept toward Oak Ridge, Menzies said, with as much ingenuousness as he could muster, "What do you think's going to happen today?"

It dripped with *precious*, so Nikolai said, "I don't know, Wilbur. What do *you* think's going to happen today?"

"Maybe not what we expect," Menzies said shrewdly.

"Something's up?"

"You could say that. In fact, a brand new wrinkle!"

"Turns everything around," Boettinger piped in.

"If you don't mind," Menzies chided. He turned back to Nikolai. "Late last night we learned that General Leslie Groves and Doctor Robert Oppenheimer will be coming in tomorrow. And one more. I forget his name. Italian."

"Enrico Fermi," Nikolai said. "They're coming in for a startup in Y-12. A new Alpha calutron."

"The point is, they're pretty important, wouldn't you say? Groves heads up the entire Manhattan Project. Oppenheimer is in charge of developing the bomb at Los Alamos. And Fermi …"

"Nobel Prize. Did the chain reaction," Boettinger remembered.

"Exactly." To Nikolai, Menzies said, "You getting the drift?"

"You think they're the target."

"Under the circumstances," Menzies snapped, "don't you?"

Nikolai thought about it. "No, I don't."

"You don't think this changes everything?" Menzies said, seeping disbelief.

"No."

With exquisite patience, Menzies said, "Look, I was stuck on a big-time plan to hit production in Oak Ridge. But all we had showing was two people, so I figured there had to be more on the way up from Mexico. Now I find out three VIPs are coming in tomorrow. That changes everything. The German plan is to kill all three of them. Can't you see that?"

"What about the truck?"

"The truck is a decoy!"

"I don't think so."

"Why not?"

"Why would the *Abwehr* want to kill them off now? It would have made sense two years ago, when the project was just getting off the ground. But the hard work is over, the technology's in the book, and word is, the bomb's almost ready. So how would killing off the top brass slow the program down?"

"Good point," Boettinger muttered.

"Not to me," Menzies said, fixing Boettinger with a scowl. He swiveled back to Nikolai. "Ever hear of a propaganda victory? You'd hear the cheering in Berlin from here."

The argument took them all the way to the North Gate and through the inner-complex gate at K-25. It ended abruptly when Nikolai wheeled up before the Webster & Co. truck lot. A cloud of smoke hovered over the lot, and fire engines were scattered about. A crowd of people was spread along the fence, watching firefighters scrambling around inside the lot.

"What the hell's going on?" Menzies said.

"I don't know, but I'll bet we're not going to like it," Nikolai said.

The gate to the lot was blocked by vehicles and people. The Knoxville and Memphis contingents stayed put while Nikolai, followed by Menzies and Boettinger, rushed inside.

Apparently, several trucks had caught fire. The fires had been tamed, but the trucks were still smoldering. The smoke was thick and black, now that the flames had been extinguished.

Nikolai peered through the swirling smoke past a sea of truck hoods. A number of trucks had been moved because of the fire, and there were many more gaps now.

Boettinger caught his expression. "Gone?"

Nikolai nodded. Standing in the spot where the truck had been was a man in blue coveralls, one of the three security men assigned to watch number 67. He looked numbed by the situation. Furious before the fact, Menzies bolted forward to confront the man, who obviously wanted to run.

"What the hell happened, goddamnit?" Menzies roared.

"Don't know!" the man wailed.

The two other members of the trio were nearby, looking like bad boys reporting to the principal. They slunk over. One of them said, "Fire started all of a sudden. Called the fire department. Next thing you know, truck's gone!"

Because you're stupid!" Menzies railed. "You fell for the oldest trick in the world!"

He told them to contact headquarters and put out a general alarm: Webster & Co.'s truck number 67 to be stopped at all costs, Heinz Baumann and Toni Graf to be shot on sight.

They ran out the gate, Menzies with the tight elbows and high knees of his freshman college days. The Knoxville car was dispatched in one direction, the Memphis car in another, fanning out in search of number 67; they were to coordinate through radio phone with base security.

Nikolai kicked the Chevy into gear and they sped toward K-25's gargantuan main building.

"Stupid bastards," Menzies growled. Boettinger, in the back seat, was noisily puffing. What hung unspoken in the air was the assassination theory, gone up in the same smoke as the fire's: Baumann and Graf had made their move one full day before Groves, Oppenheimer, and Fermi were scheduled to arrive.

"Where the hell are you going?" Menzies said irritably.

"I have an idea," Nikolai told him.

Boettinger, still puffing, leaned forward: "What?"

Enigmatically, Nikolai said, "Other end of the building."

*   *   *   *

Heinz was behind the wheel, and Toni was in the back of the truck. While it bounced along, she opened the suitcase, wedged out of sight until now among the sacks marked CEMENT. Within the suitcase were detonator caps, a timing device attached to a number of six-volt batteries taped together, and several loops of cable. The truck rode stiffly, but Toni's movements were sure and swift. When she was finished, she banged on the cab, and Heinz pulled off to the side of the road. They had just raced past the west end of K-25.

Toni jumped out of the back, and Heinz slid out of the cab. They met at the open door.

"You sure is better this way?" he said doubtfully.

"Just go by the book, Heinz. I'm better driving, you're better with a gun. Okay?"

Heinz stepped aside, and she jumped up into the cab and adjusted the seat. Heinz came around and got in on the passenger side.

*   *   *   *

Nikolai pushed the Chevy up to 88 on the half-mile stretch that paralleled the twin lengths of the huge building. When they reached the west end, he cut across a flat stretch that short-cut the paved road before leading back to it.

When they bounced back onto the road, Menzies said, "I don't see a damn thing."

"There," Nikolai said. In the distance was a thick dot. When they drew closer, the outline of a truck emerged.

"You think that's them?" Boettinger said as they closed the gap.

"That's them," said Nikolai, and the question was resolved as a figure in the truck, the bulky outline of Heinz Baumann, half swung out of the passenger side and fired a pistol.

"That son of a bitch!" said Menzies.

He took out his gun and fired back. Boettinger, from the back seat, leaned out and did the same.

They swerved with the road, and a bullet glanced off the middle of the windshield. A small spiderweb appeared.

"That son of a bitch!" Menzies said again.

The truck was swallowed up by a number of buildings bisected by a rail spur. In the distance now, Nikolai could make out the Clinch River, shrouded by the thinner foliage of late winter.

The buildings turned out to be a small village of warehouses, brand new and unoccupied. Red dirt ditches looking like bloody gashes in the earth decorated the main street and the side streets, and here and there were stretches of the sewer line piping yet to be installed. The road was almost straight through this structured area, but the truck had disappeared. There had been almost no traffic, but now an old Ford shot out of an alley; the driver hit the brakes so hard that he seemed to spring up, his arms at almost full length as he hung onto the steering wheel.

The Chevy slowed, and Menzies said, "Where the hell are they?"

"Down there!" Boettinger was pointing to a side road past one of the warehouses.

Nikolai raced into a U-turn that slammed Menzies against his door, while Boettinger grabbed a strap.

"Driving like a maniac," Menzies complained.

They shot down the side road, past the warehouse and a number of short side roads dotted with smaller service buildings. The truck came into sight again, careening past the last of the warehouses into open space.

The rear window of the Chevy suddenly shattered, splattering glass as a bullet crashed through and buried itself in the felt-covered ceiling; it was no more than inches from Boettinger's head. "Hey!" he complained, indignant.

Nikolai caught a rear-mirror glance of Baumann pulling into the shadows of one of the smaller service buildings.

Boettinger, brushing off glass, said, "Let me out! I'll get that bastard!"

"We'll get him later!" Menzies said.

They shot past the buildings into the open, the road slanting toward the river. The truck was no more than three hundred yards ahead. Looming up beyond it was yet another monster-sized structure.

Boettinger gaped. "What the hell's that?"

"Power plant," said Nikolai. "That's the target."

"The power plant?" Menzies said, surprised.

Nikolai said, "It's the only target that makes sense. Knock out the power plant, and Oak Ridge goes dead."

Awed, Boettinger said, "Big son of a bitch."

"Can't this thing go faster?" Menzies said.

"It's on the floor," Nikolai told him.

"What's she trying to do?" Boettinger said, mesmerized. "She's going straight in."

"I think that's the idea," said Nikolai.

"Kraut kamikaze," Boettinger muttered.

"Stop her!" Menzies shouted. He leveled his revolver and emptied the chamber. The shots had no effect. "Damn, damn, damn!"

The truck unswervingly held its line. The erector-set forest of condenser towers, generators, and voltage transmission lines were in sharp perspective, dead ahead now.

Boettinger, who had once scored second prize in an FBI regional small-arms contest, bit his lip and propped an elbow on the edge of the window. The gunsight bobbed like a cork in a stream. "Shit," he said. The contest had been fifteen years ago, before the astigmatism. "Hold this thing steady for a minute, will ya?" he murmured to Nikolai. He tightened his finger on the trigger, and the blasts bounced around the interior of the Chevy.

"Look at that!" Menzies said.

Nikolai was focused on the rear window of the truck cab, and he saw Toni Graf pitch forward. "You got her," he told Boettinger.

"Too late," Menzies said, in a doomsday whisper.

Toni's body was tilted against the steering wheel, and her foot was heavy on the accelerator. Far from slowing, number 67 was picking up speed on its downgrade journey.

"God almighty," Boettinger said, transfixed.

"Hey, what're you doing? Slow down, for Christ's sake!" Menzies shouted. He raised an arm against the cosmic blast that would surely envelop them when the truck hit the power plant.

"It's okay," Nikolai said.

"The hell it's okay!" Menzies blared. He was trying to figure out if he would survive jumping from the car. In the back seat, Boettinger could not take his eyes from the mountain-sized power plant swiftly filling his field of vision.

The truck plowed into it with a force of two hundred thousand foot-pounds. Even without explosives, it would have been enough to take down a moderate-sized building. But the only casualty was the truck; it was pulverized. The front end was an accordion, bits and pieces of metal and glass and seat cushioning stickily fused with the flesh, blood, and bones of what had been its driver, who in any case had died only seconds before from a .38 slug in the back of her head.

"What the hell happened?" said Boettinger, stunned.

"Didn't go off," Menzies noted gratuitously.

Boettinger was trying to read Nikolai's benign expression. His face lit up. "I'll be damned. You did it."

"With my little hatchet," Nikolai conceded.

Confused, Menzies said, "Did what?"

The Chevy braked to a stop alongside the twisted metal of the truck cab, its remains slapped against the solid base of one of the condenser towers.

Nikolai got out slowly, anticipating the messy gel that would be Toni Graf. He stopped short and let it go at that. Menzies and Boettinger came alongside but no further.

Their gazes shifted, trying to adjust to the mountainous structure that was the Oak Ridge power plant, the biggest in the world.

"Baumann," Nikolai reminded. "He's still back there." His attention was drawn to vehicles racing toward them from the river road.

Boettinger saw them too. "Cavalry."

The first vehicle turned out to be one of the FBI cars; trailing it was a base security jeep.

Nikolai slipped behind the wheel of the Chevy. "Go with him," Menzies instructed, and Boettinger climbed in alongside Nikolai as the Chevy started to roll. While Nikolai retraced the route back to the warehouse street, Boettinger reloaded his empty gun.

When they reached the west end of the warehouses, Nikolai skidded the car to a stop, and Boettinger jumped out. "Be careful when you start back," he cautioned. "Try not to shoot me in the balls."

Nikolai drove on, heading for the far end to set up a pincers. Meanwhile, he idled along at ten miles per hour, his eyes poking into glassless windows and doorless entrances. He held the wheel with his left hand, the gun in his right.

Near the end of the last building, he saw something move, but it was so subtle that it could have been imagined. It was a flash of pale brown and gray-white, perhaps nothing more than a swirling leaf or a piece of paper caught in a gust. Then the image mutated, and Nikolai realized it had been Baumann's hand, the fingers flexing around his pistol.

At the next alley, Nikolai turned in, stopped abruptly, and eased out of the car without slamming the door. He slid through an open window-frame into the cold emptiness of a storage building. There were dividing walls and hundreds of shelves, but they were empty. Nikolai crossed the room and emerged from the building onto a hardscrabble stretch that unfolded to miles of open Tennessee countryside.

He kept low and reached another service building; it was on the side street where he had seen movement. He entered the building and let out his breath, tuning himself to an odd vibration in the air, a sense of presence: Baumann's rank smell, left behind like a stain.

Something moved at the far end of the long, empty room, and Nikolai saw Heinz crouched in the shadows. Heinz blinked, focusing in the dusty darkness, but he did not fire.

Nikolai's voice bounced off the walls in a series of echoes. "It's all over, Heinz. Toni Graf is dead. I switched trucks. You were carrying cement. Real cement."

Heinz swayed a little. His gun hand seemed to droop, then it came up again.

"Drop the gun," Nikolai said, listening to his voice, not recognizing it.

Heinz was studying Nikolai like a specimen, an object so distorted in the prism of his loathing that he could only stare. He said, "You think I don't know? I know. I know everything." His eyes were bright; they seemed to have been turned on, like lamps.

"Don't," Nikolai appealed. It was a moment he had desperately sought to avoid. But he could see the lines tighten in Baumann's face.

Heinz fired. The bullet whistled through Nikolai's jacket and through his shirt; the heat of its passage seared his skin.

Nikolai's shot was a reflex. When he pulled the trigger, it took him by surprise.

Heinz looked down at his right arm. Blood was soaking his forearm. He heard a clatter and realized that he had just dropped his gun. He bent to retrieve it, this time with his left hand.

"Don't," Nikolai said again.

But Heinz seemed not to hear him. His moves were robotic; they were unhurried, because nothing could obstruct his hatred.

A shot crashed out, but it was not from Nikolai's gun. Boettinger, at an open window, watched Baumann sink to his knees, still reaching for his gun. Boettinger fired again.

Heinz went over on his face. He was dead.

Boettinger squeezed through. He was shaking his head. He bent across the body and kicked the gun free. Then he moved to Nikolai. "What the hell were you doing?" he said. "You almost let that son of a bitch kill you."

Nikolai put his gun away, but he moved jerkily, as though distracted.

Boettinger was watching him. In that second, he understood. "You had a thing with her."

Nikolai nodded: bittersweet, past tense, gone.

Driving back to the power plant, Boettinger was bubbling. "Seventeen years, and that was my first," he said. "Not that hard." It was a joke, but he meant it.

They arrived to see a dozen cars at the crash scene. An army ambulance was just driving off, and a khaki-colored wrecker was winching up the rear end of the truck, with its recently painted number 67.

Menzies' mood was unsurpassed. It had been a day of triumph, and the news about Baumann was icing on the cake. He beamed and then kept beaming, as though about to burst into song. When neither Nikolai nor Boettinger picked up on his exuberance, he gushed, "Guess who was right all along?"

Menzies showed them an army teletype addressed to the commanding officer of the Manhattan District CID. It read: *CID operatives have arrested four men this date Chattanooga. All four Mexican nationals. Do not speak English. Totally disoriented. Carrying bus tickets destination Oak Ridge, debarked Chattanooga assuming Oak Ridge. Suspects being held federal facilities here pending orders FBI and CID Pentagon.*

"How do you like that one, boys?" Menzies said, buttons bursting.

His paranoia regarding help out of Mexico had been based on expectation. He knew that the *Abwehr* was sending reinforcements.

He had kept both men in the dark up until now, and he looked first at Boettinger. "A little bird told me. Guess who?"

Boettinger barely heard him; he was thinking about killing Heinz Baumann and how good it would look on his record. "What?"

Undeterred, Menzies said to Nikolai, "Guess who?"

"Dieter Krone," Nikolai said, deadpan. He knew he should have seen it coming, because not only had Menzies waved his "reinforcements" theory like a cheerleader, but Nikolai himself had suggested that the FBI squeeze Krone.

"Right! Dieter Krone! The same one you and your partner checked out in Los Alamos!"

Nikolai gave him his lead. It had not been his day; it had been Menzies' day, and that was the way of the world. And it was not quite over.

That evening, Anna came to the Oak Ridge morgue to sign off on her father. She refused to identify him. She took his bagged belongings—lumber jacket, shirt, pants, shoes—and dropped them in a trash can outside the morgue.

Nikolai knew she would not talk to him, and at first, he kept his distance. By morning, though, a cauldron of emotions jolted him out of bed, and he tore through early traffic and pulled up sharply before her building.

Inside the apartment he found two MPs, but Anna was gone. The MPs were doing an inventory for security. Anna had apparently packed her bags and left for parts unknown just after dawn. Somebody in the building had seen her heading for the bus station. Nikolai drove there but just sat in the car without entering the terminal. It suddenly seemed meaningless to find out where she had gone.

He rummaged through their brief, fiery, futile relationship, and only now, in the emptiness of her departure, could he examine what she had been other than Heinz Baumann's daughter: a trusting child, desperately hungry for love, naive to the point of foolishness. They had had little in common, but in this carefully constructed remembrance, he supposed that their torrents of shared pleasure had exceeded the banality of sex.

Her street-smart humor had surprised him; for all his duplicity in charming her, bewitching her, and winning her, she was the one who had smoothed their time together. Nothing about his own role struck him as particularly engaging. She, the dedicated victim, had held the stage.

He wondered if he and Anna had more in common than he had thought: the commonality of hidden psyches and secret lives.

Nikolai, Menzies, and Boettinger said their good-byes in Knoxville's L & N station that same day. Menzies and Boettinger were returning to New York; Nikolai's train, heading for Washington, left first.

CHAPTER 29

▼

A cold, pre-spring March wind was blowing down Pennsylvania Avenue as they drove past the White House, and the cabbie turned back to Nikolai and said, "See them lights back around that portico, like? Means Mr. President himself in there, fighting the war."

Nikolai kept his eyes on the lights until they disappeared, and he thought about the serpentine path he had taken since his arrival in America. From his rootless European past, he had brought vengeance. His American experience had shamelessly crushed and exploited him—a hash mark for the uniform he did not wear.

The question of America ran through his mind—not the question of whether or not he belonged, but whether or not he wanted to belong. He looked back at the White House and was surprised at the flicker of a spark.

He remembered that Churchill, among others, had graded democracy as the worst of all possible systems, except for the rest. Which said a lot for man's ingenuity but not much for man.

*　　　*　　　*　　　*

He dumped his bag on the living-room floor and soaked up the moment. Not the sense of coming home, because the apartment was never homey; rather, it was a little dark and a little gray and a little drab, but he and Dancer had shared its time and its space, so there was the mystique of memory to consider.

McKennan had arranged to remove Dancer's things, and if that did not entirely remove Dancer, it helped. Nikolai opened a kitchen cabinet. There were a number of bottles, mostly scotch, and not always the best, because Dancer was guided by what he called "the spirit of the thing," the alcoholic content, rather than malt breed. But one bottle stood out, tall and proud and bearing an elegantly simple label: McKennan's Best.

Glenallen McKennan's welcome home. Once, in a weak, personal moment, McKennan had offhandedly mentioned a "family still." This was its product. Nikolai poured. He toasted Dancer and, one drink later, McKennan.

In the morning, he sorted through a pile of mail the super had left on the kitchen table. There were bills and ads, a registered mail notice for Dancer, an appeal to buy bonds, and a flyer supporting a canned-food drive.

The phone rang. It was McKennan with his usual brusque burr, which softened when Nikolai said, "You should have stayed in the family business, Mac."

"So you found it. Well, they do a nice job, but it's a foul-tempered cousin on my mother's side runs the distillery. Not a good man to be around for any length of time."

"Speaking of which, I want to talk to Guthrie."

"And he wants to talk to you," McKennan said. He was calling to pass on an invitation to a party at Guthrie's home that very evening. It was a well-known annual affair. Not to be missed.

Nikolai said, "I'm overwhelmed. I think."

"As well you should be. You'll be rubbing elbows with the Washington hoi polloi."

"Me?"

"Look, he knows what you've done. The fact is, Mr. Menzies telephoned this morning and gave us an informal report. Of course, he soaked it in FBI glory, not least of which was his own valor, but one could read between the lines, so to speak—after which I spoke at some length with Oak Ridge security. You did one hell of a job, lad."

"Still, we know it isn't generosity of spirit that prompts our Mr. Guthrie. What's he got in mind, Mac?"

"That I do not know. And kindly do not attempt to beat it out of me."

"You're too tough to have anything beaten out of you. So I'll have to find out for myself, is that it?"

"That's it."

For the occasion, the blustery weather stunningly reversed itself. It was mild and pleasant. Guthrie's neighborhood, though something less than the grandness implicit in his overbearing nature, was unpretentious upper middle class. It was a highly patriotic neighborhood, filled with flapping flags and banner-filled windows, and here and there a gold star for a dead hero.

Guthrie's house was a handsome red-brick Georgian located in a cul-de-sac dotted with maple trees. Cars filled the street on both sides: guests at the party. On the front lawn were a laid-aside bicycle and a laid-aside scooter.

Nikolai got out of the taxi and moved up a flagstone path across a front lawn hardened by winter. He stopped before a black-lacquered front door with an elegantly gold-lettered *G*.

A woman, pleasant-faced and modestly plump, opened the door and warmly welcomed Nikolai. She introduced herself as Roberta Guthrie. "Do have a wonderful time," she said warmly, aiming him past cream-colored rooms filled with Regency furniture and out through a door that led to the back lawn and the sudden bedlam of the party.

Several dozen adults swirled about, an older and more privileged crowd in casual costume, along with the usual assortment of service plumage. They grouped around two bars, a half dozen outdoor tables brought in for the occasion, and a long table with hors d'oeuvres and petite sandwiches. The promise of more substantial fare wafted out of the kitchen.

Uniformed servers navigated the lawn, and now a woman with a tray of wine and champagne came before Nikolai. He plucked a glass of wine from the tray; it was chilled and dry and very good.

Nikolai wandered, observed, smiled, nodded, sipped.. He stopped before a sea of hors d'oeuvres that brought back memories of the backstage parties at the Riga National Theater, where Tati, always addicted to the consumption of strange life forms, would gobble microscopic creatures dredged from the bottom of the Baltic. On one such occasion, eleven-year-old Nikolai had watched something gelatinous move on a cracker and thrown up.

McKennan came alongside. "Well, lad, you made it. Talked to him yet?"

"Haven't seen him," Nikolai said.

"Ah, then he's still in the study with the other great man, J. Edgar himself. I saw him early on. He knows you're here."

That minute, J. Edgar Hoover came out of the house. He bulled his way to the bar and backed out clutching a ginger ale. Nikolai and McKennan watched him go by. In person, Nikolai could see that the resemblance was strong: barrel shapes, pie faces, pig eyes. Hoover had a bulldog chin, and Guthrie had a squashed nose.

Guthrie was bearing down on them, face plaited in smiles. No less alien was his attire: a gray tweed sports coat, slacks, loafers, and a bright regimental tie. He wrung Nikolai's hand vigorously, as though with the heartfelt thanks of a grateful nation. "Mac, would you excuse us?"

He steered Nikolai toward the house, but two boys of about eight and ten intercepted. Guthrie put his arms about them. "What are you two up to? Mr. Granger, I want you to meet Ronny and Rudy. Boys, say hello to Mr. Granger. Shake hands. That's it. And how about a couple of hugs for your daddy?"

They hugged and ran off. "Great kids," Guthrie said, flushed with pride. "Wonderful kids."

He led Nikolai into the house and down a hallway to a leather-saturated study. Here were busts of Washington, Lincoln, and Franklin D. Roosevelt, and a shiny new bust of J. Edgar Hoover—of no more than fifteen minutes standing, Nikolai guessed.

Guthrie sat Nikolai down in an armchair and settled on the catty-cornered sofa. He offered a cigar, which Nikolai declined, then lit an intricately carved meerschaum pipe. "The road hasn't always been smooth," said Guthrie, "but I am pleased as punch with your performance. Pleased as punch. Now, to business. As you know, the Special Assessment Unit has been the subject of reevaluation for some time now. In line with decisions reached over the past week, the organization will cease to exist as of the first of the month."

It had been coming for some time, but it was still a bombshell. Guthrie clucked, as though in memoriam, before moving on, surprisingly upbeat. "Still and all, bad tidings often usher in new opportunities. And that's what I want to talk to you about. I have been honored with a new assignment. You are one of the first to know of it, by the way. It will be a new enterprise, under my stewardship. It will be semi-independent, loosely connected to the Justice Department.

"It will deal with the problem of Nazi war crimes. The war in Europe is almost over. Soon, the United States will be faced with the massive problem of sorting out war criminals. Investigation, interrogation, evaluation—that will be the function of this new department. A department with a high sense of purpose, I might add. It will consist of no more than two dozen uniquely qualified people. You speak German, I believe. That is one of the vital qualifications, among many, and I am convinced that you possess them all. Therefore, I am happy to offer you a transfer, with an equivalent government grade of G-eleven in this new organization."

He revealed a smile of kinship no less bewildering to Nikolai than the rest of the surreal night. "Let me suggest one more qualification," Guthrie said intimately. "It is a healthy dislike of the German. I believe we share that qualification. Am I right?"

"Yes, sir."

"Good," said Guthrie. He made a small joke: "A little prejudice goes a long way. Well, what do you say?"

"In what manner would one exercise that prejudice, sir?" asked Nikolai.

Guthrie took on a swaddling-babe look, then he seemed to understand. "Oh, no, no, no," he said, with all the shyness of virtue. "Nothing like that, nothing like that. Everything perfectly in order."

"I'm wondering, sir, where you stand on the alien issue."

"The alien issue."

"People like me," Nikolai said. "Aliens."

Guthrie was apparently so embarrassed that he put out his pipe, as though to pay penance for his pleasure. "That was a very foolish statement on my part. It was an ignorant charge, made under the pressure of a particularly trying period. It failed to take into account your obvious worth. Indeed, Nikolai, your value to me should be evident by now. I do not embrace new colleagues lightly."

As a measure of this embrace, he stuck out a hand. Nikolai took it. It was fat-fingered and weak.

"Why don't you take two weeks off and report in on 9 April?" Guthrie suggested. He pulled out a card and handed it over. "Call me at this number—temporary quarters over on E Street."

"Sir, we haven't discussed my pardon," said Nikolai.

"Your pardon? Oh! Of course! Your pardon!"

"Yes, sir."

"Well, they've taken their own sweet time about that, haven't they?" Resolutely, he said, "Time to get that show on the road, Nikolai."

"How long do you think it would take?"

"No more than three months." He smiled. "I think I can guarantee that."

"In the meantime, sir, I'm out in the open. As far as the Commonwealth of Massachusetts is concerned, I'm an escaped convict."

"Not with me taking care of you, you're not," said Guthrie

"With all respects, sir, that still leaves me vulnerable."

"Now you listen to me, Nikolai," Guthrie said. He bent forward and tapped Nikolai's knee for emphasis. "It will be handled. Personally, and with all due speed."

Exiting the house, Nikolai waited for McKennan, just behind him in the short good-bye line filing past Roberta Guthrie; Guthrie himself was off somewhere with Hoover. A couple came out, then McKennan.

"Car's down the street," he said, and they walked to it in silence. They piled in, and McKennan said, "Well, let's have it."

"You know all about his new setup, of course."

"I do. The question is, what did you say?"

"If you mean 'did I commit,' the answer is, he made it sound as though I did, but I did not."

"Why not?"

"Because Guthrie promised a pardon again. This time, no more than three months. I half believed him for two and a half years. Now I'm supposed to half believe him for three more months—and on and on."

"He told you that? Three months?" It was rhetorical, and McKennan sniffed the air with an uncertain look. "Out of curiosity, lad—would you have signed up if he handed it over, right then, right there?"

"Absolutely," Nikolai said. "Promise to stay and be gone in five minutes."

McKennan nodded and looked away, curiously adrift. "It's a remarkable thing about Mr. Guthrie. He's a bit of a monster, but he can work you up to a froth of loyalty. I stayed with him longer than I should, because there was a certain amount of right in our work. But so far, and no farther. This which he has done to you, I do not countenance. Do you understand?"

Nikolai studied him and said, "I think so."

"Reckless abandon for the good of the whole is one thing, but duplicity for its own sake serves no one."

"In other words," Nikolai said, "he's got the pardon, but he's holding out on me."

"The miserable lying toad. He's had it for months. He's had it since Christmas. He told me it would be presented as a holiday present. I had no way of knowing. I expected you to have it by now. I should have asked."

"Not your fault, Mac."

McKennan raged in silence, while Nikolai mulled.

"It's all wrong, lad. It cannot be allowed."

"I was thinking the same thing."

McKennan pondered this, then said, "I believe it was Robbie Burns—or was it Moffat?—who said, 'There can be no wrong in that which is right.'"

*　　*　　*　　*

On the face of it, "that which is right" should have been a hair-raising adventure, but it turned out to be absurdly simple. McKennan provided keys to the building, inner-office keys, a security guard timetable, and most importantly, the combination to Guthrie's file.

Within eight minutes, Nikolai had located the document: Certificate of Pardon, Commonwealth of Massachusetts. Ten minutes later, he was out of the building. That left only the awkward business of facing Guthrie..

In fact, Guthrie showed up at the apartment at ten o'clock the next morning, pounding madly at the door, along with two District of Columbia policemen.

"You lousy, stinking thief! You're the lowest scum on the face of the Earth! You have the gall to steal from me? From me!"

Nikolai, holding a cup of coffee, said, "Would you like to come in, sir?"

"Goddamn right I'm coming in! I want this man under arrest!"

The last, of course, to the two cops, who had no idea what to do. They had been dispatched to accompany Guthrie—some sort of government official with a line to the chief of police—but they had no jurisdictional powers.

With this limitation in mind, Guthrie shouted, "Stay there!" to the two cops and slammed the door in their faces.

"You're not getting away with this!" Guthrie erupted again. "Nobody steals my underwear, Mr. Polack!"

"Latvia, sir," Nikolai said.

Guthrie switched to old shoe sly. "At nine o'clock this morning, you were officially deleted from the roster. That means all pay and benefits cease." His face lit. Malevolence oozed. "Not that it matters. Where you're going, nothing's going to matter, because what you did was write yourself a ticket back to the Bastille, and before I get through, they'll pile on ninety-nine years plus. You know what that pardon is worth? Absolutely nothing. You know why? Because I'm going to have it revoked." He smiled. "Did you really think I was just going to sit still? What happens now, Mr. Granger, is you get to pay. And pay."

"I don't think so," Nikolai said.

Guthrie looked up sharply. The tone was a warning bell.

"You don't think so," he said. "Why is that?"

"Because I can't imagine that you want the American people to know your wartime record. All those bodies on the pile."

"You're threatening me? Are you actually threatening me?"

"Yes, sir."

"With what, you sick-brained half-wit?" The last was a shout. He looked toward the door. He snarled but lowered his voice and said, "Accusations are a dime a dozen. They're useless unless you can back them up. And you've got nothing to work with. Not a single scrap of paper. And even if you did, what good would it do? Go public and cut your own throat?"

"If I'm going to prison for ninety-nine years plus, sir, why would I care about my throat?"

"You don't have a thing," repeated Guthrie

"No, sir, I don't."

Guthrie did not like the sound of it. Where was the dread? "What is it you think you have?" he said, amused.

Nikolai thought about it and said, "It's more of a team thing, sir."

Guthrie understood immediately. He blanched. Then he snorted. "That stinking ingrate McKennan! That miserable goddamn traitor!"

Nikolai said nothing.

"He's backing the wrong goddamn horse!" Guthrie thundered. His eyes narrowed. "You're not going to get away with it."

"I can understand how you feel, sir," Nikolai said. "The instinct to hit back is strong. Especially in a person of strong instincts—a characteristic I share. In this case, however, you're wide open and have nowhere to turn."

Guthrie had not been defeated often, and defeat dried his lips. He wet them. It was the sort of game, like chess, where even brilliant strategy could be overcome by position.

To his credit, he turned it into farce. "Shall I assume a safe deposit box somewhere, in which my name is prominently mentioned?"

"You might want to assume a backup too, sir."

Guthrie was not the kind to waste time on things over and done. He popped out of his chair and moved to the door. In a curious reversion to another time, he said, "I bid you good day, Mr. Granger."

CHAPTER 30

▼

No sooner had Guthrie and his entourage tramped down the stairs and out of the building when the telephone in the kitchen rang. It was a wrong number, but it brought Nikolai back to his set-aside mail, and now he discovered that the post office notice, apparently addressed to Dancer, was actually a notice of registered mail *from* Dancer to *him*.

He walked to the post office and signed for the letter. He tore it open and read:

> Should I have mentioned this earlier? I was never sure, so I kept putting it off, but I can't put much off much longer, and here it is. Liquid-dining at the Old Mill some time back, I happened to see Guthrie and a friend. Guthrie did not see me—they made a point of staying out of sight. But this is about the friend—a fellow with strange eyes and a lot of peculiar tics. It hit me that this odd-looking bird had to be no other than Guthrie's informant. I watched him, and I was sure of it. For all his eccentric, nervous moves, he was European as hell—the way he lit his cigarette, the way he held it, etc.
> Here's the point: the cigarette came from a case, and son of a bitch if it didn't sport the same design as yours—no question.
>
> Never knew exactly what it was all about—what the hell, your business—except it was eating you up alive, so maybe this will help. If you need anything else, let me know.
>
> Dancer

P.S. I dumped my bank account into yours. It's healthy, because I never spent on anything but cheap booze, so don't go fucking noble and donate it to the National Turtle Preservation Society.

For some time, Nikolai stared at nothing. Then he shook it all off and set out for the Pentagon and then FBI headquarters. His ID, still valid, allowed him to tweeze a Plymouth from the motor pool. Soon, he was crossing the Arlington Bridge, heading south.

It was a picturesque place of rolling hills and surrounding pine forests, and the army had done a good job of maintaining what had been a pleasant resort. He parked in a visitors' lot, flashed his credentials, and set off down a network of charming paths cut through the woods. He saw picnic tables, benches made of split logs, dozens of small waterfalls, and a clear stream.

This was the exclusive section of the VIP cottages, not simply sequestered but thoughtfully distanced from each other, so that neighboring cottages could be barely made out through the camouflage of foliage and trees. Here, wounded and battle-strained officers of rank were assigned to regenerate torn minds and bodies. Those who did not wish to dine in the VIP mess hall—known, not surprisingly, as the Brass Ring—could have their meals sent over on a bicycle towing an insulated hamper.

From time to time, medical orderlies visited the cottages, bringing medication or changing bandages. But these were not regular visits, and doctors' visits were even rarer; the prime objective was tranquility.

To gain entry into the installation was to gain status, and Nikolai was barely noticed as he wandered the area. In the welcome center, all but deserted because a staff meeting was in progress, Nikolai was able to examine a large, leather registration book exclusive to the VIP section.

In the pampering nature of a fine hotel, it contained a great deal of information, such as SLEEPS LATE, HOT COCOA NINE P.M., and ARRANGE TENNIS, FULL BAR.

Nikolai had no idea who he was looking for, other than the fact that it would be a nom de plume, probably at general rank, given the ego involved, and probably a European-sounding name from an Allied nation.

There were two French, one Dutch, one Belgian, and one Polish—along with the expected high-ranking officers of the U.S. military.

The name he stopped at was the Pole, Jerezy Novik, major general, whose personal requests included champagne, with a preference for the Bollard marque.

Nikolai found the cottage without trouble, but it was empty. Its occupant, only recently departed, had left the stub of a cigarette, and its pungent Turkish scent was heavy in the room. He exited the cottage and wandered down the path; it was still soggy from the last rain and here and there revealed the dainty imprint of a small foot.

Nikolai followed the stream and paused just short of a narrow pedestrian bridge. A solitary figure was hunched at the crest of a gently arched railing, staring into the water. The location was remote to the point of mystery. The silence was enormous.

In all the tens of thousands of his fantasized confrontations, this one had never manifested itself. Prescient, the man brought his head up. He looked around and saw Nikolai, but there was no recognition.

Nikolai came closer. The man's face was much changed. It was bloated, and the skin was mottled and pocked by sores. His hair was much thinner, and when he opened his mouth, there was a gap on one side.

"Do you bring me the shot?" the Baron asked. The English was serviceable but multi-accented, the voice cracked but still imperious.

Nikolai replied in German, "Do you know who I am?"

"I do not get the shot until seven o'clock," the Baron said, still in English. Oddly enough, the German had not surprised him at all, and now he switched to it. "What is the time?"

"It's 4:35," Nikolai said. He moved closer. "You don't know me?"

The Baron struggled to focus rheumy eyes. "Do you want to give the shot early?" he said, the words as broken as a child's. "Come."

He tottered off the bridge and moved past Nikolai in a broken gait. Nikolai followed, caught up in the irony of the moment. He had been thinking more in the nature of a violent duel to the death, a clash of titans. Instead, he had overtaken a wretched cripple.

He remembered now what McKennan had once said about Guthrie's mysterious source—that the man was out of business because he was overstressed. Now it was obvious that his condition had been hugely played down.

For years, Nikolai had sharpened his teeth for this moment. He had no sense of compassion; this was the same heinous monster he had hunted down in his dreams. But now there was confusion.

The Baron led him into the cottage. It was, in effect, a handsome one-bedroom suite. There was a modern kitchen, a bar, a rustic living room, and a view to a thick, wooded rise. It was getting dark, but the Baron apparently liked the dark and left it that way.

Everything was German now. The Baron said, "Where is your kit? How can you give me a shot without the kit?"

"I don't have a kit," Nikolai said. "What is the shot for?"

"What do you think?" the Baron roared. Froth bubbled at his lips, and he collapsed into a lounge chair as though lead-weighted. He said, "I must sit."

"Do you have syphilis?" Nikolai asked.

The Baron looked up. His mental processes were obviously scrambled, but the blatancy of the question cut right through. With an ancient contempt, he said, "Don't you know? You're the one who gives the shots."

Nikolai realized that, ego or alter ego, the lordly Baron von Hartigens-Hesse would surrender nothing of his breeding. It was wondrously easy not to feel pity for this man. "Shall we have a drink?" Nikolai asked.

"A drink?" the Baron said in surprise.

"Yes, why not? Do you have Bollard Classique?"

"Bollard!" the Baron snarled. "The so-called richest country on Earth, but they cannot find a single bottle! White Star they bring me! White Star!" The Baron began to mutter unintelligible fragments, whether about his treatment by an ungrateful America or the inconvenience of madness, Nikolai could not tell.

He said, "Let's drink it anyway."

"Yes, yes, why not?" the Baron agreed. He tried to rise, a series of faint tremors that left him unmoved and his mouth open.

"Shall I?" Nikolai said. He moved to the refrigerator and opened it to two trays of champagne. There were two chilled champagne glasses, a stick of butter, and a tin of sprats.

Nikolai pulled out a bottle and cheerfully noted the label. "It's not White Star, general, it's Roederer."

"Roederer," the Baron considered. "You may open it."

Nikolai found a dish towel and uncorked the bottle. It was nicely chilled. He poured and handed the Baron a glass. He filled his own glass, and at the Baron's invitation, he settled in a nearby cane chair, a high-backed affair with green padding and exaggerated wings. "You call me 'general'," said the Baron.

Nikolai said, "You are listed as General Novik, a Polish officer. But you are actually not Polish. Am I correct?"

"No, and neither are you American. Am I correct?"

"Technically, that is also true."

"You are not part of the staff," the Baron said.

"No, I am not."

"And you come here to speak to me."

"Yes."

In this phase, the Baron had been irrepressibly articulate and normal to the point of shrewd, but all at once it fell away. "Roederer, Roederer, Roederer, Roederer," he blurted out, the syllables running all over each other until a final "Roederer" came out in one mushy shout.

His head drooped. The glass of champagne was tilted precariously in his right hand; it splashed gently but somehow did not run over. And just as suddenly, the seizure was over. He noted the champagne and sipped it again. "Are you here for the shot?" he asked.

"We were talking about Roederer," Nikolai said politely.

"What is your name?" the Baron asked.

"Granger."

"Should I know this name?"

"I think so. We dined together once. We drank Bollard."

The Baron's eyes widened as he searched the long corridors of his memory. "Are you sure?

"Oh, yes."

Bitterly, the Baron said, "It affects the brain, this cursed business! You pay for a bit of fun in this world, my friend!"

"By the way, what ever happened to Helger?"

The Baron shook distinctly, as though electrically prodded "Who?"

"Helger. Your majordomo."

The convulsions ceased, and the Baron said, "Majordomo. What an amusing thought."

Nikolai rose and refilled their glasses. "I understand you served in the Wehrmacht as an intelligence officer of high rank."

The Baron raised the glass just above his lip so the bubbles would tickle his nostrils. "From where do these fantasies spring?" he asked in mock fascination.

"From Mr. Simon Guthrie," said Nikolai.

"And do I know him too?"

"Yes. But here's something you may not know. We worked together, you and I. We worked for the same clandestine organization, and neither of us knew it. It's an incredible irony, don't you think?"

"Irony, yes, if any of it made sense," said the Baron. His eyes opened and closed. He was drifting again, lips moving, spittle leaking from one side of his mouth.

"Are you all right?" Nikolai said, not particularly kindly.

The Baron understood this enough to take it as a challenge, and he fought his quivering flesh and bit his immodest lips until they were white but motionless.

"So they called you up," Nikolai said.

"In February of '43, after Stalingrad. And where do they send me?!"

"The Eastern Front?"

"I am to abandon my estate! I am to report to Manstein in the middle of that filthy Russian mud in Voronets! Army Group Center! Well, well, well—!" His brain tangled his tongue, and his voice dropped off.

"But you managed to change things around," Nikolai suggested. "Göring, perhaps."

"My good friend Göring!"

"Teutonic knights take care of each other," said Nikolai.

"He arranged a new posting, to Berlin, to the *Abwehr!*"

"You handled the saboteur file for North America," Nikolai speculated.

"A situation not without its problems," the Baron cautioned.

"Such as?"

"Such as the treatment accorded non-party members!" the Baron fumed. "And there were problems of the war. Almost every day they bombed, and almost every night." He tugged at an earlobe. "Do you see this? A perforated drum. They blew the building to pieces, the swine. The annex next to the ministry. Floors came crashing down." He tugged the ear. "Perforated," he said again.

"You have my sympathy," Nikolai said. Accommodating the minute, he took the platinum case from his jacket pocket and opened it in offering.

The Baron paused on seeing the soldierly lineup of cigarettes. "I am forbidden to smoke, of course, but—" He reached for one in naughty defiance and paused again, this time frozen in shock. "Where—?" he said, more of a gasp.

"*Ehre bis zum Tod.* Honor to the death," Nikolai said.

The Baron blinked but did not respond.

"Where did I get it?" Nikolai said. "I got it from you."

The Baron was confused again. "From me?"

"The night you took us in."

The Baron struggled with this. A decayed fragment of memory slipped into place. "Yes, it was taken from me. I was forced to duplicate it. But of course I could not—silver only. Where would I find platinum in time of war?"

Greedily, his fingers reached for the platinum case. Nikolai relinquished it, and the Baron fiercely clutched it, then stroked it. "It is mine," he declared.

"Yes, of course. I wanted you to have it again."

The Baron clutched it all the tighter. Finally, foolishly, he grinned. "I shall reward you," he declared. "You may have the other, the replacement."

"That won't be necessary." Nikolai said..

The Baron stared at the platinum case. "Hartigens-Hesse," he read with a schadenfreude lilt.

"A noble family," said Nikolai. "Tell me, was Helger with you? In Berlin?"

"Helger?"

"Helger."

All at once, the Baron vibrated with remembrances, not all of them pleasant. "He was a fool, Helger. He would only accept an officer's commission, but this was impossible. In truth, he was a Pomeranian, you see, and not from the best family. And what was he, at the villa, if not a servant?"

The Baron splashed champagne down his throat and choked, but he came out of it with a sly smile. "So he left me—this was in Berlin—but they scooped him up soon enough, and off he went to the same Russian front, and there he was blown to pieces by an artillery shell."

Nikolai grinned. "Poor old Helger."

"Pieces everywhere!"

"Scattered like manure."

They shared a laugh. Nikolai opened another bottle and filled their glasses. "So you were in Berlin. But how did you get here?"

The Baron's face, a remarkably versatile instrument, flashed with rage. "A disgrace! An injustice! There was an SS general—an impudent swine who proposed to confiscate my estate for his headquarters."

"General Pforzheim," Nikolai said.

"Yes. You know him?"

"Only by reputation. You mentioned him at dinner."

The word "dinner" brought back perplexity to the Baron's face, but he continued. "This Pforzheim—not a Prussian, I can tell you. A lowborn boor of a man, but then that's the SS for you." He looked over apologetically: where was he?

"Pforzheim, the SS general," Nikolai prompted. "He took over the estate while you were in Berlin."

"Filthy weasel! The minute my back was turned!"

"You informed Göring, of course."

"Of course, but my fat friend Göring had his own problems, so this Pforzheim and his Nazi pigs moved in! And what was I to do? Was I to let them shit all over me?"

It was a self-conscious vulgarism, and he paused, but only for a second. "What did I owe that National Socialist rabble?"

"Nothing," Nikolai agreed.

"Nothing! So I evened the score!"

"You defected," said Nikolai.

"I defected!" the Baron said.

They drank to it, and Nikolai said, "But you still don't remember me?" For this question, he had switched to Latvian.

The Baron looked him over, as though for the first time. "No, I cannot say that I do." The response was also in Latvian, and they continued that way.

"It was the second day of the German invasion. I had to get out of Riga. My cousin was with me, a girl. It was difficult. We were chased. There was a massacre. We saw a possible place of refuge—it was the villa. Your estate."

The Baron amiably shook his head. He could not remember.

"You took us in. We had dinner, and a great deal of champagne."

"Nothing, nothing," the Baron lamented of his memory." He put down his empty glass, looking pained. "I am afraid …" He registered his all-too-human need to pass water. He rose slowly and made his way past Nikolai to an alcove that led to the bathroom. The bathroom door closed.

The toilet flushed, and there was the sound of running water in the sink. Then the door opened, and the Baron reappeared, bent a little as he walked, and muttering again.

When he came to the back of Nikolai's high-winged chair, he stopped very suddenly and brought up his right hand; in it was a small Beretta. It kicked and roared six times as he emptied the chamber into the back of the chair. Splinters of cane and particles of the green padding flew through the air.

But something was not quite right. The Baron sensed the slightest variance in the way things should be, and he realized that it was in the fading silence of the echoing shots. There should have been the rustle of clothing in the slumping of the body, an awareness of movement as the body eased or pitched one way or the other.

He went around and faced the empty chair. A thin curl of smoke rose from the gun. He stared at the Beretta in disbelief, as though it had arbitrarily changed its function and caused its target to literally disappear.

He turned again. Nikolai was at the bar, only half-visible in the encroaching darkness. He approached. One hand still held champagne, and the other flashed the platinum cigarette case.

"I took this from you that night. I hope you don't mind. Now, as a reminder—first we had dinner. Then it was after-dinner sport. With me, it was Helger. For my cousin Katya, it was a bullet through the backdoor, up through her guts, and out through her head. Do you remember?"

"I told you—nothing like this happened. You are mistaken."

"I'll tell you the single most interesting thing about that moment. It is the fact that you hardened me for everything that would follow. Right up to the moment. Right up to this moment."

With an alacrity and strength that a sick man could not possess, the Baron swung his gun hand at Nikolai's head. Nikolai caught the hand and twisted it until there was the distinct crack of a bone, and the Beretta dropped to the floor. The Baron let out a cry of pain; a finger was splayed at an odd angle.

"I can see the penicillin is helping," Nikolai said. He took his gun from his pocket.

"People know you're here," the Baron said. He gave away nothing. "You can break another bone. What else can you do?"

Nikolai extended his gun hand and pulled the trigger. Disbelievingly, the Baron clutched his groin. His hands were immediately soaked in blood. He sank to his knees.

"That was for Katya. This is for me."

The shot caught him in the stomach. The Baron's right knee gave way, and he half-rolled to one side. His eyes were wide. blood was pouring across the thick, beige carpet. His mouth was moving, and this time, his unintelligible muttering was very real. His eyes rolled up in a feeble plea. They began to flicker wildly. Blood was trickling out of the Baron's mouth now.

"One more for Katya." Nikolai pulled the trigger again. The Baron shuddered violently and died.

EPILOGUE

▼

The sun was to the south in a slow race with the train, throwing the scrub country of west Texas into dazzling relief. From his compartment, Nikolai, electrically charged with new beginnings, found the spectacular vastness of the empty land soothing.

Guthrie would, of course, easily piece it together: the Baron's death would neatly tie in with a description of Nikolai from the gate guards at the camp. The connection would be obvious.

But Guthrie would be helpless to act. To shine a light on Nikolai would be to shine it on himself. There would be an investigation, but Guthrie would testify that although his former department, the Special Assessment Unit, had had certain confidential dealings with the former prisoner of war Reinhard Emil von Hartigens-Hesse, he himself, former SAU director Simon Guthrie, had no knowledge of personal enemies of the murdered man. Because of the delicate nature of the victim's work with the United States government, it would be his recommendation that such investigation be discreetly and swiftly closed.

For Nikolai, there was a bonus in the fact that Guthrie would remain deliciously in the dark; he would know that Nikolai had killed the Baron, but he would never know why.

Nikolai watched Texas slip by and thought about his freedom. It had taken literal and figurative prisons to bring him to the moment. He could savor the luxury it brought, but patriotism was still a distant concept.

He had arrived at freedom through pain and perversity and had embraced evil extolled as justice; for a flickering moment, he could even wonder what portion of his glorious freedom he deserved.

It was a delicate business, this sorting out of right from wrong. The pendulum swung, and nations and human beings swung with it, preaching morality and sanctioning murder.

For himself, there was nothing to regret. His revenge had been just. It had settled comfortably inside his soul, as sweet as love and no less satisfying. It would lodge there for a long time, but it would eventually give way to something stronger.

He thought of Tati and the last of her Polonius lectures on the day it all started, the day everything changed and nothing would ever be the same again. She had told him to find a direction, to steel himself to the future, and here he was, forged in the fire and poised for the grail.

He was headed west—the symbolic West, the West of new beginnings. As to America, he had come to realize that it suited him. It was beguiling in its excess and exuberance. It was imperfect, but nothing was perfect, so it was home. And Tati would approve; she had warned him against rootlessness. *"Wandering is for gypsies."*

He knew that the lessons of survival had not come cheaply. Gone with his irrecoverable youth was virtue. But not entirely—if everything inside him that was decent was gone, he would not, as he did, long for change and seek resurrection.

The scabby hills and the drying arroyos of the moon-like land crawled by. His eyes grew heavy, but just before he fell asleep, a thought tumbled into his brain:

Surely, if there was no God, there was at least a frolicsome force that arranged things, like an eccentric uncle.

*   *   *   *

One week later, on April 12, 1945, Franklin Roosevelt died in Warm Springs, Georgia.

Eighteen days after that, Adolf Hitler killed himself in the *Führerbunker* in Berlin.

In July, the first atomic bomb was exploded at Alamogordo, New Mexico.

On August 6, an atomic bomb destroyed Hiroshima.

On August 14, a second atomic bomb, dropped on Nagasaki, ended World War II.

Two months later, in San Francisco, in the advertising agency where she worked as a copywriter, Nikolai found Anna Brenner.

978-0-595-41024-8
0-595-41024-3

Printed in the United States
75449LV00003B/109-135

9 780595 410248